GREATSHADOW

BOOK ONE *of the* DRAGON APOCALYPSE

JAMES MAXEY

SOLARIS

First published 2012 by Solaris
an imprint of Rebellion Publishing Ltd,
Riverside House, Osney Mead,
Oxford, OX2 0ES, UK

www.solarisbooks.com

ISBN: 978 1 907992 73 5

10 9 8 7 6 5 4 3 2 1

A CIP catalogue record for this book is available from the
British Library

Printed and

For Greg Hungerford,
and other ghosts who haunt me.

CHAPTER ONE
BONE-HANDLED KNIFE

WHEN INFIDEL GRABBED me by the seat of my pants and charged toward the window, I didn't protest. Partly this was due to the speed of her action, but mostly due to my inebriation from the sacramental wine we'd stolen. Plus, it wasn't the first time I'd been defenestrated by her. Of course, this window was five hundred feet up, in a lava-pygmy temple carved into the sheer cliff face of a volcano.

In my semi-drunken haze, I admired the view as I departed the temple, surveying the landscape around me. The night sky was bright orange as the bubbling caldera above reflected against belching steam. Far below, the dark, vine-covered canopy of trees draped like a casually tossed blanket down slopes stretching to the moonlit ocean. A lovely tropical night, one might even call it serene, save for the steady pulse of war drums and the nerve-jangling pygmy battle cry. It's difficult to relax when five-hundred waist-high men are barking in unison, "Yik-yik-yik-yik-yik!"

I reached the apex of my arc and began to fall. The pygmies were drowned out by the whistling wind and a deafening, high-pitched shriek tearing from my throat.

I don't know why I was screaming. If experience was any guide, Infidel had aimed me toward a particularly bushy looking patch of forest. While my brain had faith in her, my vocal cords had doubts. I quickly saw that my brain was correct as I fell toward a living net of blood-tangle vines. I threw my hands over my eyes. My leather gauntlets spared my face from the worst of the thorns as I punched into the canopy, the vines popping and snapping beneath my weight. I bounced from branch to branch on the trees below. Even with my leather armor, the beating was as bad as anything I'd ever received at the hands of a mean-spirited bouncer.

Seconds later I jerked to a stop, completely tangled. I spread my fingers and found my face inches above a jagged obsidian boulder. The sobering realization I'd just escaped a messy death negated the effects of the stolen wine. I reached for the steel flask in my back pocket and took a quick gulp to restore myself. As much as I wanted to hang in the vines until my nerves calmed, I knew that the pygmies wouldn't need long to find me. I reached for my bone-handled hunting knife and chopped at the tendrils, my body lurching, until I slid onto the boulder and tumbled to the ground.

I looked up at the hole I'd punched in the canopy. Far above, a dark speck shot from the window through which my hasty exit had been facilitated. The speck quickly took on the shape of a woman as she hurtled toward the gap in the trees.

Infidel was laughing. She had both hands wrapped around the dragon skull, hugging it to her chest like an oversized watermelon. Her long blonde hair trailed out behind her. She was still wearing the loose-fitting white blouse and navy breeches from her recent stint as a mercenary in the pirate wars. She was barefoot, the soles of her feet black as coal. The orange light caught the string of yellow beads around her throat, a necklace of human molars that she'd kept as a diary of sorts while she'd served aboard the *Freewind*.

If she'd been aiming for the hole I'd left in the vines she missed, overshooting by several yards. I lost sight of her, but heard curses and grunts as she bounced from branch to branch, the blood-tangle snapping as it slowed her fall.

I managed to find my feet as she stumbled out of the darkness. Her blouse and breeches had been torn in a dozen places, but there wasn't a scratch on her enchanted skin. She had blood-red flowers jutting from her hair, and thorny vines draped over her shoulders. She held the dragon skull above her head one-handed, as if it was carved from balsa. With her other hand, she used her cutlass as a machete. Her lips were pressed together tightly as she spotted me.

"Are you okay?" she asked.

"Nothing's broken," I said, my voice trembling. I took another swig from the flask. "Your aim's still good."

She giggled. "I'm glad you're fine, because I'm looking forward to teasing you for the next ten years about that scream. Even I can't hit a note that high."

I held a finger to my lips and whispered, "You can laugh later. The pygmies won't be far behind."

"We've got a good head start," she said, looking up at the temple. She plucked a few flowers from her hair and flicked them away. "You worry too much."

For most of my life, I've earned a reputation as a man who doesn't worry enough. It's only around Infidel that I play the role of responsible adult. She's been magicked up to be as strong as ten men, with skin as tough as dragon hide. Her supernatural gifts have left her fearless, an aspect of her personality that draws me like a moth to a flame. Like many a moth, I sometimes get singed.

She held the dragon skull toward me, admiring it in the dim light. "The Black Swan's going to slip in her own drool when she gets a look at this."

Since I was presently in hock for a life-endangering sum of money to the Black Swan, I hoped that would be the case. There are blood-houses throughout the Shining Lands that pay handsomely for dragon bones. A single knuckle can be worth its weight in gold. An entire skull, complete with lower jaw and all the teeth, was a fortune so large that adjectives fail me. It would cover my debt, and, more importantly, once more restore my line of credit at the bar. The cheap river-pygmy hooch I'd been swilling since the Black Swan cut me off was unbefitting of a connoisseur of fine spirits.

I whispered, "Let's get going. The pygmies know this jungle better than we do, and—"

There was a tapping sound, like raindrops hitting a leaf. Infidel looked over her shoulder, stretching out her long, slender leg. Three porcupine quills were caught in the torn fabric of her pants. Suddenly, the air around her was thick with flying quills, some tangling in her hair, some bouncing off her impervious forehead. My own armor sprouted a dozen of the missiles. None made it through the leather, which was good. Lava-pygmies tip their darts with poison.

"Follow me!" Infidel shouted, slicing at a wall of vines with her cutlass and leaping through, the dragon skull balanced on her shoulder. She could have stayed and fought without risk. By running she was protecting both me and the pygmies. We'd come out here to rob them, not to kill them.

I ran as fast as I could, slashing out with my bone-handled knife to better clear the path. In the darkness, I focused on Infidel's bright hair bobbing before me like a ghost. The pitter-patter of pygmy feet echoed in the canopy. Darts tapped across my shoulder blades as they continued to fire.

I kept falling farther behind. I was only a week away from my fiftieth birthday, too old for this profession. Once this was over, I swore I would find a safer, more gentlemanly way of earning a living. My breath came in ragged gasps. A stabbing pain ran up my side. I could barely raise my knife to chop away the remnant vines Infidel left in her wake. I felt sure that if I pulled off my boots, sweat would pour out like stale beer from a pitcher.

I wiped the perspiration from my eyes and when I pulled my hand away, Infidel was gone. I kept running. The darkness in front of me had an Infidel-sized hole torn from it, and beyond I could once more see the rolling clouds of the eerie orange sky. There was a bass rumble ahead, a sound like a waterfall. I skidded to a halt on the lip of a cliff and looked down into a deep scar in the earth. Infidel dangled from a mass of roots just beneath my feet. She was still carrying the dragon skull, but her cutlass was nowhere to be seen.

"I know where we are!" she yelled, her voice nearly drowned out by the rushing water beneath her.

I knew as well: the southeast slope of the volcano is cut through by a whitewater river that cascades all the way to the sea, about ten miles distant.

"We're practically home!" she shouted.

I was of a different opinion. Many years ago, a palm-reader in Commonground told me I'd die of drowning. More poetically, she'd told me, "The sea will swallow your bones." It had been one reason I hadn't joined Infidel on the *Freewind*. I extend my caution by never imbibing anything weak enough for a fish to live in.

"Jump!" Infidel yelled.

"Let's weigh our options!" I shouted back.

Of course, arguing was pointless. Infidel pulled herself up on the thick root she held, clamping onto it with her teeth. With her now free hand, she punched the cliff wall. The root-draped stone beneath me crumbled.

As I dropped, Infidel grabbed me by the shoulder, pulling me toward her. She wrapped her arm around me, pressing me tight against her unbreakable body. Her breasts flattened against my back as she spooned me, curling us into a ball with her powerful legs. Her breath was hot against my neck. We fell through darkness, weightless.

I couldn't breathe. Partially because Infidel's arm across my belly was as gentle as a python, but, even more, because I so often dream of Infidel's embrace. She'd been a mere teen when I met her; I a worn-out drunk twice her age. I'd watched as she'd ripped the arm off a bold warrior two feet taller than her who'd pawed her lithe body as she'd stood at the bar of the *Black Swan*. I wasn't the only man to witness this that quickly decided an attempt at seduction wasn't worth the risk.

I was, however, the only one who bought her a cider that evening and told her tales of the ruined cities hidden in the jungle. I've always been quick to make friends. Fate has brought me many fortunes over the years, and I've spent those fortunes making sure the patrons of the *Black Swan* never go thirsty. Yet, I've never had a friend quite so true as Infidel. Her lightness balances my darkness; her recklessness makes the ongoing foolishness of my life look like sage wisdom. The two of us laugh together freely, and trust each other with our lives. I'm the one person who would never betray her for the obscenely large bounty on her head. She's the one person who never abandons me when my money runs out and I'm suddenly begging for drinks.

Never once in ten years of friendship has a night passed in which I didn't fantasize about her touch. I've never spoken a word of my secret passion. She means too much to me. It's not my arm I fear losing; it's her company. Our time together is so much sweeter than our time apart.

As dreamlike as her embrace might be, there was the unfortunate reality that we weren't in a bed, we were hurtling toward a dark, raging river. With a horrible jolt, Infidel's shoulder cracked a boulder. We bounced into the torrent and her grip loosened. I inhaled, a bad move since my head was under water. We slammed into another rock and I slipped from her grasp. My face popped above the surface for a second and I coughed, water spraying from my lips. I sucked a cupful of air and croaked, weakly, "Infidel!"

She didn't answer as I bobbed along, careening from rock to rock. In moments of panic, the mind can grasp onto the most trivial details, and I noticed I'd lost my knife. Infidel either misplaced or broke her weapons on a daily basis, but I'd carried this knife for forty years; it had been a gift from my grandfather. For a fleeting second, finding the knife felt like a priority. Then, from the thunder ahead, I realized that I was about to be swept over a waterfall, and my new priority became not to do so. I clawed desperately at boulders, but my hands had no strength. I still could only gulp small mouthfuls of air. The rocks pummeled me like the fists of giants. The knife-sharp pain that had torn my gut while running sliced me from groin to gullet. The water pushed me under and I went numb.

They say that drowning men see their lives pass before them. I could only see the fortune teller, an old woman with dark eyes, her ears sporting gold rings and thick tufts of gray hair. Her voice crackled like dry leaves as she traced the line of my palm and told me how I'd meet my end.

Of course, she'd told Caleb the Crusher that he'd die by hanging, and he'd been the man whose arm Infidel had torn off on her first night in Commonground. You have to question the skills of a diviner who misses such a fate.

I slammed into a rock face first. Stars danced before me, changing to snowflakes as they showered down in the darkness. I found myself standing before Aurora, the ice-ogress who serves as the main muscle at the *Black Swan*. She was discussing the small matter of my bar tab. In the three months Infidel had been at sea, I'd been a little freer with my purse than usual. When I confessed that I had no money, Aurora had pointed out that a man was never completely without assets. Artfully butchered, human flesh could pass for pork; only a few coins per pound, but for a grown man that added up. I assured her that once Infidel returned, my fortunes would improve. She gave me thirty days. It was thirty-two days later when Infidel got back. Unfortunately, the *Freewind* had been on the losing side of the pirate wars. This was in no way Infidel's fault, but it meant that she'd not received the bonus promised to her in the event of victory. Given the way the Black Swan calculated interest, the handful of coins Infidel had been paid failed to dent my debt. Thus, not for the first time in my life, I was off to plunder the ancient tombs and temples of the Vanished Kingdom.

As I was swept over the lip of the waterfall, I took some small measure of comfort that my corpse would be sufficiently mangled that Aurora couldn't even sell it as dog food.

The drop proved to be the shortest distance I'd fallen

that evening, a trifling fifty-foot plunge into a broad pool. The water at the base of the fall roiled. In the turbulence, I couldn't even guess which direction was up and which was down. The shallow gulps of air I'd gotten bobbing in the river were exhausted in seconds. My leather armor was heavy as steel plates. The pounding water pinned me. Yet, the pain and pressure felt distant. The water was warm, heated by the volcano, almost pleasant. The polished gravel beneath me was as comfortable as a feather bed. I went limp, all my weariness flowing from me like bubbles from my lips. There were worse ways to die.

As I was about to discover.

Just as I was on the verge of sleep and surrender, a strong hand grabbed my hair. I was tugged into the air and tossed over Infidel's left shoulder like a sack of sodden potatoes. She was still carrying the dragon skull, her fist shoved inside the base. She waded through knee-deep water as I draped across her back, my eyes at the level of her heart-shaped buttocks. Water poured out of my lips and nose, but I couldn't muster the will to inhale.

Infidel laid me on a beach of black sand, dropping the skull beside me, then straightened, shaking her head to get the hair from her eyes. She looked as soggy as a drowned rat; her torn pirate blouse hung from her arms like flaps of skin on a once-fat man. Her hair was plastered to her scalp, knotted so horribly that she needed a razor more than a comb. At some point, her necklace of molars must have snapped. The only evidence it had ever been there was a single tooth wedged between her hip and the top of her broad belt. Despite her sorry condition, her waterlogged clothes revealed the magnificent paradox of her body, the sleek and sultry curves that sat atop angular, iron muscles.

I spotted something amiss on her flawless form. A dark red stain glistened atop her left shoulder. I sucked in a spoonful of air, the effort making me tremble, and whispered, "You're bleeding."

She frowned as she followed my gaze to the crimson circle that seeped out across her blouse in ever-lightening shades of pink. Her eyes grew wide. In the adventures we'd shared, I'd only seen her bleed three times. Once, No-Face had caught her square in the mouth with his ball and chain, producing a split lip. He'd hit her by accident and she didn't hold grudges, which was the only reason he was still alive. The same couldn't be said for the bounty hunter who'd gone after her with a shadow sword. He'd crisscrossed her arms with a dozen cuts before she wrestled the blade away. They'd had to carry out what was left of him in buckets. And, of course, there had been the tussle with that mechanical tiger with the diamond-tipped claws. The only scars on her otherwise flawless legs had come from that fight.

Her face turned pale as she pushed the remnants of her pirate blouse down her shoulder, revealing streaks of red across her ivory skin. She wiped away the blood with her fingers, leaving behind smooth, unblemished flesh.

She looked back at me, her face turning whiter still.

I looked down. I understood why I couldn't breathe.

The good news was, I'd found my knife.

The bone handle was jutting from the waist of my leather armor. Eight inches of honed steel were lodged in my gut. I couldn't feel a thing, but blood pulsed from the wound with every fading heartbeat.

Infidel dropped to her knees. I looked up at her, her face so bright as the world around me darkened. I took in another thimble of air and mumbled, "Tell the f-fortune teller... I want... my m-money back."

Infidel frowned, then just as quickly grinned. "You faker," she giggled. "It's nothing more than a scratch." She grabbed the edge of my vest with both hands. The thick leather tore like tissue paper in her superhuman grasp.

Her jaw went slack.

It was something more than a scratch.

Her gaze met mine once more, and for the first time ever I saw tears gleaming in her eyes, her lovely eyes, a pale blue-gray, the ephemeral color sometimes found on the horizon of the ocean, where you can no longer tell where the sky ends and the water begins.

I couldn't let my final words to her be some joke, some quip that hid the great secret truth of my life. I managed to swallow another mouthful of air and whispered, "I... have always... l-loved you."

"Stagger," she whispered back, eyes closing, tears rolling down her cheeks. "Oh, Stagger."

I closed my eyes as well, unable to spare the strength to keep them open. My heartbeat fluttered in my ears, faint and failing. I hoped I could die at peace now; I'd confessed what I should have revealed ten years before. And yet... and yet there was one thing more. One last secret haunting me as I slipped toward my final rest. My blood turned cold as the guilt of my only betrayal of Infidel's trust pulsed through me.

I mouthed the words, my voice barely audible, "I... didn't lose... the m-map. I... s-sold it... to the... the... f-fishmon—" My voice failed. I tried to breathe but couldn't. My body refused to obey, save for my eyes, which opened once more.

Infidel's face was inches from my own. Her lips were puckered. I had the distinct impression she was about to kiss me. Then her eyes snapped open. She jerked upward as my final words sank in.

"You did *what?*" she asked.

I tried to answer, but it was no use. My body was done for. I couldn't even close my eyes. Her lips moved, but I couldn't hear what she said. Her words were lost beneath the roar of waves from a distant, invisible ocean. Behind her, I could see the bright orange faces of lava-pygmies as they emerged from the forest, holding spears tipped with glassy black rock above their heads, preparing to strike. I couldn't warn her. I couldn't do anything except drift upward. Whatever essence there may be of a man that is separate from his body had come loose as my heart went silent. I found myself floating, a shapeless, formless thing, a fog composed of memories and broken dreams, cut free from my flesh.

I looked down though non-existent eyes at the scene beneath me. Spears were bouncing off Infidel's back. She rose with a snarl, yanking the bone-handled knife from my belly. Normally, I love to watch Infidel in combat. She fights like the unholy union of a bobcat and a ballerina, a whirlwind of blades and laughter that traces the landscape around her with long and looping arcs of blood.

But, I paid little mind as she raced toward the first pygmy and delivered a kick that sent him flying above the treetops. Instead, I looked down at the sorry, sodden thing that I'd once thought of as me. I hadn't made it to fifty, but the mask of wrinkles around my eyes could have belonged to a man twice that age. My cheeks and chin were speckled with scraggly white stubble; I couldn't grow a decent beard on a bet. My shoulder-length hair was streaked through with gray, and my pony-tail did nothing to hide the scaly bald patch at the back of my skull. I was tall, and in my better days my torso had been shaped like a V, with broad shoulders and a narrow waist. Until this moment, I always pictured myself with that body, and had never accepted that the bottom of the V had gotten lost beneath an O, a big, oval jug of jiggling fat that must inevitably attach itself to a man who loved his liquor as much as I did.

With my eyeless vision, I could see the truth of who I'd been: a fat, half-bald old drunk who'd been vain enough to fantasize that a woman whom the gods must surely envy might one day love him.

As my consciousness expanded, ever wider, ever thinner, I was dimly aware that I'd miss that man.

Then, I had no awareness at all.

Or, more accurately, I had awareness, but no will, no ability to guide my perceptions or ponder the scenes I saw. I was spread through all things. I was present in the dark depths of the ocean, floating beside hideous fish with lantern eyes and jaws like bear-traps. I was present in the jungle, slithering among the branches crawling with snakes and toads and beetles, all in rainbow hues brighter than gemstones. I was present in the bars of Commonground, where battle-weary veterans of the pirate wars stumbled along the uneven boardwalks as whores called out for their company. I could feel all the lust and loneliness of their moments, all the sorrowful joy that spills into the universe when two strangers touch in intimacy.

And, far, far above the squalid city, I was present in the clouds, looking out upon a night sky full of glittering diamonds, keenly aware of every point of light. The sky shimmered with distant suns and unseen planets, and I could hear the murmur of countless voices, the indecipherable echoes of life on worlds too numerous to number. What was left of my mind shrugged and surrendered, unable to absorb the infinite majesty of a creation in which my life had been of no consequence at all.

It was into this vastness that I would disappear. The final spark of my consciousness calmly dissipated. Like a stream of stinking urine spreading into the ocean, I was absorbed once more into the Great Incomprehensible All.

Then, blood pulsed within my non-existent heart.

There was another pulse, then another, and I began to feel as if I once more had veins and arteries, as if I once more had lungs. The atoms of my awareness raced back from the ocean, from the forest, from the sky, coalescing into a specter above my still very dead corpse. Where I'd been only a formless mass of thought, I could now look down at ghostly fingers, wraith-like toes, and a phantom wang. I was hanging naked above the shell of my body. I reached down to touch it, but my ghost hands found no purchase in the dead flesh. Yet, I was definitely me again. Something had halted the dispersal of my soul.

Around my body, the ground was wet with blood. Far more

blood, I knew, than had ever pumped through my heart. I quickly spotted the severed limbs and mangled torsos of half a dozen pygmies. I felt a shiver of guilt that I'd brought this fate upon them. I spun around, searching for Infidel.

She looked as if she'd been doused with buckets of tomato juice. She had a pygmy dangling in her grasp, a chief judging from his feathered head-dress. She had my bone-handled knife pressed against his throat.

"Call them off!" she growled, as more pygmies emerged from the trees. "Just leave us alone and no one else gets hurt!"

The chief responded by spitting in her eye. Two seconds later, his head was separated from his shoulders.

As his blood flowed across the bone-handled knife, life flowed back into me. I inhaled, my ghost lungs filling, and shouted, "Infidel!"

She didn't react. She was too lost in her anger to hear me as she charged the newest round of warriors, a dozen spearmen clustered in a frightened clump at the edge of the clearing.

I grabbed at her arm as she raced past me. My fingers passed right through her skin.

"Infidel!" I screamed again.

She didn't even blink as she crashed into the wall of spears, splintering them. The wide-eyed pygmies turned in unison to flee. She gave chase for only a yard or so, then, either in frustration or as a warning, she punched the nearest tree, splintering the trunk.

The tree groaned, then toppled, as Infidel lowered into a half crouch and scanned the area, her eyes as intense as a cat searching a bush for a bird.

Infidel remained alert for several minutes as her panting breath returned to normal. At last, she relaxed, straightening up. The pygmies had taken the hint. She twisted her head in a slow arc, her bones popping as the tension in her neck and shoulders slackened. Her lips parted slightly as she took a deep breath. Looking at my body, her shoulders sagged.

She walked toward my corpse, her arms limp at her sides, my bone-handled knife barely dangling in her grasp. When she reached my remains, she stared down, breathing slowly. The music of frogs and insects began to hum and strum as the violence of the moment before was swept away by the unceasing flow of time.

She shoved my knife into her broad leather belt and knelt before my body. Placing her arms beneath my knees and shoulders, she lifted me. I twisted my ghostly form to occupy the space of my corpse, trying to feel her hands upon my dead flesh, to no avail. I could no more grasp my body than I could grasp the wind.

She carried my cadaver into the calm end of the pool, walking ever deeper until I was submerged. She ducked her whole body beneath the water. I didn't know what she was doing. I was mystified, unable to read the blank mask of her face and eyes. She bobbed back above water to breathe. The blood from the battle washed from her face. As the water carried off the gore that caked my grandfather's knife, my ghostly body faded from my sight. I was no longer dispersing into nothingness, or allness, but was instead simply invisible, intangible, a memory of a man haunting the woman he once loved, his soul somehow bound to the blade that had killed him.

Beneath the water, she undressed me, peeling away my torn armor, still studded with pygmy darts. She washed the blood and mud and sand from my pale skin, her fingers gently tracing the lines of my face. She calmly worked the tangles from my hair, then let my body drift in the still water as she ducked back beneath and pulled off the shreds of her own clothes, scrubbing her skin, her hair spreading through the water like a halo as she patiently pulled out bits of vines from the numerous knots. Twenty minutes later, she carried my now clean corpse from the water. She was naked save for the thick black belt that sat upon her angular hips. The blade of my knife pressed against the smooth arc that traced where her belly met her hip, the tip resting near the thick blonde curls of her pubic hair.

She laid me gently on the black sand and sat beside me, her legs folded beneath her. I looked as if I was sleeping. The hole from which my life had drained was just a jagged flap an inch or two across, not so fearsome. She folded my arms over my chest, cupping the uppermost hand in her slender fingers. Free of blood, her skin gleamed like marble.

She sat for a long time, her lips twitching. Sometimes, she looked on the verge of tears. In other moments, I was certain she was about to curse, and beat my battered corpse with her fists. In the end, her lips curled upwards, as the faintest hint of a smile managed to claw its way up from beneath grief and guilt and rage.

She shook her head gently as she looked into my face. As the jungle crescendo grew with the approaching daylight, and song birds lent their voices to the drone of bugs and frogs, she swallowed deeply.

"You old fool," she whispered. "I loved you too."

CHAPTER TWO
THAT DAMNED MAP

INFIDEL BURIED ME on a high bluff overlooking the sea. She'd carried me here wrapped in a colorful cloth she stole from the lava-pygmy village not far from the base of the falls. She'd met no opposition. It would be a long time before members of that tribe would come anywhere near her. The village emptied out as she walked into it. She could have robbed them blind, except, of course, they didn't have much to steal. The village was nothing but stick huts with dirt floors, with a few scrawny chickens the only livestock. It brought home the magnitude of my sins.

When the monks who raised me had had taught me about hell, they'd painted vivid pictures of barren landscapes in which the damned are tormented by horned devils. I never feared it. But, if I'd been told that I'd linger on after death, forever confronted by the people I'd hurt the most... maybe I would have tried to be a better person.

After making my shroud, Infidel had fashioned an impromptu sarong from the remaining cloth. The fabric had a crimson base looped through with green lines and yellow circles. The yellow circle motif could be found all through the ruins of the Vanished Kingdom. My grandfather had speculated that the yellow circle represented Glorious, the primal dragon of the sun, who had been worshipped as a god in ancient times. I don't know if the pygmies gave the same symbolic value to it, or just liked the design. The festive pattern was remarkably inappropriate for wrapping a corpse, but Infidel valued practicality over propriety. Despite its failings as a shroud, I thought the cloth looked good on her. She normally didn't wear vivid colors; she especially disliked bright greens for some reason.

She'd spent much of the day following the river to the sea. Given the rugged terrain, she made better time with me as a limp corpse across her shoulder than if I'd still been alive. Her endurance matched her strength. Even with my weight, plus the dragon skull, she never stopped to rest or eat.

By the end of the day she'd reached my final resting spot. I don't know if she'd planned to bury me here. Perhaps she intended to take me all the way to Commonground, to have me outfitted for a proper coffin by one of the city's numerous undertakers. Unfortunately, after a single day in the jungle heat, I was beginning to spoil. Dark, foul-smelling fluid stained my shroud, and by the time we reached the bluff the fabric would go black with flies faster than Infidel could shoo them away.

Infidel placed me at the foot of a shaggy, wind-blown tree as the sun set behind us. Shadows danced on the waves as she rested. A cool, steady breeze blew up from the sea, drinking up the sweat beaded on her face. Her hair danced around her eyes as she stared out at the darkening sky, watching the stars flicker to life above the water.

At last, she began to dig. She had no tools other than her bare hands and my old knife. The soil was sandy, covered with a layer of scraggly grass. She worked through the night, digging until she had a pit deeper than she was tall. She lowered my body into the ground with a look of utter weariness, then proceeded to cover me with the mounds of damp earth heaped on both sides of the hole. She finished just before dawn, running her hands over the sandy grave as if she was smoothing out the wrinkles on a sheet.

She thrust the bone-handled knife into the soil above my head, where it stood like the world's smallest tombstone. I felt a flutter of panic. Would she leave the blade there? My spirit was now tied to the knife. For my soul to remain anchored here so close to my body was, I suppose, appropriate. Yet, I no longer felt any connection to the rotting meat six feet below. I wanted to remain with Infidel.

I had no lips with which to speak, so I merely thought the words, *Keep the knife. Keep the knife.* I suddenly understood what the monks had tried to teach me about the fierce urgency of prayer. *Keep the knife. Keep the knife. Keep the knife.*

She sat down, resting her hands on her knees as she glanced at the yellowed handle. The humble bone gleamed like precious ivory, polished and oiled by a lifetime spent in my sweaty hands. *Take it*, I prayed. *Take it.* Her face was lined with deep furrows around her lips as she frowned. She looked as if she was about to cry, but, always when she was on the verge, she'd swallow. Her fists would go tight, and the moment would pass. Her eyes turned away from the tiny tombstone. I sensed that my prayers would go unanswered. Still, as long as she still lingered by my grave, there was hope.

At last the sun came up. The water danced with colors to rival the sarong still draped around her shoulders. Gulls wheeled in the air above the cliff, calling out to one another. Clouds drifted leisurely overhead, white as lambs in a distant field. I wanted to tell her that she'd done a good job. My bones had to rest somewhere, and this was a fine choice, a grave any ghost could be proud of. As much as I wished to continue to journey by her side, I knew my time had passed. If I was now a prisoner to eternity, this peaceful, sun-drenched bluff would be an acceptable jail.

By my count, Infidel had been awake for almost forty hours. Her endurance was superhuman, but not infinite. Her head sagged as she watched the endless dance of the waves. At last, she stretched out on the white sand of my grave. She used her arm as a pillow, and her fingers brushed against the handle of the knife. She looked at it again, her eyes bloodshot and bleary. She snatched the knife free of the soil, clutching it to her invulnerable breast like a doll. Then, with a shudder, she gave herself to sleep.

She slept fitfully through the day, undraping the cloth of her sarong and using it as a blanket pulled over her head to block out the light. As someone who'd shared campsites with Infidel, I knew she talked in her sleep. Mumbled, more accurately. Many a night I've lain awake and tried to make sense of her slurred half-words. Usually, I can't interpret them. But, as she turned from one side to the other, three unmistakable syllables escaped her lips: "So sorry."

She thinks she killed me. She thinks that as we fell toward the river, she was the one who drove the knife into my gut.

Perhaps.

I wish I could tell her that I don't blame her. She shouldn't ignore the fact that we were out robbing that temple because I was the one in debt, because I'm the one who needs to buy the company of crowds, because I'm the sucker who can't resist a good sob story from any down-on-his-luck bum who begs me for a few spare coins and winds up with my entire purse.

Of course, I wouldn't have been in debt when she got back from the pirate wars if I'd sold the map for even a fraction of what it was worth.

That damned map.

A year ago, Infidel had hunted down a fallen Wanderer by the name of Hurricane. Wanderers have a longstanding pact with Abyss, the primal dragon of the sea, that prevents them from ever drowning as long as they spend their lives without touching dry land. Their behavior is guided by ancient and elaborate laws; transgress these laws, and a Wanderer can find himself put ashore on some distant desert island. Hurricane had suffered that fate, due to acts of piracy against fellow Wanderers. But, he didn't live out his days on his island prison. He'd built a raft, fled to the Isle of Fire, and resumed his piracy. The Wanderers placed a bounty on his head, a price large enough to catch Infidel's eye.

Finding Hurricane was no great challenge. He'd set up camp in a sea cave on the western side of the island. Infidel made swift work of his crew, and took Hurricane out with a single punch. We were searching his treasure chest when we found the map in a hidden compartment at the bottom. Even before we opened the thing, we knew it was something special. It was embroidered onto metallic cloth spun from threads of gold far finer than silk. When we unrolled it, it made a musical sound, like tiny guitar strings plinking. It showed the central volcano of the Isle of Fire and plotted out several key buildings from the Vanished Kingdom. I knew this area well, both from my own explorations and my grandfather's detailed surveys. At the building I call the Shattered Palace, the map showed a tunnel leading into the volcano. Depending on how you held the map to the light, different layers were revealed; there were tunnels beneath tunnels. Someone had used ordinary ink to trace out some of the pathways, and there were notes near these paths, written in a code I couldn't decipher. I could only scratch my head as I turned the map from side to side, pondering the different images. Beneath the overlapping layers I spotted an 'X', and two words written in old-tongue that were perfectly clear.

Greatshadow. Treasure.

Greatshadow is the primal dragon who lives in the central volcano of this island. I've never seen Greatshadow, but my grandfather wrote that he'd been on the island once when the dragon was awake, and he said that the big lizard had a wingspan half a mile wide. The heat of Greatshadow's breath will turn iron armor into hot white syrup dripping off the blackened bones of any knight foolish enough to face him. Like all dragons, Greatshadow has an eye for gems and precious metal. What he does with them, I can't even guess. It's not as if he strolls down to the *Black Swan* from time to time to buy a round. Still, he's been hoarding riches during the rise and fall and rise of at least two civilizations. If a man could sneak into that treasure vault for even five minutes, he could snatch up enough wealth to carry him through a dozen lifetimes.

While I deciphered the map, I was thinking out loud, pitching my thoughts and theories to Infidel. Almost instantly,

I regretted it. I could hear the wheels turning in her mind. We'd been tomb-raiding together for a long time. Why not go after the ultimate treasure?

Here's why: Greatshadow isn't just another monster. He's the living embodiment of fire. He may be wrapped in scaly hide, but he's fundamentally an elemental being, a sentient force of nature. A fraction of his intelligence is present in every flame. You can't kill something like this with just a strong arm and sharp sword.

Infidel is tough, but her skills as a thief tend toward the smash and grab. There was no way she could reach Greatshadow's treasure without confronting the dragon, and, if it came to that, good as she was, Greatshadow would win.

So, at my first convenient opportunity, I 'lost' the map.

This was really the only time I've ever deceived her, other than the daily, ongoing, unspoken lie that I wanted nothing more of her than friendship. It's weighed heavily on my conscience for the last year, mainly because she'd accepted my lame explanation of how I'd lost the map down a privy hole on the docks in Commonground. She'd reacted to my story with her easy-come, easy-go shrug and never mentioned it again. Maybe she'd known all along the adventure was too big for her. If so, that makes my lie even worse. If she could have been dissuaded from the lair by simple reason, we could have sold the map for a small fortune, perhaps even a large one. I didn't need to betray her trust. We could have been living it up in Commonground rather than out robbing pygmies with the same foolish bravery of young boys throwing rocks at a hornet nest.

She turns again in her slumber, moaning softly.

I'm sorry, I pray to her. *So, so sorry.*

INFIDEL RETURNED TO Commonground the following day, making good time as she bounded along the shore. In open terrain, she's fast as a jack-rabbit, using her super-strong legs to propel herself in skips that cover a dozen yards a stride. Around mid-morning she found the wreck of a ship; it couldn't have been more than a few weeks old. She didn't take long to explore it, but did manage to pull a damp, sand-covered yard of canvas from the wreckage. She wrapped the dragon skull in this — a wise precaution. Even with Infidel's reputation, Commonground is full of thieves who would be tempted by the sight. It's a lawless city, a bad place to call home. Of course, there's not a lot of choice in addresses when you live on the Isle of Fire. Commonground is the only real city on the island.

Actually, there are a couple of things wrong with that statement.

For starters, the city isn't on the island, but out in the bay. The whole place is up on stilts. Plus, it's not really a city in the ordinary sense of the word. It's a collection of docks. It's like a city that exists entirely of streets where the homes come and go on a daily basis. Wanderers gather here, taking refuge in the sheltered bay, and on any given day you can find a hundred or so of their ships at the port, and several thousand of their ilk milling about. But, the Wanderers don't live in Commonground. They stay only a little while, then move on, replaced by the crews of other ships.

The only permanent residents of Commonground are people who've come there due to the lawless nature of the place. The Wanderers don't impose their codes on outsiders; they care nothing of the actions of others as long as it doesn't harm them. So, over the years, Commonground has become a haven to men and women not welcome in the more civilized parts of the world. Along the docks you'll find barges housing bars and brothels and blood-houses. These draw visitors from distant ports, mainly young, hedonistic men escaping the chains of morality that confine them in places like the Silver City. Also drawn to the place are criminals who've fled their homelands to seek out the one place on earth where no one ever asks about your past. It's taboo even to ask a person's real name in Commonground. Everyone goes by nicknames. It wasn't like my mother looked at me in the crib and said, "I bet he'll be a drunkard. Let's call him Stagger."

Commonground is just a lousy name. As noted, there's no ground at all. And you'd be hard pressed to find anyone who's common.

A few hours after she'd plundered the wreckage for the canvas, Infidel reached one of the boardwalks leading out into the bay. She strode purposefully through the maze of docks, ignoring gawkers as she passed. The sight of her in the colorful sarong was turning heads. Infidel normally dressed in a more masculine fashion, often wearing leather armor even though she didn't need it.

Not that there were that many people out to gawk at her. The late afternoon sun was unbearable. The docks didn't really come to life until darkness fell. The algae-green water of the bay was as smooth as jade in the windless heat. Fortunately, the tide was in. When the tide was out, a strong sea wind was the only protection against the raw sewage and fish-rot stench. With the water high, the stink wasn't so bad, though I was left to ponder why I could smell at all, since I no longer had a nose. Of course, I was seeing without eyes, and hearing without ears. If I wound up near whiskey, would I be able to taste it?

Of course, the best place to put that to the test was exactly where Infidel was heading. Near the heart of Commonground, Infidel reached the largest barge anchored at the docks — the *Black Swan*. This was a saloon and gambling house that catered to the high rollers from the Silver Isles. Wealthy men could visit the *Black Swan* with little fear for their safety. Thieves knew that messing with a guest of the barge could result in a visit from the Three Goons. Not many people would risk that for a bag of gold. A dragon skull on the other hand...

Infidel stepped through the door of the bar, pausing as her eyes adjusted to the shadows. The bar was decorated with a level of opulence that stumbled across the fine line separating good taste from garishness. The walls were lined with dark, polished teak; large paintings of scantily clad goddesses hung there. The various gaming tables sported crisp velvet surfaces. Only a single poker table was fully occupied. Everyone else was likely sleeping in the well-furnished rooms above. The main room was at least twenty degrees cooler than the air outside. Behind the bar at the far end of the room was the reason why.

A first timer to the bar might mistake the creature who stood there as male, given the broad shoulders and looming height. Few people have ever seen an ice-ogre of either sex. Aurora's nine feet tall, with pale blue skin mottled with patches of white, like a sky full of clouds. She's bald save for a tuft of dark blue hair in a knot at the tip of her scalp. Tusks jut up from her lower jaws, reaching to her eyebrows. Her clothes offer no hint of her gender; she always wears a long sleeved, walrus-skin coat that hangs down to her ankles. Aurora exhaled as she spotted Infidel, her breath coming out in a fog. The ogress is in charge of security at the *Black Swan*. While most of Infidel's visits are peaceful, she's been known, occasionally, to cause a bit of property damage.

"Where's your shadow?" Aurora asked, squinting at the doorway behind Infidel. Crystals of frost on her cheeks sparkled like diamonds.

"My shadow?" Infidel asked, walking toward the bar.

"Stagger," said Aurora. "I never see you without him hang-dogging behind."

"Stagger's dead," said Infidel, placing the sack onto the bar. There was no emotion as she spoke the words.

"Oh," said Aurora. She shook her head slowly. "I'll miss him. Most drunks think they're funny and charming. He really was, sometimes."

"He was more than just a drunk," said Infidel.

"No offense," said Aurora, in a tone that sounded as if she had, indeed, meant no offense.

Infidel looked directly into Aurora's eyes. She knew about Aurora's threat to sell my body for meat; Aurora probably knew she knew. Of course, Aurora was just the enforcer. If Infidel had come here looking for revenge, she'd be looking for the woman who really called the shots.

"I need to see the Black Swan," said Infidel.

Aurora crossed her arms, her biceps bulging beneath the walrus leather. She and Infidel had never lit into one another; Infidel probably had an edge, but Aurora wasn't going to be a pushover. Her strength was supplemented by a formidable array of ice magic; for a tropical town, Commonground has a surprising number of residents who've lost limbs to frostbite. "The Black Swan has a busy schedule," Aurora said. "I'll see if I can work you into her calendar."

"I need to see her now," said Infidel.

Aurora shook her head. "She'll see you when she wants to see you."

"She'll want to see me now," said Infidel, pulling the canvas away from the dragon skull. All the people at the poker table suddenly placed their cards face down and stared at the bar. Whatever stakes they were playing for, a dragon skull would trump it.

The ice-ogress let loose an appreciative whistle as she eyed the priceless object. "The lower jaw and everything," she said, reaching out to touch it.

Infidel caught her by the wrist. Aurora tried to pull back, but Infidel held her arm immobile. I had my answer as to who was strongest. Then Aurora grinned, and Infidel grimaced as her whole arm turned blue.

"Hold me too long and you'll lose those fingers," said Aurora, coolly.

"No one touches the skull but me and the Black Swan," Infidel said, through chattering teeth.

Aurora nodded. Infidel released her wrist.

"Given the nature of this transaction, I'll see if the boss is available," said Aurora, drawing her arm back. Infidel rubbed her frosted fingers as the ice-ogress vanished behind a red silk curtain at one end of the bar.

I sincerely hoped the Black Swan wasn't available. Whatever Infidel was planning to do, it couldn't be good.

As Infidel waited, a tall man in chain mail peeled away from the shadows in the far corner. He was broad-shouldered, his hair cropped short, his face rugged, probably handsome once, before his nose had been broken one too many times. His proboscis perched over his lips like a scaly red vulture. His hands were large and rough, his knuckles thick with calluses. I'd never seen him before. Perhaps this was some new enforcer that the Black Swan had hired, though more likely he was employed by one of the clients as private muscle. The man's gaze kept darting between the dragon skull and Infidel's bosom, accentuated as it was by the sarong.

"That's a mighty expensive thing for a little lady to be carrying," Vulture-nose said, easing up to the bar. "Seems like you could use a little security."

There was a commotion at the poker table. Everyone was standing up and stuffing their chips into their pockets. One by one, they bolted for the door.

Infidel gave him a sideways glance, and said, with remarkable restraint, "Go away."

The big fellow grinned. "Aw, don't be like that. For a pretty gal like yourself, I wouldn't have to work for money. We could work out things out in trade. You scratch my back, I scratch yours."

To demonstrate what he had in mind, the doomed man placed one of his meaty paws on the small of Infidel's bare back. His hand was nearly as large as her slender waist as he began to gently rub her.

It's easy to rub Infidel the wrong way.

When Aurora poked her head back into the room a second later, Infidel was in exactly the same pose as when she'd left.

Above her was a hole about a yard across. Sunlight filtered down. A naked man in the room directly above sat up in his bed, looking up at the hole that had suddenly appeared in his ceiling. He looked down at the matching hole in the floor. He rubbed his eyes, perhaps not certain if he was awake. A single boot tumbled from the sky, landing with a *thump* on the floor next to Infidel.

"Some guy knocked a hole in your ceiling," she said. "You should be more careful who you let in this joint."

Aurora grimaced. "The Black Swan will see you now."

THE SALON WAS dark save for a red glow from the glass window of the cast iron stove. A ceramic crock of potpourri simmered on the stove, filling the room with a cloying floral perfume and a level of humidity worse than anything out in the jungle. Despite the heat, the Black Swan had a shawl of black feathers draped across her silk dress; save for its ebony hue her gown looked like something she might have worn at her wedding. Like a bride, a lace veil concealed her face. Her hands were wrinkled claws, speckled with dark brown liver spots, her long nails painted to match her wardrobe.

In a city of outlaws who would rob their own grandmother, the rise of the Black Swan as its most powerful denizen was something of a mystery. It seemed improbable that this frail old woman commanded the respect of ogres and half-seeds, but Aurora kept her head bowed as she approached the leather couch where the Black Swan lounged and said, in a reverent hush, "Madam, Infidel has come to discuss a matter of commerce."

"Thank you, Aurora," said the Black Swan. Her scratchy, dry voice made me imagine that, should she cough, dust would come out.

The old woman turned her head toward Infidel, then motioned her to have a seat on the padded leather chair across from the couch. As Infidel sat down, the Black Swan said, "Aurora informs me your lover has passed away."

"He wasn't my lover," said Infidel, somewhat over-emphatically, I thought.

"I see. I had assumed—"

"You assumed wrong," Infidel snapped. "Stagger was my friend. With the life I've led, I needed a friend more than I ever needed a lover."

"Ah, friendship," said the Black Swan. "It's a commodity I find sorely overrated. You cannot pay someone to be your friend; they may pretend to be so, but you would always know the truth. In my experience, if a thing cannot be purchased, it has no true value."

"Or it may have the greatest value of all," said Infidel.

"Your naiveté is charming." The Black Swan shifted on her couch. A handful of downy black feathers drifted to the floor. "Though, perhaps I've underestimated your judgment if you didn't take that old drunkard as a lover. You must have known that when the desire for alcohol gripped him, he would have gladly walked over any of his so-called friends to reach a bottle. Even you, my dear."

If I'd still had teeth, I would have ground them.

Infidel pressed her lips together. I was surprised at how calm she seemed. She said, "I haven't come to discuss my personal life. I've come to pay off Stagger's debts."

The Black Swan tilted her head. "This is most honorable of you."

"Honor has nothing to do with it," said Infidel. "I want to clear the balance sheets once and for all. I know you think of Stagger and me as a team; I don't want the money he owed you to influence any business we may undertake."

The Black Swan nodded. "The skull will cover Stagger's debt, and more. I will arrange an auction. Aurora will deliver the balance of the proceeds to you."

"Keep them," said Infidel. "I want to open my own account to make use of your services."

Aurora raised an eyebrow, obviously surprised by this news. The Black Swan's face showed no reaction.

"I want to hire the Three Goons," said Infidel.

Aurora's other eyebrow shot up.

"This is… most unusual," said the Black Swan.

"Is it?" asked Infidel. "They're hired muscle. People purchase their services every day."

"Despite your many limitations, my dear, you are hardly lacking in muscle. Why would you possibly need their help?"

"I've got a robbery in mind. A smash-and-grab with a payoff that will make this dragon skull look like a hunk of tin. As good as I am, I'll need backup. The Three Goons can get the job done."

"Undoubtedly," said the Black Swan. "Alas, I cannot give you what you ask for. Another client recently engaged the Three Goons in an open contract. I don't know when they will be available."

"I'll buy out the contract," said Infidel. "Just name the price."

"My dear, I admire your ambition, but you cannot possibly match the resources of this client. For all practical purposes, their purse is infinitely deep."

"Who is it?" Infidel asked. "I'll talk to them. Make them an offer."

"You know that is a confidential matter."

Infidel frowned as she crossed her arms. Negotiations weren't Infidel's strong suit. I used to handle this sort of business.

The Black Swan said, "Perhaps there are others who could serve your needs? Commonground is thick with mercenaries. Post a bill and you'll have a hundred men standing in line for the job within an hour."

Which was true, but the Three Goons were worth a lot more than a hundred men. Remember No-Face? The only man who ever gave Infidel a split lip? He's one of the Goons. And he's not the one that most people are afraid of.

Infidel's hands balled into fists. Aurora tensed up. Infidel's eyes narrowed as thoughts danced in her mind. She still hadn't given up. "You've tried to hire me before," she said. "I'll work for you for the next year. Take any job you give me. At the end of the year, you give me the Goons, no questions asked."

The Black Swan nodded, smiling faintly. I quickly sensed this was a bittersweet smile. She wanted to accept Infidel's offer, but couldn't. "Tempting. Quite tempting. There are men who would pay a lifetime of wages to use you for a night."

The color drained from Infidel's cheeks.

"My darling, you don't think I would waste a year of your service on fighting, do you? As you note, I already have access to the finest mercenaries on the island. I have a high priestess for my chief enforcer. Why shouldn't I have a princess for a whore?"

Aurora scowled deeply. It took me a second to realize that she had to be the priestess. It seems I wasn't the only one with a religious background that never got discussed. But I was even more intrigued that the Black Swan referred to Infidel as a princess. What did she mean?

Infidel jumped to her feet. Snow began to fall in the room as the temperature dropped to single digits. A sheen of ice glistened on Aurora's clenched fists, with icicles growing down like spiky claws.

"That wasn't what I was offering," Infidel said, her voice trembling as she tried to control her temper. "Don't twist my words!"

"You should be more careful with what you say, my dear," said the Black Swan. "You've offered a binding contract. Alas, I cannot act upon it. My word is my bond, and my previous contract for the Three Goons is sacrosanct. Your virtue — such as it may be — is safe."

Infidel stared at the Black Swan, then cast one more glance

at Aurora, now encased in a shell of ice that resembled armor. Infidel unclenched her fists, her shoulders sagging. I could sense she wasn't afraid of Aurora; she just knew that she wouldn't get what she wanted by hitting anyone in this room. She turned toward the door, then glanced back. "I want the balance of the skull in diamonds."

"Of course, my dear," said the Black Swan. "I've often thought you'd look good in jewelry. This new fashion of yours is a step forward, but could benefit from a few simple adornments."

Apparently, the Black Swan had never seen one of Infidel's molar necklaces.

The poker players were back at their table as Infidel stalked across the main room. The hole in the ceiling already had planks laid across it. As Infidel reached the door, Aurora called out to her.

"Hey," she said.

Infidel paused at the door, but didn't look back.

"I… I wanted to say that the Black Swan was wrong about Stagger," said Aurora. "He'd do a lot of things for a bottle. But he'd never sell out a friend. And everyone could tell you were much more than a friend to him."

Infidel sighed, shaking her head.

"Not everyone," she whispered, as she stepped outside.

CHAPTER THREE
RIPPER

I FELT SENTIMENTAL as Infidel climbed from the creaking gangplank onto my old boat. She grabbed at rigging and rails as she moved across the slanted deck. I've lived my life askew — the mud-locked boat sits at a ten-degree tilt. An objective man would describe the place as a hovel. To me, the place was the closest thing I've ever had to home.

If you witnessed my vagabond lifestyle, you'd never suspect that not so long ago my family was wealthy. My great-grandfather was the famous — or perhaps infamous — Ambitious Merchant. Merchant is a family name stretching back generations, and it's common for followers of the Church of the Book to name their children after desirable virtues. Seldom has a man been more suitably monikered. Ambitious made a fortune in the slave trade, with Commonground as his base. The river-pygmies have enslaved forest-pygmies for centuries, but it was my ancestor who realized that these squat, muscular men could be sold as a commodity to the mines on the Isle of Storm. The trade goes on to this day, though my family no longer has any role in it.

The so-called pirate wars had more to do with the slave trade than with actual piracy. Many Wanderers regard slaves as just another cargo, which doesn't seem to mesh with their claims to hold freedom as the highest virtue. A band of radical Wanderers had taken a stand against the slave trade, going so far as to raid ships and free the captives. For this, they were branded as pirates, and wound up with every navy in the world united against them. Infidel had signed on to a losing cause from the start.

While I've never gone so far as to take up arms to oppose the slave trade, I've always had a gut dislike of the practice, and have never been shy about sharing my views. The business corrupts everyone, especially the river-pygmies. They think of forest-pygmies as animals, when anyone can see they're the same race, just of differing hues. Each of the three major pygmy tribes dye their skin with jungle berries: forest-pygmies are green, river-pygmies blue, lava-pygmies orange. Wash them off with vinegar and they're all fish-belly white. My grandfather, Judicious Merchant, son of Ambitious, discovered that the bitter dyes were an effective mosquito repellent, which is why I remember him with dark green skin.

Judicious had been trained to take up the family business until he made the mistake of actually talking to the pygmies. They told him tales of the Vanished Kingdom, a once great nation on this island, its monuments now buried beneath roots and vines. My grandfather burned through a great deal of the family wealth with his elaborate expeditions into the jungle. Judicious bore a son by a forest-pygmy woman; this was my father, Studious Merchant. As a teen, Studious aided his father by traveling to the Monastery of the Book, home of the world's most extensive library. He went to these archives to read everything that had ever been written about the Vanished Kingdom. But, while he was there, he grew to love the prayerful, contemplative life of the monks and joined their order. As a monk, father had his flaws. My existence is testimony to his difficulty with the vow of celibacy.

I'm told my mother was a prostitute who abandoned me on the monastery's doorstep. I've never even learned her name. I was raised in an orphanage run by the monks. My father taught there, but barely acknowledged me. Every three or four years, my grandfather, Judicious, would visit and tell me stories about his jungle adventures. He said that when I was old enough, he'd take me with him. I never saw him after my tenth birthday, when he'd given me the knife. I eventually reached

Commonground on my own when I was seventeen, but no one had seen my grandfather in years. The jungle had swallowed him long ago.

My grandfather had owned the sailboat Infidel now stood upon; in his day, it was quite a vessel. As years passed with my grandfather absent from Commonground, the boat had been looted. Pretty much everything that hadn't been nailed down had been stripped, along with a fair share of stuff that had been nailed down. The husk was still anchored at the docks when I got to town, and no one protested when I moved in.

Infidel pushed aside the torn curtain that led into the small shack I'd built from cast-off lumber. She found the duffel bag of clothes she kept stashed in the rafters and tossed her sarong onto the floor. I'd never seen her naked when I was alive, but this was the second time since I'd died I'd gotten to see her full glory. Yet, her nudity didn't provoke lust. All my ordinary desires seem muted. Since dying, I haven't felt hungry or sleepy. Of greater interest is that I haven't felt thirsty. Perhaps I should be relieved. My afterlife truly would be hell if I were tormented by desires I had no hope of slaking. Still, it seems wasteful to finally look at Infidel's body and feel only dispassionate appreciation of her symmetry.

She pulled on a pair of canvas breeches, but frowned as she looked through her various blouses. Many were blood stained and torn; she always was hard on clothes. She pitched aside the duffel and picked up one of my old shirts from the back of a chair, holding it to her face to sniff it. At first, I thought she must have found the scent unpleasant; her eyes began to water. Then, she hugged the shirt to her chest as she closed her eyes tightly. After a moment, she composed herself, slipping the shirt on, rolling up the too-long sleeves and cinching up the dangling shirt tails with her thick leather belt. She dug around under the bunk and found an old pair of boots she'd left here. In the jungle, she normally went barefoot. However, the boardwalks of Commonground were littered with things no sane person would want squishing between their toes. She shoved my bone-handled knife into the boot sheath, then rooted under the bed until she produced the scabbard that held my old saber.

For the first time in two days, she ate, raiding my pantry for dried herring wrapped in seaweed and a jar of pickled peppers. She washed it all down with the ceramic jug of rotgut I kept by the bed. Infidel rarely drank anything stronger than cider, but she chugged down the hard liquor like it was cool water. Afterward, she wiped her mouth on her sleeve and belched.

Usually, my shack felt cramped with the two of us. Now that it was just her, the place looked larger than it used to. Infidel scanned the room, her eyes surveying the clutter. There were books everywhere. Like my father, I'm an avid reader. A muddied pair of my boots sat next to the door. The oil-cloth coat I wore during the rainy season was still slumped on the floor next to them.

But the dominant feature of the room were all the empty bottles — wine, cider, ale, whiskey. Somewhere in the world was a glassblower who earned a living due to my habits, though the bastard had never bothered to write me a thank-you note.

This mound of mildewed books and dirty bottles was all the evidence left that I'd once been alive. Whatever the quirks of my sundry ancestors, at least they'd all successfully reproduced. I'd died childless. The only legacy I left the world amounted to little more than litter.

THE SUN HAD set by the time Infidel departed my shack. The tide was flowing back out to sea. She wrinkled her nose as the stench of the muck wafted around her. She wound her way through the maze of gangplanks and piers, heading west. I knew where she was going. I had, after all, managed to choke out most of the word 'fishmonger' in my feeble dying effort to shed my guilt.

JAMES MAXEY

Bigsby was a rarity in Commonground, a man who made his living in an honest profession. Bigsby did brisk business selling barrels of dried and pickled fish to Wanderer ships, and supplying the more upscale establishments, like the *Black Swan*, with fresh oysters and rock lobsters to serve their clientele. Of course, Bigsby wouldn't live in Commonground if there wasn't something wrong with him. In his case, it's physical. Bigsby is a dwarf, barely four feet tall, with the torso of a normal man but stubby legs and arms. He spends much of his time haggling with river-pygmies, buying their daily catch. Perhaps he came to Commonground to feel tall.

I'd sold Bigsby the Greatshadow map for a handful of coins. I'd been quite casual about it. I told him the map had belonged to my grandfather, but was a fraud that he could probably sell as a historical curiosity. My conscience had been assuaged because I knew that Bigsby wasn't likely to raise a band of adventurers to go after the fortune. Nor would he drunkenly boast in one of the local bars about his treasure map. He was a quiet, timid man, who survived in this rough city by keeping — please pardon the expression — a low profile. If Bigsby did sell the map, he'd do it discreetly.

The fishmonger rarely went out at night. He was up at dawn every day to buy the night's catch. As Infidel came within sight of his warehouse on the western edge of the bay, all the windows were dark. I guessed he'd gone to bed. Then I noticed a single dim light in one window, no brighter than a candle. As I focused on the window, I thought I could hear muffled voices. But the voices fell silent as Infidel stepped onto the gangplank leading to Bigsby's door. The plank squeaked; the candlelight went dark.

As Infidel neared the door, I noticed that something was off. Specifically, the door was off its hinges. It was merely leaning in the frame, the wood around the lock and hinges freshly splintered. Infidel didn't notice this detail. Instead, she paused a few feet away and kicked, cracking the door in twain. The

43

halves fell into the room, clattering loudly as Infidel stomped inside.

The door that Infidel had entered led to the room that served as Bigsby's office. Bigsby sat on short stool next to an empty pickle barrel he used as a desk. He was scribbling in the ledger he used to record the day's trades. An extinguished candle sat beside the ledger, a plume of pale smoke rising from it.

He stared at Infidel, slack-jawed. His face was covered with sweat; dark stains seeped from beneath his armpits. He looked terrified, but this wasn't fresh terror. His clothes had been soaked before Infidel had kicked in the door.

"C-can I-I-I... can I help you?"

"I'm here for my map," said Infidel.

"Y-y-yuh-yuh... uh... huh?" All the blood was gone from Bigsby's face, apparently taking with it the capacity for coherent speech.

Infidel stalked forward. She slammed her fist on the barrel, which all but vaporized in a spray of splinters. She reached for Bigsby.

"I don't... I don't... I don't..." Bigsby's voice fluttered as her hands slowly neared. I thought he was about to faint.

As her hands reached his throat, Infidel sighed. Her mouth relaxed from its menacing snarl as she stared down at Bigsby's frightened face.

She stepped back and crossed her arms.

"Look," she said. "I'm having a bad day. Let's pretend I didn't just kick in your door and start over. Stagger gave you a map. I want it back. It's rightfully mine; I killed the last guy who owned it."

Bigsby wiped sweat from his eyes as he contemplated this bit of mercenary logic.

Infidel continued: "I'm willing to pay a reward for the map. We'll call it a finder's fee."

Bigsby swallowed hard. His eyes kept darting from Infidel toward the door on the side wall. I'd been in this shop a hundred times; there was nothing behind that door except for a small porch, and stairs leading down to the dock where he traded with the pygmies. Was he thinking of making a run for it?

As I looked at the door, I felt a strange sensation, like the hair on my neck rising, if I'd still had hair, or a neck. I could barely hear a faint, distant buzz. I watched Bigsby's eyes. He wasn't thinking of running. He was afraid of whatever was lurking on the porch.

He whispered, not looking Infidel in the face, "I'm sorry, b-but I don't know anything about a m-map."

"We both know you're lying," said Infidel, cracking her knuckles. "I'm trying to be nice, but I'm prepared to be nasty. Don't be stupid."

The Bigsby I knew wasn't stupid. Nor was he all that brave. Which made his next move all the more shocking. On the short stool, he barely came up to Infidel's waist. This meant that the hilt of my bone-handled knife, sitting in the boot-sheath, was at the level of his bent knee, on which his hand rested. It took only a fraction of a second for his hand to dart out and grab the knife. He thrust it upward into Infidel's belly, shouting, "I'm sick and tired of being bullied!"

The knife had the expected effect, ripping a button from my old shirt as it slid along her impervious skin.

She reached down and hooked two fingers into Bigsby's nostrils and lifted him to eye level. Bigsby raised his hands to grab at her fingers, a dumb move considering he had a knife in his hands. He cut a gash across his cheek, nearly blinding himself. The blade tumbled from his fingers, landing upright in the floor as Infidel growled, "And I'm sick and tired of your little game!"

I barely paid attention to her words. There was a line of blood along the edge of the knife. As it slowly rolled down, forming a red bead, I once again had the sensation of a heartbeat. I waved my phantom fingers before my face as they materialized. I sucked in a ghost breath, savoring the sensation.

"If you like to play games so much, let's play one called 'hotter, colder,'" Infidel said as she spun Bigsby around like a fish on a gaff. He squealed from the pain. "When I get closer to the map, you call out 'hotter!' When I move away from it, say, 'colder!'"

Bigsby's eyes flicked once more to the door to the porch.

"Outside, huh? Through that door?" she said. She didn't wait for his answer.

He didn't say 'hotter' or 'colder' as she reached for the doorknob. Instead, he jabbered, "No, no, no, no, no, no, no, no, no!"

My foggy guts knotted as she touched the doorknob.

She yanked the door open and stared into the burlap-covered crotch of a man who had to be a dozen feet tall. Only his legs and lower torso could be seen. The rest of his body was above the level of the doorframe. An impossibly large hand with nine fingers clamped over Infidel's face. Bigsby tumbled from her grasp. The giant jerked Infidel from her feet and flung her far out over the dark waters of the bay. I could hear her curses fade off into the distance, until at last there was a faint, faraway splash.

Bigsby curled into a fetal position where he fell, his hands clamped over his bleeding nose. A hunchback suddenly stuck his head into the room from behind the giant. His whole body was concealed beneath a tattered gray cloak; his head hung so low beneath the misshapen lump of his back that it was nearly even with his waist. He supported his ill-distributed weight with a gnarled staff, grasped with equally gnarled fingers. His hands were wrapped tightly in filthy brown gauze; not a single inch of flesh was visible. Beneath his hood, his face was concealed by a burlap sack; blood-red eyes peered through two holes. The inhuman eyes made my ghost skin crawl. I moved in closer for a better look, trying to fathom what manner of creature this might be. The hunchback cast a baleful glare toward me.

Though he didn't say anything, I heard a voice whisper,

his cloak, then walked back to the door. Suddenly, the whole room shuddered. The pots and pans in the kitchen next door clattered as they fell from their ceiling hooks. The hunchback was nearly thrown from his feet, staggering until he reached the wall, where he regained his balance. He peered once more out the open door.

Infidel was tricky to see in the darkness, as she was now black as ink, the twin specks of her eyes the only clean spots left on her. She was perched in the center of the giant's shoulders, pounding his head with rapid-fire blows. The sewn-together scalp had come apart, revealing bones held together with thick copper wires. The beast groped around, awkwardly fumbling, until he found her leg. He snatched her free and slammed her into the dock with his full strength. The building shuddered from the shockwave. The giant tried to pick Infidel up again, but she grabbed the edge of the dock with her iron grasp and his fingers slipped from her mud-slicked leg.

She spun around, eyes narrowed as he tried once more to grab her, this time aiming for her head. As his arm closed in on her face, she clamped his wrist with both hands, then kicked both legs into the pit of his arm. She stretched out, her body straight as a board. With a sound like a branch breaking, the arm snapped free of the shoulder and she fell back to the deck with the severed limb. The giant stumbled backwards, off balance. No blood came from his wound.

Infidel rolled, rising to her knees, shaking her head slowly. Her body shuddered as she took a deep breath. She seemed not to notice that the patchwork man had regained his footing. He lumbered toward her, his remaining hand outstretched.

At the last second, she sprung up with a growl, swinging his liberated arm back over her head, two-handed, like an axe. Her growl turned into a grunt as she swung the limb, smashing it directly into his face. The blow knocked Patch from his feet and he fell to the dock on his back. Infidel sneered as she stomped down on his left ankle, pulverizing the bones.

Infidel lighted on the center of his chest, digging her fingers into the folds of sewn together flesh, ripping it open. She made short work of his rib cage, bones and wires flying into the night. The creature possessed no internal organs. Where his heart should have been, there was only a small golden box secured by silver rods. The giant's remaining hand grabbed her by the hair as she reached into his chest cavity and tore the box free. She popped it between her fingers, the lid flying open. It was difficult to see clearly, but what looked like a large, white mosquito buzzed up from the open container. It was at least two inches long, and glowed with an internal fire. It shot upward, like a shooting star in reverse, and vanished among its brethren in the sparkling firmament.

The giant no longer moved. Infidel made certain it never would again, as she snapped every bone and dried up muscle that she touched, tossing the fragments out into the bay. In a matter of minutes, the beast was completely disassembled; all that remained were the shredded remnants of his impossibly large pants.

She turned her face toward the doorway, twenty feet above. The hunchback met her gaze. Without warning, she leapt.

The hunchback calmly stepped aside as she flew into the room. She nearly tripped over Bigsby, who was still curled up on the floor, whimpering. Skidding to a halt in her muddy boots, Infidel whipped around. A trail of black mud splattered the walls like paint, stinking of dead fish and rotten eggs. She quickly spotted the hunchback, who held an open palm toward her.

"You seek the map," he said. "It's not here. Calm yourself, and I will tell you all you wish to know."

Infidel straightened up from her fighting crouch. She was still seething. The hunchback held his ground as she moved toward him. I was certain the creature had misplayed his hand. She paused before him, reaching out to grab his cloak. But, instead of yanking the hunchback off his feet, she wiped her muddy face, using the gray tatters of his cape like a towel. Ordinarily, these dingy rags were the last thing anyone would use for cleaning, but after you've rolled in Commonground muck, pretty much everything is more sanitary than you are.

I was heartbroken when she dropped the edge of the cloak. She was bleeding, her own blood this time. Her right eyebrow sported a gash at least an inch long. There was a knot just above this big as a hen's egg. Her nose was bleeding from both nostrils. When she spoke, I could see blood pooling around her gums.

"I'm listening," she said.

"Bigsby sold the map to a man named Ivory Blade. You know him."

Infidel nodded. "He's King Brightmoon's top spy."

"Correct. The king was quick to recognize the importance of the map. Even now, a ship of his warriors is under sail, heading for the Isle of Fire."

I suddenly put two and two together. I knew why the Black Swan hadn't been free to give Infidel the Three Goons.

The hunchback continued: "Blade has been recruiting local talent to aid in the quest. I intended to offer the services of Patch. Now, I intend to offer you."

"I'm not yours to offer," said Infidel.

"You need not play coy," said the hunchback. "We share a mutual goal. We each have our reasons for wanting to reach Greatshadow's lair. The simplest path forward is to assist the king's team. He's assembled the finest warriors at his command, masters of both physical and spiritual warfare. Earlier this evening, you sought to hire the Three Goons. You'll still be able to fight by their side; you just won't have to pay their wages."

Infidel shook her head as she walked away from the hunchback. "I'm not really a team player. I could get along with the Goons for a couple of weeks, but put me together with a bunch of knights and priests and I kill someone."

"Indeed," said the hunchback. "You're perfectly suited to such a task."

Infidel toed around the shattered slivers of barrel that littered the floor.

"You see a knife around here?" she asked. I saw she'd also lost my saber; it was probably out in the middle of the bay.

The hunchback produced the blade from his pocket and held it toward her.

"This knife belonged to your friend," he said. "You think of it as your last link to him."

She scowled as she snatched the knife from his grasp. "What are you, some kind of mind-reader?"

"Yes," he said. "Your thoughts are not a secret from me, Infidel. I could deceive you and not reveal this fact. But, I want you to know that I am not without my talents. If we form a partnership, we each have something to gain."

Infidel kicked most of the muck off her leg, then slid the knife back into her boot. Dark sludge bubbled up around the hilt as it sank into the sheath. "Thanks, but no thanks. I'm not looking for any new friends."

"I'm not offering friendship, Infidel. Only an alliance."

She stared at him. "It seems unfair that you know my name, while you get to remain a mystery. Who the hell are you?"

The hunchback chuckled. "Who indeed? As difficult as it may be to believe, I've lived my life without a name. I was cast out to die at birth."

"How tragic. But you still must have a name." Infidel said. "A relic like you can't have made it this far without someone calling you something."

"And yet, it is so."

"Well, today's your lucky day. From now on, you'll be called 'Lumpy.'"

The hunchback cocked his head, unsure if she was joking. I

was pretty sure she wasn't. Infidel didn't like her own nickname much, and compensated by sticking others with bad ones. After her debut at the *Black Swan*, people called her Ripper and she liked it. Then, a month later, she'd been sitting at the bar when a wild-eyed man in a black robe burst through the door, shouted, "Infidel!" then broke his knife stabbing her in the back. The name might not have stuck, except the scene repeated itself about nine times over the next year. Everyone at the bar started calling her Infidel, and eventually I made the switch as well. She's never volunteered what she did to piss off the fanatics, and I've never asked. The rule is, what happens outside Commonground, stays outside Commonground.

The hunchback rubbed his chin as he contemplated his need for a sobriquet. "You called me a relic. This will suffice."

"Relic?" she said with a smirk. She thought it was a lousy name.

The hunchback nodded.

"Well, Relic, it's nice meeting you, but it's been a long day, and I've got a headache like you wouldn't believe."

"I believe you," said Relic. "I feel your pain."

"Whatever," she said, heading toward the door with a dismissive wave. "Have fun on your dragon hunt."

"Lord Tower is leading the quest," said Relic.

Infidel froze in her tracks. Her eyes widened. I wasn't surprised she knew who Lord Tower was; he was easily the most famous knight in the Shining Lands. Still, what did that matter to her?

Relic said, "He's carrying a weapon that can actually slay Greatshadow."

"Which one?" she asked, not looking back. "The Gloryhammer?"

"Something much, much more dangerous."

Infidel pondered this, shook her head, then kept walking.

"After Tower slays the dragon, your job will be to kill the knight."

Infidel spun on her heels. She eyed Bigsby, who'd uncurled sufficiently from his fetal ball to stare at her. "Go fix me a tub of boiling water," she said. "And find me soap. Lots and lots of soap."

Bigsby nodded as he stood, then scampered off.

Infidel leaned against the wall. She spat a gob of pink spittle into the middle of the floor.

"I'm not promising anything," she said. "But let's hear your plan."

CHAPTER FOUR

GOONS

FOR THE THIRD time since I croaked, I watched Infidel strip off her ruined clothes, dropping the tar-black rags into a growing pile of goop. The candle-lit tub of steaming water before her filled the air with a pale haze. I was intrigued that Bigsby had such fancy private quarters. The fishmonger may not have flashed his wealth around in public, but his bathroom was opulent to the point of stupidity. Did a bath brush with a gilded handle scrub his back better than a plain wooden one? Even his toothbrush was studded with gems. And why did he need all these bejeweled bottles of perfumes and ointments? As Infidel moved around the room, my consciousness floated through a black lacquer cabinet decorated with inlaid mother of pearl. Even though it was dark in there, I thought I spotted an ivory wig stand sporting a curly blonde wig. What a very odd thing for a bachelor like Bigsby to have spent money on.

I did, however, admire his bathtub, a long, deep vessel carved from a single block of polished black marble. It was large enough that I, with my lanky frame, could have stretched out comfortably. Bigsby must be able to swim in it. Infidel sank beneath the surface, resting there a moment as the muck that still clung to her hands, face, and hair began to dissolve. She reached for a bar of bright white lye soap and the bath brush. The steamy air grew foul with the low-tide stench, cut through with the burning fumes of the lye. The bathwater quickly turned dark gray; I could no longer see her clearly through the haze.

Perhaps I've never seen her clearly. The truth is, while I've known Infidel all these years, I know so little about her. I've kept few secrets from her. I've talked about growing up in the monastery, and about my convoluted family history. I've freely shared my innermost thoughts on politics, religion, and the human condition. She, in return, has revealed that her favorite color is black (despite my insistence that black isn't a color), that she likes dogs more than cats, and that she hates carrots. Everything else I know about her, I've learned by observation. She's obviously from the Silver City; her speech has become much rougher and more colloquial over the years, but she still has traces of the accent and a vocabulary that hints of good breeding. It's not unusual to meet young men from wealthy families visiting Commonground, seeking vices they can't find at home. But most women in Commonground are usually coming from the other end of the economic scale. It's hard to imagine what she was looking for when she came here — or what she was running from.

After Infidel finished her bath, she spent time examining her wounds in the foggy mirror. It wasn't just her face that had taken a beating from Patch; her whole body was mottled with dark blue bruises, fading to yellow. I wondered how long it would take her to heal. The few times I'd seen her injured, she recovered much faster than a normal person. Why? She made no secret she'd been enchanted, but by whom, and for what purpose? Why hadn't I pried deeper about these things when I'd had the chance? I'd always hoped that, one day, she'd open up to me, and tell me of her life before Commonground.

"It's not the role of the dead to be inquisitive," Relic had said.

I felt like proving him wrong. I'd messed up my chance to learn Infidel's secrets while I was alive. Perhaps, in death, I had a new opportunity to unravel her mysteries. It seemed unethical, perhaps, to spy on her unseen and unsuspected. On the other hand, did I even have a choice in the matter? I suspected that by being around her at all times, a lot more than her naked body was going to be revealed.

Bigsby had left a small pile of fresh clothes for Infidel. They were decidedly more feminine than anything I'd ever seen her wear. Lacy underwear, a short black leather skirt, a black silk blouse with a low neck. Again, it seemed strange he'd just had these lying around. Bigsby wasn't married and I'd never seen him consort with whores. The clothes hung horribly on Infidel, both too big and too short, but would have fit a pot-bellied dwarf just fine.

I dropped the line of thought before I had a picture in my head I wouldn't be able to get rid of.

WHEN YOU'RE UP on the slopes of Tanakiki, (the central volcano, which translates from lava-pygmy as 'the Farting Dragon') you see that the Commonground bay must once have been a volcanic caldera. The water is almost a perfect circle three miles across, with a gap several hundred yards wide at the far end open to the sea. Twin arcs of land lead out to the gap. The southern arc is mostly low, rolling dunes surrounded by marshes. The northern arc is rockier, and the ocean beyond is unimaginably deep. There's a place out near the tip called the Old Temple. It's a long stretch of hexagonal basalt columns bunched tightly together; there's some debate as to whether it's a natural formation or man-made. I've poked around out there a time or two and don't have a strong opinion, other than the place is damn spooky. The rock is black as coal, but etched with white rings of salt left by evaporating seawater. Nothing grows there, not even lichen. Pygmy lore says that Greatshadow once landed here to drink from the sea, then pissed on his rocky perch, poisoning the ground.

It was still a few hours before dawn when Relic led Infidel out to the Old Temple. Her skin was pink in the moonlight, raw from the lye soap and vigorous scrubbing. She looked ridiculous in the clothes Bigsby had provided. The outfit could have come from a whore's wardrobe, but the scowl on Infidel's face would likely discourage any customers. She was barefoot again. My knife was stuck into the waistband of her skirt.

Bigsby had been dispatched by Relic on an errand. I'd missed the specifics while Infidel was bathing, but apparently the dwarf was supposed to bring someone out to the Old Temple to meet with Infidel.

Relic no longer seemed to be aware of me. With my knife free of blood, I was unable to shout at him. He may have been able to read the minds of the living, but the dead lay outside his awareness, as long as they weren't drunk on blood. Still, he knew I was haunting the knife. I couldn't help but wonder what other uses he had in mind for me. If he talked to me again, what was I going to say? Should I try to use him to convey messages to Infidel? Tell her I was haunting her? Would that make her feel better, or worse?

Infidel leaned against one of the basalt columns, gently kneading the knot on her forehead. After she'd been mauled by the iron tiger, she told me that it was interesting to be hurt. She'd been fascinated by her scabs for days. She acted like she'd made it through her entire childhood without so much as a scratch.

A fog started to gather, masking the edges of the salt-crusted platform on which we waited. The lanterns aboard the ships at Commonground faded as the mist thickened. The damp night turned decidedly cold. Infidel folded her arms across her chest, tucking her hands into her armpits for warmth.

Relic looked toward the thickest clump of fog and said, "There's no point in hiding. You've come this far; you won't turn back."

The fog swirled as a dark shadow moved through it, then parted as Aurora stepped onto the basalt platform. I don't remember ever seeing the ogress outside the *Black Swan*. Bigsby emerged from the fog right behind her. I wondered what he'd said to her to convince her to leave the bar.

Aurora glowered at the hunchback. She was easily twice as

tall as him. She said, "The dwarf gave me your message. How did you learn my true name?"

Relic chuckled. "I plucked it from your mind, Aksarna. I have the gift, and the curse, of hearing the thoughts of others."

"Do you have the gift of an iron neck?" Aurora asked as her eyes narrowed. "Since you know of my past, you leave me little choice but to strangle you."

Infidel spoke up. "The Black Swan knows your past, and you don't strangle her. Give ol' Lumpy here five minutes."

Aurora looked at Infidel, pausing for a second to study her odd attire and bruised face. "What's your role in this, *princess?*"

"I think I'm auditioning for the villain."

"Infidel has agreed to kill the king's men once they've slain Greatshadow," said Relic.

"You know about the mission?" asked Aurora.

Relic tapped his brow with a gnarled finger.

"Right, right. Mind-reader," said the ogress. "Fine. Why have you dragged me out here?"

"Ivory Blade negotiated with you to hire the Three Goons," said Relic. "We need you to arrange for him to hire us as well."

"You've already confessed that you're planning to kill the king's men. As of now, that includes the Goons. I'm no traitor."

"You've been accused of treason in the past. I've come to offer you a chance to clear your name."

Aurora shook her head. "It doesn't matter what you offer me. My loyalty lies with the Black Swan. I could never betray her."

"You have deeper, older loyalties, Aksarna."

"Don't call me that," said Aurora. "Aksarna died long ago. Commonground and the Black Swan are all I have now."

"You didn't die," said Relic. "You failed. The difference is significant. The dead are devoid of hope, but the fallen may dream of redemption. I know you are haunted by the possibility that you could one day return to Qikiqtabruk with the Jagged Heart, restoring the temple and erasing your shame."

"The Jagged Heart was destroyed," said Aurora. "My soul

was bound to it. My spirit died when the tip was shattered. It's only my stubborn body that carries on."

"Wrong, wrong, and wrong," said Relic. "The Jagged Heart was never so much as scratched. Your soul was never bound to it, despite the teachings of your religion. You may have loved it so much that it felt like a part of you, but this attachment was emotional, not supernatural."

"I know what I saw."

Relic shook his head. "The eyes are the easiest sense to deceive. The weapon was switched in the moments it was out of your sight; the raiders masked the true shard with dream magic. When you reached the raiders, they brandished a duplicate. It is this you saw shattered."

Aurora clenched her jaw. She placed her giant hands over her left breast as her eyes grew moist. "You know nothing. I *felt* it shatter. You can never understand."

"Cling to this falsehood if you wish," said Relic. "But the Jagged Heart still exists. It's carried by Lord Tower on his quest. With it, he'll slay Greatshadow."

Infidel rapped her knuckles on the basalt column, a sound like a hammer striking brick. "Sorry to interrupt, but what the hell are you two talking about? What's the Jagged Heart and why is it any more likely to kill Greatshadow than, say, a pointy stick?"

Aurora contemplated her question. The sea mist beaded on her leather coat, running down in rivulets, pooling at her feet. At last, she said, "The Jagged Heart was a ceremonial harpoon. As High Priestess, I would use it to hunt the spirit whales in the Great Sea Above. The shaft is carved from the tusk of a narwhale; the blade itself is a knife-sharp fragment of pure ice taken from the shattered heart of Hush, the primal dragon of cold. In shape, the blade resembles the heart from a deck of cards."

"A fragment of Hush's heart?" Infidel asked. "I thought that Verdant was the only primal dragon ever to be slain."

"Hush didn't truly become a primal dragon until her heart was broken. It was only then that the elemental cold filled the vacant space inside her. My people revere Hush; our land rests upon her slumbering back. In exchange for our worship, the dragon grants her followers magical gifts."

"Back to the topic at hand, Tower is seriously going to try to kill Greatshadow with a harpoon made of ice?" Infidel rolled her eyes. "This is going to last, what, five seconds inside the volcano?"

"The Jagged Heart can negate any heat it encounters. Cold is the true condition of all existence; heat is merely a local aberration. If the Heart still exists, it's the perfect weapon to destroy Greatshadow. Of course, someone would need to carry it within striking distance of the dragon. That's a nearly impossible task."

"'Nearly impossible' is semantically the same as 'possible,'" said Relic. "With Lord Tower involved, it's probable. He wears the Armor of Faith. It will shield him from Greatshadow's powers."

Infidel nodded. "Yeah, I guess that would work."

Now it was Aurora's turn to look puzzled. "Armor of Faith?"

"It looks like a suit of plate armor," said Infidel. "It encases Tower completely and is filled with a lot of gears and ratchets that enhance his strength. Pretty much nothing can penetrate it."

"Greatshadow's breath melts armor," said Aurora.

"If it's metal. But this armor is made of prayer. The Church of the Book has a team of monks whose sole job is to pray Tower's armor into existence. One monk does nothing but pray for the helmet, another prays for the greaves, another guy prays for the shoulder pads, and so on. Every single gear and rivet on this thing has a monk — actually a whole squad of monks — whose only spiritual duty is to maintain their unceasing faith that the armor can't be so much as scratched."

Aurora nodded slowly. "Very well. Let's suppose the armor

works. Tower can reach Greatshadow and slay his body. Then what? This is a primal dragon, the very spirit of fire. There's a little of Greatshadow's essence in all flame. You need to extinguish every fire in the world at once to truly kill him. If you overlooked a single flickering candle, he could eventually weave a new body and seek vengeance."

"This is why Lord Tower doesn't travel alone," said Relic. "The Voice of the Book has issued a Writ of Judgment. A Truthspeaker will read this writ aloud before Greatshadow's spirit, slaying it."

Aurora stroked her chin, rubbing the bulges where her tusks were anchored in her jaw. "I still can't believe they have the Jagged Heart. Maybe they're the ones fooled by a replica."

"But you would know when you saw it," said Relic. "And you *can* see it again. Arrange for Infidel and myself to be hired as mercenaries on the quest, and when we kill Lord Tower, we'll return the harpoon to you."

Aurora shook her head. "I see no reason to trust you with this task. I owe the Black Swan my life, but it's my sacred duty to recover the Jagged Heart. I'll resign my position with the Black Swan and petition Lord Tower to join his team on my own. You may attempt the same. I won't speak against you."

Relic glared at her. I could tell he hadn't considered the possibility that Aurora would take a more direct path toward recovering the artifact.

Aurora seemed unconcerned by Relic's baleful gaze. She looked over at Infidel.

"First the sarong, now a skirt. What's with your wardrobe lately?"

Infidel shrugged. "Once I have Greatshadow's treasure, I'll hire a team of tailors to follow me around. Until then, I'm getting by with whatever's handy."

"Why are you so confident you can kill Lord Tower? If he's good enough to take down a primal dragon, I don't see how an undisciplined brawler like you will stand a chance."

Infidel chuckled. "Armor or not, I've thought of a thousand different ways of killing Tower. He'll be dead before he knows what hit him."

"A thousand?" asked Aurora, sounding amused. "What's your grudge against the knight?"

"It's kind of a long story," said Infidel, raising her hand and pinching about a half inch of air between her thumb and forefinger, "but I once got *this* close to marrying the bastard."

To my great frustration, Aurora didn't ask to hear the long story, not even a short version of it. Her devotion to the unwritten rules of Commonground was admirable to a fault.

Relic dismissed Bigsby, telling him his services were no longer needed, as he and Infidel set off for the *Black Swan*. Aurora walked alone, a few hundred feet ahead. Relic, despite his bent form and hobbling gait, proved to be rather spry, keeping up with Infidel's tireless pace with no sign of effort.

The sun was rising by the time we reached the docks. The daylight revealed a half dozen corpses floating in the brine. It was a rare night in Commonground that didn't yield a few murder victims. Bleary-eyed river-pygmies in dugout canoes poled their ways under the docks, gathering the bodies. Commonground bred strange industries. Pulling the right corpse out of the drink could be the equivalent of winning a lottery. Any given body might turn out to be an outlaw with a price on his head, payable dead or alive. Or, you might recover the corpse of a wayward son of a wealthy family and demand a ransom to return the remains for proper burial. In contrast, my career of looting temples and ruins seemed like honest work.

As Relic and Infidel approached the *Black Swan* barge, I noticed that the stream of clients leaving the bar was a bit heavier than usual. It was like the place was emptying out completely. Patrons grumbled as they walked past us, luggage in hand. Some of them were standing around, looking lost as they stared at empty boat slips. It dawned on me that only half the ordinary number of ships were docked this morning. What was going on?

Waiting at the front door of the *Black Swan*, arms crossed, were the Three Goons, looking stern. When Aurora walked up to them, No-Face moved to intercept her as Menagerie locked the front door. We were still too far away to hear what the Goons said, but not too far away to hear Aurora's loud and astonished reply: "What do you mean, I'm fired?"

Hearing this, Infidel launched herself into the air, covering the distance with a single bound. She landed beside Aurora, not wanting to miss any juicy details, as Menagerie said, "The Black Swan no longer requires your services. This establishment is closed until further notice."

"You're joking," said Aurora.

Menagerie shook his head. Reeker chewed a toothpick as he stared at Aurora, obviously amused by her confusion. No-Face slowly tossed the iron ball he carried back and forth between his beefy hands, his attention focused tightly on Aurora, no doubt hoping she'd make trouble. It was almost breakfast time, and it was a rare day when the Goons didn't beat up someone before breakfast.

Here's a quick primer on the Goons: I've mentioned No-Face a couple of times. He's got a flap of scarred skin that hangs down from where a normal man's eyebrows should be, covering his face like a curtain. There's a tiny gap on the left side of the flesh-mask where a single pale eye peers out. Perhaps because his eyesight is iffy, he tends to strike anything that moves when he's in combat, which is why he pegged Infidel that one time. He's bald, his whole scalp covered with pale, shiny scars from the countless brawls he's been in. They say he was sold as a baby to a traveling circus for display as a freak, but by the time he was eight he was big and mean enough to take up pit-fighting. Now, he's seven feet tall, but manages to look squat due to the thickness of his muscles. The only armor he wears is a chain-mail vest; his only weapon is a fifty pound iron ball at the end of a long chain that he keeps rolled around his forearm. I've heard he feeds himself by pounding his victims into pulp with the ball, then sucking the remains under his flap into whatever mouth is hidden there.

Next on the Goon roster is Reeker, a half-seed. Half-seeding is a variant of blood magic, suppressed by the church but never wiped out. Women who wish to get pregnant visit blood-houses to acquire specially prepared animal semen to, shall we say, supplement contributions from their husbands. In theory, the mix of animal and human sperm produces children with desirable qualities. A half-seed bull child will be strong and willful. A half-seed panther, agile and silent. No one knows if Reeker's mother meant to purchase skunk juice, or if she got burned by an unscrupulous blood-house. The product was a man who can emit odors at will from every bodily orifice. The stench can bring even the toughest fighter to his knees. When Reeker's not actively shooting out stink clouds, he's still got a wet-dog whiff to him that makes you envy No-Face's lack of nose.

Unlike No-Face, Reeker doesn't have a scar on him. No one ever gets close enough to land a punch. He's learned to spit a gob of the worst smelling phlegm you can imagine up to twenty feet, and he's more than happy to cut a gagging man's throat to put him out of his misery. Reeker matches his dastardly combat style with a personality that's all leers and crude jokes. Yet, for reasons I've never understood, he's popular with women, even women who aren't whores. He's got a dumpy physique, and, at five-foot-nine, looks tiny next to the other Goons. Maybe it's his hair. Above a pasty, round face, he's got a thick, wavy, black mane that any woman would envy, sporting two snow-white streaks running back from his temples.

The final Goon is Menagerie. He's about six four and skinny

as a rail. He's normally dressed in a loincloth and sandals, showing off the animal tattoos covering him from the crown of his shaved head to the little gaps between his toes. Most of the animals are predators. He's got lions, tigers, bears, ohmis (a jungle viper), sharks, and eagles. Being tattooed in Commonground rarely earns you a second glance, though Menagerie has taken his skin art further than the average sailor. What makes Menagerie stand out is that his tattoos are alive, inked in the blood of the various beasts, and infused with their spirits. Stare at them long enough and you'll swear they're breathing. No one has ever actually seen one move, but one day the shark will be on his right shoulder, the next day on his left thigh, like it's swimming around. That's a neat trick, but it's not what makes him dangerous. Menagerie's a shape-shifter. He can surrender his body to any of these spirits, taking on their forms in the blink of an eye. The people he fights face off with a tall, skinny, unarmed man, and two seconds later they've had their hand bitten off by an alligator, their guts raked by a tiger, and have a rattlesnake clamped down on their jugular.

Remember I told you that No-Face wasn't the Goon people were really afraid of? Menagerie is the Goon people are really afraid of.

Back to the confrontation: Aurora clenched her fists. "Stand aside. What you're saying makes no sense."

Menagerie shook his head. "We both know that everything the Black Swan does makes sense, even if we mere mortals are blind to the logic."

Reeker spit out his toothpick. "Heh. Maybe the bar ain't profitable now that Stagger's pushing daisies."

If it was possible to die from a mean look, Reeker would have joined me in the afterlife from the glare Infidel gave him. No-Face found the crack funny, judging from the muffled, farting, "hur hur hur," that filtered from beneath his face flap.

Menagerie raised his hand. Reeker looked instantly chagrined. No-Face's spooky chuckle went silent.

"I apologize for the insensitivity of my colleagues," the tattooed man said to Infidel. "Stagger was a beloved brother in the larger family of Commonground. I, for one, shall miss him."

"Yeah," said Reeker. "I kind of liked the guy. There going to be a funeral? I'll send flowers."

"The funeral was private," said Infidel. "And I don't want to talk about Stagger any more. I want to talk about the dragon hunt you boys are going on. I want in."

"As do I," said Relic, hobbling up beside the women.

Menagerie looked down at the hunchback. "Who the hell are you?"

"Infidel calls me Relic. This will serve."

"Uh-huh," said Menagerie. "I can't help but notice that you look, um... less than formidable. While I can't confirm the existence of any upcoming dragon hunts, may I ask what, exactly, would you bring to the table?"

"Knowledge," said Relic. "I've survived Greatshadow's lair before. My experience may provide the difference between success and failure."

"Is that so?" said Menagerie.

The hunchback nodded.

"Be that as it may, I am not in charge of hiring for any missions that may or may not be occurring soon," said Menagerie. "The Black Swan may have been conducting transactions of this nature, but to reiterate, she's now closed to all business."

Aurora clenched her fists. "Menagerie, who do you think you're fooling? You know I know all about the mission. Get the hell out of my way. I'm talking to the Black Swan." She stepped forward, looking ready to push the mercenaries aside.

Reeker spit a gob of pale green phlegm toward her eyes. The wad crackled as it froze inches from her skin, bouncing harmlessly off her cheek, its foul payload neutralized. She punched out with an ice-gauntleted fist, sending the skunk-man flying toward the edge of the dock. He landed on his feet with inches to spare, but momentum was against him. He stumbled backward, and vanished over the edge with a splash.

No-Face swung his chain-draped fist and caught Aurora beneath the chin, hard enough that the frost coating her face flew off in a spray. She went down, landing flat on her back, as snow danced in the air where she'd just stood. She started to rise, but before she could sit up, Menagerie leapt toward her, taking the form of a huge, black-horned ram. His head smashed into Aurora's tusks with a loud, sharp *crack*. Aurora's arms flopped to her side as she stared up into the pale morning sky, cross-eyed and dazed.

Infidel grinned. This was her oh-good-there's-a-fight-and-I-was-wanting-to-hit-someone grin. She punched No-Face right where his mouth should have been. He staggered backward, stopping when his back slammed into the locked door of the *Black Swan*. Infidel kicked him in the gut, shattering the wood behind him, knocking him inside.

Infidel spun to face Menagerie, who'd leapt into the air as a ram. In the span of a heartbeat, his body flowed into a fifteen-foot-long shark, his mouth stretched wide enough to clamp onto Infidel's face. She raised both hands, shielding herself with her forearms as the toothy jaws snapped shut. There was a loud *crunch*. Bright fragments of white teeth showered onto the docks. For half a second, the shark hung there, clamped onto Infidel's unbreakable arms. Infidel head-butted the shark in the snout. The big fish flew off, and Menagerie was once again human as he landed ass-first on the dock, blood streaming from his nose.

"Ouch," he said, spitting out broken teeth.

Infidel loomed over him, fists clenched. "Had enough?"

From inside the jagged hole that No-Face had left in the door, there was a confused grunt.

Menagerie looked toward the hole, and his face went slack. Infidel turned toward the noise as well. Her brow furrowed as her eyes adjusted to the shadows before her. Aurora rose up on her knees, shaking her head. When she finally followed the others' gazes, she whispered, "This is unexpected."

The main room of the bar was completely transformed. All the gaming tables were gone, as were the paintings on the wall. No-Face was sitting up, rubbing his skin-flap, dust swirling around him. "Whuduhfuh?" he mumbled as he looked around.

Cobwebs clung to every corner of the room. The grime was so thick on the floor that No-Face had left a little dust-angel where he'd fallen. Behind the bar, the shelves were empty, save for dirt. There was no evidence that the place had been a thriving business full of people only moments before.

Menagerie stepped into the room. Aurora and Infidel followed.

Menagerie muttered something to himself I couldn't quite catch, save for the word 'time.'

"Oh no," said Aurora, who'd apparently caught what he was saying. "She was too old to go back more than a day or two. She'd never survive a longer trip. She—"

"You aren't blind, Aurora," said Menagerie.

"Is this a private conversation, or would you care to fill me in on what's happened?" asked Infidel.

Relic hobbled into the room. "They won't betray the Black Swan's secret. I, however, am not bound by their oaths of loyalty. The Black Swan owes her power and influence to a rather tragic curse. She—"

"Guys!" shouted Reeker as he rushed into the room, water streaming from his clothes. "You gotta come look at this."

The whole building shuddered as he spoke. The air took on the stench of rotten eggs, but Reeker didn't seem to be the source of the odor.

Menagerie furrowed his brow. "Did the barge just hit bottom?"

"All the water's draining out of the bay!" said Reeker, waving his arms for emphasis.

"Luhguptaruh," said No-Face.

"Good idea," said Menagerie. "To the roof!"

Before he finished speaking, where the man had stood there was an owl gliding forward. He flapped his wings once and shot toward the cobwebbed spiral staircase in the far corner of the room, vanishing as he tilted his wings and flew up to the second floor.

No-Face and Reeker followed without hesitation.

Aurora grabbed Infidel by the arm. "You took my side," she said. "Thank you."

"What?" asked Infidel.

"In the fight with the Goons. You defended me when I was down."

Infidel shrugged. "It was three against one. I always side with the underdog. It's nothing."

Aurora nodded. "Still, I owe you one."

Relic sighed as he hobbled across the room toward the staircase.

"You women can bond another time," he grumbled. "Right now, we should follow the owl."

CHAPTER FIVE
ALL MUST BURN!

THE ROOF OF the *Black Swan* was a broad, flat deck with four large stained-glass dome skylights and a sixty-foot mast that jutted up from the middle, with smaller masts fore and aft. It had been many years since the bar had actually been moved with sails; the masts now served mainly as flag poles to fly the barge's banner, a field of pure white with a black swan in the center. Menagerie stood in the crows nest atop the tallest mast, peering out at the bay, his hand raised to shield his eyes from the morning sun. Infidel leapt, grabbing the rigging, and in seconds reached his side.

Ignoring the main reason we'd come out here, her gaze was instead drawn to Menagerie's face. It took me half a second to understand why it was so interesting at this particular moment.

"You have your teeth back," she said.

"Owls don't have teeth, so when I changed back, I grew new ones," said Menagerie. "Can we focus on the problem at hand?"

The water was flowing out from the bay so swiftly that fish were left flopping in the mud. The *Black Swan* was anchored in water ordinarily twenty feet deep at its lowest, but it now sat flat on the bottom, the whole structure shuddering as it slowly sunk into the muck. As far as the eye could see boats were stranded across the bay, except, I noted, the ships of Wanderers. These had been the ships that had gone missing during the night. They were now far out at the mouth of the bay, dozens of them, riding on a ridge of water that bunched up near the gap leading to open water.

"You ever see anything like this?" Infidel asked.

Menagerie shook his head; he was the oldest of the Goons, a resident of Commonground for over forty years. He pointed toward the bright blue forms of river-pygmies running out on the mud flats, snatching up the stranded fish. "Maybe they know what's going on."

But before Infidel could leap down to speak to a pygmy, a mountain of bright blue-green water rose from the sea just beyond the Wanderer's ships. It kept rising, as other bulges formed around it. It vaguely resembled, from a distance, an enormous sea-turtle, assuming one could grow to be several miles wide.

Suddenly, the impossibility that this was a giant turtle changed into reality as the beast's eyes snapped open. Its vast maw yawned wide, a mouth several hundred yards across. The Wanderer ships were pulled toward it by a fierce suction. Yet, these expert seafarers proved the match of the turbulent white water, guiding their schooners across the ship-studded waves as agilely as a river-pygmy steering a canoe through the pilings of Commonground. In moments, all the vessels had ridden the flow of water into the mouth of the great beast.

"It's Abyss," said Menagerie, his voice hushed in awe.

Abyss is the primal dragon of the sea. His consciousness spreads through every wave and ripple in the world's vast ocean. Due to his pact with the Wanderers, he's one of the few dragons who still intervenes in human affairs. Most of primal dragons don't even notice mankind, any more than an earthquake notices the cities it topples, or a tornado notices the villages it smashes to splinters. To witness a primal dragon personify itself, taking on at least an echo of its original form, was something few men would ever see in their lives.

With the last of the Wanderers swallowed, Abyss closed his mouth and spun, heading back toward the open ocean. The mound of water that had been heaped up by his arrival collapsed, sending a wave fifty feet high surging back into the emptied bay.

"Brace yourselves!" Menagerie shouted, before changing into an eagle and launching himself into the air. He could barely be heard as the roar of the water reached us, a thundering wall of sound that made the timbers of the *Black Swan* tremble. The tidal wave hit the far end of the docks, sending boards and pilings flying high into the air. The boats of slavers, pirates, and pleasure seekers splintered as they were crushed by the rushing water.

The wave hit the *Black Swan*. The barge was solidly built, but still the timbers cracked and snapped as the water lifted it, spinning it sideways, carrying it up over the docks and gangplanks, crushing everything in its path. Infidel clung to the railing of the crow's nest; the mast groaned, but didn't topple. The barge began to bob in the relatively smoother water behind the crest of the wave. The tsunami kept moving, reaching the normal boundaries of the shore, then beyond, carrying debris and corpses up over the marshes, into the forests.

Infidel looked down as the barge settled on the remains of docks and boats trapped beneath it. Relic was nowhere to be seen. No-Face had wrapped his ball and chain around the mast and was still on his feet, completely drenched. Reeker dangled in his hammy grasp, his normally well-groomed mane now tangled with a mass of brown seaweed. Aurora stood on the water next to the barge, seemingly walking on the waves, until the current calmed and revealed an ice floe beneath her.

The ogress shouted to the eagle circling overhead, "This is what she saw! This is why she went back!"

Infidel shouted down, "Would someone tell me what the hell is going on?"

Relic cleared his throat. Infidel spun around. He was standing right behind her. I never saw him climb the rigging, though, admittedly, my attention had been focused elsewhere. His rags were drenched; steam rose from them as if they'd been soaked in boiling wash-water rather than the tepid waters of the bay. He smelled vaguely of brimstone as he said, "On the day that the Black Swan was to be married, her groom was killed in a horseback accident. It was a senseless, pointless, random tragedy; the world is full of such moments. Unknown to her fiancé, the Black Swan was a Weaver, a member of a secret sect of witches with the power to rend the fabric of reality and knit it back into something more to their liking. Yet, even Weavers lack the power to restore life to the dead. In her grief, the Black Swan sought out Avaris, Queen of Weavers, and asked her for a boon. She wished for the power to go back in time so that she might avoid these random tragedies."

Infidel looked around at the devastated mishmash of broken ships and crushed docks that had once been Commonground. "She didn't do a very good job of stopping this."

"I didn't say she could stop tragedies," said Relic. "I said she could avoid them; the Black Swan isn't here. She's lived through this tidal wave, then traveled back in time to abandon the barge and relocate elsewhere before the destruction occurred."

The eagle lighted gently onto the rail of the crow's nest. Then, in a twinkling, Menagerie stood next to Relic.

"How do you know this?" he asked.

Relic shrugged. "Is it important? You know it's the truth. You and Aurora have experienced the time shifts enough to recognize them and remember them. I know what's happening due to... certain talents."

Menagerie scowled. "Who are you again?"

"The only name I've ever been given is Relic."

Infidel said, "You've also been called Lum—"

"Relic," said Relic.

Menagerie looked down as Aurora formed a staircase of ice to walk back onto the deck of the barge. The water was swirling all around; the mast swayed as the barge bumped along the bottom.

"She was too old," Aurora called out, looking around at the wreckage. "She'll never survive going back."

Infidel shook her head. "Has everyone but me lost their minds? You're seriously expecting me to believe the Black Swan is some kind of time-traveler?"

"Yes, but only in one direction. She can jump backwards in her own timeline to pivotal moments. She moves forward in time at the same speed as the rest of us," said Menagerie, apparently no longer seeing a reason to protect the secret. "Her curse is that, when she goes back in time, she doesn't regain her youth. If she lived through an event at age forty that she could have changed by making a different decision at age twenty, she can go back to that event, but she'll go back as a forty-year-old, not a twenty-year-old. Only twenty-nine years have passed since the Black Swan was born, but physically, she's almost a hundred and twenty. The husband she loved so dearly rejected her, disgusted that she turned into an old crone while he was still a youth. The Black Swan only cares about wealth now; everything else she regards as impermanent."

"A fat lot of good all her money will do her if she's dead," said Infidel.

Menagerie shrugged. "So far, her money has allowed her to purchase the potions needed to keep her alive. I'm in no position to disapprove of her priorities. I've made a sizable fortune from the Black Swan's business acumen."

"Really?" said Infidel. "The only thing you seem to own is that loincloth."

"Even a Goon may have a family," said Menagerie. "My loved ones are very comfortable."

By now, the bay was slowly starting to return to a normal level, as the water flowed back from the forest. The air smelled horrible, like every outhouse in the world had been overturned at once. All over the place, men were climbing out the water, clinging to overturned boats and the few strips of dock that had somehow survived.

Aurora shouted up, "There are people trapped in all this rubble. I'm going to help who I can."

Menagerie nodded. "A wise suggestion. We should all help out. We can... can...." His voice trailed off as his eyes were drawn toward the mouth of the bay. Seven large ships were sailing through the rocky gap. Their sails were a pale blue-white, catching the morning sun like silver. Flags fluttered from the pinnacles, showing a green dragon against a sky-blue field.

Infidel followed his gaze toward the ships.

"It's King Brightmoon's fleet," she said.

"Some of it, at least," said Menagerie. "Rather bold of them, just sailing in during broad daylight. Aren't they worried that Greatshadow might notice?"

Suddenly, the sky darkened. Everyone looked up, back toward the peak of Tanakiki. A mile-high jet of solid black smoke mushroomed up into the air, swiftly turning day into night. Bright red sparks shot through the atmosphere as the rim of the caldera crumpled, sending a white-orange river of molten lava spilling toward the bay. Trees exploded into flame ahead of the lava as a shimmering wave of heat spread outward.

The smoke and cinders swirled until they took on the shape of a dragon, spreading mile-long wings of black smoke. Two smaller dragons shot out of the folds of the wings, flying toward the bay. Smaller, in this case, is a relative term. These were huge beasts, a hundred yards long tip to tail, with glowing red scales edged in black. Their wings were larger than the mainsails of the king's ships. They had long tails that ended in tufts of flame. They looked as if they swam through the air, surfing the wind as they sailed down the slopes, aiming toward the king's ships.

Greatshadow himself remained in the caldera, a beast composed of flame and smoke, who roared, in a language I'd never heard yet instantly understood: "ALL MUST BURN!"

"He noticed," said Infidel.

These were the first living dragons I'd ever seen, even

76

though I've handled a lot of dragon bones in my time, and seen more than a few depictions of the beasts carved onto walls or woven into tapestries. Dragons used to be numerous, until the Church of the Book nearly wiped them all out.

The survivors are the primal dragons. These beasts were so fluent in elemental magic that they eventually became the elements themselves.

Of course, if there are no more ordinary dragons, I had to wonder just what the hell was flying toward us. The creatures looked exactly like they did in the books in the monastery; big serpents, with a long neck and serpentine tail, and a short, thick, pot-bellied torso with four legs a bit too small in proportion to the rest of its form. What they lacked in legs, they more than made up for in wings. The wings were easily as wide as the body was long, huge membranes of drum-taut flesh that reminded me of the limbs of jungle bats.

Smoke trailed from their nostrils as they passed overhead. They were at least a quarter-mile up, but the furnace-like heat of their bodies washed over the remnants of the *Black Swan* as they beat their wings in a powerful downstroke. In seconds, they were at the mouth of the bay, facing the king's ships. Their jaws gaped open and their pot bellies swelled as they inhaled uncounted gallons of air. At last, they breathed out.

Infidel shielded her eyes as a second sun formed where the jets of flame shooting from the twin dragons overlapped. As the light faded, all seven of the king's ships were aflame. At this distance, the men were little more than insects throwing themselves into the sea, trailing smoke as they fell.

The dragons spun around. Again, they sucked in air and breathed flame, the light of their assault casting long stark shadows on the roof of the *Black Swan*. When the light faded, little remained of the ships. The sea itself was boiling where the boats had been mere seconds before.

Satisfied with their work on the fleet, the dragons split,

making a more leisurely approach toward what remained of Commonground. Along the way, they spit fire at the few boats and canoes that were afloat out in the bay. The distant screams of frying men carried over the water.

One of the dragons turned its serpent face toward the *Black Swan*.

"Uh oh," said Infidel.

"Goons!" Menagerie shouted to No-Face and Reeker on the roof below. "Let's teach these oversized garden snakes some manners. Maneuver nine!"

"Rurh!" said No-Face, grabbing up a shattered roof beam.

Reeker looked pale as he shouted to Menagerie, "You're joking, right?"

No-Face handled the twenty-foot beam, thick as a grown man's thigh, like it was no heavier than a piece of kindling. The big man slapped the beam down at the edge of the roof, with about six feet hanging out, pointing straight toward the advancing dragon. Reeker held up his hands as No-Face approached him.

"C'mon, guy, I mean, you can't really—"

No-Face grabbed him by his shirt and spun him around, sitting him squarely on the end of the beam that sat upon the roof. Reeker swallowed hard. "Boys, it's been good knowing ya," he whispered.

"Guh," said No-Face, nodding.

"On the count of three!" Menagerie shouted. "Three!" He threw himself from the crow's nest. When he was over the point where the broken beam jutted into space, he changed again, taking the form of a hippopotamus.

Like most hippos who discover themselves to be sixty feet up in the air, he dropped like a stone. He hit the edge of the plank with all four of his fat, round feet expertly placed for leverage. Reeker shot into the sky, his hands clasped before him, his eyes tightly closed. His lips were moving, though I couldn't hear him. It looked for all the world like he was praying.

The Goons' aim was perfection; there was a reason why they were the best paid mercenaries in Commonground. The dragon dove toward the *Black Swan*, opening its mouth to fill its great bellow lungs with air. What it got, instead, was a damp skunk-man slapping against the roof of its mouth. Instinctively, the beast clamped its jaws shut. Instantly, a cloud of yellow-green fumes shot out from between its long, jagged teeth. Its eyes grew wide.

The creature veered away from the *Black Swan*, whipping its head back and forth, coughing violently, unable to breathe deeply enough to ignite its flames. Reeker clung to the beast's tongue, hugging it with his arms and legs like it was a greased pole. Slowly, he slipped toward the tip. His entire form was hazy, as the most powerful stenches he could summon poured out of every pore. The dragon began to convulse, its nervous system overwhelmed by the chemical assault. With a final, frantic jerk of its neck, it sent Reeker flying. Before it could recover, it slammed into the waters of the bay, hard, vanishing beneath the surface in a violent boil.

Reeker shrieked like a teenage girl as he sailed through the air before he, too, hit the surface of the water, bouncing once, twice, thrice like a skimming stone before he sank, leaving an oily film.

"One down," said Relic, casting his gaze toward the beast's twin, who was still burning ships at the other edge of the bay. "Unfortunately, we're running out of Goons."

Reeker still hadn't surfaced, nor was there any sign of a hippo thrashing about in the waters below. No-Face had run to the edge of the barge and was looking down into the water, shouting out, "Munuh! Rukuh!"

Infidel cracked her knuckles. "We don't need no stinkin' Goons."

Below, there was a loud crash. I hadn't seen Aurora in over a minute, and now her head was sticking up from a trap door in the roof. She climbed out, bearing a large wooden harpoon, nearly twice as tall as she was, with a long coil of rope looped around her shoulders.

"I've hunted whales bigger than these things," she shouted, as she met Infidel's gaze.

"Fire-breathing, flying whales?" asked Infidel.

"You wouldn't believe," Aurora said.

The ogress spun around as the remaining dragon roared angrily and shot toward the barge, apparently now aware of the loss of its twin. Aurora dropped the coil of rope to the deck and drew back with the harpoon. "For honor!" she cried as she hurled the weapon toward the approaching beast.

The harpoon never even got close. The coil snagged on a ragged board and the weapon jerked to a sudden halt not fifty feet overhead. The dragon inhaled deeply as it plunged straight toward Aurora. Aurora crouched down, covering her head with her hands as the dragon exhaled, shooting out a jet of flame, engulfing the ice-ogress. The dragon's momentum carried it toward the mast upon which Infidel was perched. The flames instantly disintegrated the lower half of the mast. Infidel jumped from the crow's nest, grabbing Relic by the cloak and hurling him out toward the bay. She dropped down, hands open wide, as the dragon's scaly back flashed beneath her. She grabbed hold of the scales near the beast's tail. The dragon reacted with the speed of thought, whipping the end of its tail down to shatter more beams on the roof of the *Black Swan*. The jolt knocked Infidel free. She bounced across the deck, flying off the edge, until a long length of chain whipped out and lassoed her ankle. No-Face jerked her back onto the roof, if it could still be called a roof. Little was left but a pile of broken boards and timbers, and half of these were on fire.

Aurora was still alive. She was crouched behind a wall of cracked and melting ice, fighting to untangle the snagged rope of the harpoon.

Infidel leapt to where the harpoon had fallen. It jutted up from the boards of the deck. She snatched it free, spinning around, racing toward Aurora, splintering the snagged board that had caught the rope. She wordlessly snatched the freshly coiled rope from Aurora's hands and jumped over the edge, flying from the *Black Swan* toward a still intact piling. She landed on this and leapt again, giving chase to the retreating dragon, who now spun slowly over the area where the other dragon had fallen. The sea still boiled furiously. The dragon again cried out; this time the thunderous roar had an edge of grief to it. The beast turned its head upward, flapping its mighty wings as it steered back toward the distant volcano. The whole south slope was aflame now, the forests forming the world's largest bonfire as the pyroclastic flow slipped through the once lush jungles.

Infidel landed on a final piling before deciding she was close enough. She dropped the coil into the water, wrapping the last few inches around her wrist. The beast was low over the waves, the down beat of its wings brushing the surface. She reared back with the harpoon, the weapon comically long compared to her. When she let it fly, it flashed through the air more swiftly than an arrow. The dragon grunted as the harpoon buried itself in its flank, but didn't look back. It flapped its wings again and flew higher, as the rope trailed behind it. Infidel grabbed hold with both hands as she was snapped into the air. She clambered up the rope like a monkey on a vine. The dragon tilted its head back, aware of her weight. It sucked in air and exhaled a long cone of flame, engulfing Infidel. For a second, she couldn't be seen at all in the conflagration. Then, her hand reached out of the flame, grasping onto the hind-claw of the dragon just as the rope disintegrated.

The flames faded, revealing Infidel clasped by a single hand onto the middle nail of the dragon's hind-claw. Her clothes were mostly burned away; her skin was flushed red, like she had sunburn, and it broke my heart to see that her long, flowing tresses were mostly gone, singed down to a frizzled mess. Her eyes were set in a look of determination.

The dragon wasn't impressed. It flexed its claw forward, bending its head toward her to bite away the unwelcome passenger. As it opened its jaws, Infidel swung her body back and forth, dangling from the claw. The creature's mouth glowed with the fading remnants of its flame. I saw a flash of light as the well-honed blade of my bone-handled knife was revealed in Infidel's free hand. She swung forward, leaping into the beast's open jaws, clearing its teeth. The creature's mouth clamped shut.

Suddenly, I was alive again. Not ghost alive; I was physically whole once more, popping into existence inches above the dragon's snout. Unlike my previous manifestations, this time the laws of gravity applied. I slammed into the dragon's scales, sliding down its snout, scraping my restored flesh on its raspy hide. I cut my hands trying to grab hold. The scales were like flakes of razor-sharp volcanic glass. I screamed as I left a trail of blood down its snout, but caught myself at last, my foot coming to rest on the ridge of its nostrils.

My stomach twisted as the beast lurched through the air. The ground seemed impossibly distant. I felt certain I'd been restored to life only to face a second death. But... why? How had this happened?

Suddenly, Infidel's fist burst through the skin only a few feet down the snout from the dragon's eyes, my bone-handled knife firmly in her grasp. The dragon's blood bubbled on the surface of the blade, quickly boiling off now that it was exposed to air. Infidel's whole arm tore through the skin, followed by a shoulder, then her bloodied head burst through. The blood boiled on her skin as well as the knife. The creature shuddered, then went limp in the air; whatever Infidel had done to it had apparently been too much to withstand. The beast's snout tilted down. I could see water far below; at some point, we'd come back out over the bay. I was thrown free of the beast's nose, my naked, bleeding body tumbling in the air. As I spun, I looked back toward Infidel, who was gawking at me, her eyes wide.

"Infidel!" I shouted, straining my hand toward her.

"Stagger?" she whispered.

Then, the last of the fresh blood vaporized from the knife, leaving only a crust of black gore. The wind once more passed straight through me. I was suspended in mid-air, no longer in the grip of gravity. Light passed through my vaporous fingers.

"Stagger!" Infidel cried, her eyes frantic as they searched the air where she'd last seen me.

Then the dragon hit the water, and I plunged beneath as well, my ghost still tethered to the knife. The sea was black as ink, full of the stirred-up silt from the tidal wave. My vision was all but useless, unable to make sense of the images that flashed past me. The dragon's hide seemed to be crumbling, breaking apart into bits of black and red gravel. For half a second, I saw a flash of Infidel's torso. There was something long and rope-like wrapped around it, covered with cup-sized suckers. The water roiled, and a giant eye flashed past me, the size of a dinner plate, glowing with a golden phosphorescence.

Then, suddenly, Infidel and my knife were back above the surface of the water. She was wrapped in the tentacle of an enormous squid, at least sixty feet long. A second tentacle held the soggy, sputtering form of Reeker.

Infidel raised her knife to stab at the tentacle that held her, but stopped herself before she thrust the blade down. The dragon blood had been washed off by her plunge into the bay. As the last bit of pink water ran down the handle, I faded once more, invisible even to myself.

The squid's tentacles gingerly placed Infidel onto the wrecked roof of the *Black Swan*. She was, yet again, buck naked save for a ring of ruined leather that had once been the too-short skirt. Aurora rushed to her side, snatching up the half-charred flag of the barge and draping it over Infidel's bare shoulders before Reeker had recovered enough to ogle her.

"That was really damn impressive," Aurora said. "But... who was up there with you?"

"What?" asked Infidel, running her fingers through what was left of her hair. The longest bits were only a few inches long.

"For a second, I thought I saw someone else clamped onto the dragon's snout with you. Were my eyes playing tricks?"

Infidel turned pale. "I thought I saw... I thought..." her voice trailed off. "It was just some poor sailor. He... he fell."

Menagerie dragged himself up onto the roof, human once more. The squid tattoo that had once been dark black upon his neck had faded to a barely visible gray-blue outline.

He collapsed against what was left of the mast, staring up toward the still bubbling volcano. "I guess the king's dragon hunt has been cancelled."

Infidel shook her head as she, too, looked at the raging mountain. "I don't think so. Greatshadow has just been suckered. Those ships were decoys; I'll stake my life on it."

"You're probably right," said Reeker, wringing water from his hair. He looked at Menagerie. "So, anyway, I quit. I'm done with dragons. Infidel can be the third Goon."

"You aren't quitting," said Menagerie. "You signed the contract." He tapped at a section of cursive text on the left cheek of his buttocks. "Didn't you read all the terms? You're in this until Greatshadow's dead, or you are."

Reeker sighed, then muttered something underneath his breath.

"Hur hur hur," said No-Face.

Infidel laughed as she contemplated Menagerie's skinny ass. "I guess that's one way of discouraging people from studying the fine print."

CHAPTER SIX

INNOCENT

MY OLD SAILBOAT had come to rest in the tangled branches of a mangrove thicket half a mile away. The gaping holes in the hull would never allow it to return to the bay, but as a tree house it possessed a certain charm. Menagerie had spotted it in the aftermath of the dragon strike, as he'd flitted over the area in his vulture form, surveying the damage. He'd quickly singled out the most likely places to look for survivors, then he and the other Goons had set forth to help who they could.

Infidel was never afraid to lend a hand to anyone in need, but she declined to take part in the rescue mission. I couldn't blame her; she looked completely wiped out after her fight with the dragon. She found Relic's gnarled staff among the shattered planks of the *Black Swan* and used it for support as she limped across the rubble in search of my boat. She was sweating, her face pale and feverish. Her invulnerable skin didn't burn, but, like anyone, when she got overheated, she could feel sick. It didn't help that the sun had come out with a fury, its tropical rays turning the humid atmosphere over the churned up bay into a pressure cooker.

At midday, while Infidel still searched through the mangroves, I noticed the Wanderer ships returning. They sailed back into the bay in droves, once again forming a boat city, held together by ropes and ladders instead of docks and gangplanks. River-pygmies were now thick in the bay as well, an entire flotilla of canoes searching among the shattered ships and buildings.

The eruption of the volcano had finally subsided. The once verdant southern slope of the mountain was black now, cloaked with smoke and steam. A shower of fine charcoal ash rained down on the bay, coating every surface.

Infidel was grimy as a miner by the time she found my boat. The once white flag she was wrapped in was now mostly gray. She was all alone as she climbed into the branches. I wondered if Relic had possibly survived. No one had seen the hunchback since she'd tossed him from the crow's nest.

My place was even more of a trash heap than usual. The piles of books had all toppled. The towers of bottles and jugs had turned into a carpet of broken glass. Infidel dug through the rubble until she'd found the thin cotton mat that served as my bed. She yanked it free of the debris and tossed it onto the deck outside. She located a few stained blankets and draped them in the branches, forming an umbrella to provide shade and shield her from the drifting ash.

She toppled onto the bed face first, her body completely slack. She lay motionless for half a minute until she raised her hand to the back of her neck, running her palm along the uneven stubble of her scalp. She groaned, a sound mixing weariness, frustration, and despair.

Then, she fell silent. After five minutes, I could hear her muffled snores. She slept like a corpse, her slumber undisturbed by the tossing, turning, and mumbling that normally characterized it. Hours passed; eventually the long day drew to an end and still she slept, without a single muscle twitching.

The ash rain had finally stopped and the stars were slowly emerging when there was a loud *crunch* in the debris beneath the boat. Infidel didn't stir as the sound repeated itself; something large and heavy was walking around.

Someone called out, "Infidel?"

Infidel remained face down and immobile, her voice muffled as she replied, "Mwuh?"

"Infidel, it's Aurora. Where are you?"

Infidel rolled over on her side.

"Go away," she said, without opening her eyes. Her voice was feeble and scratchy.

"I want to talk," said Aurora. "I brought you some food."

Infidel's unbruised eye cracked open slightly.

"Monkey?" she asked, the faintest glimmer of hope in her voice. River-pygmies sold monkey meat stuck on bamboo reeds, deep fried and served with a chili sauce. Infidel loved the stuff, though I'd never cared for it.

"Sea beans, some whale jerky, and a coconut," said Aurora.

Infidel rolled over on her back, her brow furrowed. She seemed to be caught in an internal debate, weighing her hunger against her desire not to have company. At last, she sighed. "Come on up."

She scooted into a seated position against a mangrove branch, tugging the flag she was wrapped in like a towel higher up her breasts as Aurora climbed onto the boat. Despite the devastation of the day, the night was coming to life with the chirps of frogs and birds. Off in the distance, a troop of apes howled as they scrambled through the canopy. The air was still thick with the smell of putrid water mixed with smoke. All along the slope of the volcano, remnant blazes danced. I felt a sense of longing, looking up at the mountain. It was impossible to say what ancient ruins had been wiped out by the eruption. On the other hand, the forest fires no doubt cleared away the tangles of vines that hid many a lost wonder. I wished I could go up on the slope later this week to scope out the newly revealed terrain.

Aurora sat down on the deck, cross-legged, dropping a large canvas bag in front of her. "I found you some more clothes. I have to say, that idea about a team of tailors following you around sounds like a good idea."

Infidel shrugged. "There aren't many people in the world with skin tougher than their clothing. I can be hell on a pair of pants."

"How did your skin get to be so tough?"

"You aren't supposed to ask stuff like that in Commonground," said Infidel.

"I'm not sure there is a Commonground anymore," said Aurora, glancing back out over the bay.

"Fair enough." Infidel dug into the bag and found the coconut. She cracked it in her bare hands, holding the nut to her lips as the milk began to run out. She gulped down the pale white fluid then wiped her mouth, sitting the coconut aside as she dug back into the bag, pulling out a slender plank of purple meat as long as her forearm.

"Whale jerky, huh? I guess I shouldn't be surprised. Even in a city by the bay, there aren't that many people who keep harpoons in their room."

Aurora nodded. "Whales are central to life on Qikiqtabruk. We eat their flesh, drink their blood, make cheese from their milk—"

"What?"

"What what?"

"Milk? Whales are fish. They don't have teats. How can they have milk?"

"Whales aren't fish. They breathe air like you or me. And, they suckle their young on milk. If you kill a mother whale while she's still nursing, you can harvest barrels of cream. The cheese we make from it is a great delicacy. As high priestess, I would always be given the first batch after a hunt."

"High priestess sounds like nice work if you can get it," said Infidel. "I take it the Jagged Heart was used on the whale hunts?"

"Indirectly. Before each hunt, I would summon the ghosts of whales we'd slain on the previous hunt, and vanquish the spirits so that they couldn't do evil against the ogres going out to hunt. The spirit meat was also essential provision for the dead of our people on their journey into the Great Sea Above. The Jagged Heart also had the power to open a pathway into the afterlife where I could commune with our ancestors. Its pale light would guide us as we sailed from the dragon's jaws into the Great Sea Above."

Infidel rolled her eyes.

"What?" asked Aurora.

"Nothing," she said, as she chomped down on the sheet of meat and tore off a mouthful. She chewed with her mouth open as she said, "Hmm. Not bad. Not fishy at all. I hope you got the spirit of this one; I'd hate for an angry whale ghost to give me indigestion."

Aurora frowned. "You aren't terribly respectful of other people's beliefs."

Infidel shrugged. "I'm not even terribly respectful of my own beliefs. Anyway, why should you care what people think of your religion? It certainly didn't do you much good. Banished by your own people for losing a harpoon."

Aurora's eyes narrowed. I thought she was about to scold Infidel, but then her expression softened. "I wasn't banished. I was executed. I was wrapped in chains and taken to an iceberg. My people chiseled a hole in the ice, then buried me in it. My own brother, Tarpok, filled the hole with water so that it would refreeze. Cold cannot harm me, and my people can survive for days without breathing if we do not struggle. Still, I was left to drift in my frozen tomb, completely trapped, doomed to eventually suffocate or starve."

"But you obviously escaped."

"The Black Swan rescued me. I don't know if it was by pure chance, or due to her ability to travel back in time, but she found me after I'd been adrift for little more than a week. I was near death when she freed me. I had no will to live, but she nursed me back to health anyway. She told me that, since I was dead to my people, I could make a new life with her in Commonground. I hope she's survived.

"I searched the ruins of the barge and found no sign of her. I don't know what to do if she's gone forever."

"She'll be okay. She strikes me as a survivor," said Infidel, who by now had found the sea beans. Sea beans aren't actual beans; they're a puffy weed that grows in marshes. They taste like asparagus soaked in saltwater. They make my mouth pucker, but Infidel likes their crisp snap. "You were going to quit working for the Black Swan anyway. What do you care?"

"As priestess, my whole life was devoted to serving others. Without service, I have no purpose. I didn't always approve of the Black Swan's actions. If she had any greater goal for her life other than accumulating wealth, I never learned of it. Yet, serving her gave structure to my days. I know I was only another employee to her, but she was my world."

Infidel rooted around in the sack once again and pulled out a jug with a cork in it, looking at it skeptically. "What's this?"

"Fresh water," said Aurora. "I don't drink spirits."

Infidel popped the cork and chugged down several cupfuls. "Mmm. I needed that. After a big fight, I'm always thirsty for days."

"It must take a lot of energy, to do the things you do," said Aurora. "There aren't many people who can say they've killed a dragon."

Infidel shrugged. "Yeah. It takes a lot out of me. But, not as much as you might think. My strength is more magic than muscles."

"What is the source of your magic?" asked Aurora.

Infidel stared at her, obviously annoyed by the question. Then, to my surprise, she flashed her what-the-hell grin. "Okay," she said. "You know that there used to be a primal dragon of the forest named Verdant. He was killed, like, a thousand years ago by the first Knight of the Book, the original King Brightmoon."

Aurora nodded. "I'm familiar with the legend."

"It's not legend, it's history," said Infidel. "Brightmoon killed Verdant, who had been weakened by the decimation of the forests near his lair. The blood of the beast was drained and dried, forming a dark green powder. A gilded casket of this blood was kept at the Brightmoon Cathedral. When Knights of the Book are initiated, they're given a spoonful of the stuff, dissolved in wine. It grants them a small measure of the dragon's strength and toughness."

"Blood magic," said Aurora. "I thought the church disapproved of such things."

"The Church is just a wealth of contradictions," said Infidel. "They preach peace, then raise armies of violent tempered men to impose it. They sing the virtues of forgiveness and mercy, but build torture chambers to focus the faith of those who've gone astray. Dabbling in blood magic is a sin for you and me, but priests don't have to play by the same rules. Since they decree what is and isn't a sin, a priest could eat babies and pick his teeth with the bones and still be praised for his rectitude."

"I'm starting to see how you earned the name 'Infidel.'"

Infidel shook her head. "The church doesn't give a damn about my opinions. It's my actions that put me on the naughty list. When I was fifteen, I stole their casket of dragon blood. Knights had been gobbling down this stuff for centuries, so it was almost gone, but there was still about a pound of it caked up in the corners. I went at it with my fingernails and polished off everything that was left. At first, I didn't think anything had happened to me. When the priest came to get me from the inner sanctum, he found me crouched down over the empty casket, blood caked around my lips and under my finger nails. The sleeves of my wedding gown were green with —"

"Wait," said Aurora, holding up her hand. "Wedding gown? Is this part of the story about you once being engaged to Lord Tower?"

Infidel pressed her lips tightly together, as if contemplating whether to say more. After several long seconds, she said, "Engaged isn't the right word. It implies that he asked me to marry him and I said yes. The truth isn't so pretty. I was sold to him."

Aurora raised her eyebrows.

"My birth name was Innocent Brightmoon. I was the king's third daughter, but the first to survive to breeding age."

"A princess," said Aurora.

"It's not as good a job as it sounds," said Infidel. "'Princess' is just a fancy label for a high-priced slave-whore. My wedding to the firstborn male heir of the Tower family had been arranged before I was born. The Towers were immensely wealthy; there were all sorts of political and economic reasons that the Tower and Brightmoon lines were fated to mingle. My father had decided that his first eligible daughter would marry the first eligible son of the Tower family, and that was that. No one ever asked my opinion on the matter."

"Still…" said Aurora. "You were born into luxury. Life couldn't have been all bad."

"Couldn't it?" Infidel asked. She sighed. "I guess, from the outside, it looked like I was living a life of wealth. But, it wasn't my wealth, or my life. I was little more than a doll, a pretty thing to be dressed in gowns and decorate my father's court. I was never allowed to make a single decision. I lived in a palace where court dinners were held, with meals literally fit for a king, and all I'd be given to eat would be a meager salad. I wasn't allowed to taste dessert because my wedding gown had been designed before I was even conceived, and it was important that my waist be slender enough that I might get mistaken for a wasp. I never wore shackles, but I was a prisoner all the same."

Aurora nodded. "So you decided to run away."

"I wish I could say my actions were that deliberate. My education, such as it was, didn't teach me much about making good choices. When my wedding day finally came, I could barely think. I felt like a caged rat; my mind was darting all over the place, looking for any escape, but I found nothing."

"You must have really hated the young Lord Tower."

Infidel made a gagging noise. "Hated doesn't begin to cover it. He's such a sanctimonious idiot; he can't fart without running to the nearest priest to offer repentance. He believes every lie the church has ever crafted. You wouldn't believe his awkward, ritualistic attempts to court me. I could tell he really had no choice in this matter either. If he'd been a little rebellious about it, who knows? Maybe I might have liked him. I mean, he was good-looking, and he was always winning jousting tournaments, so he wasn't without a certain physical charm. But, his attempts to write love poems were cringe inducing. They sounded like sermons! 'Praise the creator who this day has blessed me with the bounty of your chaste lips, blah blah bluhhh.'" She stuck out her tongue. "We never even held hands."

Somehow, my ghost heart felt lighter to learn this. Since hearing she'd been engaged to Lord Tower, I'd assumed that she must have loved him once. I was jealous, though, obviously, there was no rational basis for this. I found myself annoyed that she was spilling her guts so freely to Aurora. I'd been her closest companion for ages. Why had she never shared this with me? Worse, why had I never had the courage to ask?

Infidel continued her story, "Anyway, it was my wedding day. There's this ten minute ritual before the ceremony where the bride goes to the inner sanctum to pray in private; there's not even a priest present. The inner sanctum was where they kept the casket of dragon blood. The second the priest closed the door, my eyes fixed on it. It was locked, but it was also a thousand freakin' years old. I had it cracked open in about thirty seconds. And, like I said, when the high priest came back into the sanctuary, I was coated in the stuff. I'd gobbled it down like it was all the ice cream and cake that I'd been denied since I was a toddler."

Aurora chuckled softly. "You must have been a sight in your bloodied gown."

"To this day, I still don't like wearing green," said Infidel, with a small shudder. "I get bad flashbacks of looking down at the green coating my arms. The priest stared at me for about half a minute, just dumbfounded, then clenched his fists and came at me, shouting, 'What have you done? What have you done?' Even though I'd never hit anyone in my life, I gave him a backhanded slap to shut him up. And... um... and... and his face sort of caved in. After that, I kind of... I kind of snapped. I launched out of the inner sanctum and tore through anyone in my way. I jumped out a stained glass window and kept running.

I killed... I killed a lot of people on my way out of town. There might have been a puppy that got squished as well. I... my memory's fuzzy, and I don't like to think about it anyway. I was completely drunk on the blood. It's one reason I seldom drink now. I don't like feeling out-of-control. Anyway, long story short, I wandered around the islands for a couple of years getting my head straight before winding up in Commonground. It's been a while since any of the church's assassins came after me, but I'm guessing I'm still public enemy number one."

"Which makes it strange that you want to sign on to the king's dragon hunt," said Aurora. "Won't Tower recognize you?"

Infidel shrugged. "Who knows? I was just a girl back then. I have boobs now." She ran her hands along her ruined hair. "And, you know, a different haircut."

"Father Ver is with him," said Aurora.

Infidel pressed her lips together tightly. If I'd still had arms, I would have hugged her to console her. I knew what she was thinking. A few extra curves and a dragon-induced haircut weren't going to fool the church's best Truthspeaker. I had personal experience with Father Ver's powers. Infidel was screwed.

"Why do you want to go on this quest anyway?" asked Aurora. "It can't be the treasure. You've never been obsessed with money."

Infidel drew her knees up to her chest, resting her chin on her arms as she stared out over the dark bay. Boat lanterns twinkled like stars across the water.

"Maybe I'm tired," she whispered.

"Maybe?"

"Screw it," she said, raising her chin. "I *am* tired. I mean, I've had fun. Stagger led me on some wild adventures. I've had experiences I couldn't even imagine when I was fifteen. My life hasn't been boring. But..." Her voice trailed off as she shook her head.

"But?"

"But maybe I'd like boring." She took a deep, weary breath. "Maybe I'd enjoy sleeping in a real bed at night, and wearing clean clothes every day. Maybe I'd like to walk down a street where I'm not looking over my shoulder wondering who's about to jump me with a shadow blade. Maybe I'd like to meet a stranger and not instantly start thinking about how I'm going to kill him if things turn ugly. Maybe thirty-year-old Infidel doesn't want to live her life trapped by choices made by fifteen-year-old Innocent."

Her eyes were narrowed as she spoke. She sounded so angry. I'd never suspected. What kind of friend had I been that I'd missed this?

She finally relaxed, and said, softly, "The closest I ever came to feeling normal was when I hung out with Stagger. This is… this is crazy. But I used to imagine me and him getting out of here, finding some little village where no one knew who the hell we were, and settling down. Maybe find a little peace and quiet and normal."

I'd dreamed that too. Why hadn't I told her?

"Why didn't you tell him?" asked Aurora.

"We… we…." She cradled her head in her hands. Her voice cracked as she said, "There are things that are wrong with me."

"Stagger was wild about you. You have a crazy streak, sure, but anyone could see that he loved you."

Infidel closed her eyes and clenched her fists. She looked as sad as when she'd sat at my grave. She was silent for a long time. Finally, she relaxed her hands, and sniffed. She whispered, "Normal couples can… they can do stuff. Intimate stuff. And I wanted that. I wanted that so badly."

I wanted that! I wanted that so much it hurt. Why didn't I have the courage to tell her? If I'd still had lungs, I would have cursed the sky for my cowardice.

"I'm guessing Stagger would have been okay with, um,

intimacy," said Aurora, with what might have been a grin, though her tusks made it hard to tell.

Infidel shuddered. "My strength makes touching things tricky. I try to slap a man, and I smash his face in. It took me years to learn to pick up a glass without breaking it. I'm more dangerous than people know."

"You seem to have it under control."

"I could have held his hand without crushing it, sure. Maybe even kissed him without breaking his teeth. But... but *all* my muscles are supernaturally powerful. Even ones... even ones I don't always have full control over."

"Oh," said Aurora. Then, she said, "Ooooh," in a way that made it clear she understood what Infidel was getting at.

Suddenly, I understood as well. Ordinary coupling could have left me maimed and mangled, if not outright dead.

"So..." said Aurora. "You're a thirty-year-old virgin."

Infidel shrugged. "I'll die one, I guess. I'm never going to know anything like love. But, at least when I hung out with Stagger, I felt... I felt happy."

I'd been happy too. And, even with my fantasies of shared sexual bliss crushed by Infidel's physical realities, I still would gladly have gone with her to that quiet little village and lived out my days beside her. I'd loved her without even so much as a kiss for years. I could have accepted anything to make her happy.

"And now you're unhappy," said Aurora. "So what? The plan is to go get yourself killed by Greatshadow?"

"No," said Infidel, sounding deadly serious. "The plan is to go get myself rich. Not pirate booty rich, not ancient artifact rich, but filthy, filthy, filthy rich. Because if there's one thing I learned growing up in my father's court, it's that if you're filthy rich everyone will bend over backwards to tell you you're clean. If I show up in my father's court with sole possession of Greatshadow's treasure, I'm confident I'll have a full pardon in my hands inside of ten minutes. The church might not be happy about this, but I'm betting after I donate funds to build a few new cathedrals, they'll come around. I'll be rich with my own money, not my father's. I'll be free to live where and how I wish. I'll have my own palace with silk sheets on a bed so fluffy you'd think it's stuffed with clouds. Every day I'll take a hot bath while musicians serenade me and I'll get out of the water and put on clean freakin' underwear. And when I walk into my own damn dining room, people are going to run up to me with trays full of goddamn cake!"

Aurora nodded slowly, contemplating the dream. "And this is going to make you happy?"

Infidel shrugged. "I'm not shooting for happy. I'm aiming for comfortable and fat."

"You'll achieve more than this," said a voice from the branches above. Infidel jumped to her feet. Aurora jerked her head up as a sheen of ice grew across her clenched fists. It was Relic. How the hunchback had climbed into the branches without us hearing him I don't know. It seemed like a bit of a stretch that this could have been where Infidel had thrown him.

Relic peered down at the two women. His eyes glowed faintly golden in the darkness. He said, "You shall be beloved by all mankind, princess. You will be the champion who slew Greatshadow. For centuries men have perished due to the unpredictable malevolence of fire. Castles, hovels, entire towns have been reduced to cinders with no warning, killing young and old alike. Once Greatshadow is dead, fire will be a trusted tool of mankind, fully tamed, a danger no more. Children will sing songs about you a thousand years hence, just as they sing the tale of how the first Brightmoon vanquished the dragon of the forest. As for seeking the forgiveness of the Church of the Book, remember you won't just return with the dragon's treasure. You can also return with barrels of fresh blood, replacing the dwindling holy relic you stole. You can claim you were driven by divine visions to renew the blood. One day you'll be regarded as a saint."

Infidel looked up the slope of the mountain, toward the glowing caldera. "And maybe one day I'll sprout wings and fly.

Because if there's a Truthspeaker on this quest, then I'm never going to be part of this dragon hunt."

"Assuming there's still a hunt," Aurora said. "The Truthspeaker's charred bones are probably at the bottom of the bay with the rest of the king's fleet."

"Nah," said Infidel. "My father's a jerk, but not an idiot. He sent those ships in to give the dragon a chance to feel like he'd finished off the threat before it even reached shore. It had to be a distraction. Tower and his team are already on the island."

Relic nodded. "I concur. It's only a matter of time before they contact the Three Goons. We must prepare for this moment."

"Prepare how?" asked Infidel.

"You will need a disguise that Lord Tower cannot see through," said Relic. "I have just the persona in mind."

"Forget Tower. How am I supposed to fool a Truthspeaker?"

Relic's glowing eyes twinkled as he chuckled. "That, my dear, will be far easier than you may think. Few are as easy to deceive as those most confident of the truth." Then he cast his gaze toward Aurora. "The deception will require your cooperation, as well as the silence of the Three Goons."

Aurora nodded. "If you promise to help me recover the Jagged Heart, I pledge to keep my mouth shut. As for the Goons, they've been hired as muscle; there's no clause requiring them to disclose everything they know. We can buy their silence with a non-competing contract for those sub-rights."

"I vow that recovering the Heart for you will be my second goal, though ensuring that Greatshadow dies remains my top priority. If you accept this, then we have a deal," said Relic. He held out his gnarled hand. Aurora placed her giant hand upon it. Infidel laid her smaller hand against the ogress's knuckles.

Infidel said, "Excellent. It looks like we've got it all worked out for me to join a group of men sworn to kill me so we can face off with a dragon that melts stone with his breath." She grinned. "And Stagger used to complain that I never planned ahead."

CHAPTER SEVEN
SUCH CRUEL THINGS

AT DAWN THE harbor rang with a cacophony of sledgehammers and saws as the Wanderers salvaged useful lumber from the shattered remains of Commonground. Along the shores, river-pygmies gathered up scraps of wood too splintered to be of use and heaped them onto bonfires. Nearby, the bodies of dead brethren were stacked into muddy blue piles. I always found it odd that the river-pygmies cremate their dead; a water burial would seem more appropriate. I need only glance up the blackened slope of the mountain to understand the origins of the custom. Greatshadow could wipe out the pygmy tribes at any time for any reason. They pygmies believed that, as long as they let fire consume their bodies when they were done with them, Greatshadow would leave them alone most of the time. Whether Greatshadow was even aware of this bargain I can't guess.

Once or twice during the night, pygmies had come poking around the trees beneath the boat. I've no doubt they would have climbed aboard if Aurora hadn't stuck her head over to investigate the noise. Her big, tusked face had sent would-be scavengers scurrying back into the darkness.

Relic left at sunrise. I'd watched as he scrambled down through the branches of the trees then dashed off through the debris-threaded thickets, agile as a cat. His crippled routine was obviously just a disguise. I have to say that he'd sounded like he knew a thing or two about disguises when he spent the better part of the night explaining his ideas for how to hide Infidel's identity. He had wanted her to wear a suit of full plate armor, including a bucket-style helmet that would conceal her features. Infidel had vetoed this; she liked her comfort and full freedom of movement, and helmets got in the way of her peripheral vision. After a few hours of circular discussions, Relic had thrown his hands into the air and announced that he'd thought of the perfect disguise, but couldn't share it. It would be a surprise, he said, as he scurried out to gather whatever supplies he had in mind.

I still felt like they were wasting their time. With Father Ver among the king's men, Infidel would be discovered in seconds. My upbringing in the monastery had left me keenly aware of the power of Truthspeakers, and Father Ver was a legend. He was the most powerful Truthspeaker the Church of the Book had ever produced, as I knew all too well.

To appreciate the power of Truthspeakers, you need to know a little bit about the Church of the Book. High in the mountains of Raitingu, what the Wanderers call the Isle of Storm, there's a temple built into the bedrock of the world's tallest mountain. Within this temple is a chamber carved from pure white quartz. Here, on a pedestal of gold, sits the One True Book. The book is roughly five feet long, three feet across, and two feet thick. It's bound in leather black as a moonless night; it's said that if you stare at the cover, you can see stars twinkling in the void. In contrast, the pages are snowy white, thin as onion skin. The priests calculate that the book contains 7,777 pages.

Within this book, the Divine Author has written the history of the world, from the moment of creation to the final day of judgment. My life, your life, the lives of the dead and yet to be born, are recorded in minute detail on these holy pages. The One True Book is the final authority on all that has been, all that is, and all that will be.

Having access to this document would seem to give the Church of the Book a certain advantage over everyone else, save for one tiny detail: the book is far too sacred to ever be sullied by human hands. All men are too corrupted by lies to risk opening the book and actually reading it. The pure light of sacred truth would melt the flesh from the bones of anyone deluded enough to think himself worthy of sullying the pages with his unworthy gaze.

It's taught that, one day, a Golden Child will arise, a perfect being uncorrupted by lies, who will open the book and read out the final account. The world we live in is built from four fundamental and opposing forces: spirit, matter, lies, and truth. As the book is read, all falsehood will be banished; all matter will be cleansed, all spirit will be purified. The world we know will be wiped away and replaced with the world as it always should have been, with a trinity of unified forces: truth, spirit, and substance.

Until the day of that Final Account, all that we know of the contents of the Book have been learned through prayer. Truthspeakers spend years on their knees in the temple, their faces pressed to the floor, weeping, sweating, laughing, screaming as they plead with the Divine Author to reveal even a few lines of sacred truth to them. After years of effort, the Truthspeakers go out into the world to spread the received revelations.

The Truthspeakers gain certain gifts as a result of their devotion. The most powerful Truthspeakers can see the falsehoods of the world and correct them. For instance, if it's raining, and a pious Truthspeaker understands that the One True Book foretold that the day would be sunny, he simply tells the sky it's supposed to be blue. The clouds will part and the sun will come out. This may be hyperbole; I've never personally witnessed a Truthspeaker pull off such a feat. But, I have witnessed another magical gift. It's impossible to lie to a Truthspeaker. Believe me, I've tried.

The monks run a vineyard where they produce the sacramental wine used in certain church rites. The wine isn't intended to be used recreationally, but when I had my first sip at age ten, I appreciated the warmth that spread through me as I swallowed, and wanted more. By age twelve I'd sneak out at night to the pitch dark wine cellars to finish off entire bottles, luxuriating in the mellow heat that spread through my body and washed over my mind in a soothing wave. I'd lie on the frigid stone floor in the darkness and dream of using grandfather's bone-handled knife to hack away vines from ancient statues in steaming tropical jungles.

Alas, the monks kept meticulous track of their inventory. A Truthspeaker was brought in to investigate the missing gallons. I'd heard from other orphans that you can fool a Truthspeaker if you can fool yourself. You couldn't lie, but truth wasn't always black and white. I was certain I'd be asked if I'd stolen the wine, and, technically, I hadn't. The wine didn't belong to any one person. It was property of the Church, and I was a member of the Church. It was no more a theft for me to share the wine than it was to drink water from the communal well. I trusted I could slip through this loophole if the Truthspeaker interrogated me.

I remember the moment that I'd been brought into the room where Father Ver waited. He was middle-aged then, his close-cropped dark hair speckled with gray at the temples. His skin was pale from spending most of his life in a cave. There was a large callus in the center of his forehead from decades spent rubbing it against the floor. His eyes were sunk back into his skull, hidden in shadows. The interrogation room was lit by a single candle which sat on the table between us, and the light flickered like twin stars in the void of his eyes.

Despite his stern expression, I walked into the room with a confident swagger. I sat down and faced him, unafraid to meet his gaze. I waited for him to speak to me. Seconds passed and he said nothing. I slid back in my chair, prepared to wait him out, but turned my face away. It was uncomfortable to look at someone so directly without saying anything. As the seconds passed into minutes, I'd glance at him and always find his eyes locked on my face. I began to fidget. I could feel his stare boring into me. I started sweating. My palms were clammy as I wiped away the moisture on my brow. I trembled as I worried he might mistake my

JAMES MAXEY

discomfort for evidence of guilt. Which was absurd, I reminded myself, since I hadn't stolen anything. I wanted to tell him this, but my tongue had grown thick in my mouth. If my rubbery limbs had possessed the strength, I would have fled the room. Instead, some horrible internal magnet kept pulling my gaze toward his. I felt as if my face wasn't truly my own, but was instead a mask I'd all but forgotten I was wearing. The Truthspeaker's eyes were peeling back that mask to reveal the sinner beneath.

After what felt like hours, he spoke, in a low, gravelly voice. "You are the wine thief."

I collapsed to the floor, my tongue leaping to life: "Yes! Oh yes! Yes! It's true! I stole the wine!"

Hot tears erupted from my eyes as I wept, my body wracked with sobs. I was vaguely aware of Father Ver rising and walking around the desk.

"You will stop crying," he said, standing before me.

Instantly, I stopped. It was like he'd reached in and flicked some unseen switch that commanded my tears. I reached out and hugged his ankles, groveling as I pressed my cheeks against his sandal-clad feet. "Forgive me," I whispered. "Forgive me."

"You will stand," he said.

Though my body felt hollow, gutted by guilt and shame, my muscles moved to obey his words and I rose.

Father Ver frowned. "There's a weakness in you," he said. "Unfounded hope is the source. Your grandfather paid you a visit two years ago."

"Y-yes," I said, sniffling.

"He filled your head with tales of vanished kingdoms, pygmy tribes, and lost treasures. Seductive visions for a boy your age. You've turned your eyes from the path of righteousness and now dream of life outside this monastery."

I wiped snot onto my sleeve and said, "My g-grandfather is going to t-take me with him next time."

"We both know this isn't true," said Father Ver.

I swallowed hard.

103

"If your grandfather wanted you, he could have taken you on his last visit. You aren't our property, boy. We'd welcome one less mouth to feed. The truth is plain; Judicious Merchant loves the jungle more than he loves you."

I wiped my cheeks and whispered, "He... he said the jungle is too dangerous for a child."

"Do the pygmies not have children? In any case, your grandfather is a free man, still in possession of remnants of your family fortune. He need not live in a jungle like a savage. He could have raised you in comfort on some modest country estate. His actions show what he truly loves in this world. It isn't you."

I dropped to my knees, doubled over, feeling as if I'd been kicked in the gut.

"Your thirst for wine comes from your love of falsehood. In your intoxication, it's easy to feel as if the dreams you cling to are real. It's time to let go of your childish embrace of fantasy. Truth will never be found digging among the ruins of failed civilizations. Truth is revealed through prayer and obedience to the church. The great adventure for any man lies not in exploring the ruins of distant jungles, but in navigating the ruins of his own soul. Your soul in particular is a treacherous labyrinth. Your father, mother, and grandfather all live, yet you are an orphan. What a heavy burden, to be so unloved. I understand why your dreams seem more attractive than your piteous reality."

I dug my nails into my palms, trying to make the pain blot out the words. I sniffled. "H-how can... how can you say such cruel things?"

"It is a measure of your weakness that you mistake truth for cruelty," said Father Ver. "Within the One True Book, your life has already been written. I know nothing of your future; there is too much contained within the Book for one man to study it all. I have no certainty of your eventual fate, but slaking your blasphemous thirst with sacramental wine is a poor omen. My informed speculation is that one day you'll die drunk on some distant shore, leaving your bones to rot in an unmarked grave."

He walked to the door and rang a small bell to summon the monks. He didn't look at me as he said, "If I were the sole arbiter of your fate, you would be hung. A boy who is a thief will almost certainly grow into a man who is something worse. Alas, the brothers will sanction no punishment more severe than flogging. You will receive ten lashes a day with a braided leather whip for the next seven days."

My mouth went dry as I thought of the pain I would endure.

"I know you are afraid of what's to come," he said, his voice softening ever so slightly. "Look at me."

I turned my face toward him as he untied the knot that held his simple robes at the waist. He shrugged the heavy cloth from his shoulders. He turned, revealing his bare back. He was more muscular than I'd suspected. There was no fat on him; his muscles looked wiry and powerful beneath his white skin. I squinted in the candle light. Quickly, I understood what he was showing me. His back was crisscrossed with scars and countless fresh scabs.

"When the whip touches you, pain flashes through your mind like a light," he said. "Follow this light. It will lead you to truth. Pleasure leads only to falsehood; pain guides men to what is real. Truth is hard. Truth is harsh. *Truth is all that matters*. It is stark and beautiful and complete. Embrace your pain, child, and you may yet live a righteous life."

He pulled his robes back up his shoulders. "Should you not heed my words, pray we do not cross paths again," he said. "When next we meet, I will not show such mercy."

He left, and I listened to this feet pad away down the stone hall. I was all alone, his words echoing in my ears. All I could feel was gratitude. Father Ver had given me a precious second chance. I didn't fear the punishment to come; I was eager for it, ready for the whip to beat away my weakness and bring me to the same state of grace as this holy man.

I didn't find enlightenment in my floggings. The instant the whip touched me I found only hurt and humiliation and a festering distrust for all things labeled holy. I returned to wine theft within the year. When I finally fled the monastery, it was with a belly full of sacramental wine and the contents of the poor box jingling in my pockets.

RELIC HAD TOLD Infidel to wait for his return, but nothing was holding her at the boat beyond her own weariness. As the heat of the day settled over the bay, she was wide awake. Aurora's cold compresses had helped reduce her lumps and bruises. She looked like her old self as she finished off the last of the whale jerky. She and Aurora cracked crude jokes as they speculated as to what, exactly, Relic might be. There are nineteen sentient species in the Shining Lands; toss in the more popular half-seeds and there were roughly fifty different types of humanoid that could be hiding under that cloak.

There was no reason to limit the speculation to the earthly realms. Aurora's belief in a Great Sea Above was hardly the only auxiliary reality one could believe in. The Church of the Book believed there were two further realms of existence. Heaven was populated by true men, glorious creatures who had reached the final perfection after passing through the trials of life. Hell was populated by sinners and worse things. There were demons whose very existence was a lie the universe had been tricked into accepting. Only when the Golden Child read the One True Book would these false creatures be eradicated.

Of course, I take these teachings with a grain of salt. The Vanished Kingdom is proof that men lived long before the Church of the Book. I'm sure that these men believed in the stone idols they worshipped, gods whose names are now completely forgotten. If ancient men had been mistaken about their beliefs, why should modern men be any different?

All my life, I assumed that I'd finally discover the answers to

JAMES MAXEY

these philosophical questions once I was dead. What a gyp that I have more questions now than ever. Still, when I think of the scaly flesh that surrounds Relic's eyes, I can't help but think of how closely he resembles the drawings of demons from the books of my youth.

After her meal, Infidel got dressed in the clothes Aurora had found. Though the tan britches and striped shirt were tailored for a man, I thought she looked fantastic. Her sculpted perfection makes her enticing even in peasant clothing, her features unadorned by make-up or jewelry. Royalty breeds for beauty. I can only imagine that, dressed in lacy gowns in a palace, her face framed by pearls and gold, she must be breathtaking.

Aurora created a mirror of ice for Infidel to use to fix what was left of her hair. She had little choice but to crop what was left, trimming away the frizzled ends. While I'd always liked her long silver tresses, I had to admit this new style had a certain charm. It highlighted the graceful lines of her smooth, slender neck, and drew attention to her enigmatic gray eyes.

I wondered where she would go after she was done with her hair; I was certain she wouldn't simply wait for Relic. Then, fate provided her with a destination. Far out at the mouth of the harbor, dark shapes appeared, a long line of humps rising and falling in the water. At first, I thought it was an enormous serpent, but as it drew closer I could see that it was, in fact, a pod of a dozen whales, enormous blue-gray beasts big as ships. Long strands of woven seaweed trailed from elaborate harnesses that hung over their broad, flat faces. A crew of mermen swam beside them, urging them on, prodding the slower ones with tridents, and trumpeting long, low commands through horns fashioned from giant conch shells.

Behind it all, towed by the mighty sea beasts, was an enormous barge, waves breaking against its squat frame. From the center of the barge a single mast thrust into the air, sporting a banner of white and the silhouette of a black swan.

Aurora rose, shielding her eyes, staring at the barge like it was an apparition. The new arrival looked much like the old *Black Swan* barge, only larger and obviously newer. It now rose three stories instead of two. One by one, the whales were set free of their harnesses as momentum and tides carried the vessel forward. The mermen exceeded even the Wanderers in their understanding of water currents. The barge came to a halt mere feet from a newly built dock the Wanderers had finished only hours before. A crew of men leapt from the barge to lash it into place. Anchors splashed all around the vessel, sinking down to the mud. The *Black Swan* had come home.

Aurora jumped down from the boat, quickly clearing the tangled mangroves and reaching the mudflats. The ground crackled as she froze a long, rock-hard path across the mire. Infidel leapt to follow her, slipping the second she hit the icy mud. She grimaced as she waved her arms for balance, looking around for a less slippery path. She jumped toward a river-pygmy canoe floating about twenty feet out in shallow water. The two pygmies currently occupying the canoe toppled into the bay as Infidel landed in the center of the craft. The canoe spun, capsizing as the lip sank beneath the water, but Infidel had already kicked off again, flying toward a slanted piling that jutted from the water. She barely touched down before she sprang again, leap-frogging her way toward her destination. When she reached the *Black Swan*, she leaned against a wall, crossing her arms. She looked nonchalant as Aurora climbed up onto the deck.

"What took you so long?" she asked.

Aurora didn't respond, racing past Infidel toward the main door of the new *Black Swan*. There were no guards in place to stop the ogress from bursting through the door. The main room had more gambling tables than the old one, and the whole place smelled of pine varnish. It hadn't yet acquired the funk of ten thousand cigar-smoking men and the heavily perfumed women who clung to their arms. Infidel followed as Aurora vaulted over the bar and down the hall beyond. At the end of the passage she looked ready to throw her shoulder against the door there.

Before she could make a move, the door opened.

The thick, cloying scent of potpourri poured out into the hallway. Aurora stepped into the dimly lit room with Infidel at her heels. The room was little changed. If not for the smell of freshly finished carpentry, it would be easy to mistake the Black Swan's new chamber for her old one.

The Black Swan herself was stretched on the couch. In front of her, there was now a low table covered with a long semi-circle of engraved letters, painted white against the black finish of the wood. It was a simple alphabet, plus the numbers 0 through 9, and a few common marks of punctuation. The only actual words were a 'YES' at one end and a 'NO' at the other.

"Mistress," said Aurora, sounding joyful. "You're still alive!"

The Black Swan said nothing. One of her bony hands unfolded from her chest and pointed toward the 'NO.'

Infidel sucked in her breath. I followed her eyes to the Black Swan's wrist. It wasn't merely bony; it was actual bone. Beneath her black veil, I could see an eyeless skull, white as chalk.

"Oh, mistress," whispered Aurora.

The Black Swan moved her finger across the board with a surprising rapidity; she seemed much faster now that she was freed from her withered muscles.

"My work is too important to be slowed by death," she spelled.

Infidel stepped back toward the doorway. She looked... spooked. I'd never seen her react like this.

The Black Swan nodded toward her and spelled, "You need not fear me."

Infidel squared her shoulders. She put on her brave face, but I could hear a hint of discomfort in her voice as she said, "I'm not afraid. If you give me any problems, you won't be the first undead I've taken apart this week."

The Black Swan nodded.

"How did you do this?" Aurora whispered. "Why?"

The skeletal hand tapped out. "My great work is not yet finished."

Aurora furrowed her brow. "Your great work? What great work? I've never known you to want anything other than money."

The Black Swan tapped the 'YES.'

"People say you can't take it with you," said Infidel. "Guess you proved them wrong."

'YES.'

Then, she spelled out, "Priests tell us the world is built of matter, spirit, truth, and lies. There is a fifth force, most powerful of all. Money."

Infidel looked skeptical. "I've known more than my fair share of rich people, and money hasn't kept their skeletons animated after they croak."

"They didn't know how to spend it," the Black Swan tapped. "With every journey into the future, my wealth grows exponentially. My purse strings entangle all the world's kings. The future rests upon my decisions."

"Really?" said Infidel. "Because with that kind of power, you'd think you'd choose to be something other than a bag of bones stuck in a dark, smelly room."

Before the Black Swan could respond, Aurora asked, "Menagerie told me I was fired. Why?"

"You cannot serve two masters. You have chosen to recover the Jagged Heart and return to your people. I have arranged a contract with Ivory Blade on your behalf. We will not meet again after this day."

Infidel stepped closer. "Then it's true. Tower has the Jagged Heart."

The Black Swan's hand remained motionless as her empty eyes gazed at Infidel. At last, she shrugged.

"You mean you don't know, or won't tell us?" asked Infidel.

The Black Swan shook her head, the vertebrae in her neck creaking. "In my most recent trip to the future, I was unable to learn whether or not the Jagged Heart endures. All that is certain is that twelve of the world's greatest warriors set out to slay Greatshadow. They failed. Only two survived." She nodded toward Infidel. "I learned this from your daughter."

Infidel's eyebrows shot up. "My daughter?"

"Given her birth date, you may be pregnant now. If not, the child will be conceived within the month."

"Umm... no. No, I can assure you that's not possible. Whoever you met in the future, she wasn't my kid."

The Black Swan shrugged, then once more began tapping out a message. "The resemblance leads me to think otherwise, but no matter. I've returned to ensure that the future I lived through doesn't come to pass. Your daughter died soon after I met her. Everyone died. Everyone."

Aurora gave Infidel a puzzled glance.

"What do you mean, everyone?" she asked.

The room grew quiet save for the tapping of bone on wood. "All humanity is destroyed when the primal dragons rise as one to wipe out civilization in the span of a day."

"That's impossible," said Aurora. "Hush would never take part in such destruction."

"She does," tapped the Black Swan.

"Why?"

"The dragons judge mankind for their sins; none are found worthy of forgiveness."

Infidel looked pale. "Do... do we cause this? Does our quest to kill Greatshadow cause this destruction?"

The Black Swan shook her head. "The world carries on twenty years after the assault on Greatshadow."

"The primal dragons think of time differently than we do," said Aurora. "If there's a risk that Lord Tower is going to trigger some kind of dragon apocalypse, we need to stop him."

The Black Swan's skeletal hand lingered over the board,

edging toward the 'YES.' Then, her fingers returned to the letters to tap, "Rather than stop him, ensure he succeeds. We must hope the primal dragons will be weakened if Greatshadow is no longer among their ranks."

"Hope?" said Infidel. "If you're trying to change the future, shouldn't we be going on more than hunches?"

The Black Swan shrugged and sank back onto the couch, growing very still.

"So, what, your plan boils down to guessing what we should do?" asked Infidel.

The Black Swan didn't move.

Aurora put her hand on Infidel's shoulder. "Don't drive yourself crazy. I try to ignore any hints she tells me about the future. The more she tells you about tomorrow, the more she changes today, and pretty soon hunches and guesses are all you have. The best thing to do is make the choices you would make anyway. Try to pretend you're in charge of your own fate, and not a puppet following someone else's script."

Infidel nodded as they left the room. "Yeah. Sure. I've never worried what the Black Swan thought before now. I guess there's no reason to change that."

They went back outside, blinking in the light. Aurora said, "I'm still going on the quest, but if you want to back out, I understand. I mean, if you're pregnant..."

"I'm not pregnant!" snapped Infidel. "It's not possible. It's never going to be possible. Without Stagger, I wouldn't want it to be possible."

"You two never fooled around even a little? You can get pregnant just by—"

"No!" Infidel threw her hands up in the air. "This is crazy." She gave a dismissive wave toward the Black Swan. "Forget her. All I know is I woke up this morning planning to kill Greatshadow, and nothing I've heard today has changed my mind."

"What about the Truthspeaker?"

Infidel clenched her fists. "If he messes with me, he won't be the first priest I've killed."

Aurora nodded as they walked down the rebuilt dock. "For what it's worth, I don't believe the Truthspeaker's powers will affect me. Our faiths don't overlap even a little. The whole truth and lies as foundations of reality, that's just dumb. The world is obviously a flux of heat, light, cold, and darkness." She blew out rings of fog. "The evidence is right before your eyes."

"Whatever," said Infidel. "I'll let the two of you debate religion. I just want to get on with this dragon hunt. The quicker I get my hands on that treasure, the faster I can build my palace and hire my cake servants."

"There are simpler ways to get cake," said Aurora.

They reached the edge of the dock. Once it had led all the way to shore; now, crooked pilings were all that remained.

"There are simpler ways to get back to the boat," said Infidel, looking out over the water. "But simple isn't always entertaining."

Without warning, she grabbed Aurora by the hips and hefted her up, holding the oversized woman directly over her head. Aurora let out a yelp as Infidel leapt, flying out over the topsy-turvy pilings, lighting down every third or fourth post before skipping on again. They reached the mangroves in under a minute and practically flew the last dozen yards to the boat. The old boards creaked as Infidel landed and planted the ogress on the deck feet first.

"Don't do that again!" Aurora growled as Infidel giggled.

"What?" said Infidel. "You don't like short cuts?"

Aurora sighed. "I'm not as invulnerable as you. One misstep on your part could have broken my neck, for no reason other than you wanting to show off. You're reckless, *princess*. Perhaps this was charming when you were fifteen, but it's not a quality I want in an ally when we face Greatshadow."

"I was just having a little fun."

"Children have fun. A warrior needs discipline."

"I'm living backwards. I was disciplined as a child so I'm having fun as an adult."

Aurora didn't look persuaded by the reasoning. Before she could argue, someone cleared his throat from inside the tilted doorway to the cabin. Both women turned to see Relic squeezing from the opening, a large canvas bag slung over his shoulder.

"I told you to wait for me," he grumbled. "Speed is of the essence. Ivory Blade has contacted the Three Goons. We need to prepare your disguise, and the dye takes several hours to set properly."

He dropped the sack to the deck. Things within it clattered loudly, as metal hit metal.

"There's dye involved?" said Infidel, squatting down over the sack. "I like my hair blonde."

"It's not your hair we'll be dying," said Relic.

Infidel opened the sack and pulled out various objects. She paused to study what looked like two shoulder caps for a suit of plate armor. They were formed of half-inch steel and polished to almost a mirror finish. Only, as shoulder plates, they weren't very practical; the two halves were joined together by a single link of chain. And, the plates were too rounded. No one had shoulders this circular. Infidel looked puzzled as she turned the metal cups over and over in her hand.

"What the hell is this?" she asked.

Aurora chuckled. "It looks like a plate-steel bra."

Relic was very quiet.

Both women stared at him.

He stared back.

"No freakin' way," said Infidel.

"This would be easier if you'd wear a helmet," said Relic. "If not, we must choose attire that ensures none of the king's men will be staring at your face."

I expected Infidel to fling the armored lingerie into the bay. To my surprise, she shrugged. "What the hell," she said. "It's about time I had an outfit that doesn't get ripped to shreds every five minutes. But if there are chain mail panties in here, I'm drawing a line."

It turned out that there weren't any chain mail panties, which provoked a mixed reaction within me. As unfair as it was for me to have such thoughts, I would have been relieved to see a full-blown, padlocked, cast-iron chastity belt. Infidel might have shrugged off the talk of pregnancy, but I was a little worried. My poor mortal frame might not have been up to the task of fathering a child with Infidel, but the king's men were more than mere mortals. Lord Tower could fly, Father Ver can change reality with his voice, and Ivory Blade supposedly can move faster than the human eye can follow. Who knew who else might along for the trip? What if someone among the heroes matched Infidel in strength and stamina? What if what the Black Swan said about an impending pregnancy was true?

CHAPTER EIGHT

WAR DOLL

THE SUN WAS directly overhead as we rode the churning waves toward the pirate cave. Was it only coincidence that Tower's party had set up camp in the very place where all this had begun with the discovery of the map? I hadn't told Bigsby the truth of where I acquired it, so he hadn't passed on the information. Perhaps Ivory Blade had researched the map further and other sources had led him here.

The cave was located on the western side of the Isle of Fire, a stark landscape of steep, rocky cliffs scoured by ceaseless wind. The waters here are turbulent but deep; a ship can sail within inches of the cliffs if her captain is crazy enough to risk the swirling currents. The cave we aimed for wasn't the only one along this coastline. The area was riddled with old lava tubes exposed by the churning sea.

Most of the caves hold nothing but bird nests; indeed, the sky above was full of feathered creatures in every hue of the rainbow, from tiny finches no larger than my thumb to albatrosses with wingspans longer than my bar tab. The pirate cave was right at sea level; the tides here can rise and fall twenty feet, and when the tide is low the opening of the cave is a long, narrow slash amid jagged stones, just wide enough to sail a good-sized schooner through. Within lies an underground lagoon nearly a mile across, ringed by a pebble beach polished smooth by the waves. It was a safe, sheltered haven, assuming the captain was skilled enough to thread the needle.

Fortunately, Infidel, Aurora, and Relic were in a small rowboat that could navigate the gap with ease, even with the rising tide. Infidel manned both oars, and her iron muscles were more than a match for the swirling currents. She aimed the boat for the gap and rowed confidently over the waves, shooting into the cavern swiftly enough to leave a wake. Gulls cried as they dove at the churned up water.

The last time I'd been here, the room had been full of torches and lanterns. Now, the shore was lined with bright glorystones, rare gems purported to be fragments of the sun itself. Glorystones were far more expensive than diamonds, and there were more in this cave than I could count. Reflected on the dark water of the lagoon, they looked like stars. We'd definitely arrived at a camp outfitted by a king.

As my eyes searched the shadows beyond the shore, I was surprised at how empty the cave looked. When we'd come here to fight pirates, the noise in this place had been deafening, as the voices of a hundred rowdy men echoed through the chamber. The air had been foul with the smoke of fires fueled by dried guano, not to mention the stink left from using the lagoon as a toilet. Today, the air was clean and cool; everything was quiet. Off in the distance I spotted a few modest canvas tents, shelter enough for a dozen men perhaps, if they were friendly.

The only boat was a single-mast skiff that I recognized as belonging to the Black Swan. No-Face was standing near the boat, his arms crossed, his feet planted wide, looking ready to smite anyone who came too close. Reeker was in the boat, stretched out on the folded sail, snoozing, using a backpack as a pillow. Menagerie sat beneath a glorystone lantern, reading a book. The faded letters on the leather-bound tome could barely be made out: *The Vanished Kingdom*, by Judicious Merchant. My grandfather had published his discoveries years before I was born. With it, I had retraced his steps on the island, or at least attempted to. Sadly, I found most of his directions convoluted and his cartography rather cryptic. Some of the most interesting places he claimed to have explored I've never found. I can't say if he embellished his adventures, or was simply rotten at drawing maps.

Menagerie had beaten us here even though he'd remained behind the other Goons to assist Infidel with her disguise. He'd requested an eye-popping sum of money for his services as an artist; in what he claimed was pure coincidence, it was equal to the value of the dragon skull once my bar debt was paid. Infidel hadn't haggled. Menagerie had sent the other Goons on their way, promising he'd catch up to them. What might take No-Face a full day to row Menagerie could cover in mere hours as an eagle. As for whether the tattooed man's artistry had produced a passable disguise, I wasn't the best judge. I'd spent enough time staring at Infidel's face to know its subtle lines no matter what color it was dyed. And I still didn't understand how any amount of coloring and cleavage was going to hide her identity from Father Ver.

Aurora jumped from the boat and helped pull it up onto the stony beach. Relic hobbled out, placing a hand on his back as if it pained him to have sat so many hours. I could hear his bones popping as he craned his neck from side to side.

As Infidel stepped out of the boat, No-Face rattled the chain around his arm, waking Reeker. Menagerie set down his book, and shouted, "Halt!"

"It's okay, guys, they're with me," said Aurora.

Menagerie marched within inches of her and stared up into her tusked face. He shouted, "It is not okay! This is a secure area. What the hell are you doing bringing unauthorized personnel? What's wrong with you?"

Aurora thrust her finger into Menagerie's chest. "Back off. I have every right to be here, and these two are my guests. If you have a problem—"

Before she could finish her sentence, a voice beyond the Goons shouted, "Yes, we have a problem!"

Further up the rocky slope, a ghostly white figure strode swiftly toward us. This was Ivory Blade; I recognized him from his occasional visits to the *Black Swan*, though I'd never actually met him. Blade was the king's top spy, though I wondered how good a spy he could have been since everyone knew it. On the other hand, Blade is a six-foot-three albino. He doesn't exactly blend into the shadows. Hiding in plain sight might be the best strategy available. He was certainly an eye-catching figure, dressed in stark white leather armor. This was the famed Immaculate Attire, crafted for Alabaster Brightmoon, the Warrior Queen, nearly three centuries earlier. Since the armor fit him like a full body glove, I can only assume that Alabaster Brightmoon was rather tall for a woman, or else some enchantment allowed the armor to adapt to the form of its wearer. The leather truly did look immaculate, without a single scrape or scuff.

The fact that Blade's armor was unmarred might have been evidence that his reputation as a master swordsman was deserved. I've heard he can draw his sword, kill a man, wipe the blade and return it to his scabbard more swiftly than the eye can follow. He certainly possessed an air of confidence as he marched up to Aurora.

"I'm reporting for duty," Aurora said, addressing Ivory Blade over the heads of the Goons. "The Black Swan has provided the appropriate contracts."

"For you," Blade growled. "Who are these two?" His pink eyes narrowed as he stared at Relic and Infidel. "Or perhaps I should ask, what are these two?"

Relic bowed. He spoke in a raspy, trembling voice, "Long ago, I was called Urthric. Alas, the men for whom that name had meaning have long since passed away. Today, I am known only as Relic."

"Relic showed up after the attack on Commonground," said Aurora. "I wouldn't ordinarily risk the safety of a mission with a last-second recruit, especially one I can't vouch for. Still, I think his story is worth listening to. Hear him out; if you don't think he'll be useful, I'll personally snap his neck."

Blade sneered as he looked down at Relic. "What can this decrepit fool possibly have to offer us?"

I found it interesting that Blade's attention was so fixed on Relic. Infidel was standing only inches behind the ragged man, not moving or making a sound, but she was hardly invisible. Given her garb, I expected at least a little gawking.

"I may be decrepit," said Relic, "but I'm no fool. I'm the most important person you can hire for this mission."

Blade smirked. "Truly?"

As Blade spoke, a woman stepped out from behind him; only, it wasn't so much a woman as the absence of a woman. It was a bubble of air the shape of a naked female wielding a sword in each hand. No one else reacted as she silently tiptoed around the Goons, pausing to study Aurora, then moving to study Infidel up close. She placed her face only inches from Infidel's eyes. Infidel didn't even blink; the woman was apparently invisible to all but my ghostly gaze.

Relic said, "My tale is difficult to believe, yet I know you have a Truthspeaker among you. Bring me to him, so he may judge the veracity of my words."

"Why don't you try your story on me first?" said Blade.

Relic nodded. "Very well. I am the sole survivor of the Vanished Kingdom. When I was young, a great nation had tamed this island. From shore to shore the land supported vibrant cities. Our harbors sheltered armadas of trade ships that brought treasures from the far reaches of the world. Truly, it was a golden age."

Blade smirked. "I'll give you credit for imagination. But, assuming you are thirty centuries old, how does this make you an asset for our mission?"

"This quest has been set in motion by the discovery of a map. I am the author of this document. I was an engineer for the king during the construction of what is now referred to as the Shattered Palace."

Blade studied the ragged figure before him with a more critical eye. Even I was taking another look at Relic. Was he telling the truth?

"How is it that you have survived all these years?" Blade asked.

"Modern men are not the only ones to have gods," said Relic. "The gods in those days were far more active in the affairs of this world. They would travel the kingdoms, disguised as men, granting favors to those who were kind, curses to those who were cruel. The god I met gave me eternal life; alas, he was not so kind as to grant me eternal youth."

Blade rubbed his chin, contemplating Relic's words. The invisible woman now stood beside Relic, staring at his burlap-covered face. Blade gave the slightest nod and the woman raised her hands to grab the cloth, no doubt to pull it away.

Relic said, "It would be unwise for your companion to touch me."

The woman halted. Blade looked impressed. "You can see the Whisper?"

Relic nodded. "I've learned many arcane arts during the endless parade of centuries."

"So you know a little magic," said Blade. The Whisper's hands still lingered only inches from the hood. She looked to Blade for further cues. "I still don't see why we shouldn't just pull your mask off to see what you truly are."

"An understandable desire," said Relic. "Alas, long ago, I contracted a disease that causes flesh to wither and rot. It cannot kill me due to my curse, but it has disfigured me horribly. I'm not contagious as long as my scabs are closed. Much of my garb is adhered to my skin. Tearing it free could expose others to the illness."

"I see," said Blade, as the Whisper backed away. "That certainly makes the thought of sharing a camp with you appealing."

"I'm a difficult companion. But my knowledge outweighs the risks. Currently you have a map. With me, you shall have a living atlas."

Blade finally turned his gaze toward Infidel, who stood quietly on the shore. "And who... or what... is that?"

Menagerie grinned ever so slightly at Blade's confusion.

Infidel couldn't be tattooed; no needle could penetrate her skin. Still, Menagerie knew a thing or two about pygmy dyes. From scalp to toe, Infidel's skin was now a pale silver-blue, looking more like metal than flesh. Her limbs were concealed beneath skin-tight leather armor, though her torso was mostly bare save for the shiny steel bra. Her face was also naked, though bold black dyes created the illusion of a mask around her eyes. Menagerie had assured Relic the pigments would last for weeks without streaking or smearing.

"This is my War Doll," said Relic. "As an educated man, you may know that the engineers of the Vanished Kingdom have no peers in today's world. We crafted clockwork animals that mimicked life in every way, only with skeletons of steel instead of fragile bone, muscles of wire instead of meat, and veins pumping oil instead of water."

Infidel stared silently at Blade. The greatest flaw of her disguise was that to play the role of a machine, she would need to remain mute, and keep her face passive. A quiet, unexpressive Infidel was impossible for me to imagine.

Relic continued: "The men of my time were as blood-thirsty as the people of today. We constructed machines in the likeness of men to fight as gladiators in our arenas."

Blade furrowed his brow. "I would hardly call this the likeness of a man."

"We were lustful as well as blood-thirsty," said Relic. "It pleased the king to watch women in mortal combat. The War Doll, and others like her, were far more resilient than a true woman. Her performances could entertain the king for hours on end."

Blade looked skeptical. But he wasn't the one who gave voice to doubt. Instead, it was Menagerie who said, "I'm not buying it. This is obviously just a painted woman. You can see her breathing!"

Relic placed his hand on the small of Infidel's back and pushed her forward. "The engines within the War Doll produce heat.

She inhales and exhales air to maintain an optimal operating temperature. When she's active, she will appear to sweat; this is partially for cooling and partially aesthetics. She's been designed to mimic life in the finest detail."

"This is the biggest load of garbage I've ever heard," said Menagerie.

"You have the power to ensure our veracity," said Relic, ignoring Menagerie and addressing Blade. "Bring us to the Truthspeaker."

"We don't need to waste his time," said Menagerie. He reached over to Ivory Blade and drew the dagger the albino carried on his belt. Before anyone could blink, Menagerie threw the blade with a grunt. The tip struck Infidel directly at the base of her throat, in what should have been a killing blow. The dagger bounced off, landing on the pebbles before her. She continued to stare impassively, not displaying the slightest discomfort.

Relic clapped his hands. "Demonstrate your strength."

Infidel leaned over and picked up the blade. She thrust the edge into her mouth, clamping down on it with her pearly teeth, then biting through the steel before dropping the dagger. She spit out a half-moon fragment of metal. It clattered on the pebbles beside the damaged blade.

Menagerie stared, slack-jawed.

"What is your opinion now?" asked Relic.

Menagerie cleared his throat and crossed his arms. "I'm not getting paid to offer opinions. I'll shut up."

The Whisper knelt and picked up the dagger and the wedge that had been bitten from it. She returned it to Blade, who sighed as he tapped the matching pieces together. "This was my favorite dagger," he said, sadly. He gave Menagerie a stern look. "This will come out of your pay."

"I insist on it," said the tattooed man.

Blade gave Infidel one more long stare, before looking down at Relic. "I'll probably regret this, but you've earned your audience with Father Ver."

Blade led us further back into the cave, toward a broad circle of sunlight. A section of the roof had collapsed, leaving a large shaft to the sky. Blood-tangle vines hung from above, their leaves swaying in the wind. The rise and fall of the lagoon turned the cave into a bellows, with air flowing in and out through the shaft in gushes. The breeze and the sunlight made this area of the cavern less dank. It was here that the king's men had made their camp.

I watched as the Whisper slipped into one of the tents to alert Father Ver. She moved with such grace that the tent flap showed only the slightest flutter. Still, since it had moved, I deduced she wasn't intangible. That ruled out the chance she might possibly be another ghost.

Blade led us to the center of the circle and motioned that we should wait. Reeker wandered over to a large boulder at the edge of the sunlight. He reached into his jacket and produced a cigar as thick as Aurora's index finger. He flicked a match against the rough stone. The tip sputtered to life — then was just as quickly extinguished as the Whisper leaned down from the top of the boulder and snuffed the match between her fingers.

"What are you doing?" Ivory Blade cried as he ran toward Reeker.

"Catching a quick smoke?" Reeker said, looking at his dead match with puzzlement.

"That is entirely the wrong answer!" Blade yanked the cigar from the skunk-man's grasp. "Didn't you read your contract?"

"Maybe."

"I apologize for the lapse," Menagerie said as he approached. He raised his hand and slapped the offending Goon on the top of his head with a good solid *THWACK!*

Reeker cringed, whining, "Watch the hair, boss."

"I read every last line of the contract to you," said Menagerie. "You have no excuse."

"My mind wanders sometimes," said Reeker. "There's a no smoking clause?"

"Fire of any kind is forbidden," said Blade. "Greatshadow's spirit is present in all flame. There will be no campfires, no torches, no lanterns, and, yes, no smoking! Striking a match opens Greatshadow's eye and invites him to stare at us."

"That's a little paranoid," said Reeker. "I thought the no-fire clause meant something big enough to cook on. There must be a million candles burning right now. You think the dragon pays attention to what he sees through all of them? You think he even notices a match that gets lit for a couple of seconds?"

"This isn't subject to debate," said Blade. "We've arrived safely on this island by adhering to strict discipline in our avoidance of fire. I won't tolerate any further lapses."

"There won't be any," said Menagerie. "The contract says no fire. We'll comply. Right, Reeker?"

"Sure, boss," said the skunk-man, frowning as he tossed the cigar into the dark reaches of the cave.

Like everyone else, Aurora had been focused on the confrontation. As it wound down, she turned toward the center of the circle. She jumped back, startled.

Father Ver was standing mere feet behind her, staring at her massive frame. Despite the years, I recognized him instantly. His dark eyes were still set deep in a face that resembled a skull wrapped in old, crinkled parchment. He was completely bald save for bushy white eyebrows and tufts of hair just behind his ears. While his face had grown more skeletal, his body still looked robust. He stood straight as a board in his ink-black robes.

He said, with a glance toward Blade, "This... *creature*... is the best muscle you could hire?"

Blade nodded. "Aurora comes with the highest recommendation."

"She's an ice-ogress," Father Ver said, in a weary tone that made it sound as if he thought that Blade had somehow missed this fact. "Of what use can she be in the tropics?"

Aurora raised her fist as an ice gauntlet formed around

126

it. "Actually, the jungle enhances my powers. Ice magic depends on moisture. The atmosphere of my homeland was arid; here, water is plentiful. Spells that take minutes back home can be cast in seconds. Plus, though you wouldn't know it from the heat outside, it *is* nearly the winter solstice, the time of year when my powers are at their peak."

"I asked my question of Blade, not of you, ogress," said Father Ver. He turned once more to the albino. "The Whisper says you need my powers."

"These two," said Blade, nodding toward Infidel and Relic. "They showed up uninvited. Aurora vouches for them, but—"

The Truthspeaker raised his hand as he glared at Relic and asked, "Who are you and why are you here?"

Relic stared directly into Father Ver's eyes as he said, "I was once known as Urthric," before launching into his tale of being a survivor of the Vanished Kingdom and the author of the map.

During Relic's monologue, Father Ver gave no reaction beyond his default scowl. Finally, Relic finished. Father Ver continued to glare down into the hunchback's face. I noticed the Whisper slip up next to Ivory Blade. She stood on her tiptoes and placed her lips to his ear. As she spoke so softly only he could hear, I noticed that she ran her hand along Blade's face and hair in a gesture that told me their relationship was more than simply teammates.

"Oh, right," said Blade. "You should also know the hunchback is afflicted with a potentially contagious flesh-eating disease."

"This information would be important only if we were considering allowing him to join our mission," said Father Ver.

"So he's lying?"

"He speaks the truth, or believes he does," said Father Ver. "It doesn't matter. I advise we kill him, and dismantle this abomination." He gave Infidel only the barest glance as he spoke. Again, I couldn't help but suspect there was something odd going on with the way the king's men were ignoring her.

Blade leaned back against the boulder, scratching his chin as he thought. The Whisper wrapped her arms around him and began to plant soft, silent kisses along the side of his neck. Blade's voice remained steady despite this as he said, "If he's telling the truth, killing him seems short-sighted. Physically, he's no asset, but the War Doll offsets this liability."

"I don't understand why the king feels we need to hire mercenaries," grumbled Father Ver. "It shows a lack of faith."

"I'm not going to second guess the king. And, now that we're actually on the mission, the decision of who we hire isn't mine to make. Tower will have to decide."

Menagerie asked, "Where is Lord Tower anyway? Isn't it time we meet the man leading this mission?"

"Tower can only carry one other adult with him when he flies," said Blade. "He'll be back soon enough with the final members of the team."

"Flies?" asked Menagerie. "He can turn into a bird as well?"

"No. Flight is a power granted by the Gloryhammer."

"What's a hammer got to do with flying?" asked Reeker.

"Kumuk yuh fuh wut wuh," said No-Face.

"Just try it," said Reeker.

Before anyone else could ask for a translation, a shadow flickered across the cavern floor. I'd never met Lord Tower, but there was no mistaking the identity of the man who descended slowly through the shaft toward us. He was covered in plate armor polished to a mirror finish; Aurora raised her hand to shield her eyes from the glare. He had his right arm thrust straight out, grasping the Gloryhammer. The sacred artifact was a sledgehammer carved from a single glorystone, blazing with a bright white intensity.

Tower's right arm was wrapped around a slender figure; at first, I thought it was a woman, but as he drew closer to us

I could see it was a man. He had black hair gathered into a pony-tail, and priestly robes of the same style as Father Ver's, only bright red. His arms were tightly wrapped around Tower's torso, his eyes wide with terror as he gazed at the ground. Of course, the look of fear wasn't the first thing I noticed about his face. I couldn't help but wonder why he had a large letter 'D' tattooed onto his forehead in blood-red ink.

The terrified man wasn't Lord Tower's only passenger. There was also a bored-looking boy standing on Lord Tower's left boot. He balanced there on one foot, with one hand gripping Tower's belt, looking quite relaxed as Tower descended. The boy looked no older than ten. His head was shaved; he wore no shirt, only a pair of white cotton britches. He was heavily tanned, the shade of a loaf of bread fresh from an oven. The boy hopped from Tower's boot with the ground still ten feet away, dropping to a silent touchdown on the gravel. Tower's metal boots came to rest seconds later with a loud *CLANK*. The man in the red robes fell to the rocky ground, groveling at the knight's feet. It took a second to realize he wasn't showing gratitude to Lord Tower but was, instead, kissing the ground.

Tower's face was hidden behind his steel faceplate. His eyes could barely be seen through twin slits in the mirrored surface. He surveyed everyone in the room; glancing quickly at Reeker and Menagerie, pausing at No-Face. I detected a slight shudder before he moved on to Aurora. His eyes narrowed; she returned his gaze without flinching. He then sized up Relic, and, apparently judging him harmless, turned his attention to Infidel.

His eyes lingered on the metal bra longer than necessary. Infidel didn't move a muscle. He raised his eyes to her face. Again, his gaze lingered for longer than it should have.

He said, finally, "I see we have... guests."

"Trespassers," said Father Ver.

"Applicants," said Blade. "Who did quite admirably on their interview, I thought."

The sun-tanned boy had been studying everyone as well. He said, "The hunchback and the painted woman are seeking to join our mission?"

"Correct," said Blade. "I think they could prove valuable."

"All they prove is that someone has already compromised our mission," said Father Ver. "Killing them will set an example to those who might seek to betray us." He looked directly at the man in the red robes as he spoke.

I found it curious that Blade and Father Ver were addressing the boy instead of Lord Tower, the supposed leader of this mission. Just who was this kid?

The boy walked up to Relic. "You appear too old and feeble to make the journey."

Unlike Father Ver, the child spoke in a neutral, observational tone, with no hint of scorn or disdain.

"Hiring only my body would be a poor investment," Relic said. "It is my knowledge that will be of value."

"Your knowledge is of little use if you cannot survive the tests before us."

"I assure you, I will be alive long after everyone in this room has returned to dust. As for my diminished physicality, the War Doll more than compensates. She is the ultimate fighting machine; no one in this room is her match."

"That," said the boy, cracking his knuckles, "sounds like a challenge." He clasped his hands together prayerfully and bowed toward Relic. "I accept."

CHAPTER NINE
THE GOLDEN CHILD

RELIC TILTED HIS head quizzically. "Are you challenging the War Doll?"

"Yes," said the child. Despite the fact that he was well-muscled for his age, the boy didn't look like a fighter. Most boys of a combative nature were covered with scabs and scars, but this kid didn't look like he'd ever even been scratched. Despite his modest attire, his gray eyes hinted at a royal lineage. Perhaps, if he'd been in fights before, it had been against opponents who understood the political advantages of not landing a punch.

"I mean no disrespect, but you don't understand the danger," said Relic. "The War Doll is a finely tuned killing machine. Her bones are solid steel; her artificial skin is impervious to the sharpest blade. Her mesh-cable muscles can crush a man's skull like an eggshell."

The boy responded with a serene smile. "You're lying. Your companion is a woman with painted skin, not a machine. Your dire warnings are nothing but a bluff. Isn't that right, Father Ver?"

The Truthspeaker frowned. "The hunchback believes he is telling the truth."

The boy furrowed his brow. "There is an aura of magic around you, creature. Somehow, you are fooling Father Ver."

"No magic could conceal the truth from a servant of the Divine Author, could it?" Relic replied.

The boy frowned as he continued to study Relic and Infidel. Finally, he said, "If your 'War Doll' can simply knock me from my feet, we shall consider that a victory. I'll acknowledge that she's not a painted woman, despite the plain evidence of my senses."

"And if you knock her from her feet?" asked Relic.

"She is welcome to continue the fight," said the boy. "My intention is to prove that she's a fraud. I shall do so by breaking the woman's bones until she confesses, proving that there's no steel within her."

"Fierce little bastard, ain't he?" Reeker said with a chuckle.

"You will hold your blasphemous tongue!" shouted the Truthspeaker.

Reeker opened his jaw so wide I worried his cheeks would tear. He thrust both hands toward his mouth and grabbed his tongue in a death grip.

"This is the Golden Child," said Ivory Blade, glaring at the skunk-man. "He is the culmination of generations of pious men and women who have faithfully adhered to the teachings of the One True Book. He is the perfect blend of body, spirit, and truth, untainted by falsehood."

Father Ver placed his hand upon Blade's shoulders. "Be careful with your words," he counseled. "While there is evidence that Numinous Pilgrim is the Golden Child, we do not have the final proof. Perhaps one day he shall be the Omega Reader; first he must conclude the seventeen sacred tests."

Numinous? I felt sympathy for the boy. His name was even worse than the one I'd been stuck with as a baby. Menagerie apparently found the name amusing as well, since he looked as if he was fighting back a laugh.

The Truthspeaker glowered as he saw the look on Menagerie's face. "Do you have something to say, mercenary?"

The tattooed man gave Reeker a sideways glance. His fellow Goon was still wrestling with his tongue. "I'm good," said Menagerie.

"Now that you know who I am," said Numinous, "you know it is futile to attempt to deceive me."

"Of course," said Relic. "I wouldn't want a person of your sacred esteem to doubt my claim. I accept your challenge."

Infidel, standing beside Relic, casually placed a hand upon his shoulder. There was a faint crunching sound.

"If you'll excuse me," said Relic, speaking through clenched teeth, "I will require only a moment to fine tune the War Doll before battle."

He hobbled toward the shadows, with Infidel clamped to his shoulder. Once they were out of earshot, she leaned close and whispered, "Are you out of your mind? I can't fight a little boy!"

Relic nodded. His voice was barely audible as he said, "From the mind of Ivory Blade, I've learned that Numinous has already completed twelve of the seventeen sacred tests. If the boy truly is the Omega Reader, all our planning may be for naught. Your fear may be justified."

"Fear? I'm not... look, I just won't beat up a kid. I only fight people bigger than me."

"You've fought pygmies," said Relic. "You've slaughtered them and stacked their bodies like firewood."

Infidel frowned.

Relic continued, "I know you don't wish to be a bully. But if you fail to beat Numinous, we shall be exposed."

Infidel glanced back toward the circle of light. The Golden Child stared into the shadows as if he could see them clearly. "He's so skinny. I'm worried I'll break him."

"Break him if you can," said Relic. "The Golden Child's senses are uncluttered by falsehood. He can hear your heart beating. He can smell your sweat. He alone can expose you."

"What about Lord Tower?" asked Infidel. "Have we fooled him? I thought I saw something in his eyes. I don't know if it was recognition, or... or something else."

Relic shook his head. "While he wears his armor, I cannot read his thoughts, let alone manipulate them."

Infidel cocked her head. "You manipulate thoughts?"

"To a degree," said Relic. "I'm no puppet-master, controlling the actions of others. But, I have the power to subtly guide the focus of men. Our ruse would crumble if Father Ver thought to ask you the truth of your identity. Fortunately, I've managed to keep his attention fixed upon me. Even though he can see you, he's too distracted to focus on you. The same is true of Blade. Alas, Numinous and Tower are beyond the reach of my powers."

"I wondered why I was being ignored in this outfit," said Infidel.

"Back to the matter at hand: you need only knock Numinous from his feet to silence him. He's given his word and dare not go back on it. If he is the true Omega Reader, he must never make a false promise."

"I don't think knocking him down is a real problem," she said, clenching her fists. "This is going to be my shortest fight ever."

Relic shook his head. "Don't be overly confident."

"C'mon. Let's get this over with."

They headed back toward the sunlit circle.

"The War Doll is ready," Relic announced as they returned.

Lord Tower's eyes narrowed as he looked at Infidel. She had a sword on one hip, a mace on the other, and still had my knife in her boot. The knight held up his gleaming gauntlet and said, "There's no need to shed blood. Your gladiator must relinquish her weapons."

"As you wish," said Relic.

"This is an unnecessary precaution," said Numinous. "Even if she was armed with the Gloryhammer, she could not harm me."

Infidel's face was passive as she handed Relic her weapons. I felt a shiver pass down my non-existent spine as he grasped the hilt of the knife.

The king's men and the Goons retreated to the edge of the sunlit circle, forming an impromptu arena. I noticed that Reeker had finally let go of his tongue; apparently the Truthspeaker's command wasn't permanent. The boy stood in the center of the circle, his stance loose, his arms dangling. His eyes were fixed on Infidel's face. She stopped about six feet away and raised her fists, planting her feet in a boxer's stance.

Seconds passed into moments as the two studied each other. Infidel bobbed back and forth as she waited for the boy to make his move. I could tell she still worried about hurting the kid. With his placid face, Numinous looked more like a bored observer of the fight than a participant.

Infidel was the first to lose patience. She jumped toward the boy, kicking out, her foot aimed at his gut. Numinous stepped aside fluidly, placing one hand on her ankle, another behind her knee as she flew into the space where he'd just stood. With an ear-splitting cry of "Yiaiiah!" he spun her in the air, slamming her face-down into the gravel. Before she could pick herself up, he leapt into the air, shouted, "Hiaaayah!" and landed with his full weight on the back of her neck, burying her head deeper into the small stones. He bounced off, landing gracefully. He looked down at Infidel with a smug expression. Infidel didn't move a muscle.

"That didn't take long," Ivory Blade said from the edge of the circle.

"It's not over," said Numinous. "She's still conscious."

As he said this, Infidel's fists closed around big handfuls of gravel. In a flash, she sat up and whipped her arms toward the Golden Child, letting the gravel fly in a dangerous hail of stone shrapnel. Yet before the gravel had even left her fingers, Numinous dove toward her. His body twisted as he spun through the stony cloud, avoiding every last piece. The gravel sparked as it struck the boulders beyond.

Infidel was still sitting with her arms out when the boy reached her. His leg blurred as he kicked her three times in the throat with cries of "Hyia! Hyia! Hyia!" She went down, flat on her back, her arms limp. The boy landed, hopping on a single foot. His placid expression was replaced by an unmistakable frown. He winced as he placed weight on his kicking-foot.

Infidel sat back up, rubbing her wind-pipe. "Son of a bitch," she muttered.

Among the king's men, there was a simultaneous furrowing of brows.

Relic cleared his throat. "The War Doll has been programmed to utter simple phrases to simulate pain or frustration. The old kings demanded this verisimilitude."

The boy wasn't distracted by the conversation at the edge of the arena. His eyes were locked on Infidel as she rose. The kicks to the throat might have decapitated an ordinary woman. Right about now, the Golden Child was probably starting to wonder about the possibility of steel bones after all.

Infidel made it back to her feet. She took a deep breath, steadying herself. She leaned forward slightly and the boy danced back. Even with a sore foot, he was still as nimble as a cat. Maybe he was going to have a hard time breaking Infidel, but she faced an equally tough challenge in knocking him down.

Infidel lunged toward the boy. Instead of aiming a blow at the child, she raised both fists above her head, then dropped to her knees, delivering a powerful two-fisted strike to the ground. Gravel flew into the air in a wave. I gave the cave roof a worried glance as the shock toppled boulders and popped tent pegs. Numinous merely lifted his feet into the air as the destructive energy passed beneath him. When he landed, he somersaulted toward Infidel. She rose, punching out, and he used her outstretched arm as a springboard. He landed behind her and shouted, "Hyuh!" as he kicked into the bend of her knees. Infidel's legs folded beneath her, but before she hit the ground, the boy unleashed a whirlwind of blows —"Hyi! Hyun! Haih! Yah! Huu!" — as he aimed precise strikes at nerves in her spine, elbows, and shoulders.

Infidel sucked in air as her face twisted in pain. She rolled to her back as the Golden Child dropped toward her, sinking both knees into her gut just beneath her ribs, then rolling forward and cuffing both ears simultaneously as he shouted, "Kiii!" His momentum carried him out of Infidel's reach as she flailed her arms uselessly in the air.

"I've seen enough," said Lord Tower, raising his hand. "The War Doll has failed the test."

Relic sighed. "Centuries of wear have cost the War Doll some of its former prowess. Still, you must admit, it has withstood the best the boy can throw at it without breaking."

I prayed that he was right, that Infidel wasn't broken, but I wasn't sure. Her eyes were unfocused as her legs uselessly pushed at the gravel. Her arms were splayed to her side, fingers twitching.

The Golden Child paced in a circle around his victim.

"The fight continues!" he cried, his voice a fierce growl. "She has not yet cried out for mercy! I will not rest until she confesses her ruse!"

"Your holy urchin is a sadist," Aurora said, from across the sunlit arena.

"He has an unwavering passion for truth," said Father Ver.

"Nonetheless," said Lord Tower, "The fight is over. We should—"

He never got to complete his sentence. The Golden Child leapt into the air above Infidel, spinning like a top, as he unleashed an ear-piercing battle cry. Gone was the placidity that had gripped his features earlier. Blood-lust blazed in his eyes.

Then, to everyone's surprise, Infidel moved, grabbing a fist-sized rock in her right hand, a slightly larger one in her left. She swung her arms together as the boy dropped toward her, his feet aimed at her belly. Numinous tucked up his legs, and the rocks passed beneath his toes. The stones collided with a *BANG* that raised everyone's hands to their ears. The rocks were pulverized, concealing Infidel and the boy inside a cloud of smoky gray dust.

From inside the haze there was a sharp high-pitched shout of "Aiigh!" It took a fraction of a second to realize that this wasn't another war-cry. Numinous trailed dust as he shot skyward, a good fifty feet up the shaft, both hands grasping his crotch. Infidel sprang up as the boy reached his apex. The Golden Child's eyes went wide as he spun his body, trying to avoid landing in Infidel's grasp, but, as I knew all too well, no amount of arm-flapping and desperate kicking can change the trajectory of a falling body.

Infidel lifted an arm and grabbed the boy by the ankle, then swung him in an overhead arc to plant his face in the gravel.

"The fight is over!" shouted Lord Tower, jumping toward the combatants.

"The hell it is," growled Infidel, whipping the boy up again, painting the gravel before her with a line of bright blood.

"The War Doll is programmed to taunt its enemies," Relic said, though I don't know if anyone was listening. Everyone's eyes were wide with horror as Infidel spun the boy's limp body around overhead and flung him. The child smashed into the stone wall above the Truthspeaker. The boy bounced off, completely limp, as the Whisper dove to catch him. She lowered his battered body gently to the ground. He was bleeding from both ears. His arms were bent at odd angles, as if they had too many joints.

Everyone was paralyzed as they stared, slack-jawed, at the bloodied child. Ivory Blade was the first to recover his senses. He whirled around, drawing his sword, as he shouted, "You've broken our Golden Child!" He leapt toward Relic, the tip of his sword aimed for the hunchback's eyes.

Lord Tower reached out his gauntleted hand and caught the albino swordsman in mid-strike. The sword sliced the air six inches away from Relic's hood.

"Let me go!" Blade cried out.

Father Ver turned from Numinous and shouted, "You will calm yourself!"

Instantly, the look of rage vanished from Blade's features. He straightened his clothes as Tower set him back on the ground.

"The boy is not the Omega Reader," said Father Ver, coolly.

"He failed the thirteenth test; he faced an ancient monster, and could not defeat it."

"But—" said Blade.

"The truth is before your very eyes. The boy misjudged his opponent; the true Omega Reader would never deceive himself so. This boy was just the latest in a long string of false hopes." Father Ver glanced at the fallen boy with a look that was half pity, half contempt. "Numinous was poisoned by arrogance. This is one of the most insidious forms of self-deception."

Infidel wasn't paying any attention to the conversation. Instead, she moved slowly toward the boy, her eyes full of guilt. Relic intercepted her, taking her by the arm as he said to Tower, "Aurora has some skill as a healer. Let her look at the boy; perhaps his life can be saved."

I doubted that Aurora was up to the task. Barely a minute had passed and both the boy's arms were swelling up, turning purple from where bone had punched through muscle. His body trembled as he sank deeper into shock. A cold compress on the forehead wasn't going to fix this.

However, the question of what Aurora could do was rendered moot as the man in red robes stepped toward Lord Tower. "You threatened to cut off my hands if I touched your precious Golden Child," he said. "Now that he's failed you, do you mind if I save his life?"

The knight nodded. "Do what you can, Deceiver."

I suddenly had an explanation for why this man had a big 'D' tattooed on his forehead. I had thought that Deceivers were only bogey-monsters that monks used to frighten orphans. A fundamental tenant of the Church of the Book was that truth was truth; there was nothing subjective under the sun. The reality recorded in the One True Book was the only reality, inviolate, inflexible.

Deceivers, on the other hand, believed that nothing at all is true, not even the experience of our own senses. Everything we assume about reality — that the sky is blue, that grass is green, that snow is cold and fire is hot — is merely a shared delusion, constantly reinforced by people desperately clinging to the illusion of stability in a world where nothing is absolute. The One True Book was merely a work of fiction in the Deceiver's world view. The Deceivers thought of themselves as shared authors of this fiction, and, as such, were free to edit reality to their liking. They were the greatest enemies of the church. What was one doing here, alive? I couldn't believe Father Ver hadn't slit his throat the second they met.

The Whisper recoiled as the Deceiver knelt beside the boy, stepping back several feet, as if she didn't want to risk breathing the same air.

"Can you help him?" asked Aurora, as she knelt down next to the Deceiver.

"I possess the power to heal any injury," the Deceiver said, running his hand along the boy's arm. "Though I believe we were all mistaken in thinking the boy was seriously harmed. Wipe the blood away, and he's suffered little more than a few scratches and bruises."

And, indeed, as the Deceiver wiped the blood and grit from the boy's limbs, the flesh no longer looked so distorted. Perhaps it had only been a trick of the light that had made the wounds look so serious before.

"He's just had the wind knocked out of him," the Deceiver said, cradling the boy's face, pushing back the eyelids to look at the dilated pupils. "He'll come out of it any minute."

Everyone had fallen silent as they watched the Deceiver tend to the fallen boy. The only sound was a faint rasping noise. The sound was coming from the Truthspeaker, grinding his teeth. His eyes were narrowed into slits as he watched the Deceiver restore the boy to health. Finally, he could stand no more.

"Get your unholy hands off him!" He jumped forward, his robes flying as he kicked the kneeling man in the head. "I would rather see the boy die than be tainted by your filthy lies!"

Numinous, still unconscious, gasped as his left arm twisted

once more, obviously broken. Yet, the boy still looked better than he had before. The Deceiver lay beside the boy, glaring at Father Ver with naked hatred as he rubbed the sandal-print on the side of his jaw.

Tower grabbed Father Ver by the nape of his neck and hauled him back before he could kick the Deceiver again. "Control yourself," he said. "Zetetic is using his power for good, as promised."

"Promises mean nothing to his kind!" Father Ver shouted. His spittle flecked Tower's faceplate. "He swore only to use his power to alter his own form, and already he has broken this vow by altering the boy's body!"

Zetetic, the Deceiver, said, "Technically, I gave myself the power to heal. The boy's body wasn't altered, only restored, until you meddled."

Father Ver went bug-eyed. He once more lunged toward his enemy, but Lord Tower held him back. "His presence is an abomination! The king is mad to include him on this quest!"

Tower sighed. "If the king is mad, so be it. He is still the king, and it's our duty to obey him. I forbid you to strike Zetetic again."

"There are greater authorities than the king," Father Ver growled. "You cannot honestly expect me to simply stand and bear witness to such blasphemy!"

"You could always close your eyes," Zetetic said.

Father Ver sputtered a string of meaningless syllables as his rage stripped him of coherent speech.

"Get back to work," the knight said to Zetetic as he lifted the Truthspeaker from his feet and carried him back several yards.

The Deceiver looked at the boy and shrugged sadly. "I've done all I can. Father Ver has aborted the newborn reality we created where the boy was cured. Still, I think it persisted long enough to save the boy's life."

Aurora still knelt beside the unconscious child, probing his arm tenderly with her beefy fingers. She looked up and said, "I can set the arm in a splint. For a boy this age, the bone will heal in a matter of weeks."

Father Ver turned away in disgust. He grumbled to Tower, "At the command of an earthly king we ally ourselves with liars, ogres, and rogues. What does it matter if our quest succeeds when we corrupt our very souls in the journey?"

"The primal dragons are the enemy of all mankind," said the knight, resting the Gloryhammer on his shoulder. "If I must be damned in order that the world can be free of their tyranny, I shall pay the price. You, of all people, understand the importance of our mission."

Father Ver's shoulders sagged. His voice trembled as he whispered, "Very well. But the boy must remain behind. If he isn't the Omega Reader, we have no business endangering a child."

Tower nodded. "I concur."

Father Ver gave Relic a rueful glance. "The hunchback doesn't believe he's lying, but I still don't trust him or his whorish toy. Given all they know of our quest, I must advise you to destroy them."

Blade stepped over to the conversation.

"I second that opinion," he said. "I was impressed with the War Doll's strength, but now that I've seen its savagery, I fear it's a danger to us all."

"Thank you for your counsel. However, since we can't have pack animals on this mission, it seems wasteful to destroy the War Doll. It would make a good substitute for a mule." Tower looked up the shaft. The sun was no longer directly overhead, and the shadows in the cave grew deeper. "Our emotions run high at the moment. We won't be ready to leave until morning. I shall make my decision then."

Despite the fact that he was the subject of the ongoing conversation, no one was paying attention to Relic. He walked to the wall where the Golden Child had hit. There was a spattering of blood dripping down the stone. Casually, he reached out and dabbed the gore with a rag-covered finger.

Then, since he still carried Infidel's weaponry, he drew the bone-handled knife from its scabbard, and ran his blood-damp finger along the steel.

My ghost lungs gasped for air as I materialized once more. I was fainter than my previous incarnations; I could see through my ghostly fingers to the bones of fog beneath.

He spoke to me in his soundless voice: *It seems I have need of you after all, Blood-Ghost.*

I looked down at my body, on the verge of tears from the joy of seeing myself again. As a thought-fog, my emotions are muted; now that I once more felt ephemeral blood pulsing in my veins, I was terrified at the thought of having the knife cleaned once more.

Obey me, and I will see that the knife is never bare of blood.

"What would you have me do?" I asked.

The king's men are a dangerous lot. While the boy is no longer a threat, I cannot read the mind of Lord Tower while he wears his armor. Were he the only one immune to my powers, I would have few fears. But the Whisper's thoughts are dim; the harder I concentrate on them, the fainter they become.

"Is she a ghost?"

Doubtful. Your thoughts are clear to me. Blade may know her true nature but I've yet to find her origins among his thoughts. What worries me even more is the Deceiver. His mind is unlike anything I've encountered. His true thoughts are buried beneath veils of hallucinations. I risk my very sanity probing him.

"What am I supposed to do about this?"

You will be my spy. In your phantom form, you aren't tethered as tightly to the knife. You may wander, listening in on conversations I will not be privy to. Have a care, however. Should Father Ver suspect your presence, he has the power to banish you forever to the spirit world.

I furrowed my brow, confused. "Aren't I already in the spirit world?"

Obviously not. You are a spirit in the material world.

Actually, that was kind of obvious. But, if there was a spirit world, what was it like? Why hadn't I gone there?

I will help you reach the spirit world at the proper time should you assist me.

"Maybe I don't want to go. I'd rather stay here. I'll help you only if you promise to let me speak to Infidel."

A fair bargain. I will grant this if you serve me well. Have a care, however. You may desire to speak to the woman, but the feeling may not be mutual. The living seldom wish to be confronted by the dead.

I clenched my jaw as I thought over his offer. If I refused to cooperate, he could just wipe the blood from the blade, and banish me once more. But, while he had the power, perhaps, to grant me what I wanted, I had to wonder what, exactly, he wanted, beyond my immediate services as a spy. Aside from a desire to kill Greatshadow, I knew nothing of his plans or purpose.

Relic's eyes glimmered. *You are wise to be suspicious of me, Blood-Ghost. Yet, my motives are simple. I hate Greatshadow with every fiber of my being. The world can hold no joy for me as long as he lives. Tower would sacrifice his soul. I would sacrifice this, and more, for the pleasure of watching Greatshadow die.*

"And then what?" I asked. "You take his treasure?"

Relic gave a low, soft chuckle that chilled my vaporous guts. *Then, my dear Blood-Ghost, I take the world.*

CHAPTER TEN
FLAWED VESSELS

THAT EVENING, EVERYONE dined on hardtack and dried beef; I would have expected an expedition backed by a king to have food fit for one, but apparently all the funds had gone into buying glorystones and Goons. Tower still had his helmet on as Blade handed him his rations. I waited for him to pull off his helmet to eat, but instead he retreated into his tent.

"Guess he's too good to eat with us," Aurora said as she sat cross-legged on the ground by the Three Goons.

"I heard he never takes off that tin can because his face is covered with scars," said Reeker.

"Boo hoo hoo," No-Face answered. For once I didn't need any translation.

Relic came over to the circle of mercenaries. "Perhaps he has other reasons for hiding his face. Most warriors, in my experience, are eager to show off their battle scars."

"It ain't battle scars," said Reeker. "According to what I heard, about fifteen years ago on his wedding day, one of Tower's enemies launched a sneak attack. Half the chapel got knocked down by a catapult and a fire broke out. Tower kept running back into the conflagration, saving the lives of a dozen people even though he was getting all burnt up himself. But he never pulled out the one person he was searching for: his bride. Now, when he sees his scars, he thinks of her."

"A tragic tale," said Relic.

"A stupid tale," said Reeker. "Ain't no dame worth risking your life for. They're like stray cats; one gets killed, two more show up the next day."

"Tower must not have felt that way," said Menagerie. "My sources say he's still unmarried."

"Maybe that's just proof he sees things my way now," said Reeker.

"Mubuh huh duug guh buhn uf," said No-Face.

"Maybe we should stop gossiping about the man who's paying our wages," said Menagerie. "Don't forget they have an invisible spy."

Infidel was several yards away from the ring of dining Goons. She was standing with her back to the others, looking into the shadows of the cave. I moved in front of her and waved my ephemeral hand before her eyes, though I knew it was futile. Her face was completely blank, with no hint of a reaction to Reeker's tale. Save for the occasional blink, she really looked like nothing more than a statue.

THE FOLLOWING MORNING, Tower announced his decision: "Relic and his War Doll can join the expedition. We'll use the War Doll chiefly to carry gear. Aurora will also have pack duty as punishment for revealing our location."

Reeker raised his hand. "We're going to hike to the dragon's lair? The caldera's, like, fifty miles away. Can't you fly us?"

Tower shook his head. "The Gloryhammer glows most brightly when I'm in the air. Flying low over the ocean in midday wasn't a problem, since the glare of the sun upon the waves masks the weapon's radiance. Short bursts of flight to help us over obstacles are probably safe, but I don't dare risk making a dozen long trips back and forth over the jungle canopy. Greatshadow would surely spot us."

"So he spots us and comes down to kill us," said Reeker. "We fight him on the slopes instead of in the volcano. What's the big deal?"

Ivory Blade nodded toward Lord Tower. "If I may?"

Tower nodded back.

"First," said Blade, "Our mission is more than to simply kill the dragon's body. We must also slay his spirit, and forever sever his intelligence from the element of fire. This can only be done in his lair. Second, you're being paid to do what we tell you to, not to question our commander's decisions before we even leave the base."

Reeker looked as if he were going to say something back, until he spotted Menagerie glaring at him. He crossed his arms, and gave a subservient nod.

Aurora apparently was undeterred from asking questions. "What will happen to the boy? He still needs medical attention."

Numinous was sitting near the main tent, gazing toward Lord Tower with a look that bordered on hatred. He'd been furious when he'd been told earlier that he was no longer taking part in the mission. Gone was the placid, supremely confident Golden Child of the day before. In his place was an ill-tempered ten-year-old boy who'd always gotten his way until now. I felt sympathy for the kid. Every day of his life until today, he'd been surrounded by adults who treated him like he was the salvation of the world. Now, the adults had decided he was nobody important. That can't be easy to swallow.

Tower said, "Numinous may not be the Omega Reader, but he is still exceptionally educated and trained. Despite his injuries, he's able to fend for himself until we return. He can use this time alone to reflect on whether life in the priesthood will suit his future, or perhaps a more martial life as a knight will be his calling. When this mission is over, I will ensure that his education continues for a new, more suitable, role."

This answer seemed to satisfy Aurora, though not Numinous, who rose and went back into the tent.

"If there are no more questions, we shall begin. First, allow Father Ver to bless our mission with a prayer."

Father Ver's left eyebrow shot up. He looked surprised by the request, which I found curious. A man in his position was no doubt asked to lead prayers a dozen times a day.

The look of surprise was quickly wiped away by his omnipresent scowl. He stepped forward into the middle of the circle and looked up the shaft of sunlight spilling into the cavern. He then looked down at his hands, bony and wrinkled, covered with age spots. He cleared his throat.

"The question before us," he said, in what sounded more like a sermon than a prayer, "is one of predestination."

Tower, Relic, Ivory Blade, and even Zetetic, the Deceiver, all nodded reverently as he began. The Goons and Aurora just looked bored. The Whisper, apparently, wasn't all that religious. She slipped in up behind Blade as the priest spoke and began to kiss him gently on the nape of the neck.

"The future was written long before we were born. We know in our hearts that the Divine Author would not have written a story in which the wicked are allowed to triumph and the righteous meet endless defeat. In the end, good shall triumph over evil."

I gave a little ghost yawn. I'd heard this generic prattle about the inevitable victory of good ten times a day growing up.

"There can be no doubt that Greatshadow embodies evil. No honest man has ever stared into a flame without perceiving the malignant intelligence behind it, the predator spirit that waits to pounce upon the weak and unwary. The Divine Author has left no room for doubt as to the identity of the villain of our tale. The only question that remains is: Are we good enough to be the heroes? Do we undertake this mission in complete honesty regarding our motivations? Do we seek to vanquish evil purely because it is our duty, or have the seeds of our defeat already been planted in falsehoods buried deep inside our hearts? Will our tale not be one of triumph, but of instruction, a warning against vanity, or greed, or lust?"

It may have been my imagination, but Ivory Blade looked chastened by these words. He hung his head low, his lips pressed tightly together, even as the Whisper gave him a comforting hug. Tower's shoulders also sagged a little as Father Ver spoke.

The only person who looked inspired by Father Ver was Zetetic, who was grinning broadly.

Father Ver concluded by looking back up the shaft and switching from sermon to something more like a prayer. "We ask, oh Author Of Our Fates, that even if we are flawed vessels, you still will use us as vessels of your will. Help us, oh Lord, to bring the world one page closer to its perfect ending. Your will is our will. Amen."

"Amen," echoed Tower. Then he raised his head and said, "Relic, get your War Doll loaded. We'll use it to cart our gear up the cliff, with Aurora's help. I'll ferry the others one by one. As long as I don't rise above the treeline, this flight shouldn't draw attention."

Tower grabbed Ver by the arm and pulled the cleric to his chest. "You first," he said, sounding somewhat terse. The holy man didn't have time to say a word before the knight launched skyward.

Follow them! Relic screamed in my mind. *If they have a private conversation, I want to know the details.*

I looked at him and said, "Maybe you didn't notice that they're flying?"

And perhaps you haven't noticed that gravity no longer holds you to this earth?

I had noticed that, but I'd still been hovering at pretty much the same eye-level I'd been at when I was alive. In my ghostly form, I could wander around where I wanted to just by thinking. Did it work the same way going up?

I moved toward the shaft and spotted Tower high overhead. I furrowed my brow as I willed myself to follow him. Then — *whoosh!* — not only did I fly, I flew fast, shooting up along the rugged cliffs to reach the knight and the cleric in a matter of seconds. The terrain atop the cliff was still a fairly steep slope, but had soil enough to support trees and shrubs in a nearly uniform canopy of green. Tower punched through the foliage into the shadowy forest beyond. There were huge boulders among the trees. Tower landed on one, releasing Father Ver, before asking, in a voice that was almost a shout, "What was that?"

Father Ver looked undaunted by the anger in the knight's tone. "You are unhappy with my prayer."

"I wanted an invocation to our inevitable success, not some admonition that we might be too vain or lustful or whatever to defeat the dragon. Where is your faith?"

"Faith is a crutch for the spiritually weak," Father Ver said. "It's something used by women and children and the feeble-minded who may be unprepared to handle truth. I have never thought of you in this category."

"You've been unpleasant company since this expedition was announced," said Tower. "I've always looked up to you and respected you, Father. I can't understand your sudden embrace of pessimism."

Father Ver closed his eyes and rubbed the thick callus on his forehead. "Truthfulness sometimes precludes optimism. You of all men should understand this."

"And you, of all men, should understand that the righteous always defeat the wicked. It is the only conclusion that will satisfy the Divine Author."

Ver shook his head. "You're a warrior, not a priest. You overstep your bounds when you claim insight into the mind of our creator."

"I'm only repeating what you've taught!"

"You are only repeating the teachings you find convenient to remember," said Ver. "You remember that good triumphs over evil in the end. But you fail to recall that we may not be at the end. The One True Book is a very thick document. There may yet be centuries, even eons, before the final victory. In the intervening time, the outcome of any given battle can never truly be known."

Tower sighed. "Fine. You are technically correct. We may not actually know how this particular story ends. But I'd appreciate it if you would be a little more inspirational, to help motivate the troops."

"What troops?" asked Father Ver. "There are eleven of us. The Goons are not believers in the Book, nor are the ogress and the hunchback. Blade and the Whisper walk a middle path and are not so pure as you may wish to believe. And they are saints compared to Zetetic, who twists all truths he encounters into lies. The only one among us whom my words may truly inspire is you."

Tower crossed his arms, tapping his gauntleted fingers on his iron biceps with little clanking sounds. His feet were hovering a few inches above the ground. He shook his head slowly and said, "Perhaps I need the inspiration."

"What you need is to know yourself," said the priest. "Are you honest regarding your reasons for leading this mission?"

"I seek only to defeat evil and improve the lives of my fellow men. You would know if I was lying."

"I would know if you were lying to me. I cannot know if you're lying to yourself."

"You think I have some other motive? What? Treasure? I'm already wealthy. Fame? Glory? The streets of the Silver City are lined with statues erected in honor of my previous victories. It matters not at all if they erect another."

"So you say."

"Such is the truth," said Lord Tower. "Years have passed since I first saw my image carved in stone. Any pride I once felt has passed as I've aged. A statue is an empty legacy to leave the world. My only goal now is to leave the world a better place than what I inherited. The death of Greatshadow is a step toward that goal."

"Very well. Even if your motives are pure, you must know your chosen allies are motivated by nothing other than greed."

"True. But experience shows me I need not share the same motives as an ally in order to achieve a common goal. I've had years of battle experience to learn these truths. Still, I understand it must be difficult for you. This mission is forcing you into alliances with men you wouldn't normally associate with."

"You're being too polite," said Ver. "I would normally order these scoundrels and heretics flogged, imprisoned, or hanged."

"Understood. Now, try to understand that I've fought beside rough men and unbelievers in previous battles," said Tower. "Against some foes, power is more important than purity. We could lead an army of ten thousand pilgrims up these slopes, and Greatshadow could kill them in a matter of seconds by unleashing an inferno. These scoundrels and heretics are survivors. I'm confident we have assembled the perfect team to defeat Greatshadow. I want you to feel this confidence also."

Ver pressed his lips tightly together. "If I believed this to be a doomed enterprise, I wouldn't have accepted your invitation to join. I'm not blind to the difference between principle and truth. I respect the power of the team you've assembled. We stand a good chance of success. But I cannot pretend that victory is certain."

"I suppose I'll have to settle for that," said Tower.

"Yes, you shall. Go get the others," said Ver, with a dismissive wave. "They'll wonder what's keeping you."

Tower nodded, then shot back over the cliff side. I started to follow him, but was distracted by something I spotted out on the water. I raised my hand to shield my eyes from the sun, though, alas, it proved pointless, since the rays passed right through my spectral skin. As I got used to the light after the shade of the trees, there was no mistaking I was looking at a clipper ship, still a mile out, but heading toward the cliffs at a breakneck pace.

A few seconds later, I spotted Tower rising back up from the cave, now with Zetetic in tow. Tower sat the red-robed figure on a boulder facing Father Ver, then swung back out to grab another passenger.

"Nice little prayer you gave down there, Ver," said Zetetic.

"Did I detect a little bit of a guilty conscience in all that talk about whether you're good enough for this mission? After all, given what you've done to me…"

"You've suffered nothing you haven't earned," said Father Ver. "Count each breath you draw as a blessing from the Divine Author. If I were the master of your fate, your bones would have long since been picked over by ravens."

"No doubt. But, since a higher authority than you has seen to it I'm along for this journey, could you maybe try to be more courteous? Or at least try not to kick me in the head any more?" He rubbed the side of his skull for emphasis.

"I can make no such promise," said Father Ver.

Zetetic shrugged. "I can't be blamed for asking."

No-Face was next up, followed by Reeker and Menagerie in the form of a parrot. I might not have recognized Menagerie among the other parrots flitting through the trees if not for his voice. "Looks like trouble," the bird said, as it landed on No-Face's shoulder. It pointed seaward with a wing.

By now, the ship had gotten much closer, and seemed to be heading directly for the pirate cave below.

"Suh hurs," said No-Face.

I squinted. He was right. It was the *Seahorse*, a pirate ship. I could even see Captain Stallion on the deck, in case there had been any doubt. Stallion is a distinctive figure. He looks like a half-seed, but is really just a man's torso jammed onto the body of a donkey, though he tells everyone his equine parts are prize-winning stallion. He got this way after a badly thought out double-cross of a Weaver, who have a flair for this sort of magic.

"This is inconvenient timing," said Tower, glancing down. "He's heading straight for the cave. So much for the thought of leaving Numinous behind."

"Or we could just kill Stallion and his crew," said Menagerie. "We'll be glad to do it for no charge, as long as we don't have to split the bounty for his head with you."

While Tower pondered this offer, I drifted back down toward the cave. The *Seahorse* was moving toward the entrance at a speed that no sane sailor would risk. But then, Captain Stallion wasn't known for being timid. I passed Infidel and Aurora on the way down. They were climbing the cliffs, lugging large bales of gear from ledge to ledge. Relic was nowhere to be seen. I slipped back into the cave just as the *Seahorse* reached the mouth. Numinous, Ivory Blade, and the Whisper were still inside. The *Seahorse* carried at least fifty men, battle-hardened cut-throats who would give even the Goons a run for their money. Whatever Tower decided, I hope he decided it fast.

Within the cave, Ivory Blade stood on the shore, watching the pirates set anchor in the cove. Numinous came out of the sole tent remaining in the camp. A handful of glorystone lanterns were still scattered about the place. It took the pirates all of ten seconds to notice the precious rocks. The *Seahorse* leaned starboard as the entire crew rushed to the rails to look at the glowing gems.

Captain Stallion leapt from the deck, his pirate hat flying off as he sailed across the water to land in the shallows, splashing onto the shore with a few more jumps. He had a saber drawn as he eyed Ivory Blade.

"Well, well, well!" Stallion shouted. "Look who we have here! Mister Ivory Blade! The deal-breaking, cowardly dog who I swore would walk the plank if ever we met again!"

"Didn't know you were the type to hold a grudge, Stallion," said Blade.

A dozen men jumped from the ship, swimming ashore quickly, blades in their teeth, to stand beside their captain. Stallion said, "A grudge?" as he pranced closer to the albino. His donkey body left him a little taller. While Blade was a figure of composure, every hair in place, Stallion looked as if he'd gone feral. His long hair was tangled and matted around his sunburnt face. His clothing was half rotten on his back. "A grudge is a small thing, Mr. Blade. A grudge is like weak beer. My feelings for you have been distilled ten times into a brew of pure 200-proof hatred. Whatever happens from this day forward, I'll die a happy man to have finally learned if your entrails are the same spook-white as the rest of your unholy flesh."

"Don't make any hasty decisions until you hear what I have to say," said Blade.

"I'll not be listening to your lying tongue ever again!" cried Stallion. He turned to his men, and cried, "Kill him!"

And in the blink of an eye, the dozen men that surrounded him fell to the ground, grasping their slit throats, as the silhouetted form of the Whisper danced silently through their midst. She ended her dance by slicing up with her sword and chopping Stallion's blade in twain four inches above the hilt. The impact made no sound; what was her sword made of?

Stallion frowned as he looked at his abbreviated weapon. He glanced around at the dying men surrounding him. Then, he grinned broadly. "Blade! Old friend! Can't you recognize a little joke?"

"Only when dead pirates are the punchline," said Blade, still with his arms crossed. "Shall we discuss business now?"

"What do you have in mind?"

"I would like to hire you as a shuttle service. We have a boy here who is far from home. You can return him to the Silver City."

"Ah," said Stallion. "That could be a problem. A man such as yourself has perhaps heard of the small matter that your own king has placed a sizable price on my head?"

"Among other body parts," said Blade. "Which is why, as payment for your services, King Brightmoon himself shall grant a pardon for your crimes. I can give you a letter of safe passage that all members of his navy will respect."

"His pardon would carry no weight with the Wanderers. Or the Stormguard, for that matter."

"No. But it will open an entire archipelago of ports where you could legally dock. Any number of towns where you could trot the streets a free man. And, the king recently lost several ships. Perhaps he'd find a position for you and the *Seahorse* in his navy."

"I seem to recall similar promises being made five years ago, when I handled the small matter of bringing you the Book of the Abyss."

"If it had been the genuine article, and not a blatant forgery, all promises would have been kept."

Stallion ran a hand along his tangled mane. "Aye, it was a piss-poor forgery. I knew you'd discover it sooner or later."

"It was sooner," said Blade.

Stallion chuckled. "This boy must be precious to you, that he'd bring a king's pardon."

"Indeed. And if a person of a mercenary nature were to try to hold the boy against his will and seek a ransom, I can give you my solemn vow that his corpse would be rendered into glue."

"I'm sure you would. Fortunately, I can't imagine a person of a mercenary nature wanting a treasure greater than the king's pardon… especially if these glorystones are thrown into the agreement."

Blade shrugged. "Why not? We were leaving them behind anyway."

"Very well, sir. We have a deal."

The albino and the pseudo-centaur sealed their verbal contract with a handshake.

Blade said, "I was certain you were still a reasonable man, despite the haircut."

"Aye," said Stallion. "It's been many years since I've been able to dock in a port with a barber I'd trust with a razor."

"A shave and a haircut will make you feel like a new man," said Blade. He glanced back over his shoulder and shouted, "Numinous."

Numinous was already standing behind him.

"I've heard every word of this transaction," he said. "I approve. The thought of waiting endless weeks in this cave in solitude held little appeal to me."

"He's got a busted arm," said Stallion, studying Numinous. "Is there a bonus for being a floating hospital?"

"The bonus is that if you stop trying to haggle on an already closed deal, I won't sever your testicles and hang them from your earrings."

"That is an excellent bonus," said Stallion, nodding.

Later, after the letter of safe passage had been written, Blade left the pirate cave, following the same path that Aurora and Infidel had taken. Tower met him at the first ledge.

"I was waiting in the shaft the whole time, listening," said the knight, carrying them skyward. "It seemed as if you had the situation in hand. But, are you certain you can trust him with Numinous?"

"Stallion wants that pardon. He wanted it five years ago. Other pirates can slip into towns in disguise from time to time to spend their ill-gotten gains. Stallion doesn't have that option. He's got to be the most recognizable pirate in the world. Just as I'm probably the most recognizable secret agent in the world. We understand each other."

The reached the top of the cliff. Blade sat down on a rock and the Whisper slipped behind him and wrapped her arms around his neck. Tower hadn't carried her up. Could she fly? Or was she just as fast at climbing as she was at cutting throats?

CHAPTER ELEVEN
EVERYTHING THAT CAN BE IMAGINED IS TRUE

TOWER HADN'T BEEN joking about using the War Doll as a mule. After the gear was all brought up from the camp, they began to test how much weight she could carry, piling more and more tents, rations, and tools upon her shoulders until the mound was almost comical. Infidel bore it all with mechanical stoicism. After a certain point, the roped-together pile on her shoulders was so large it risked getting tangled by branches as they walked, so they gave the rest of the gear to Aurora before reaching the limits of the War Doll's strength. I wasn't surprised. Infidel was probably strong enough to carry all the gear and the rest of the party as well, along with an actual mule if we'd had one.

Of course, pack animals were out of the question. The part of Greatshadow that was still a big hungry lizard had a taste for livestock. Paintings and sculpture from the Vanished Kingdom showed that cows, horses, and oxen had once had a home here. After Greatshadow rose to power, he stripped the land of any mammals larger than pygmies. It's rumored that the pygmies' bitter dyes protect them; more likely, Greatshadow doesn't hunt pygmies for the same reason that men don't hunt mice. The meat you get isn't worth the effort.

I floated next to Relic as we set off into the jungle. I said, "The Black Swan was a bit off. She said a dozen adventurers would join the hunt for Greatshadow. With Numinous down, there's only eleven."

Perhaps she's counting you, said Relic.

"Was she? She can see me?"

Relic shrugged. *I could read her thoughts before she became undead. Now, her thoughts are lost to me.*

"Eleven against Greatshadow doesn't seem like good odds," I said.

The king has chosen quality over quantity. As to whether the king has chosen well, we shall see.

Progress up the slopes was frustratingly slow. The terrain was steep and rugged, dotted with boulders as big as houses all tangled with tenacious vines. No-Face was armed with a machete and turned loose on the foliage, but we still barely covered a mile by mid-day. Despite the thick canopy above us, the sun directly overhead soon raised the temperature from sweltering to unbearable. As we paused for No-Face to chop away a particularly nasty tangle, Father Ver leaned wearily against a tree, looking pale. His heavy clerical robes were better suited to a chilly mountain monastery than the tropics. Aurora, taking pity, approached him. She cupped her oversize hands and, within seconds, crafted a bowl of ice, filled to the rim with cool water drawn from the soggy air.

"Have a drink," she said.

Father Ver wrinkled his nose at the offering. "I must decline," he said. "I'm certain you mean well, but it would be a sin to drink water created by your pagan magic."

"I didn't create the water. I just gathered it. But, suit yourself." She turned around, only to find Reeker standing just behind her. He took the cup from her hands without asking and gulped it, rivulets running down his chest.

I didn't notice if Aurora took offense at this because from the corner of my eye I caught a glimpse of the Whisper giving a canteen to Ivory Blade. As Blade drank the water, the Whisper unbuttoned the top few clasps of his armor and folded back a flap of white leather to expose the skin around his collarbones. Then, in a move that probably warmed him rather than cooled him, she leaned her invisible face to his chest and began to lick at his sweat. I looked around, feeling squeamish about witnessing such an intimate act.

After a few more hours of hacking, we eventually made it

through the worst of the vines into the denser jungle beyond. It's counterintuitive, but the deeper you go into a jungle, the easier the going becomes. The canopy above is so thick with plants growing on other plants that most of the available sunlight gets captured long before it reaches the ground, creating a semi-permanent twilight in which only a few hardy, broad-leafed plants grow. You might expect the ground to be covered by fallen leaves and branches, but the soil is constantly scoured by ants and beetles that make short work of anything that hits the jungle floor.

With most of the machete work behind us, Menagerie took the lead, scouting ahead of the party as a panther. Ivory Blade and the Whisper followed, then Lord Tower, Father Ver, and No-Face. No-Face, when not on machete duty, was assigned as Father Ver's bodyguard. Despite his deformity, No-Face wasn't a half-seed, nor did he openly dabble in blood magic. Apparently, this made him acceptable to walk within an arm's length of the holy man.

Reeker and Zetetic were next. Reeker was the Deceiver's bodyguard, or perhaps just his guard, period, since he had orders from Lord Tower to give the Deceiver a snoot full of skunk juice at the first sign of anything suspicious. I had to wonder why the Deceiver was part of this team, if he couldn't be trusted.

Relic took my private musings and turned them into a prompt for a telepathic exposition.

The Deceiver is immensely powerful. He is the master of falsehoods, and the things that are false in this world far outnumber the things that are true. Zetetic may be the greatest threat Greatshadow faces, assuming he can find the courage to stand up to the dragon. He's definitely not undertaking this quest out of choice.

"How can you know that?" I asked. "I thought you couldn't read his mind."

His mind is labyrinth of hallucination that protects his innermost thoughts, but I am slowly navigating that labyrinth.

I've learned that he blames his presence here on the Black Swan. She paid a substantial fee to persuade King Brightmoon of the importance of including him.

I scratched my ghostly scalp as I contemplated this. It was difficult to wrap my head around the idea that the Black Swan had already witnessed the next twenty years. I wondered what else she'd changed on this mission, beside including Zetetic and Aurora? I glanced back at the ogress, who was bringing up the rear along with Infidel. One thing conspicuously absent from the mountains of gear upon their backs was a harpoon. From the way Aurora had described it, the shaft of the harpoon was over fifteen feet long. It plainly wasn't with the gear, and Tower wasn't carrying it either. Could it have been broken down into something smaller?

I spent most of my time drifting near the two women, mostly because of my craving for Infidel's company, but also because of the circle of chilled air that surrounded Aurora. Even as a ghost, the jungle heat was unpleasant. Still, being a traveling ghost wasn't all bad. On my trips through the jungle while I was alive, I was normally too exhausted by hiking to enjoy the scenery. In my weightless, ogre-cooled comfort zone, I had time to appreciate the rich tapestry we walked through. If everything around us was the work of the Divine Author, he had a sense of playfulness when it came to the colors surrounding us. Translucent pink salamanders the size of bananas crawled over dark jade leaves big enough to use as a tent. Parrots and parakeets the color of lemons and oranges flitted between chocolate-brown tree trunks, devouring iridescent copper beetles and finger-length ants red as chili peppers. Orchids blossomed in every nook and cranny, flowers I'd only seen in botany books — yellow and black tipsy tigers, snow-white wedding gloves, pale purple danglers. The breeze was a heady mix of their perfumes; though, little by little, the floral aroma was getting drowned out by the low-tide stench of Reeker as he and the Deceiver slowed their pace to skirt the bubble of cool air surrounding Aurora.

"Allow me to apologize for Father Ver," said the Deceiver, looking back at Aurora with a friendly smile. "His church teaches that ogres and mermen and the like are false beings, existing as sort of a shared dream that will all be wiped away when the world finally awakes to the truth. I pity him for the limits of his worldview. I personally am happy to be in the company of someone who knows ice magic."

Aurora gave him a suspicious look. Even a compliment felt dangerous coming from the man. Still, I wondered if I was giving him a fair shake. I distrusted Deceivers mainly because the church had drilled into my brain from an early age that heretics like Zetetic were the incarnation of evil. That same church harbored a supply of knife-wielding maniacs dedicated to stabbing the woman I loved. Perhaps I needed to keep an open mind.

"I've always been fascinated by the magic of your people," Zetetic continued. "It's based on completely different theories of reality than those that are taught by the Church of the Book. Since Father Ver believes he is in possession of the sole path to truth, your mere presence is a threat to him. The undeniable evidence that your magic works undermines everything he believes. No wonder he hates you."

Aurora shrugged. "I don't care what he thinks."

"A healthy attitude," said Zetetic. Then he turned toward Relic, who was hobbling along near Infidel. "The ruins of the Vanished Kingdom are filled with idols of gods long since forgotten. I'd love to learn more about who these gods were, and what the men of your time believed."

Relic shrugged. "The men of my time were no different than the men of today. There was no one great, universal truth accepted by all. In the end, it mattered little who or what was worshipped. Time wiped away both the just and unjust. The followers of the dog-god vanished from the world just as completely as the followers of the snake-god. The temples where a thousand men gathered to sing the praises of their makers are now hidden beneath roots and rocks. I cannot help but think that, no matter what men believe to be true, over a long enough time scale, it will be proven false."

Zetetic smiled. "Just because an idea is eventually false doesn't mean it wasn't true once. We Deceivers are smeared as believing that the world is created from shared lies. It's more accurate, however, to say that the world is composed of contradictory truths."

"How can truths be contradictory?" asked Aurora. "Things either are, or they aren't. It can't be both night and day at the same time."

"It can if the world is a sphere," said Zetetic. "In your homeland it is always winter; here it is always summer. If I could travel instantly between the two physical spaces and ask the season, I would receive two contrary yet true answers. People are limited to thinking that their immediate experiences represent all that is real. The Church of the Book believes one model of reality, while Weavers, blood magicians, and somnomancers all are certain that they are in sole possession of the actual truth of the world. You can't blame people for thinking that these competing ideas can't all be correct. But, what if reality is large enough to accommodate everything? What if we live in a world where all truth is local? What if, on the grand scale, everything that can be imagined is true?"

"Remind me not to ask you any more questions," grumbled Aurora.

"I'm merely trying to pass the time with some intellectually stimulating conversation."

"The only thing I need stimulated is my spine," said Aurora, with a hint of strain in her voice. She shifted the oversize pack she hauled to redistribute the weight to her left shoulder. "What the hell does Tower have in the packs? Anvils?"

"If your load is heavy, perhaps I could be of assistance."

Aurora gave the Deceiver's slender form a quizzical look. "What? You'll tell me some lie about the gear? Convince me that it's lighter?"

Reeker suddenly became much more alert.

"Uh-uh," he said, grabbing Zetetic by the arm and pulling him a yard further up the trail from the ogress. "If you try to use your powers, I'm supposed to give you a full blast of juice."

Zetetic frowned. "You wound me, sir. I was merely offering aid to a member of the fairer sex. Have you no sense of chivalry?"

Aurora snorted. "He's the wrong guy to ask that question."

The faintest trace of a snicker flickered over Infidel's face.

"Reeker's the worst womanizer I've ever seen," said Aurora. "He's slept with every whore in Commonground without paying a dime. Treats them like something you'd scrape off a boot, and still they line up outside the bar waiting for him."

Reeker didn't look offended by this summary of his character. Instead, he slicked back the white streak in his hair and said, "Aurora, honey, I'd be happy to show you what the women are so hungry for."

Zetetic stroked his chin as he studied the skunk-man. "I suspect his secret is musk."

Reeker cut him a sideways glance.

Zetetic wasn't deterred. "Most mammals use scent to convey sexual signals. With his control of aromas, perhaps Reeker is seducing women on a primal level with odors they aren't consciously aware of."

Reeker poked the Deceiver in the chest. "You don't know nothing! Women like me for my good looks and charm."

Zetetic held up his palms. "I meant no offense. However, since I lack your striking features and erudite manners, I'm left with only simple kindness with which to befriend women. This is why I'd like to help Aurora."

"No magic!" said Reeker, again with a finger-poke.

"I don't really do magic," said Zetetic. "I only tell lies. What have you to fear from a mere liar?"

"I'm not afraid of you," said Reeker. "But you're lying in saying you're a liar. Or not a liar. Or not lying about... I mean, you're not telling the truth in... what I'm saying is..." He furrowed his brow as he got lost ever deeper in the thicket of the sentence he was attempting to construct.

"You're trying to say I'm lying about being merely a liar," said Zetetic. "That's an astute observation. Any man can tell a lie. I know how to make the universe believe it."

Suddenly, for no apparent reason, Relic gasped loudly. His staff fell from his gnarled hand as he collapsed to the ground, completely limp.

"My head is not a safe place to eavesdrop," Zetetic said, sneering down. Then, while Reeker was looking at the fallen hunchback, the Deceiver casually placed a hand on Aurora's pack. His gaze met the ogress's eyes as he said, in a matter-of-fact tone, "I'm big enough to lift this pack with one hand."

Reeker spun around and spat, sending a gob of yellow goo toward Zetetic's face. Only, by the time the spit had crossed the five-foot gap between them, Zetetic's face was replaced by a giant ankle, and Aurora was jerked from her feet.

Everyone looked up through the hole that had suddenly been punched in the canopy. Zetetic was now two hundred feet tall, holding the pack by a single finger looped under a rope. Aurora dangled beneath the pack, looking no bigger than a rat.

"I do believe I've remembered another appointment," Zetetic said, laughing, his voice booming like thunder. He flicked his arm toward the ocean, sending Aurora and her pack flying in a long arc down the slope.

Infidel knelt next to Relic. She whispered, "You alright?"

Relic sucked air through clenched teeth, then said, "His thoughts... like razors... my mind... is bleeding..."

Infidel shrugged off the shoulder straps of her pack, letting it drop to the ground in a clatter. She cracked her knuckles and looked up with the same eager grin she always brought to fights where she could beat up someone bigger. Her face fell into shadow as Zetetic's sandaled foot flew down toward her and Relic. Infidel whirled around, kicking, catching Relic in the gut and launching him out of the stomp-zone. She crouched to jump away but was too late. The giant foot slammed into her with a shudder that shook the whole mountain.

Zetetic jumped, knocking over trees, flying down the slope a good fifty yards before crashing back to earth, waving his arms to maintain his balance on the uneven terrain. Off in the distance, perhaps a half-mile away, I caught a glimpse of Aurora and her pack tumbling head over heels, on the verge of vanishing once more into the canopy. Then, in a sudden flash of light, her downward arc was intercepted by the shining silver form of Lord Tower, catching the ogress in his outstretched arms. Her pack tore loose at the impact, sending a spray of camping gear out over the treetops.

As difficult as it was to tear my eyes from this spectacle, I turned back to Infidel, who was splayed out in the center of a giant footprint. With a grunt, she popped her face up from the earth. She spat out a mouthful of black jungle dirt as she sat up, rubbing her eyes.

Satisfied she wasn't hurt, I turned my attention back toward the Deceiver. He had leapt again. His robes were tattered below his knees, shredded by the ancient trees he pushed aside like tall brush. Long streamers of blood-tangle vines trailed behind him as he fled down the mountain.

Lord Tower had circled around and now shot like an arrow toward the Deceiver's chin, the Gloryhammer blazing like a second sun in his outstretched arm. Aurora hugged his chest for dear life, in a death-grip that probably would have crushed anyone not encased in enchanted armor. Yet, before the knight could strike, Zetetic swung out with his tree-sized right arm and back-handed the knight in mid-air, sending him shooting back toward the ocean, looking like a spiraling comet as Aurora left a trail of bright snow in their wake.

Infidel rose back to her feet just in time to see Father Ver fly past, his hands locked onto the hide of a large tiger that effortlessly carried the old man. I followed as they caromed down the mountainside, leaping from rock to log, covering the quarter-mile to the giant's ankles in a span of seconds. The Truthspeaker cupped both hands around his mouth and shouted, "You will go no further!"

The Deceiver smirked as he spun away from the Truthspeaker's voice. His smirk changed to a frown, however, as his feet remained firmly planted on the ground. He raised his hands, feeling the air before him as if it were an invisible wall.

"You are no giant! You are a vile fabricator who will turn and face me at your true size!"

Zetetic's face contorted as his limbs jerked. "Graaah!" he cried out as he began to shrink, swinging his arms before him as if swatting at unseen bees. "Graaah! Naayaaah!"

With each second that passed he shed size, dropping to fifty feet, twenty, ten, and then he was only a man again, face to face with a panting tiger and a very angry cleric.

Zetetic held up his hands and gave a sheepish grin. "You can't blame a fellow for trying."

Father Ver had a different opinion, which he expressed by leaping off the tiger and planting his bony fist squarely in the center of the Deceiver's mouth. Zetetic spun from the blow, falling to his hands and knees.

He spat out blood and growled, "You bast—"

Father Ver silenced him by kicking him in the throat. The Deceiver fell to his back, his arms flopped out to his sides. Father Ver dropped with his knees, straddling the Deceiver's chest as he pummeled the man's face.

"Blasphemer!" Father Ver screamed. "Accursed malignancy! May your filthy name be erased from the Book!"

Zetetic raised his hands to block the blows, but the priest simply knocked them aside and continued to rain down punishment. Menagerie changed from tiger back to human and leaned against a fallen tree, his arms crossed as he watched the whirl of violence. Reeker and No-Face reached the area a moment later, saying nothing as they stared at the beating unfolding before them.

The Deceiver's arms fell limp. He'd never gotten in a single blow. Father Ver's fists trailed blood as he cut his knuckles pounding his victim's teeth. The Deceiver's pale face began to resemble a scary clown, as bright red blood painted his cheeks with a lopsided grin.

Ivory Blade and the Whisper suddenly bounded into the triangle formed by the Goons. Blade grabbed the Truthspeaker by the shoulders and tried to pull him off the fallen man.

"You're going to kill him!" he growled, as he tugged at the cleric's robes. With the Whisper's help he pulled the elderly man back to his feet. Blade grabbed Father Ver by the collar and said, "Calm yourself. You don't need to sink to his level."

"You will take your freakish hands off me," Father Ver said, his voice a low hiss.

Blade snapped both hands into the air, his fingers spread in a gesture of surrender.

"Now you will go away!"

Blade spun on his heels and bounded off up the trail, running at breakneck speed, quickly disappearing among the trees. The Whisper looked after her fleeing lover for a few seconds, slack-jawed with surprise, before she shot off in pursuit.

Father Ver looked back down on his bloodied victim. Blood bubbled from the Deceiver's nostrils as his breath came out in gurgles. The Truthspeaker knelt beside his victim. Zetetic flinched as his hand approached. The Truthspeaker grabbed the Deceiver's chin and turned his barely focused gaze to meet his own, then asked, "Where is it?"

Zetetic looked back with sad puppy eyes.

"Don't pretend you don't know," Father Ver said. "You wouldn't have dared this without the sketchbook. You will hand it over."

Zetetic's hands reached into the folds of his red robes and producing a small leather-bound notebook, barely six inches tall. The cover had no words on it, but it was scuffed and scratched, the parchment pages within looking dog-eared and folded over. Father Ver snatched the book away.

"Your wicked imagination exceeds my ability to think of prohibitions," said Father Ver. "Let us keep this simple. I gave my word to the king that I will not kill you. I've made no vow that would prohibit me from cutting out your blasphemous tongue. Attempt to escape again and I swear you will never utter another lie."

The Deceiver glared at Father Ver with a mix of hatred and terror, then nodded slowly, indicating he understood. Father Ver let go of the man's chin and wiped his gore-drenched hands on his victim's red robes, looking disgusted. He glanced toward the sky as Lord Tower drifted down toward them. Aurora was still clamped onto his chest; her hair had come undone from its top knot and lay against her scalp in a chaotic tangle.

She looked a bit wobbly as Tower set her on the ground.

"You believed his lie, ogress," grumbled Father Ver, without looking at her. "Your pagan faith makes you an easy target for his falsehoods. If he speaks to you again, feel free to break his jaw."

Before Aurora could reply, Lord Tower looked down at the semi-conscious Deceiver and said, "Why would he try something like this? Even if he'd reached the sea, we could have stopped him at any time."

"Not without this," said Father Ver, holding up the small book.

Tower reached both hands to his hip, popping open a compartment in his armor exactly the right size to hold the book. He stared silently at the emptiness within. "By the sacred quill," he mumbled. "How did...? When could he...?"

"The Deceiver fails to respect reality itself," Father Ver said. "It would have been a simple matter for him to become a master pickpocket." The priest cast a glance toward Reeker. "You were supposed to keep this from happening."

Reeker shrugged. "He caught me by surprise."

"Of course it was a surprise!" Father Ver shouted, throwing

his hands into the air. "Did you think he would be considerate enough to send you a detailed letter explaining his plan? Are all half-seeds half-wits as well?"

Reeker's eyes flashed with anger as he drew back his shoulders and pressed his lips into a pucker. Menagerie nodded toward No-Face. The giant man's hand clamped over the skunk-man's mouth.

Menagerie said, "This is twice I've had to apologize for my colleague's behavior. I assure you, there will not be a third incident. For now, he's going to go help gather up what gear we can find from Aurora's pack. He won't grumble while he's doing it. Right?"

No-Face lowered his hand. Reeker swallowed his pride and whatever else he might have been holding in his mouth, then said, "Sure, boss." Then, to Father Ver, "Won't happen again."

Lord Tower scanned the treetops, paying no attention to Infidel and Relic as they joined the rest of the party. Relic was limping more than usual; his whole body was wracked with tremors. Infidel was holding his arm, supporting him.

Lord Tower sighed. "Since we aren't under attack right now, maybe Greatshadow didn't notice this incident. Perhaps the worst that has come from this is that our supplies are scattered halfway back to the sea. We're going to lose the rest of the day gathering them." He looked at Menagerie. "I need more than just Reeker on the job. You'll all help recover the gear."

Menagerie nodded. "We're on it. I can work the treetops as a monkey."

Tower turned to Father Ver. "While Zetetic's stunt has cost us time, it's also proof that he has skills no one else brings to the mission. Help him get cleaned up and stitch his wounds."

Father Ver's left eye began to twitch. He looked as if he was about to explode, but he said, softly, "As you wish."

Lord Tower looked down at the Deceiver, who had managed to sit up. The beaten man probed his bloodied mouth with his fingers, wincing as he pulled out a broken molar. The knight said, "Before you fell into heresy, you earned renown as a scholar. Some priests tell me you were the smartest man they'd ever met. How can you be dumb enough to pull a stunt like this? Even if you'd escaped with the book, you would not be free. Should ten days pass without word from me, the monks will initiate the X sanction. You understand the consequences?"

The Deceiver nodded. His wet voice whistled as he said, "I undershtand the damned conshequencesh."

Tower turned back to the others. "Let's get busy. Goons, gather gear. Blade, I need you to… to…" His voice trailed off as he looked around the clearing. He turned to Father Ver and asked, "Where are Blade and the Whisper?"

CHAPTER TWELVE
SOMNOMANCER

"I CAN FOLLOW their scent," said Menagerie, shifting into the form of a wolf. His voice was a yelping growl as he said, "I'll take the War Doll for back up, assuming it can act independently. It's the only one with a chance to keep up with me."

"Agreed," said Relic, his voice still weak.

"There's no need for a search party. Blade won't run forever," said Father Ver. He didn't sound apologetic for having caused the problem. "Once he trips, or runs into something, he'll return to his senses."

"Given Blade's agility, he might run a long time," said Lord Tower, as he rose into the sky. "With the thickness of this canopy, I'll never spot him from the air. Menagerie's plan is a sensible one. I'll help gather gear while they're gone."

Stay with me, Blood-Ghost, thought Relic. *I dare not look into the Deceiver's mind again. You must watch him with complete vigilance.*

The Deceiver didn't look as if he was going start mischief anytime soon. Father Ver knelt before him, examining the man's torn face. Zetetic was oddly passive as the priest reached out to touch a gash on his upper lip. "This will require stitches," Ver said. "It will hurt."

Menagerie sniffed the ground, then bounded up the trail at breakneck speed with Infidel at his heels. Or rather, his paws. I looked at Relic and said, "I go where she goes." I spun around before he could answer and surrendered myself to the tug of the knife in her boot sheath. My ghostly feet lifted from the ground and I flew after them far more swiftly than I could have run.

A mile up the trail, the wolf slowed to sniff the ground next to a shallow stream. The vegetation here thickened again due to the presence of the water, and I searched the dense foliage in vain for any sign of Blade. Infidel caught up a few seconds later, panting heavily. Even with her strength, running a mile uphill in the furnace-like heat was no easy task.

"I thought you might like a chance to talk," said Menagerie in his wolf-yips. "It's got to be killing you keeping quiet around those assholes."

"It's not all that tough," Infidel said. "It's not like I'm eager to chat with any of them."

"I find Father Ver moderately entertaining," said Menagerie, pausing to take a few laps from the stream. "Have you noticed that he and the Deceiver seem to have exactly the same power? They both say things that aren't true and make them come true."

"Actually," said Infidel, "the Deceiver's power is less creepy. He says things that change himself. The Truthspeaker says things to change others."

"Creepy or not, I could have laughed my ass off when Reeker had to hold his tongue. I went into the wrong line of business with blood magic. I'd trade all my tattoos for the ability to shut Reeker up whenever I wanted to."

"I thought you guys were friends," said Infidel.

The wolf shrugged. "I'm not in a career where it pays to have friends. The people I grow close to have a depressing tendency to die. Reeker and No-Face are my companions chiefly because they've proven themselves as survivors."

Infidel pressed her lips tightly together and swallowed hard.

"You okay?" asked Menagerie.

"Just thinking about Stagger," said Infidel. "He'd still be alive if he hadn't been my friend."

"You can't blame yourself," said Menagerie.

"Can't I?" said Infidel with a feeble grin. "I'd trade Greatshadow's treasure for the chance to go back and do things differently. Sometimes, I forget that he's gone, and feel like I'm going to look back over my shoulder and find him standing there, giving me a reassuring smile."

"I'm here!" I shouted, waving my arms. "I'm here!"

"You'll always have his memory, at least."

"Maybe I don't want the memories," she said. "Because, when I do turn around, and see that he's not there, it feels like hands grab my heart and squeeze, and squeeze, and squeeze."

She closed her eyes and clenched her fists, drawing a long, slow, breath.

"It helps some, pretending to be a machine," she said. "To think there's only a mechanical pump in my chest, not a heart. I'd pay any price for a head full of gears instead of memories."

Menagerie sat down, scratching behind his ear with a paw. He took a moment to let Infidel compose herself before he said, "I know it's trite, but time does make the pain go away."

Infidel shook her head. "When I think about the Black Swan in her cobwebbed wedding dress, I wonder if that's true."

"You've never lost anyone close to you before?"

"Stagger's the only one who ever got close," she said. "My mother died when I was thirteen. I was told I should mourn her, but I didn't really feel anything. I was raised by servants; my mother was just this pretty china doll who decorated my father's palace. She barely ever spoke to me. I can't remember the sound of her voice."

"My mother was my world," said Menagerie.

"Was? She passed away?"

"She's still alive. I just don't see her."

"But you used to be close?"

Menagerie looked up and down the trail, as if making sure no one else was listening. Finally, he said, "My mother was a prostitute, sold by her parents to a brothel when she was eleven. She was fourteen when she gave birth to me, and I was swiftly followed by two baby sisters. She gave us the best life she could; stashing away a few coins here and there in the hope that she might one day purchase her freedom and raise us in a better home. From the age I first understood what was going on, I dreamed of having enough money to make her dream come true. I joined a street gang when I was seven and began shoplifting and picking pockets. I committed my first murder at age nine. Got involved in blood magic not long after; by age thirteen, I was running my own gang, and earned enough to send my sisters off to a boarding school. By the time I was sixteen I bought my mother's freedom and set her up in a house with servants."

"That's very noble of you," said Infidel.

The wolf let out a series of low barks that it took me a second to recognize as a bitter chuckle. "Noble is not a label often applied to me. The evidence is before your eyes; I've surrendered to blood magic so completely, I'm no longer fully human. I've killed hundreds of men, too many to count, and am incapable of remorse. My sisters are both married to respectable men and have large families, but I've not seen them in twenty years. I send them the fortunes I earn so that they may live like royalty in the heart of the Silver City, in homes surrounded by high walls and armed guards, specifically to protect them from men like me."

As he finished, he tilted his head. He raised his nose and sniffed the air.

"Blood," he said.

"Whose?" asked Infidel. "Blade's?"

Menagerie leapt across the stream and raised his ears, cocking his head from side to side.

"Do you hear something?" she asked.

"Someone running?" Menagerie said, but he sounded confused. "It might be Blade, except—"

Suddenly, a green-skinned midget shot out from the undergrowth and splashed into the stream. He was naked save for a gourd codpiece, and bleeding profusely from his neck. He slid to a halt as he saw Menagerie and Infidel. He opened his mouth to scream but only gurgles escaped his lips. His eyes rolled up into his head and he fell face first into the water as blood loss won out over panic.

"Quickly," said Menagerie, leaping into the hole the pygmy had left in the greenery. He bounded along the blood trail, panting as he leapt over logs and boulders. Infidel chased after him, pulling out her long sword to use as a machete. They ran no more than a quarter--mile before anguished cries reached them, the sound of men dying.

In their haste, the wolf and Infidel raced right past a cluster of knotted vines laced through with palm fronds. I paused to study it; I knew this sign. It marked the edge of a forest-pygmy clan line. It announced to other pygmies that this area was off limits to all but members of a single extended family. My pygmy knot literacy wasn't fluent, but I think this clan called themselves the Jawa Fruit.

Since the others were well ahead now, I again surrendered myself to the tug of the knife and flew to join Infidel, flowing through trees and rocks as if they weren't even there.

I caught up in seconds. Infidel and Menagerie had stopped. I couldn't see past them at first. I did notice, however, that the ground around them was slick with blood. Beyond them, I could hear more screaming.

"This will come out of our pay for sure," Menagerie grumbled.

I moved to see what he was looking at. I wished I hadn't.

Ivory Blade was slumped up against a rock. At least, what was left of him was. His head was missing from his shoulders. There was a heavy log hanging from vines, swaying back and forth. One end was wet with blood, and worse things. Remnants of white-haired scalp were pressed into the grain of the wood. Infidel had triggered one of these traps by accident a few years ago. Trip over the wrong vine, and suddenly a log swings down like a hammer. Infidel had escaped her trap with a minor headache. Ivory Blade, alas, had popped like a balloon. Despite the gore coating every nearby surface, Blade's Immaculate Attire was still spotless.

"Whisper must be taking revenge," said Menagerie as he tilted his ears toward the screams coming from further upslope. "Sounds like she's tearing through some pygmies."

"Déjà vu," said Infidel. "Still… it's not really their fault. That damned Truthspeaker caused this."

"She'll get to him next," said a voice behind me.

I turned around, and there, like a pillar of fog, stood Ivory Blade.

Blade looked down at his wispy form. Blood from his corpse was trickling down the stony ground to form a little pool, and he rose from this pool like steam. He looked at me with sad eyes, shaking his head. "How ironic. As a somnomancer, I always assumed I'd die in my sleep."

"You can see me?" I asked.

"Can you see me?" he asked.

We both nodded. Infidel had no reaction at all to the words being spoken mere inches behind her, but Menagerie turned his head slightly, his ears twitching.

"Hear something?" Infidel asked.

"I… don't think so. Dog ears are so sensitive, they play tricks on me. I'm picking up faint voices, but they must be coming from miles away."

"She's free now," Blade said, his voice trembling. "She was my dream while I was alive. Now, she'll be the world's nightmare."

"What? Who? What's going on?"

"The Whisper," he said, holding his ghostly hands toward the sky, watching the light filter through his ethereal skin. "I died with a heart full of rage. She'll be trapped in this emotion. She'll kill and kill and nothing will ever slake her anger."

"Let's start over," I said. "I'm not following you. I mean, I understand she'll be angry, but—"

"Whisper was my wildest dream, brought back from

178

the land of sleep by my experimentations in somnomancy. Dream magic," he said, his voice sounding choked and tight. "She's a dream creature who pretended to be human to make me happy. She became the living embodiment of my lust and vanity. I've walked in the shadows for so long I grew to love the darkness. Now..." He frowned, the saddest face I've ever seen. "Now I will have nothing but darkness."

He shuddered and the wispy edges of his body began to blur.

"Don't surrender!" I shouted, offering him my hand. "You can stay behind if you hold on to something hard enough."

If he heard me, he didn't respond. The tower of mist no longer looked like a man; then, it didn't even look like mist. All that was left was the pool of blood where he'd stood and the light and shadows of the forest dancing upon it.

I dropped to my knees before the pool of blood. I was desperate to bring him back; until this moment, I hadn't known that I could talk with other ghosts. I plunged my hand into the gore. "Come back," I cried out. "Come back, please!"

Nothing happened. Though my condition was no different than what it had been a moment before, I suddenly felt desperately lonely, like a fallen Wanderer left on a desert island. I was surrounded by the living, but was not a part of them. Were there other ghosts in the world? Or was I the only soul who'd failed to move on? Was I just as much a failure at dying as I had been at living?

I lifted my hand from the blood, expecting it to come away clean. Instead, it was coated red, the warm fluid running down my naked arm. Yet, the drops that fell didn't ripple in the pool below. It wasn't real. It was ghost blood. I smeared it between my fingers and it faded away.

Suddenly, there was a loud canine yelp; I turned and found that Infidel and Menagerie had pressed ahead toward the fight up-trail. Now, a gutted wolf was hurtling through the air straight toward me. It tumbled in mid-flight, trailing loops of blue-gray intestine. The wolf crashed into a tree with a sickening wet-meat slap. Menagerie shifted back to human form as he slid to the ground, still gutted. His eyes were glassy as he stared at the gore in his lap. I noticed two bloody prints on his shoulders, about the size of a woman's hands. Infidel?

I flew to her side, tugged by the knife. She stood on a vine-draped stone platform, all that remained of some lost temple. She was surrounded by dead forest-pygmies, but, this time, she wasn't the person who had killed them.

Instead, that was the work of the Whisper. My ghost skin crawled as I saw her. She was no longer an empty hole in space, as she had been when I'd seen her earlier. She was now a creature of flesh, though it wasn't human flesh. Her skin looked as if it had been carved from onyx; her eyes and lips and nails were gems of dazzling ruby. In her left hand was the hilt of a sword, the blade nothing more than a jagged stump. Despite her mineral skin, she moved fluidly as she lunged toward Infidel.

I noticed that fragments of a broken sword lay at Infidel's feet. She was looking down, confused by where the metal had come from. She didn't seem to see the stone demon about to strike her.

The Whisper caught Infidel beneath the chin with a two-handed uppercut that lifted her from her feet and made her lose her grip on her long sword. Infidel fell on her butt as her sword spun in the air. The Whisper caught the sword with a fluid back-swipe, lifted it over her head, then chopped down with a vicious grunt, attempting to cleave Infidel in half. The sword snapped as it crashed into Infidel's skull.

"Ow!" Infidel said, raising her hands to her scalp. She drew her fingers away. No blood.

The Whisper leaned back, howling, shaking her clenched fists at the sky in frustration.

"Leave her alone!" I shouted.

The stone woman spun around, her eyes narrowed into slits as she glared at me.

"She's done nothing to you!" I shouted. "It's the Truthspeaker who you should be pissed off at."

The Whisper growled and leapt toward me. I felt no fear, certain her hands would pass through my ghostly form. Instead, I sucked in air as her ice-cold fingers grabbed me by the throat and jerked me from my feet.

She licked my cheek with a tongue rough as sandstone. She whispered in my ear, "A spirit untainted by matter! What a delightful treat! We dream-dwellers feast upon souls, which are too often made foul by the filth of the bodies they cling to. Once I've choked down the Truthspeaker and the others, I'll come back for you as dessert."

She tossed me aside like I weighed no more than a kitten; I suppose, in hindsight, that I don't even weigh that. Then, she bounded from the platform, darting back down the trail. I was very happy at that instant not to be Father Ver. My cheek burned where she'd licked it. It wasn't all that good to be me, either. What had I done to deserve this?

My eyes were caught by movement. Menagerie raised a trembling hand to his neck and touched the jellyfish outlined there. He collapsed into a puddle of quivering, glassy snot. I don't know what he'd thought he'd been reaching for, but I doubted this was it. Then, a heartbeat later, he was once more back in his human form. His guts were back inside his body. There was no sign he'd ever been injured other than the dazed look on his features.

Meanwhile, Infidel was back on her feet, the bone-handled knife in her hand, spinning around, thrusting the blade toward any stray sound. As much as I wanted to stay with her, I did some cold calculations and realized that if I didn't want to become nightmare chow, I needed to get back to Relic and warn him of what was coming down the mountain. He'd been aware of the Whisper earlier; apparently he could see dream-women as easily as ghosts.

I leaned in Relic's direction, picturing him in my mind. *Go!* I thought, and I went. I shot back down the mountain, flashing through trees and blood-tangle vine, moving in a straight line unencumbered by the tortuous terrain of the volcanic slope.

I whipped to a stop inches from Relic's burlap-covered face. "Relic!" I shouted.

He winced. *So. The disobedient dead man returns.*

"The Whisper! Nightmare! Kill us all! Dessert!"

Relic sighed. *Calm yourself, Blood-Ghost. You need not try to form sentences. If you will still the turmoil of your thoughts, I will pluck what you wish to tell me from your mind.*

I surrendered all attempts at speaking a coherent warning and allowed the memories of the past five minutes to wash through my mind.

"A nightmare loose in the material realm," said Relic. "This is bad. This is very bad."

Relic looked around. Everyone able-bodied was off in the jungle collecting the scattered gear. Father Ver and Zetetic were left sitting in the center of an enormous footprint.

Relic hobbled toward Father Ver. "Sir, if I may interrupt, you are in great and imminent danger."

Father Ver looked up. He had finished stitching together the Deceiver's torn lips. Despite his hatred for the man, I couldn't help but notice he'd done a clean and competent job. The priest asked, "What are you babbling about?"

"Ivory Blade is dead," said Relic. "The dream-lover he crafted is on her way to take revenge against you. I suggest you call Lord Tower back from his work."

Father Ver stood and looked toward the sky. The knight was nowhere to be seen. He looked at Relic skeptically. He was used to only being told the truth, but I could see he didn't trust Relic. He said, "If there is a danger—"

He never finished his sentence. There was a sudden crash from a nearby bush. A spray of leaves flew out as the Whisper leapt. She cast no shadow; no doubt I was the only person who could see her as she flew with hands outstretched toward the Truthspeaker's neck. Her mouth opened wide, revealing diamond teeth, then wider still, far beyond a human jaw-span, as she prepared to bite out the Truthspeaker's throat.

Relic moved with a speed that proved he wasn't as crippled as he pretended, striking out with his staff, catching the Truthspeaker at the back of the knees. Father Ver was knocked from his feet as the Whisper flew through the space where his throat had just been. She thrust her leg down, catching the priest dead in the center of his face with her stony knee. He gave a sharp cry of pain as he went down hard, blood streaming from his nose.

The Whisper tumbled like an acrobat as she hit the ground, rolling to her feet, spinning around, prepared to leap again at her fallen opponent. Before she left the ground, a small brown bat flitted over the treetops, diving right for her face. She swung her hand to knock it away, but the bat changed in mid-slap into a water buffalo. The beast dug his horn into her jaw as he slammed into her. They both bounced and rolled into the brush beyond the edge of the clearing.

Clever, thought Relic. *As a bat, he could see her.*

Suddenly, the water buffalo went flying up through the canopy. The Whisper was apparently at least as strong as Infidel, and just as tough if she'd survived a blow like that. Seconds later, she staggered out of the brush, trailing vines. There was enough greenery enveloping her that you could make out her form. She paused a second to tear away the vegetation. She turned back toward Father Ver, only to find that Reeker had run out of the forest to stand between her and the priest.

He sucked in a lungful of air as she dropped the last of the vines. She stepped toward him, a sneer on her ruby lips. Reeker exhaled, a billowy greenish fog that rolled through the air before him, spreading quickly to cover the space where she stood. She was faintly visible as the miasma clung to her. A tendril of the cloud reached me and I quickly retreated. It stank like awful, eye-watering, fetid cheese, after it had been eaten, half-digested, and vomited back up.

Reeker stood with his hands on his hips, looking pleased with his work. His eyes widened as her hand thrust out of the cloud and she jerked his face close to her own.

"A good trick," she said, "assuming I needed to breathe."

The Whisper flung the skunk-man skyward. She stepped from the cloud, coated with pale green droplets of condensation like jade on her onyx skin. Her gaze lowered once more to the Truthspeaker, who by now had risen to his hands and knees. She stepped toward him, only to be intercepted by an iron ball at the end of a chain that caught her in the gut. She folded over, carried backward by the momentum of the blow. No-Face charged out of the brush to pounce on top of the Whisper as she hit the ground. Straddling her, he pounded her face with a chain-draped fist, striking sparks. He struck again, but she opened her jaws to reveal her diamond teeth. She bit down on his fist as he struck.

"Haurrg!" No-Face howled as he jerked his hand away. She'd bitten straight through the chain. His little finger and a fair chunk of the side of his hand were missing. She slapped him where his ear should have been, knocking him off her. He writhed as he clamped his good hand over his mangled fingers. Blood spurted between his knuckles.

The Whisper stood and chuckled as she looked at Father Ver. "Is that the best you have to defend you?" She stalked toward the Truthspeaker. "If you'd like, I'll wait around and finish off the ogress and the knight as well, crushing your hopes one by one. You're going to die, Truthspeaker. There is absolutely nothing you can do about it."

"There is no need to wait," Father Ver said, kneeling before her.

The Whisper raised both hands above her head, knitting her fingers together, then swung with all her might to bash in the priest's skull.

Father Ver lifted his right hand and caught the blow, stopping it with no more effort than he might have spent to catch a drifting leaf. He looked at her with a look of utter calmness, and said, "I do not fear you. You are nothing but a dream, and your dreamer is dead."

And then she wasn't there. The stink mist that had clung to her hung in the air for a fraction of a second, then dispersed in the breeze.

A shadow grew on the ground as Lord Tower dropped from the sky, cradling Reeker in his arms. He landed with a *clang*, spinning around swiftly to survey the scene. No-Face still writhed on the ground. Father Ver was on his knees with a bloody nose and a placid look in his eyes.

"What attacked you?" Lord Tower asked.

"Nothing," said Father Ver.

I could see Lord Tower's eyes narrow through the slits in his faceplate. "This is a lot of damage for nothing."

Father Ver nodded. "This nothing mistakenly believed it was something. We won't be bothered further by it. We've lost both Blade and the Whisper, by the way."

"What? How did... how...." He paused, sniffing the air. "By the sacred quill, what is this wretched odor?"

"The scent of victory," said Father Ver. "Without the half-seed's miasma clinging to her, I wouldn't have seen the Whisper about to strike."

"Wait," said Tower. "The Whisper did this?"

Father Ver nodded. "It is good that we culled her out this early. Blade endangered us all with his reckless dabbling in dream magic. Our chances are improved without him." There was no hint of remorse that he'd caused Blade's death with his ill-thought command.

No-Face sat up, cradling his injured hand. "Yurga bunnah juh!"

"He's right," buzzed a hummingbird that hovered into the clearing. The bird flitted closer to Lord Tower, and suddenly Menagerie stood before the knight. The contrast between the two couldn't have been more striking; the tattooed man in nothing but a loincloth facing the knight encased scalp to sole in spotless armor. "You came here with a team of six and you're three down before we've even gotten close to the dragon. We're professionals; we don't like to work for amateurs."

"That's enough of your insolence," growled Father Ver.

Menagerie opened his mouth to speak, but no sound came out.

Lord Tower said, "Your concerns are noted, but matter little. I've taken a sacred vow to complete this mission. You are free to retreat if you wish, but I must carry on until the dragon is dead, or I am."

Menagerie took a deep breath then said, in a respectful tone, "You have something better than a vow from us. You have a contract. We'll continue on as long as you do."

Tower looked up the slope. "I spotted a stream a short distance from here. We'll make camp there while we continue to gather our gear and tend our wounded. If Blade is dead, we have a burial to perform. Tomorrow we'll press on."

"We're right on the edge of forest-pygmy territory," I said to Relic. "They'll be out for blood after what the Whisper did to them. We should retreat back to the cave."

We have nothing to fear, thought Relic. *Even with these setbacks, we still have the power to kill any pygmy that dares to threaten us.*

"You're right. We'll slaughter them when the come to drive us out, which they will. I've seen enough dead pygmies lately. Let's retreat."

I had no idea you were so tender-hearted, Blood-Ghost. Very well. Relic turned to Lord Tower he said, "I believe we are on the edge of forest-pygmy territory. It would be wise to go back to the cave. We can be assured of our safety there."

Lord Tower shook his head. "We've paid dearly to cover even this small amount of ground. I won't give up the progress we've made."

Relic nodded. "As you wish."

"Where is your War Doll?" Tower asked. "Have we lost her — I mean it — as well?"

I didn't wait for Relic to answer. It struck me that Infidel should have been back by now. I tuned myself to the knife and mentally leaned in its direction, flying to it at the speed of thought.

I found myself once more upon the vine draped platform where I'd left her. She was surrounded by forest-pygmies, easily a hundred of them. To my relief, they weren't fighting her. Instead, they were gathering up the dead. A dozen of them stood around Infidel, holding her at bay with pointy sticks. I knew that Infidel could have easily fought her way out of the situation, but instead she just stood there with her hands in the air.

"Look," she explained, in a calm voice. "I didn't do this. I've got no grudge against you. Just put down the sticks. You're only going to hurt yourself."

"Ugamadebasda!" the lead pygmy shouted. "Ugamadebasda!" Every forest-pygmy tribe had its own dialect; I could understand most east-slope pygmies, but these west-slope pygmies slurred all the syllables of a sentence together into a single word, which made it tricky to follow. Still, from the general tone I gathered he was saying, "Shut up and keep your hands up."

"I don't speak the lingo, guys," said Infidel. "I do know a little river-pygmy. Nanda chaka? Gratan doy bro?" Her accent was atrocious. She probably meant to ask if anyone knew river-pygmy, but instead she was asking if anyone had a canoe in their mouth. It didn't matter; the forest-pygmies didn't seem to understand her anyway.

She sighed. "I'm not getting of here without hurting a lot of you, am I?"

"I think there's been enough hurting here today," said a man's voice from high in the trees above. The speaker used the crisp, finely enunciated syllables of a Silver Isle accent; it could have been Lord Tower speaking, except the voice wasn't as deep or forceful. "Are you responsible for this slaughter?"

"Not me," said Infidel. "There was this invisible woman who went crazy and, uh... hell, that's just not believable at all is it?"

"Not terribly," said the voice above.

Infidel shrugged. "If I was any good at lying, I'd make up something. But, there really was an invisible woman. She cracked a few swords over my head as well. I'm not here to hurt anyone."

The branches above rustled. Suddenly, a patch of green, the color of moss, lowered down toward the platform on a slowly descending loop of vine. It was no pygmy. It was an elderly man of normal stature, wearing only the same gourd codpiece as the pygmies, his skin dyed green. He was all bones and skin, his flesh covering his thin limbs like aged leather. His hair was a few long green strands braided down the back of his scalp. His eyes were a sharp and penetrating blue.

"Who are you?" he asked, as his vine brought him to the platform.

"Who are you?" Infidel answered.

The old man scowled, then cocked his head, as if he was searching for some bit of information just beyond his grasp. "It's been a while since anyone asked that question. The Jawa Fruit tribe calls me Tenoba. It means old long gourd. Among your people, my name... my name was..."

He paused, trying to remember how to say the words. It didn't matter. I knew what he was about to say before he said it.

A light flickered in his ancient eyes. "My name," he said, "was Judicious Merchant."

CHAPTER THIRTEEN
ENOUGH

I WAS TOO stunned by my grandfather being alive to closely follow the swirl of activity that unfolded. A wounded pygmy at the edge of the platform verified that they had, indeed, been attacked by something invisible, and confirmed that Infidel hadn't hurt anyone. Forest-pygmy scouts were rushing up, telling about the fight further down slope, and how a group of long-men had killed the invisible assassin. I would have focused more on what they were saying, but I was too busy doing math in my head. My father had me when he was twenty-three. Judicious had been twenty-five when he sired Studious. So... that meant the man standing before me was ninety-eight.

For a man two years shy of a century, he looked pretty good. He still had all his teeth, for starters, even if they were the same jade hue as the rest of him. When he moved, he was as fluid as a jungle cat, without a hint of the stiffness or weakness that hampered most people his age. There wasn't an ounce of fat on him; his wrinkled leather skin sat atop wiry muscles so sharply defined you could have taught an anatomy class using them. Of course, I was seeing more of that anatomy than I truly wanted to. It's one thing to discover your long lost grandfather is still alive. It's another thing entirely to learn he's a grass-colored nudist with his privates stuffed into a dried fruit.

"I knew your grandson, Stagger," said Infidel.

Grandpa frowned.

"His real name was Abstemious Merchant."

I winced on hearing my birth name. I must have been really drunk to have told her. Abstemious means someone with control of his appetites… perhaps my father's lapse on his vow of celibacy inspired the choice. Stuck with this moniker, it was only a matter of time before I became an incurable drunkard.

My grandfather frowned even deeper. "I'm sorry," he said. "I've had seven wives. My children have produced scores of grandchildren. I'm afraid the name isn't triggering any memories."

The words were like a slap in the face. I'd revered this man. I lived on the Isle of Fire in imitation of his greatness. He didn't even remember my name?

Infidel produced the bone-handled knife. "You gave him this when he was ten."

My grandfather took the blade, sliding it in and out of the sheath. He scowled as he saw the dried blood smeared along the metal. "He didn't take care of it. It's dirty."

"He took great care of it," said Infidel. "He kept it clean and sharp for forty years. If it's dirty, it's my fault."

"Hmm." Suddenly, a light flickered in his blue eyes. "I remember this knife. The handle was carved from the tibia of a dragon."

Or so he thought. He'd told me this when he gave me the knife, but one of the monks who specialized in the study of anatomy had assured me the bone was merely that of a bull. But, what if the monk had been wrong? If the hilt truly was dragon-bone, could the magic that infused dragons explain how my spirit had become ensnared by the knife?

As Judicious turned the knife over in his hands, he nodded slowly, as if he were accepting the memories flooding back to him. "I had a son who became a monk. Studious, I think? He had a bastard child raised in an orphanage. That was Abstemious?"

"Yes."

Grandfather grinned. "I recall him now. Bright kid. Voracious reader. He became a monk?"

"He became you," said Infidel. "Or, at least his dream of

ou. He was an explorer, a scholar, and a storyteller. No one knew more than him about the ruins of the Vanished Kingdom. He lived in your old boat in Commonground."

"I notice you're speaking in the past tense."

Infidel nodded.

Grandfather sighed. "I outlive many of my relatives." He looked down the slope, in the direction of Tower's party. "I suppose, if you're friends of the family, I should show a little hospitality. Go tell your companions they're welcome to stay the night in our huts."

"I'm not sure they'll take you up on the offer," said Infidel. "The leader of the party is kind of snooty."

"Still, extend the offer."

Infidel nodded. "If they accept, you need to know that I'm pretending to be a machine. I don't talk around them."

"Ah," said Grandfather. "I wondered why you were dyed silver. I thought it might be some new fashion. You fooled me, by the way. When I first saw you from the trees, I mistook you for one of the ancient engines, and wondered how you were still intact. You reminded me of a mechanical dancer I once excavated. A lovely, wondrous thing, though I never found her head. The clockwork that used to drive her had long-since corroded, but I'm still left breathless by the cleverness of the men who once lived on this island."

THE PYGMY HUTS were better described as tree houses. I'd never been in one before, though I'd caught sight of them often enough. The floor of the forest can be a quiet place; the real action is unfolding high above in the canopy. Here, the forest-pygmies had woven together seemingly endless ropes from blood-tangle vines and strung them together in a complex network of swinging bridges. Houses were built with floors of dense netting spread from branch to branch, with roofs of still-living vines and branches woven together overhead. The floors seemed solid enough when the pygmies flitted across them, but once Lord Tower began to carry the party up to the huts, the platforms sagged ominously beneath the weight. The floor weavers had probably never planned for someone as large as Aurora to visit. No-Face swiftly moved toward the thick trunk of the tree that formed one corner of a large communal area and wrapped his chain around it, with his good arm still coiled in the links. It was hard to read the mood of a man who didn't have expressions, but I got the distinct impression he didn't like heights.

The forest-pygmies seemed especially wary of Aurora. None dared look directly at her, though behind her there was a crowd of small green people pointing and gawking.

"The blue tint of your skin makes them think you're some sort of oddly sized river-pygmy," Grandfather said. "The river-pygmies work with the slavers, so they're wary."

Aurora took a seat near the edge of the netting, looking out over the lush forest. She didn't seem bothered by the sagging floor or the drop off. "Since I left the north, I've gotten used to people being cautious around me," she said. "At home, I was a runt and a weakling. If not for being born with the mark of a shaman, I doubt they would have fed me as a child."

Zetetic stayed as close to the center of the floor as possible. I remembered his reaction when he'd first arrived in the cave. Apparently, No-Face wasn't alone in his acrophobia. Yet, though Zetetic clung to the woven floor with white knuckles, his voice was curiously enthusiastic as he said, "Mr. Merchant, I've read everything you ever wrote about the Vanished Kingdom. The world lost quite a scholar when you vanished."

Father Ver glowered as Zetetic spoke, ready to pounce if the Deceiver attempted anything. Reeker also kept his gaze fixed on the man, no doubt intent not to be taken by surprise again.

My grandfather seemed unaware of the tension in the air. He dismissed Zetetic's compliment with a shrug. "The world lost nothing. I've come to understand that scholarship has very little to do with actual knowledge. In the world I grew up in, knowledge was something found chiefly in books. It was information that gets passed on as scribbled marks on paper. When I first started exploring this land, I wrote down everything I learned, because that seemed like a validation. It was as if nothing I was doing mattered until I committed it to paper."

"It's the echo of the divine that makes you feel this," said Lord Tower. He had never actually landed on the platform; instead, he was hovering a few inches above the netting, perhaps worried about adding his weight to the already strained vines. "When we write, we imitate, in our own pale way, the original act of creation."

Grandfather chuckled. "You're my guests, so I'll say this as respectfully as possible: books aren't real. I mean, yes, books as physical objects exist, but they contain no reality or truth within them."

"Have a care," said Father Ver. "Your words venture dangerously close to the heresy of the Deceivers."

"No," said Grandfather. "The Deceivers think that everything is a lie. Reality itself is a fiction, which clever men are free to rewrite."

"Actually—" said Zetetic.

Grandfather kept talking, ignoring the interruption. "The Deceivers are wrong, as is the Church of the Book. Neither accept the obvious truth: the only thing that defines the world is the world itself. Reality is the tree we sit in; it's the sun on your face, the evening breeze, the bitter burst of jawa fruit on the tongue. The things we write in books are only daydreams and memories, mental constructs pleasant and useful, but not real. By the time a man writes of an experience, that experience is forever gone. The past vaporizes behind us; the future is devoured voraciously by the present. It is only in the now that we are alive. The physical world surrounding us is the only truth." He looked out over the green mountain, toward the azure sea. "It is... enough."

"Bah," said Father Ver with a dismissive wave. "These are the pointless musings of the spiritually weak. The here-and-now is but a trap; the pleasure of the moment seduces men from contemplation of larger truths. Feeble-minded youth sometimes fall prey to the desire to glamorize the now, but I'm disappointed a man of your advanced age has made this error. Look around you, old man. You live in a bug-infested tree, among primitives who don't even know how to make clothing. Without accepting a greater spiritual truth, man can be nothing more than another beast."

Grandfather smiled as he looked at the leaves above him. He lifted up his skinny arm and snatched a bright green katydid from the nearest branch. The insect was perfectly blended with its surroundings, but my grandfather seemed to have spotted it effortlessly. "You call them bugs," he said. He popped the leggy creature into his mouth and crunched down. "We call them snacks."

During this philosophical debate, a stream of pygmy women had been flowing onto the vine platform across the rope bridges, carrying dark green leaves the size of dinner trays. And, dinner trays were precisely what they were. A buffet was laid out on the floor; bright blue jawa fruit adorned one leaf, plump white maggots writhed on another. There were speckled eggs the size of grapes, dark red snails the size of oranges, and at least a dozen kinds of nuts, half of which I didn't recognize. One leaf held what looked like raw meat, chopped and ground to a paste. Nothing looked cooked.

"There's no formality here. Dig in," said Grandfather, snatching up a snail and a jawa fruit. "Since we live in trees, we don't built fires." He squeezed the fruit and the bright blue juice sluiced through his fingers and into the snail shell. "Fortunately, jawa juice is acidic enough that it effectively cooks most meat. Your *civilized* guts won't suffer."

Father Ver looked aghast as Grandfather sucked the snail out of its shell, giving it a tug as the last of the meat fought to hold onto its casing. The coil of pale flesh smacked into his lips before it disappeared into his mouth. Grandfather lay back on the floor-net, looking up at the sun-dappled branches. "Eat meat while it still has life in it. Keep fruit in your belly and sun on your skin. Sleep when you are tired and drink when you are thirsty. This is all a man needs to enjoy a long life."

"There are elderly among the civilized as well," said Father Ver. "Your recipe for life will not keep you alive a single day longer than the span the Divine Author has recorded for you in the book."

Grandfather scratched the dark green pubic hair around his gourd, seemingly unconcerned that anyone was watching. "You are free to think what you wish. I wouldn't trade my life for the wealth of a king. I live in the eternal moment, while a civilized man worries only about tomorrow, or longs for yesterday."

While Grandfather and the Truthspeaker sparred, Menagerie dug into the food with gusto, not bothering with the fruits, just tearing into the raw meat directly. Reeker was more dainty, picking through the nuts and berries and less wriggly-looking insects. He carried a leaf full of food over to No-Face, who squeezed the fruits and bugs into a colorful mush, which he slurped loudly from his palm into a fold beneath his face-flap.

The Deceiver went straight for the nastiest looking dish, a sort of chopped spider salad laced with bright green chilies. He washed it down with a freshly opened coconut, the pale milk spilling down the corners of his damaged mouth.

"Doesn't the spice hurt the cuts in your mouth?" Reeker asked, still keeping a close eye on the man.

Zetetic shrugged. "I've learned to enjoy pain. Plus, I've always had a sense of adventure in my diet. In my travels, I've been delighted by the different attitudes regarding what one is supposed to put in one's mouth. One man's spoiled milk is another man's cheese. Some men hunt with dogs, others eat them in stews. What half the world believes is true about food, the other half thinks is false. It's left me with an open mind and a daring stomach. I'll put anything in my mouth at least once."

Neither Lord Tower nor Father Ver made any move toward the dishes.

"Aren't you hungry?" asked Grandfather.

"We have our own provisions," Tower answered. "It would be a sin for me to partake in this food. Your people live in such poverty."

Infidel's eyes kept flickering toward the buffet. All the earlier excitement had probably built up her appetite, but she did an admirable job of just standing at attention, her face devoid of obvious longing.

"I assume you'll see she gets fed later," I said to Relic, who had a fistful of maggots.

Of course, he answered, as he shoved one of the plump larvae into the shadows beneath his hood. *We have all the details planned out. You need not worry for her comfort.*

Meanwhile, Grandfather had responded to Lord Tower. "Poverty? What poverty? None among us are hungry. We all have a safe place to sleep in the company of our family. There is not a single physical need we go without."

"You dwell in spiritual poverty, separated from the Church," said Father Ver.

Zetetic said, with a mouthful of spiders, "Why do you have to be such a jerk, Ver? Show a little graciousness for a fellow who's giving us a roof to sleep under." He glanced up at the leaves. "So to speak."

"I'm not bothered by his attitude," said Grandfather, as Father Ver eyed the Deceiver with a murderous gaze. "It's nice to be reminded of all I left behind. Which I suppose leads to the question, why are you here? You didn't come looking for me. You're too heavily armed for tomb raiding. Are you going after Greatshadow?"

"Yes," said Lord Tower. "King Brightmoon has decided to rid the world of his tyranny."

"I don't think tyranny is the word you're looking for," said Grandfather.

"I chose the word with precision," said Tower. "The dragon has crushed every attempt to colonize this island. He's shown nothing but hatred toward humanity. We must destroy him now, before he one day destroys the world."

Grandfather smiled softly. He said, "If he hates humanity so much, why does our tribe live in peace in his very shadow? Presumably, he could kill us at any time. He could daily scour the slopes of this island with lava. Nothing at all could grow here. It would be as dead as the Silver Isle."

"You know nothing of the Silver Isle, sir," said Tower. "I've flown from shore to shore; there is no inch of it I have not witnessed. It's a lovely, green land, an emerald jewel amid the vast dark sea."

"Green, yes," said Grandfather. "Green with crops and orchards, grape arbors and olive groves. The hills are lush with grass, planted so that cattle may graze. Well-tended oak trees still decorate the gardens of wealthy men. But, at no point when you flew over the island did you find a forest, or any wild thing. Men murdered the Silver Isle, then decorated the corpse with flowers. It doesn't compare to the untamed beauty of the Isle of Fire."

"We are of a different opinion," said Tower.

"Again, I must disagree. I have an opinion. You have narrow-minded dogma." Grandfather paused for a second to squeeze jawa juice into a second snail. "Greatshadow is no tyrant. Is the sun a tyrant when drought kills crops in the field? Is the stream a tyrant when it overruns its banks and floods a village? Greatshadow is merely an aspect of nature, the embodiment of fire. You civilized men need fire to cook your meals and forge your swords. You bring it into your homes to survive the winter, and your fields would be unmanageable if you didn't burn them at the start of each planting season. To wage war against the natural world is madness."

"Nonsense," said Lord Tower, speaking calmly. Unlike Father Ver, he didn't seem angered by Grandfather's bluntness.

"It isn't waging war against a stream to build a dam to control flooding. We do not wound the earth by digging into it with plows. As you must know, there was once a primal dragon of the forest. The church defeated him after a long struggle, banishing his spirit. Yet, all around you is evidence that trees have endured. We didn't wage war against the forest; we waged war against an unholy spirit that had laid an unjust claim to an elemental force. The same is true of Greatshadow. When he is gone, we will still have flames in our foundries and candles in our homes. They will simply be free of his all-watching eye."

"You're not the first to come this way, you know," said Grandfather. "Every generation sends a team of men against the beast. Every generation fails."

"You've met previous parties?" Zetetic asked. "Do you know the fate of the Castlebridge expedition?"

Grandfather nodded. "I believe you are referring to the two hundred soldiers who hacked their way up the mountain almost twenty years ago."

Zetetic nodded. "My father was with the expedition. We know the Wanderers delivered them safely to landfall. After this, they simply vanished from the face of the earth."

"Into the face of the earth is more accurate," said Grandfather. "Their ashes are no doubt well-mingled with the soil by now. Lava-pygmies witnessed it all. Greatshadow sent out his avatars as they were halfway up the slope. All flesh was burned away. The armor they wore turned to slag amid a field of blackened glass. It was a horrible scar upon the earth for all of a month; the jungle has long since swallowed all evidence of their passing."

"He attacked Commonground with two of these avatars," said Menagerie. "They were enough to get the job done, but I still wonder, does he have limits? Could he have created a dozen if he wished? If he animates these forms with his spirit, does his spirit weaken as he divides himself? No magic comes without a price. Blood magic costs a man his humanity, dream magic withers men's souls, the Deceivers pay for their powers with their sanity." Zetetic opened his mouth to dispute this, but Menagerie finished by saying, "Elemental magic can't be an exception. The dragon must have some weakness."

"True," said Grandfather. "For the primal dragons, the price they pay for their elemental magic seems to be their sense of identity. A dragon's mind is no more infinite than a man's mind. Rott, the primal dragon of decay, spread his essence so thinly that he hasn't been seen to manifest himself in a body for centuries. No one knows if he even remembers that he was once a dragon. However, Greatshadow has avoided this fate. He maintains his original body, feasting, sleeping, and fornicating; his sense of identity is in no real danger."

"Fornicating?" Zetetic asked, with a raised eyebrow. "Wouldn't this require another dragon?"

"You've already witnessed his ability to create avatars."

"But they're part of him. Wouldn't they...?"

Grandfather shrugged. "According to pygmy lore, he can create avatars with female aspects. I assume he enjoys the act of mating from both his original body and his second form."

Zetetic's face brightened. "That seems to be a fantastically practical—"

"Perversion!" snapped Father Ver. "All the more reason to kill the depraved beast."

"Just because you don't let yourself have any fun is no reason to be angry with the dragon," said Zetetic.

"Let him be angry if he wishes," said Grandfather. "It won't matter to Greatshadow. You've witnessed his power. I'm sure you wouldn't have come to this island if you didn't have some tricks up your sleeve. A flying knight, a shapeshifter, an ice-ogress; I admire Brightmoon's imagination in assembling this team. But, in the end, if you continue toward the dragon's lair, you will die. Even if ice-magic and enchanted armor can protect you from the heat of Greatshadow's breath, he still is in possession of teeth harder than diamond and claws that can rip through steel like tissue paper."

"My armor is made of something more enduring than steel," said Lord Tower.

"So what if it is?" said Grandfather. "Odds are, you won't even face the dragon. Greatshadow has had centuries to perfect his magic. It's said he's populated his lair with guardians summoned from ethereal realms. The most powerful magical artifacts that survive from the Vanished Kingdom are his to command; you cannot even imagine the forces he may throw against you. And while you may enter his lair in possession of some secret plan to beat the beast, it will all be for naught. The pygmies say that Greatshadow's mind spreads so completely through his lair that a visitor's thoughts will become the dragon's thoughts. First, he will strip your mind of all its secrets. Then, he will pour his mind into your bodies, and you will dance for him like puppets on strings."

The Goons and Aurora looked sobered by this recitation of the challenges before them. Relic, of course, remained an enigma beneath his rags. Zetetic's mouth was puckered with pain, but that was probably from the hot peppers. Lord Tower's eyes looked unconcerned; perhaps he already knew all the dangers they faced.

Father Ver's lips were turned up into something almost resembling a smile.

Zetetic took note. "Perhaps I'm not the only one here who enjoys pain."

Father Ver shook his head. "I'm merely thinking that the beast has had centuries to become overconfident. Think of Numinous, brought low by a mere decade in which to grow arrogant. No doubt, the beast's soul is rotten to the core from believing his own lies. Perhaps we have reached the page in the One True Book where he falls before the greater truth."

"Amen," said Tower, slapping the Gloryhammer against his gauntleted palm with a true-believer's fervor.

No one else echoed his sentiment. Instead, everyone sat

quietly, staring down at their food as they contemplated their fates. The only sound was the *slup, slup, slup* of No-Face eating.

CHAPTER FOURTEEN
HEART TO HEART

THAT NIGHT, AS everyone else slept spread out on woven platforms across the tree village, Infidel stepped down onto a thick branch. Relic stirred from his sleep and held out a leather sack the size of a saddlebag. She took the bag and climbed down the vine-draped trunk in silence. When she reached the ground, she followed a trail to the nearby stream, then followed this to a large pool. Looking around to make certain no one was watching, she shed her clothes and plunged in. Her body gleamed beneath the water's surface like a silver-skinned fish darting about. She surfaced with a gasp, rubbing her face, ridding herself of the sweat of the day. Whatever dye Menagerie had used wasn't smeared by her fingers. Now that she was wet, the illusion that her skin was metal was especially strong.

After only a moment in the pool, she rose from the water and opened the sack, producing a rolled up towel. Wrapped within it were fresh jawa fruits and several of the snails. She gobbled them down as she dried her hair. Mosquitoes crawled over her arms and legs, denting their noses on her impenetrable skin. She paid no attention to them as she finished off the snails in record time. She wiped her mouth then leaned over the pool, looking at her faint reflection in the still water. Her face went slack as she studied herself. Her eyes had a distant focus, as if she wasn't watching her reflection but was, instead, lost in memory.

She looked, if you will forgive the expression, haunted.

Was I causing psychic harm by sticking around? Did she sense me watching her and feel guilt? Should I leave and spare her any further pain? Could I leave if I tried?

My musings were cut short by Relic's voice in my head.

Return to me.

"I'm busy," I said.

Return to me!

The command felt like a thousand fishhooks tearing into my brain. He reeled me in as I flopped about. Fortunately, my agony was short lived, halting the second I stood before him. He was curled up on the netting, completely still; to anyone else he would have looked asleep. I saw the bone-handled knife clutched securely in his gnarled claw.

"I don't like being pushed around," I said.

We have our bargain.

"Do we? I agreed to watch Tower and the others. I don't remember signing on to be your slave."

And yet, you aren't watching Tower.

"He's probably asleep," I said.

I am certain he is not. He and Father Ver are outside the range of my mental powers, but I can still hear the murmurs of their voices on the night breeze. Go and listen to their conversation.

He shoved me with his mind out into the open air beside the central tree house. Tower and Father Ver slept separated from the rest of the rabble on a platform a good fifty yards distant. Apparently, Relic's telepathy didn't extend terribly far. The knight and the cleric had hung sheets of canvas for privacy. A glorystone cast their shadows on the cloth walls. I misted straight through the canvas into their room. To my surprise, Tower had shed his armor. For some reason, I'd expected him to sleep in it. If the monks could pray that the armor be invulnerable in battle, couldn't they also make it pillow soft come bedtime?

Out of his armor, Tower looked... ordinary. Not average, by any means, but nothing like the iron-clad warrior feared by evil-doers everywhere. Rumors of terrible scars proved unfounded. The few nicks and divots around his eyes and lips testified he'd taken a few hits over the years, but the scars were hardly disfiguring. If anything, they gave character to a face so symmetrical it was boring. He had a square jaw and a nose that jutted from his face at a perfect thirty degree angle. His black hair was cut in a bowl style that would have been unflattering on almost any other head. Here, it served to draw attention to the sharp lines of his cheek bones and his pale gray eyes. The only person I'd ever met who shared this eye color was Infidel.

Save for stray silver hairs, he had the appearance of a man in his early thirties, though, if I understood the chronology of Infidel's life, he must be closer to my age.

He was dressed in a simple linen shirt and tight-fitting cotton pants that showed off his muscular legs. He was kneeling by the side of the platform, his head bowed to touch the floor. I drew closer just in time to hear his whispered prayers come to an end. He closed his supplication to the Divine Author with, "… and grant me the wisdom to tell lust from love, desire from devotion. Amen."

It seemed like a prayer most men would find handy, though I was a little surprised lust was high on Lord Tower's list of concerns. He rose, a little closer to the edge of the sagging platform than most men would find comfortable. Perhaps he spent so much time flying with the Gloryhammer he'd lost all fear of heights. I wondered where the legendary weapon was. Or the armor; it should have made quite a pile once it was off him. Not to mention the Immaculate Attire, which they'd removed before they buried Blade. And, for that matter, where was the Jagged Heart? There still was no evidence that Tower had the harpoon.

Father Ver was sitting nearby, also kneeling, his head beaded with sweat. He was stripped from the waist up, his robes bunched around his hips. Before him lay a two-foot-long braid of leather. I drifted around behind him and saw bright red welts raised among the constellation of scabs along his back.

Tower pulled a small leather notebook from the waistband of his pants. This was the book Zetetic had taken. As he flipped through the pages, he said, softly, "There's no point in blaming yourself. Blade was the one who chose to dabble in dream magic. You couldn't have known."

"We both know that isn't true," Father Ver said, closing his eyes. "I could have known." His voice sounded wet and raspy, as if he'd been crying. "I've made too many bad bargains. My pursuit of the greater good has forced me to accept the unacceptable. Ten thousand years of lashings can never erase the harm I've done to my soul by agreeing to these compromises."

"The Divine Author would not have given you these trials if he did not feel you could endure them," said Tower. "I need you, Ver. You're the wisest man I've ever known. I wouldn't have accepted this mission without you on the team. But you'll be of no use to me if you're too paralyzed by guilt to do the job."

"I have no guilt," said Father Ver. "Undeserved guilt is a form of self-deception. Instead I feel shame, regret, and anger."

"Well, try to work on those," said Tower dismissively, looking away from the holy man and gazing out of the jungle. "I'm going to go get a little fresh air."

Without warning he pitched forward and dropped off the edge. We were a hundred feet up. He hadn't struck me as suicidal. I drifted over the lip of the platform. A light suddenly sparked below, casting shadows upward. I looked down and saw the Gloryhammer in Tower's right hand; the small notebook was still in his left. His forearm bulged as he gripped the glowing weapon and shot off through the trees, deftly avoiding vines and trunks. I followed, though I didn't need to follow far. A knot formed in the pit of my stomach as I realized where he was heading. The night went dark again as his feet touched down and the Gloryhammer suddenly disappeared. I blinked as I caught up to him. What had he done with the hammer? Could he simply summon it at will? He stuck the notebook back into the waistband of his britches.

The mystery of the missing hammer was the least of my

concerns. Tower had flown directly to the pool, landing barely five yards in front of Infidel, who still perched on the rock, buck naked. Her eyes were wide with shock. She had one arm across her breasts, and the towel draped over her lap. Tower dropped to one knee before her and bowed deeply.

"Princess Innocent," he said, in a voice just above a whisper. "I offer thanks to the Divine Author that you are still alive."

"Ummm..." said Infidel. She furrowed her brow. "Hmm."

"I presume you wear this disguise because you fear retribution from the church," he said. "You have nothing to fear, my princess. The king has long since used his influence to revoke the sentence of death placed upon you in absentia. Given the unmistakable perfection of your lineage, the Voice of the Book agreed that a proper trial was in order before any punishment is decided."

Infidel bit her lower lip. She opened her mouth as if to say something, then closed it again. I couldn't tell if she was still maintaining the ruse that she was a machine, or if she just didn't know what to say.

Tower continued: "When you disappeared on our wedding day, I suspected you were kidnapped by one of my political enemies. My investigation eventually led to Lord Claypot. He possessed some magic that confounded the Truthspeakers, but I had him tortured until he confessed the plot. Alas, he expired before I learned the full details of the events of that fateful day fourteen years, seven months, and nine days ago."

Infidel continued to silently stare at the knight.

"I did discover that you had escaped, but were in hiding because you feared retribution from the small segment of fanatics within the Church of the Book who blame you for the destruction. I assure you, I will protect you from them with all my powers. You were a pure and chaste young woman untainted by any hint of wickedness. I'm certain of your innocence, and trust you have the best of reasons for not returning home after you escaped from your captors."

"Well, yeah," she said, rolling her eyes. "Like, this 'pure and chaste young woman' crap. What the hell? If my father's spies are even halfway competent, you have to know I support myself primarily by killing people for money. Don't you think, maybe, just maybe, I don't exactly fit the definition of pure?"

"I, too, have killed men," said Tower. "Yet, my heart is pure. Motives matter when judging actions. You've done what you must to survive."

"Motives?" Infidel shook her head sadly. "You idiot. My number one motive was to get away from you!"

"Bu... but... but..." Tower's face fell as her words sank in.

"Turn around," said Infidel. "Did you have to wait until I was naked to have this little heart to heart?"

Tower turned around. "I didn't know you'd be naked. Since I knew you were in the area, I had the Gloryhammer guide me to you. It was poor timing that you are unrobed. I promise I haven't seen anything. I kept my eyes toward the ground."

"'I promise I haven't seen anything,'" Infidel said in a mocking tone. She jumped from the rock and grabbed her pants. "By the sacred quill! You're still the same simpering bore. I wouldn't expect you to know this, but some women are actually flattered by the idea that men want to look at them. When we were engaged, I couldn't even get eye contact. You acted like holding my hand before marriage might get us sent to hell! I used to have nightmares that you'd show up in our wedding bed with full plate armor, a blindfold, and a pair of tongs."

She pulled up her pants, buttoning them hastily, getting one of the buttons out of order, so that the leather sat on her hips at an odd angle. She turned around and found the steel bra she'd been wearing, pulling free the cotton slip inside. "If you've known since the damned cave who I really was, you should have said something so I could get out of this damned metal bra. My nipples are killing me!"

She spun back to face him, preparing to pull on the slip, and jumped slightly when she found Tower standing only inches from her. He was staring at her with fire in his eyes. "You dreamed..." he said, breathing heavily, "of our wedding night? Don't you think I had such dreams as well?"

She didn't get a chance to answer. He suddenly grabbed her by both arms and pressed his mouth to hers. Her eyes bulged as he pulled her to him, pressing her still naked breasts against his chest. He worked his lips against hers for a long moment. I watched in gruesome anticipation, certain that at any moment Infidel would decapitate this lustful fool. But, to my growing horror, she didn't move a muscle. She let him kiss her for five seconds, ten, a minute, as her eyes stayed wide open. Finally, she pushed him away, with frustrating gentleness.

"Ooookay," she said, pausing to wipe her lips with the back of her hand. "Let's stop for a minute. I've spent fifteen years avoiding assassins sent after me by the Church of the Book. I'm telling you point blank that I found you boring beyond all imagination when we were engaged. Can you understand I might be a little confused that you show up fifteen years later finally wanting to kiss?"

"I want much more than a kiss," Tower growled, pulling her against his chest once again. He looked down into her eyes. "When you were young, I found you utterly uninteresting. I was a battle-hardened warrior who'd traveled the world. You were a spoiled child, completely ignorant of life beyond the palace gates. You did nothing to stir my baser passions. But you... you are no longer sweet, virginal, Innocent. You're a warrior with blood on her hands. Indeed, not just on your hands... you have a dragon's blood pumping in your very veins. Having witnessed your strength, I know that rumor that you consumed Verdant's blood must be true."

"You know I could crush your head like an eggshell?"

"Yes! Whatever the reasons for your actions, you are now the perfect match for my passion! I am a man of fiery needs. You will find no plate mail or tongs in our wedding chamber.

There will only be an endless bed covered in the finest silk, upon which we will crawl and scream and bite and scratch! We shall smother each other with our lust! The earth will tremble as I hammer you with my—"

"Whoah!" said Infidel, raising a finger to his lips. "Calm down."

He closed his lips over her finger, and shut his eyes. He let loose a moan of pleasure as he sucked her slender digit.

"Nnyarg!" I cried out, gripping my ghost hair, tugging with all my might. This was the most horrible thing I'd seen in my entire life — you know what I mean — and there was nothing I could do to stop it. Nor could I turn away. My traitorous eyes remained fixed on the lustful display. Tower ran his hands along Infidel's bare back as he embraced her tightly. Why wasn't she stopping this?

"Wow," she said, pulling her finger free, then pushing him with her other hand. She spun around, swiftly pulling on her slip. "So... wow. Wow. I, uh, I really don't know what to say, Tower."

"What is there to say?" I shouted at her. "Tear his lips off!"

"Just say that you want to surrender to me," said Tower, coming up behind her, wrapping his arms around her waist. "Say that you long for me with all your heart—" he lowered his lips to her ear and finished in a whispered growl "—and all your body."

He blew gently on her ear. She shivered, gently raising her hands to his, before peeling them away and putting a little space between them.

She didn't look at him as she said, "It's funny you should show up now."

"It's destiny. All things unfold according to the One True Book. We parted so that we each could grow, to become the perfect match for the other."

"Yeah," she said, crossing her arms. "I mean, no. I mean, look, I don't know what I mean. Lately, I've spent a fair amount of time thinking of how to get back to a life of royalty. Then, boom, here you are, telling me you can make it happen. And, I have to say, if I'd seen this level of interest from you fifteen years ago, maybe things might have played out differently. But you can't just show up and start slobbering all over me. What the hell ever happened to courtship?"

Tower dropped to his knees once more. He grabbed her hand, cupping it with both palms in a prayerful pose and said, "If it's courtship you desire, I promise you romance beyond your imagination. I shall fly to the moon and carve your portrait to decorate the night sky. I shall part the sea and pluck pearls from the depths. I will search every corner of the world for flowers and perfumes and silks to adorn your bedroom. You will wear a wedding dress spun from pure gold, beaded with priceless gems from Greatshadow's treasure. The entire world will—"

"I get the idea," said Infidel, again silencing him with a finger on his lips, then snatching the finger back as his lips parted. "How about cake? Would you go get me a slice of cake?"

"For you, my love, anything," he vowed.

"Make it chocolate."

Ten seconds of silence passed as she looked down at him. Tower furrowed his brow. "Right now?"

"Why not now?"

"We... um... we're in the middle of a jungle. The nearest town is Commonground and it's in ruins. At top speed, I would need a full day to fly back to the Silver Isle to find a baker."

"So... no cake."

Tower frowned. Then, he said, in utter seriousness. "If... if you demand it, I will go."

She shrugged. "I guess I can wait."

"Thank you," he said.

She leaned back against a tree and took a second to fix her mis-buttoned pants. "So you saw right through my disguise. What about the Father Ver?"

"I don't know why he accepts that you are a machine. It doesn't matter, in the end. If he suspected the truth, he'd have already ordered that I apprehend you and secure you until a trial could be held."

"Would you?"

Tower looked like he wished he'd left for the cake.

His features sagged as he looked to the ground.

"I would have no choice but to obey Ver's direct command," he said. "Even without his powers."

Infidel placed a hand on his shoulder. "You know, I kind of like that. I mean, five minutes ago you were a lust-crazed teenager. Now, you're a knight with a sense of duty and honor. Somewhere between these extremes is my idea of a pretty good man."

"No!" I shouted. "No, no, no, no, no!"

The faintest ghost of a smile flickered across her lips as he gently kissed the back of her hand.

"Thank you for understanding," he said.

She shrugged. "No problem."

I spun around, growling, and found the nearest tree. I attempted to slam my head into it, but wound up staring at a family of possums dwelling in its rotted out center.

I took a deep, phantom breath and calmed myself. With any luck, Greatshadow would swallow him.

TOWER FLEW OFF as Infidel continued dressing. She paused as she found the boot sheath empty. She started pacing as she chewed on her fingernails. She reached the finger that Lord Tower had sucked on and regarded it with an expression half curiosity, half disgust. You can guess which half of the expression I appreciated.

At last she muttered, "Did it fall out in the tree?" She started back toward the village. She hadn't gone but a few dozen feet before she froze, turning her head toward a rustling sound from a nearby thicket. I poked my head through the screen of leaves and found myself face to face with Aurora squatting on the ground with her pants around her ankles. I quickly jerked my head back. Infidel took note of the wisps of fog drifting across the ground. Aurora had trouble with stealth in humid climates.

"Aurora?" Infidel whispered.

There was a rapid rustle from the other side of the bushes. "Infidel?"

They each poked their heads around the leafy wall and grinned.

"I'm glad to see you," said Aurora. "I need to gripe to someone. This whole mission is turning into a big, stinking pile of yellow snow."

"You don't know the half of it," said Infidel.

"I'm not even sure what I'm doing here," said Aurora. "I thought I'd feel the Jagged Heart's presence. I don't. Tower plainly isn't carting it around with him, and it wasn't in the gear. If he doesn't have it, I'm wasting my time."

"The Black Swan wanted you on the mission," said Infidel. "She must have seen something in the future that made her think you needed to be here."

"She's not always right. The whole point of her going back in time is to change the future. Sometimes, little things she does wipe out whole events she was counting on. She went back quite a ways to order a new barge built. What if some guy she hired to build it would have otherwise joined the raiders that stole the Jagged Heart? Maybe it never wound up in Tower's possession."

"I'll ask Tower about it when I see him again," said Infidel.

"Ah ah ah!" Aurora wagged her finger. "You're a machine around him. You cart gear, not pump knights for information."

"Funny you should mention pumping," said Infidel.

"How so?"

"Because Tower just caught me bathing at the stream and confessed that he knows who I am. He says he wants to take me back, clear my name, and go ahead with the marriage.

I'm suddenly really glad the Black Swan didn't tell me who the father of my daughter would be."

Aurora's jaw opened slowly, until her tusks were almost pointing straight out. She snapped out of her shock and said, "I, uh, thought you couldn't... I mean, there's still some, um, issues. Of crushing. Accidentally. Certain important parts."

"We only have to do it once," said Infidel.

I jammed my fingers into my ears to keep from hearing more. It didn't work.

"And if he's not any good, maybe I won't have any, you know, involuntary muscle spasms."

I screamed, "La-la-la-la-la!"

She continued, "I mean, it's not like I'd actually feel anything for him. It wouldn't be like it would have been with Stagger."

I stopped la-la-ing and lowered my fingers.

Infidel swallowed hard. "If Stagger were still around, I would have head-butted him when he kissed me."

"Stagger?" Aurora looked confused. "Why would you head-butt him?"

"No! Tower!"

Aurora's brow knotted with bewilderment.

Infidel looked up toward the tree village, then said in a hushed voice, "Tower kissed me."

"You're joking."

Infidel raised her hand and resumed biting her nails.

"You're not joking."

Infidel shook her head.

Aurora crossed her arms, tapping her beefy fingers on her biceps.

"So," she asked, casually. "Was he any good?"

Infidel rolled her eyes. "It... it was... I really have nothing to judge by. I've never been kissed before."

"You've never kissed? For a battle hardened mercenary who wears necklaces of human teeth, you've lived kind of a sheltered life."

Infidel threw up her hands. "What's the point of me kissing anyone? I mean, what's it going to lead to? Look, I've made it this far without any kind of intimacy. I've been perfectly content without it. I mean it. Who needs it?"

Aurora smirked. "In my experience, when people say, 'I mean it,' they don't mean it."

Infidel folded her arms across her chest. "Fine. Maybe, just maybe... maybe I'm curious. Maybe this is one of those choices made by fifteen-year-old Innocent that I'm not so sure about any more. I mean... this is going to sound stupid... but... I ... well, there was this thing he did, when he, um, sucked, uh, my finger and..."

Aurora's eyebrows shot up.

"And... I dunno. I could feel his tongue. It was, like, soft. Warm. I thought it would be slimy, but it felt clean. It was... I don't know. It wasn't nice. I mean, I didn't want it to happen. But... it wasn't unpleasant, either. I felt... this is stupid."

"What?"

"There was like... like a spark. Like, a voice in my head going, 'He's sucking your finger! What a pervert!' and... I... I guess I'm just... curious. About perversions."

Aurora laughed.

"It's not funny," said Infidel.

Aurora shook her head, and wiped a tear from her cheek. "No," she said, gasping for air. "I know. It's not. I haven't seen another female of my species for twenty years. I'm not going to judge anyone for feeling sexually frustrated. The dreams I've had..."

"You mean male," said Infidel.

"Hmm?"

"You said you hadn't seen another female. But it wouldn't do you any good if you had."

"Ah," said Aurora. She pressed her lips together. "This is awkward. You see, uh, the priesthood, it's all female, and, um, sexual release is a big part of fertility ceremonies, so, we spend a lot of time engaged in—"

"I don't think I need to hear more," said Infidel, holding up her hands.

I sort of hoped Aurora would at least finish her sentence. I was to be disappointed. She changed the subject back to the issue at hand.

"So, you've got a sex-crazed ex-boyfriend in charge of the dragon hunt. What about the Truthspeaker?"

"He hasn't seen through the disguise. Relic said he's distracting the priest. Don't ask me to explain, I still haven't figured out all of that weirdo's powers. But, anyway, if the priest finds me out, apparently he has orders to capture me instead of killing me outright."

"That's good, I guess."

"Not really. If the Truthspeaker gives me grief, I'll probably just twist his head off. I'm not sure that Tower's going to be quite as forgiving after that. And, if I twist Tower's head off, I'm suddenly short on candidates to father my daughter."

"Do you want a child?" asked Aurora.

"Until the Black Swan mentioned it, I hadn't wasted any time thinking about motherhood," said Infidel. "Now... I mean, if it's, you know, fate... then maybe I wouldn't be terrible at it."

Aurora looked skeptical.

"I know," said Infidel, shaking her head. "I mean, it's hard to imagine making the jump from bounty-hunter and tomb-looter to breast-feeder and diaper-changer. The person I've been would be a lousy mother. But, the whole purpose of this dragon hunt, for me, is to make a new life. And there are... there are nurturing instincts I have that I've never really explored. I just... maybe I should keep an open mind."

Aurora nodded, but didn't ask any follow-up questions. Instead she said, "Speaking of the dragon hunt, it's worth noting that of twelve would-be dragon slayers, the three we've lost have all been put out of action by other team members."

"Technically, Blade was killed by a pygmy deadfall."

"Blade was killed by the damn Truthspeaker," grumbled Aurora.

Infidel nodded. "What's your point?"

"My point is that our dragon hunt is going to be over before it even begins if we kill each other before Greatshadow gets a shot."

"We won't all kill each other," said Infidel. "I've got your back. You've got mine. And I think we can count on the Goons to side with us."

"Don't fool yourself," said Aurora. "Menagerie's willing to mess around with stuff that's not spelled out in his contract, like keeping your secret, but if it comes down to a fight between us and the Truthspeaker, he's being paid to protect the priest."

Infidel nodded. "At least you and I are a team," she said.

"Sure," said Aurora. "As long as you don't try to protect the future father of your child if he does have the sacred harpoon."

Infidel nodded, but she was no longer looking directly at the ogress. Her gaze was once more unfocused; I could practically hear her thoughts churning. As Aurora turned away, Infidel stared off into the distance.

Straight at me. Straight through me.

Haunted.

CHAPTER FIFTEEN
SIZZLE

I'D HEARD ALL I could stomach about finger-sucking and motherhood, so I decided to get back to the job and watch Lord Tower. I floated up to his tree house. While I hesitate to say that anything about being dead is fun, freedom from gravity is not without advantages. I drifted through his floor and found him flat on his back, eyes wide open, staring at the leaves above him. He looked as if he was unlikely to get any sleep, and not just because Father Ver was snoring. Tower didn't look all that happy for a man who had just kissed the woman he'd obsessed about for fifteen years.

"Forgive me," he whispered, as tears welled in his eyes. "Forgive me."

He swallowed down his emotions with a loud, snotty snort, then turned onto his side, hugging the thin blanket draped over him.

I sighed. I hated the guy, but I understood what he was going through. What if I'd thrown myself at Infidel years ago and confessed everything I felt for her? She'd said a lot of nice things about me since my death, but what if she'd reacted with the same lukewarm confusion Tower had received? I wouldn't have gotten any sleep either.

Angry for feeling any sympathy, and rapidly tiring of the Truthspeaker's snoring, I drifted back toward Relic to tell him about the encounter. With any luck, he was fast asleep and I'd wake him.

As I air-walked back across the gap to the main platform, my eye was caught by movement on the tree where the Goons were staying. I moved closer. In the shadows, I could make out

Menagerie. He had a row of small glass vials laid out before him as he studied the faint outline of a bat on his inner thigh. A drop of black ink glistened on a needle held in his right hand. His lips were pressed tightly together as he jabbed the bat in rapid, repeated motions. On his left forearm, a tiger glistened with fresh black ink. I was curious how he'd ever reach the faded wolf tattoos on the small of his back, but I didn't get the chance to find out.

As Menagerie concentrated, oblivious to the world around him, I noticed Reeker peek at him from beneath his blanket. Deciding that Menagerie wasn't watching, Reeker rolled slowly to the edge of the platform and carefully lowered himself down to the woven vine ladder.

If he hadn't been so quiet, I'd have assumed he was going down to use the bathroom. But, he kept looking over his shoulder, and was taking care not to make a sound. He'd never struck me as someone who worried about disturbing other people's sleep. Suspicious, I drifted closer to him, though not too close. Even though my sense of smell was muted as a ghost, I knew to keep several arm lengths between us.

Reeker reached the forest floor and stealthily crept toward the edge of the village. He went to the far side of a huge tree trunk and pressed his back to the bark. He took one more look around, then crouched and pulled out a small leather pouch, placing it on his knee. Quickly he produced a small rectangle of paper, flattened it out, then placed a large pinch of tobacco in the center. He glanced off to his right, then his left, as he rolled the paper into an untidy tube.

Finally, satisfied that he was truly alone, he pulled a wooden match out of the pouch. He ignited the tip with a quick flick of his thumbnail. A brief breath of sulfur scented the air. He brought the tiny flame to the cigarette and puffed once, twice, three times, firing it to a bright cherry ember.

He shook the match to snuff it. The small fire kept burning.

He shook it again, harder. Still, it didn't go out.

He frowned, staring at the miniscule blaze as it sputtered down the wooden dowel, nearing his finger and thumb. He reached out with his free hand, and closed his forefinger and thumb upon the feeble flare to be done with it.

He screamed. A sizzle sounded from his fingers as white tendrils of smoke spun into the air. A yellow-orange flame danced over his hairy knuckles. He waved his hand frantically, crying, "Yowowowow!" as the fire grew brighter.

Now, his sleeve was on fire. He dropped and rolled on the forest floor. The ground was damp, but his efforts only stoked the flames to greater heights. In a matter of seconds, his clothes were engulfed. His screams grew ever louder.

With a sudden *whoosh*, Lord Tower shot down from the sky. He was fully enveloped in his armor; there was no way he'd had time to put it on in any ordinary way. The Gloryhammer turned night into day as the knight flashed toward Reeker. He grabbed the flailing skunk-man by the ankle, then streaked off in the direction of the stream. I followed at the speed of thought as he threw Reeker into the pool where Infidel had bathed. Reeker vanished beneath the surface with a loud hiss and a mushroom cloud of steam.

Tower spun around. There were flames dancing on the forest floor where Reeker had rolled. They flared higher and higher, the ground crackling and whistling as dampness boiled away. Tower gripped his Gloryhammer with both hands as the flames took on a decidedly serpentine form. At first, I thought a vine was on fire, curling from the heat. Then, I realized I was looking at a dragon — a small drake, no taller than a man, made of pure flame. It reared up on its blazing legs and sucked in air. Tower charged as the beast spewed a cone of flame. The fire engulfed the knight as he swung his enchanted hammer with a grunt. The weapon went right through the flame-beast.

"I'm on it!" shouted Aurora, running toward the conflagration with her hands outstretched. Snowflakes the size of saucers began to fall, vaporizing as they hit the beast with a staccato *sss sss sss.* Aurora was iced up and took a swing at the fire-dragon with her frozen gauntlet. She spun around, off balance, as her punch failed to connect. There was nothing solid about the beast to hit.

The fire seemed to laugh as it blazed brighter. Aurora raised her arm to cover her eyes as she stumbled back, her armor cracking.

Suddenly, Infidel dropped straight down toward the drake, holding an outstretched blanket. The fluttering edges engulfed the small dragon as she landed, dimming the light. The beast screamed as sparks swirled around the edges.

Off to one corner, there was a tiny remnant of flame curling around a small twig, no bigger than a cockroach. It leapt to a stick, and flashed into a tiny dragon the size of a mouse, then leapt again toward a fallen branch to grow as big as a cat.

Tower charged toward it, trying to stomp it beneath his gleaming boots, but the fire-cat darted away, burning leaves and twigs as it grew to the size of a dog. Aurora pointed both hands at the ground and the forest debris it needed to grow was suddenly coated in ice. The creature darted back toward Infidel, stretching its neck out to nip the edge of the blanket. Infidel jumped back with a yelp as the cloth flared; in the blink of an eye, the creature was man-sized once more.

"You guys are a frickin' joke," grumbled a voice from the shadows. The creature craned its blazing neck to discover Zetetic standing directly behind it, hiking up his tattered robes. The Deceiver grumbled, "I can piss out a fire no bigger than this."

The creature roared toward him, reaching out with claws of flame.

The Deceiver began to pee.

The creature hissed, drawing back. It writhed as streams of urine spattered the ground where it stood. The flames flickered and danced, reaching for new fuel, but the Deceiver kept a steady aim and soon the ground around it was drenched.

Fifteen seconds later, the flame flickered out, and the last pale red ember went black.

Aurora demurely covered her eyes as Zetetic stuffed his manhood back into the briefs he wore beneath his robe.

"Good job," said Tower, his eyes on the Deceiver's face. "Fast thinking."

"I'm sure it seemed fast to *you*," said Zetetic. He dropped to one knee, studying the blackened ground. His eyes flickered over it like he was reading a map. He reached out and picked up a twisted black twig a few inches in length, right where Reeker had first been standing. He studied it closely, then asked, "Which idiot lit the match?"

"The half-seed!" exclaimed Lord Tower. He turned and bounded through the forest, his armor clanging. Up above, there were a hundred voices jabbering; we'd probably awakened every pygmy in a five-mile radius.

Tower leapt into the pool with a splash, fishing around in the waist deep water with his gauntlets. He jerked upright suddenly, pulling a limp, blackened form back into the air.

Reeker wasn't moving. His hair was completely burned away; his scalp was raw and red, with charred black flesh peeling away from the bone in places. Tower laid him on the stone by the pool. He pressed on the skunk-man's chest, forcing out a fountain of water.

Menagerie rushed onto the scene, with No-Face trailing behind him. He didn't pause to ask what had happened. He pushed Tower aside and dropped his ear to his friend's chest. His brow knitted as he listened. Then, he jerked his head away and placed his mouth on Reeker's lips. Reeker's belly rose as Menagerie blew breath into him.

"Gluh," said No-Face, sadly.

Menagerie continued to work, breathing in air, then pushing it out, pausing between breathes to listen to the chest.

"Is there a heartbeat?" Aurora asked.

Menagerie shook his head.

"I can't believe he's dead," said Aurora, sounding sadder than I would have expected.

The Deceiver looked down at Reeker's charred form and said, "Why not? He's not breathing, there's no heartbeat, his skin looks like charcoal. It's not a difficult diagnosis."

Menagerie looked at the Deceiver as if he was ready to pounce on the man. Then, his body slackened, and he said, in a soft voice, "Fix him. Please."

The Deceiver shook his head. "The Truthspeakers stripped me of the power to raise the dead. I'm sorry."

Menagerie ground his teeth together and clenched his fists, his anger rising. But instead of attacking Zetetic, he looked down at the fallen Goon.

"You moron," he said, his voice trembling.

"That's a fine goodbye," said Reeker's voice from the pool. I looked toward the rippling water and found a bilious yellow vapor rising, coalescing into the familiar form of Reeker. The pale spirit lingered for a few seconds as it looked down on the scene.

"Reeker! It's me! Stagger!"

Reeker's eye widened as he saw me. I drifted closer. His naked, barefoot ghost seemed shorter than he had been alive. There had been whispers that he wore lifts in his boots; apparently these rumors were true.

"Stagger?" he asked. "What are you doing here? You're dead!"

"So are you," I said. "I'm haunting Infidel. Well, technically, I'm haunting a knife. If you pick something and focus on it, you might be able to stick around."

He looked down at his burnt body. "Why would I want to stick around?" he said. "Look at what's left of me. It's going to hurt like hell popping back inside."

"I meant you can stay here as a ghost."

Reeker laughed. "How pathetic would that be? Life was fun because my body was fun. I could eat, drink, and fool around. Can a ghost do any of that?"

"No. But it beats just fading out to nothing, doesn't it?"

"What? You don't believe in heaven?" Reeker asked.

"You do?"

"Sure. Like a *Black Swan* barge in the sky. I'll just keep on eating, drinking, and sleeping around, only there I won't get bossed around by tattooed shapeshifters. And in heaven, all my friends will have, you know, faces." He looked on No-Face with a look of unconcealed disdain.

The giant man was standing over Reeker's body, shuddering, tears rolling over his blank features from his one visible eye, as he gurgled, "Guh huh huh huh. Guh huh huh huh."

"The big baby," Reeker said.

"Kind of a cold thing to say about the only man crying over your death."

Reeker shrugged. "Remember that little calico cat that used to hang around the bar? No-Face cried like a little girl when it got run over by that cart. Him crying over me is nothing special."

I had an epiphany as I looked into Reeker's remorseless face.

"I never liked you," I said.

"What a disappointment," he said with a sneer. "You were the biggest loser in Commonground. You had the most gorgeous girl on the island giving you goo-goo eyes, and you never had the guts to sneak a kiss. You acted like you were smart, reading all those damn books, but what did you ever do that was important? You wasted your life."

I ground my ghost teeth, sorry I'd called out to his wraith.

Reeker glanced up at the tree houses. A hundred dark faces looked down at us. Among them was the tall, thin form of my grandfather. "Must run in the family. Hard to get less ambitious than living up a tree like a damn squirrel."

Before I could think of a retort, he turned his eyes toward the stars and drifted upward. "I've stuck around long enough. There are women waiting in the next world. I can hear them calling to me now." His phantom body remained intact as he rose, not dissipating the way Blade had. He cast one last glimpse down at his battered, broken body.

"Damn," he said, as he cleared the trees. "I was one handsome devil."

Meanwhile, Relic and Father Ver had joined the others at the pool. The assembled dragon-slayers glanced at one another.

"This is insane," said Zetetic, the first to state the obvious. "The dragon knows we're here. Let's call this off and try again some other century."

"Maybe he does know we're here," said Tower. "But does he know who we are? If he knows the danger we pose, why such a feeble attack?"

Relic nodded. "I concur. This was merely a test to see what he was up against. If he was worried by what he'd seen, lava would now be flowing down the slope toward us."

"We've lost a third of the party without reaching his lair," Zetetic said to Tower. "How many of us will have to die before you call this off?"

"All of us," said Tower. "We have a duty."

"*You* have a duty," snapped Zetetic. "What's in it for the rest of us?"

"Munuh," said No-Face.

"Money was going to be my answer too," said Menagerie.

"Was it worth losing a friend?"

"Reeker broke the contract; he paid the price." Menagerie's face was hard as he said, "The next Goon I recruit won't be such a pain in the ass."

"That's a very mercenary attitude," said the Deceiver.

"Is that surprising?" asked Aurora. "We're mercenaries."

Zetetic looked at Relic. "Fine. So Tower and Ver are here for duty, and the others are here for money. What are you after?"

Relic pulled back his hunched shoulders and said, in a firm voice, "I'm surprised a man of your learning has to ask. Greatshadow's hoard is more than a collection of gold and gems. The greatest treasures of the Vanished Kingdom may be found amid his trove. There are scrolls containing plays that no man has seen performed in centuries, sculptures that once adorned the gardens of kings, and paintings and carvings that show the long forgotten world of my youth. I would pay any price to look once more upon these arts."

"You sound almost like you mean this," I said.

I thought it would sound plausible. It's simpler to say this than to reveal my true motive.

"Which is?"

Hatred. Pure and simple hatred of the beast. Every moment that he survives torments my very soul.

"Fine," said Zetetic. "Let me set you all straight on the real reason we're here. The Isle of Fire is the largest wild plot of land left in the world. It's covered in virgin timber, beneath which lies rich volcanic soils begging to be cultivated. The island has fresh water rivers and deep harbors perfect for cities. The king isn't trying to rid the world of some great evil by slaying Greatshadow. He's trying to expand his empire. Are you willing to die for that? Because I think that the greedy dreams of an already rich king are a lousy thing to die for."

"The king's motives are of no importance," said the Truthspeaker. "It matters only that you obey. Remember the X sanction."

Zetetic looked at Aurora, Menagerie, and No-Face. "Don't any of you wonder what he's talking about? Do any of you care what kind of monsters are paying your salaries?"

"Enlighten us," said Menagerie.

"I told you the Truthspeakers stripped me of the power to raise the dead," said Zetetic. "When *I* do it, apparently, it's 'evil.'" He formed little quote marks with his fingers as he spoke the word. "But the Church is rife with hypocrisy when it comes to necromancy. I was captured a year ago. I didn't go down easy. I killed... what? Fifty knights?"

"Forty-three," said Lord Tower, tersely.

"They wasted no time when I was captured. I was bound and gagged and given a trial that lasted less than an hour. Ten minutes after my conviction, I was marched to the gallows where a noose was placed around my neck. Father Ver himself gave the order to hang me. I still have nightmares about the trapdoor swinging open beneath my feet."

"Apparently, you survived," said Aurora.

"No," said Zetetic. "I died."

Aurora furrowed her brow.

"King Brightmoon knew of my powers, and how useful those powers might be if he commanded them. So, he paid the church a bribe. He had the monks who pray Tower's armor into existence pray that my heart would once more start beating. I awoke from death to learn I'll stay alive only as long as they keep praying. Tower can send an order through his little magic book at any time for them to stop. That's the X sanction. Tower and Ver act all high and mighty and righteous, but they aren't above enslaving the unwilling dead if it will help the king expand his empire."

Father Ver said, "You are no slave, Deceiver. You're merely employed. Your wages are paid in heartbeats."

Zetetic looked at Aurora with a desperate look in his eyes. "I've no choice but to obey these bastards. But you and the others are free to resist!"

Aurora shrugged. "The Goons and I work for the Black Swan. We aren't all that shocked by a boss motivated by greed."

Zetetic shut up, a moderate pout upon his face. I suspect his feelings ran deeper, but his stitched lips prevented him from showing a full-fledged frown.

As interesting as it was learning what the X sanction was, I was more intrigued by the idea that Tower could communicate with the monks through his book. The notebook had been the only thing in Tower's hand when he stepped off the platform, and two seconds later he'd had the Gloryhammer in his grasp. Did the notebook contain some kind of portal spell? Maybe the Jagged Heart was still at the monastery, and could be sent to Tower when he was ready for it.

Before I could ponder the puzzle further, Grandfather lowered himself down from the trees on a looped vine. He stopped with his penis-gourd at eye-level and said, "You've worn out your welcome, long-men." Our packs and gear rained to the ground around us as the pygmies tossed them from the platform. "Leave at once. Return to the sea. You may not pass through our territory."

"We'll go where we wish," said Father Ver. "Should your kinsmen threaten us, we will meet any attack with deadly force. You have no—"

Lord Tower raised his gauntlet, motioning for the Truthspeaker to stop speaking. "You were gracious to show us hospitality," he said to Grandfather. "We will not cause you any further bother. We're here to fight the dragon, not fellow men, pagans though you may be. We will find another path."

The knight cast his gaze toward Relic. "It seems we must put your knowledge of this island to a test after all."

Relic nodded. "I know a way."

"Do you?" I asked.

Not really, he thought back at me.

I smiled. For the first time since I died, I finally felt useful. All these years of poking around the island were going to prove valuable after all.

"It looks like I've finally got the upper hand," I said. "I know how to get to the lair from here while avoiding Jawa Fruit territory."

And what is the price of this information? asked Relic.

I pressed my lips together, feeling horrible about what I was going to say. But... what choice did I have? "I'll keep spying on Tower. And in return... in return, you'll tell me what Infidel's thinking. I have to know. Is she really interested in him? Is there any danger at all that he'll win her over?"

Relic's eyes glowed in the shadows of his hood. *A fair price. And what will you ask if you find that she does feel attraction?*

I clenched my fists and said, "Nothing you're not already planning to do. Tower was never going to come out of Greatshadow's lair alive."

CHAPTER SIXTEEN

OMENS

To EVERYONE'S ASTONISHMENT, nobody died during the next week. I'll take credit. Having been turned away from Jawa Fruit territory, I had Relic guide the party along the cliffs to reach the north slope. This was the harshest terrain on the island; I knew it well, since the ruins of the Vanished Kingdom here had been left relatively untouched by previous generations of tomb raiders. Treasure seekers have a tendency to look for the easy score; if they had the taste for actual work, there were more reliable careers available. So, most of the explorers stuck to the relative ease of the southern and eastern slopes, as I had done early in my career. It was only after I'd forged a friendship with a woman who could toss half-ton rocks around like bales of hay that the northern slope had opened up to me. Some of my most profitable discoveries had been made here.

There were no substantial navigable rivers on this side of the island, just cascading streams, so there were no river-pygmies. The few trees that clung to the rocky slopes were gnarled and stunted, unsuitable for forest-pygmies. That left only lava-pygmies to worry about, and since the Shattered Palace sat near the dead center of their territory, I didn't see anything we could do to avoid them.

As luck would have it, in the chaos that followed Infidel meeting my grandfather, she'd never bothered to clean the bone-handled knife. Relic had returned it to her, and I was still free to move about. I felt like a child opening gift-wrapped presents, flitting from ruin to ruin as the others slogged slowly along narrow tracks that would give a mountain goat vertigo. The men of the Vanished Kingdom had regarded this rugged landscape as a spiritual place, carving countless small temples directly into the steep rock faces.

On my last trip through the area, I'd spotted some dark spots high up a jutting cliff that looked more like windows than natural cave openings. Infidel had been willing to risk the climb, but we'd spotted it near the end of our trip and our packs were already bulging, so we'd decided to save it for another day. As Tower's party crept along the yard-wide lip of rock that led beneath the windows, I could see from Infidel's expression that she remembered the place. I felt a pang of regret over this and a thousand other plans we'd made that we never got around to doing.

I fixed my eyes upon the windows and lifted toward them, as if carried by the updrafts that swept across the slope. I drifted inside, eager to discover if we'd passed up some priceless treasure.

Even before I went in, I saw clues that this wasn't an old temple. I'd looked at enough weathered rock over the years to tell the difference between stones dressed centuries ago and relatively fresh work. These windows looked no more than a few decades old, which meant they were likely the work of lava-pygmies. Once inside, the truth was even more evident, since the ceiling was low, only about five feet high, black with soot from a fire pit lined with stones. The fire pit was still warm, and the gritty floor was covered with fresh footprints. At the back of the cave was a tunnel leading deeper into the mountain.

The whole volcano was honeycombed with these passages, carved by lava-pygmies with obsidian pick-axes. Despite all the work the little orange men put into digging these tunnels and caves, they didn't actually live underground. They used these tunnels mainly for religious rituals. For forest-pygmies and river-pygmies, Greatshadow was *a* god, but for lava-pygmies, Greatshadow was *the* god, and these tunnels normally led to pools of lava where sacrifices would be made.

When I first discovered these areas, my instinct was to back out. For one thing, exploring them meant crawling for hours, which was rough on the knees. Plus, you never knew when you'd turn a corner and find yourself face to face with a band of pygmies armed with poison darts and a sense of righteous indignation.

Once I started exploring with Infidel, the balance of power had shifted enough that lava-pygmy temples had become targets. While the lava-pygmies lived in the same relative poverty as the rest of the islanders, their sacred sites were often decorated with a commodity too valuable to ignore: dragon bones.

In theory, there were no dragons left other than the primal dragons. A scrap of dragon hide or a single dragon tooth were exceedingly rare in the rest of the world. Yet, somehow lava-pygmies always had dragon bones aplenty, along with hides that looked like they could have been tanned the week before. In *The Vanished Kingdom*, Grandfather had argued that these were the remains of ancient dragons, mummified and preserved by the dry, hot air inside the volcanic chambers. I'd never liked the theory. I'd spent enough time around the volcano to know that it might be hot, but it definitely wasn't dry. Things rotted in a heartbeat in these areas.

I may have been given a key to the mystery when the two dragons attacked Commonground. Maybe the remains came from Greatshadow's avatars once his spirit no longer animated them. Yet, when they'd been killed, their bodies had turned into slag and stone. No bones or hide had been recovered.

Since the party was creeping along the narrow path at a pace somewhere between snail and turtle, I decided I'd probe the tunnel a little deeper. The narrow passage was pitch black, yet my ghost eyes proved worthy to the task. In the absence of true light, the walls glowed with a soft, pale luminance. I wondered if the eerie illumination was some spiritual energy I had been unaware of when I was alive.

I followed the winding passageway long enough to get bored. Just as I decided to turn back I heard faint whispers ahead. I willed myself more swiftly along the corridor, in pursuit of the sound. The feeble, colorless spirit light gave way to a red glow. The dank tunnel air began to stink of smoke and rotten meat. I floated out of the narrow passage into a relatively large room, a rough circle twenty feet across, with a ceiling high enough that I was able to stand up straight again, assuming standing means anything when your feet can't actually touch the floor.

A dozen pygmies were gathered near a jagged crack in the floor, casting long shadows from a dull red glow. Lava bubbled at the bottom of the crack. A shaman dressed in feathers was tossing sticks into the hole, where they exploded into bright flares. The smoke had the sweetness of eucalyptus.

They pygmies jabbered excitedly; I think they were discussing the patterns of the smoke, reading them for omens. My lava-pygmy vocabulary wasn't all it could be. The only phrase I ever heard directly from lava-pygmies was "Yik! Yik! Yik!" which loosely translates as, "It's a long-man! Kill him!" Still, as best as I could piece together, the shaman was telling the men that the fire-giver had once again blessed them. The pygmies were standing shoulder to shoulder in a circle, looking down at something other than the smoking lava. I peered over the short wall they created and gasped.

A dragon lay before them.

Unlike the beasts that had attacked Commonground, there was no question this creature was flesh and blood. It was quite dead; its burst belly revealed entrails writhing with white maggots. The pygmies leaned down and began cutting into the scaly hide with obsidian knives. I'd used these blades before. They didn't hold an edge well, but when they were fresh, there wasn't anything sharper.

The pygmies peeled the flesh away from the skull. I winced as I saw that the left half of the skull was bashed in. That would certainly hurt its market value.

In size, the dragon wasn't much bigger than a goat. Its leathery wings had already been hacked off and were folded up along the edges of the lava pit. The snout had a bony horn similar to ones that baby lizards have to help chop themselves free of their eggshells.

Off to one side, a team of three shamans dressed in parrot feathers were scraping bright red scales from the hide into a large stone bowl. One of them grabbed a stone pestle and started grinding up the jewel-like scales. All three men spit frequently into the bowl, until it turned into a dark orange paste.

I'd always wondered what lava-pygmies used to dye their skins. Mystery solved.

Sadly, the dragon was decayed well past the stage where it had anything that could be called blood. I remembered my brief return to corporeality when Infidel had hacked into the dragon in Commonground, and my ability to touch Ivory Blade's ghost blood. What would happen if I could put my hands onto some fresh dragon blood?

Hoping that Relic might have some insight on the matter, I surrendered to the ever-present tug of the bone-handled knife. A second later, I shot out into bright sunlight and hot, gusty winds, where the others still inched along the rugged path.

I flitted down to Relic. "I just saw a dragon. Not a flame drake like Reeker let loose, but an actual corpse that was probably alive as little as a week ago."

Relic nodded. *I see it in your mind.*

"I thought all ordinary dragons were dead."

And that is all you saw. A dead dragon.

"Yeah, but freshly dead. Well, not fresh, but recent."

Relic didn't respond as he kept hobbling along the path.

"If human blood can restore my ghostly body, could dragon blood bring me back to life?"

Relic shook his head.

"But when Infidel—"

Regaining corporeality isn't the same as regaining life.

"I had a heartbeat. I was breathing. I was solid enough to get cut by the dragon's scales. If it wasn't exactly life, it was still better than what I've got right now."

Relic dismissed my reasoning with a wave of his gnarled hand. *Dragon blood possesses more life energy than human blood, but it is far more volatile. Human blood will dry on the knife, sustaining your phantom form indefinitely. Dragon blood will vaporize in seconds. The illusion of life will be powerful during those seconds, but it will be unsustainable.*

"In theory, if I had a herd of dragons to stab, I might stay alive for a long time."

Relic rolled his eyes.

"What's wrong with this idea?" I asked. "That baby dragon can't be the only one. It must have parents, uncles, aunts, cousins. I mean, what are the odds that I just happened to stumble on the very last one of its kind?"

I admire your reasoning, but it is deeply flawed. The dragon you saw had but one parent: Greatshadow.

"This wasn't like the slag or fire dragons we've seen. It had entrails. It was meaty enough to rot."

Judicious provided you with the solution to the puzzle.

I scratched my ethereal scalp. What was he talking about?

Greatshadow is among the more physical of the primal dragons. Just as he hungers for meat, he also still possesses sexual urges, and has the magical abilities needed to satisfy these instincts.

"You mean Grandfather wasn't joking when he said that Greatshadow can make extra bodies with female aspects?"

Judicious also told you that the primal dragons pay for the vast scope of their powers with a loss of identity. The female bodies Greatshadow creates sometimes become so confused they believe themselves to be true dragons, separate from Greatshadow. They unconsciously use the magical energy that sustains them to shape their bodies further, to the point that mating with Greatshadow is capable of producing fertilized eggs.

"That is just disturbing."

Greatshadow isn't pleased by the consequences either. Some females are wily enough to conceal the eggs; once or twice a decade, an egg actually hatches, and a new dragon is born. Despite being born with a portion of Greatshadow's own memory and intelligence due to their inherited telepathy, they never survive long. Greatshadow eventually discovers them and kills them. Lava-pygmy shamans harvest the remains.

"How do you know all this?" I asked.

He again tapped his forehead. Maybe he'd read the thoughts of lava-pygmies. For all I knew, he'd read the thoughts of Greatshadow himself.

He looked up the slope and thought to me, *We are near. I smell it on the air.*

He was right. In another mile we'd leave the worst of the cliffs behind and have a clear path along the relatively tame terrain leading to the Shattered Palace. It was still ten miles away, but once we were off these goat-tripping pathways, we'd make good progress.

I glanced back to Infidel, who'd fallen once more into her War Doll role. Her face was utterly blank as she inched along the narrow stone, the oversized pack balanced upon her shoulders. A single misstep and she'd be over the edge; it might be a mile before she stopped rolling. Of course, Tower would probably swoop in to save her.

"So... have you been keeping track of her thoughts? About Tower?"

Yes. Would you like to know her true feelings?

I stared at her for a long moment. When I'd been alive, I'd lacked the courage to ask about her feelings. Now, I was going to learn them in the most cowardly way possible.

I turned away from both Infidel and Relic. "Not yet," I said.

And maybe never. Because, if there was even a sliver of hope that I might be briefly reunited with her, I wanted to be able to look into her eyes without shame.

WE ARRIVED AT the Shattered Palace barely an hour from sunset. I hadn't visited these ruins in years; they hadn't gotten any less spooky in the intervening time. The entire area is surrounded by a stone wall that used to be sixty feet tall, but most of it has collapsed into overgrown mounds. A few lone towers still stand, leaning at precarious angles, the stones held together by their corsets of vines. Beyond this was the grand courtyard, a quarter-mile of barren, pitch-black stone rumored to be cursed. The fine ghost hairs of my arms rose as I followed Infidel across the ebony earth.

The palace itself had once been carved into the side of the mountain. In classic Vanished Kingdom style, it had been adorned with high, narrow pillars, large stone heads, and numerous windows and balconies. At some point in the distant past, the palace had collapsed in on itself. The columns were broken, the stone heads split in two, and the walls shattered into gravel. If you scrambled over the rubble, there were passages leading into the mountain, but these, too, were mostly filled with broken stone and more bat guano than any sane man would want to crawl through.

Of course, men who came this far into the jungle were seldom the model of mental health. In any tunnel, you could find evidence of previous explorers — lanterns with broken glass, block and tackles locked with rust, various spikes and pinions draped with the rotting remains of rope.

The sheer scale and scope of the ruins called out to any treasure hunter. I'd come here long before I met Infidel. I'd turned back when I found the crushed remains of an earlier explorer. There's a chance the guy had been someone I knew; the stench of the corpse, if corpse was the right word, was still relatively ripe. The reason I hesitate to use the word corpse is that it implies there was a body, and, really, what remained was best described as a smeared paste, vaguely man-shaped, coating a smooth stone wall. Whoever he'd been, he'd had a shovel, and whatever had smacked into him had caught the blade on the edge and folded it up like an accordion. After two days of wheezing in the ammonia rich air, slipping in the guano, the sight of the flattened body had dampened my curiosity and I turned back.

"This is a good place to set up camp," said Tower, touching down in the center of the courtyard.

"I respectfully disagree," said Relic. "Lava-pygmies conduct rituals here. If they find us on their sacred ground, we'll have to fight."

"They already know we're here," said Menagerie, in the form of an ocelot, scanning the mounds of stone surrounding the courtyard. "I've spotted a few dozen, but they seem wary. My gut tells me they'll keep their distance. They may not be as kind to the others."

"Others?" asked Tower.

"Explorers. Tomb looters. They have a camp about a half-mile down the mountain. I can smell them."

Zetetic raised an eyebrow. "You can tell they're looters by the way they smell?"

"In this case, yes," said Menagerie. "I know those scents well. It's Hookhand and his Machete Quartet. They always fence their stuff at the *Black Swan*."

"Of all the people to survive the tidal wave," I said, giving Infidel a knowing look. Hookhand and I had a rivalry that ran back twenty years. More than once I'd gone off chasing the rumor of some newly discovered ruin to find the bastard had beaten me to it.

"I don't think the pygmies pose a serious threat," said Lord Tower, rising up to survey the area. "The walls may be in ruins, but they're still formidable barriers. To attack en masse, the pygmies would have to come through the gate. We'll simply post a watch there, and frighten them away with a show of force if necessary. Aurora and Father Ver can start the night. No-Face and Menagerie will follow them. The War Doll and I will take the final shift to see us through until dawn."

Aurora winked at Infidel, though I don't think anyone else saw it. Infidel simply stared straight ahead, still playing the emotionless machine.

WITHOUT THE STEADY winds of the north slope to shield us, the mosquitoes came on strong that evening. Father Ver was particularly afflicted by the buzzing bloodsuckers. He was in a foul mood as he waited at the gate, his scowl lines and bald pate covered with red welts.

Aurora had little to fear from the insects. They froze stiff the second they touched her pale skin, tumbling into an ever growing pile around her.

"I can soothe those if you'd like," Aurora said as Father Ver scratched his face.

"I want no part of your pagan magic," said Father Ver. "Under any other circumstances, I would have already banished an abomination such as yourself."

Aurora leaned back against the stone pillar. "Is there something in your holy book that demands that you be nasty to people?"

"You don't qualify as people," said the Truthspeaker. "Ogres, along with pygmies, mermen, and the shadowfolk, are merely distorted reflections of true humanity, lies given substance by the false beliefs of fools. When the Omega Reader opens the One True Book, your kind will vanish from this world like a nightmare fading from a waking mind."

"Whatever," said Aurora. "You know, I hope I'm around when your book is finally opened. It would be priceless to watch your face fall as you discover everything you believe is wrong."

Father Ver didn't respond.

Aurora kept talking: "You Truthspeakers spend the majority of your life hidden in a remote temple, purposefully set apart from the real world, so that you can be brainwashed into a 'truth' that has nothing to do with reality." Aurora looked up at the sky. There were very few stars shining through the tropical humidity. "I come from a land where truth is stark and tangible, a landscape white as paper for as far as the eye can see. You quickly come to grips with what is real, or you die. Spend a single week out on the tundra, old man, then come back and tell me if you still believe reality is found in some book."

Father Ver slapped a mosquito on the back of his hand. "I find discussions with unreal beings tedious. Let us pass the guard shift without further attempts at conversation."

Aurora said, "I'd be fine with that, except we're going to be fighting for our lives together against Greatshadow. Among my people, it's important to know the mind of the person you're standing shoulder to shoulder with. If you and I must be allies, shouldn't we make at least some small attempt to be friends?"

"My mind is no great mystery," said Father Ver. "I've come here to make a stand for what is good; against an evil as strong as Greatshadow, I grudgingly agree to stand shoulder to shoulder with monsters. I don't like you, ogre, and will never be your friend. But, in battle, know that I will surrender my life to save yours should victory demand it. You do not need my friendship. You have something far more valuable: my sacred word."

Aurora nodded slightly, then returned to her star-gazing, letting the rest of their shift pass in silence. And though Father Ver never acknowledged it, let alone thanked her, the air around the gate was cold and dry, and frost-covered mosquitoes fell like snowflakes around them.

"MUH HUHN HURS," moaned No-Face, rubbing his bandaged hand as he leaned against the stone gate and peered out into the darkness.

Menagerie sat cross-legged on the ground, his hands resting lightly on his knees. He said, "I know your hand hurts. Talking about it won't make it feel better. Listen."

No-Face tilted his head. The forest was cacophonous with life; frogs, bugs, and night-birds shouting with all their power to catch the attention of potential mates. It took a moment's concentration to pick out a distant, dull, *doom, doom, doom.*

"Guh?"

"War drums. They say the Death Angel has returned."

No-Face pointed a finger at his own chest.

"Don't flatter yourself. They mean Infidel. Apparently she did something to piss them off."

No-Face chuckled, low and gravelly, then said, "Muhbuh shuh fuhd. Huh huh huh."

"Yeah, right."

They both fell silent, listening to the bass pulse beneath the thrumming ocean of sound.

Menagerie craned his neck, following the bouncing signals. He allowed himself a slight smile. "The Cracked Earth tribe reports a bad omen. The goat they tossed into the lava screamed three times before it died. Attacking tonight would bring certain disaster."

"Grah," said No-Face, his shoulders sagging.

"Don't sound so disappointed. You'll see plenty of action. We won't have Reeker around for wide area control. I'm already out of blood for some of my big cats. I need you to fight smart."

No-Face wrapped his chain around his damaged hand, then spun around and punched the stone beside him, sending out a spray of sparks. The sharp crack of the blow momentarily silenced the nearest wildlife, leaving only the throb of the drums, which suddenly quickened their pace. No-Face lowered his hand, his one eye gleaming with satisfaction at the dinner-plate-sized crater he'd made in the solid rock.

"Gut duh jub dum muh wah!"

"Fine then," Menagerie said, shaking his head. "Fight the way you always fight."

The bugs began to buzz again as the two men fell into silence. Soon the drums vanished once more beneath the sonic waves of life.

"Duhm," said No-Face, rubbing his knuckles. "Muh Rukuh."

"I know," said Menagerie, staring into the darkness. "I miss him too."

SINCE WE'D LEFT the Jawa Fruit tribe, Tower had barely made eye contact with Infidel. When I spied on him at night, his prayers had been especially heavy with the whole "wisdom to know lust from love" theme. With any luck, he'd decide to just forget Infidel and find some nice girl whose life wasn't an affront to all he held holy.

The two of them walked up to relieve the Goons. Lord Tower was fully dressed in his armor; I couldn't see his face. Infidel strolled behind him, biting her lower lip. Her expression could have been nervousness... or it could have been anticipation.

"You hear the war drums?" Menagerie asked as Tower reached the gates.

"No," said Tower.

"The pygmies aren't happy we're here. But, the Cracked Earth tribe is refusing to take part in an attack tonight. Bad omens."

"Excellent," said Tower. "We won't be here tomorrow night. I see no reason for unnecessary bloodshed."

"Hukhuh," said No-Face.

"He's right," said Menagerie. "They aren't going to attack Hookhand either. With your permission, we'll slip down to their camp and finish them off."

Tower cocked his head. "Why would we want to do that?"

Menagerie looked genuinely startled by the question. "We're going to be too busy fighting the dragon to secure any treasures we might find along the way. We don't want Hookhand to slip in behind us and start looting before we even have time to make an inventory."

"They don't even know we're here," said Tower.

"Which makes this the perfect time to take them by surprise," said Menagerie, grinding his fist into his palm.

"I'm not going to order innocent men be put to death simply because they had the misfortune of camping near us."

"Innocent?" Menagerie stared at the knight in shock. "You don't earn a name like Hookhand and the Machete Quartet by being good citizens. We need to—"

"I've heard your concerns," Tower said. "I've made my decision. If Hookhand bothers us, we'll deal with him. For now, get some rest."

Menagerie opened his mouth to argue further, then caught himself. He said, tersely, "Yes sir," then headed back to the sleeping area with No-Face close behind, rattling his chain.

Once they were several yards away, Tower pulled off his helmet. He produced the small leather-bound book from his hip compartment, opened it to a blank page, and tapped his helmet against it. There was a bubble of light, a sound like ripping paper, and the helmet was gone. The blank page now had a drawing of a helmet upon it.

"That's damn convenient," said Infidel, her eyes wide as she looked at the book. Her expression changed to a frown as she rubbed her jaw. "Man, it feels weird to talk after being quiet for so long." She pursed her lips, licking them. "The words tickle my mouth."

"I have something else to tickle your mouth," said Tower, leaning forward, his eyes closed, his lips puckered.

He kissed only air. She stepped backward at the last second.

"Careful," said Infidel, glancing back toward camp. "The Goons aren't in bed yet. You don't want them to see anything."

"Let them see," said Tower, stepping toward her, grabbing her by the arms. "Soon, I shall declare my love to the entire world!"

"Soon, maybe, but not now," said Infidel. "We don't want to get Father Ver all riled up."

Tower's grip loosened on her arms at the mention of the holy man. His eyes locked on hers in a look of fierce confidence. "Since last we spoke, I have searched my soul. You asked if I would obey Father Ver if he ordered that I arrest you. At the time, I was greatly troubled by the question. Now, I have no doubt. I would fight to the death to protect you, even against Father Ver. My love for you is greater than blind obedience to authority."

"Ooooh," said Infidel. "That kind of attitude will get you put on the naughty list. Believe me, I know."

"Let it be so. I would suffer the torments of hell for a single night in your arms, my love," he said, his voice low and serious.

Infidel pushed his hands off her arms and turned her back to him. "Let's hope it doesn't come to that. I mean, I'm flattered. Really, it's a very nice thing to say. But, I hate to think I just lugged a half-ton of gear across a million miles of goat trails for nothing. We've got a dragon to hunt. After we kill it, we can start discussing, you know, romantic stuff. For now, we need to stay focused on the task at hand. Like... well, for instance, I was wondering if you had, I don't know, any sort of special weapon to use against Greatshadow? I mean, your hammer didn't even make a dent in that little fire lizard we fought."

Tower smiled. "We would not undertake this quest if the proper weapon for the job hadn't fallen into our hands. Have you heard of the Jagged Heart?"

"Nope. Never. Tell me about it," said Infidel.

"The Jagged Heart was a weapon revered by the ice-ogres. It's a harpoon tipped with a fragment of the shattered heart of Hush, the primal dragon of cold. Once, she was in love with Greatshadow, but she betrayed his trust in an affair with Glorious, the primal dragon of the sun. After Glorious went on to reject her, Greatshadow spurned her as well. Hush's heart broke into a thousand shards, the largest of which was turned into a harpoon by the ice ogres."

"Sound's painful. Must not have been fatal, however. Hush is still a power up north."

"As elemental creatures, primal dragons obey different physical rules. Hush endures, but her bitterness still chills much of the world."

"And this Jagged Heart is pretty powerful, huh?"

"It's cold is such that it extinguishes any heat or flame. Anything it touches shatters, be it steel or dragon hide."

"Anything? How about your armor?"

"My armor could resist the cold. It's composed of prayer and faith rather than base matter. As long as the monks maintain their vigilance, I'm immune from all harm."

Infidel leaned close, placing a hand on his chest. "So... nothing can break through it? Nothing at all?" She ran her fingers along his breastplate. "Oh," she said, her eyes widening. "It doesn't feel like metal. It's warm. And sort of... silky." She breathed on it, then rubbed her finger. "I notice it doesn't show fingerprints, either."

"You may touch it as much as you desire," said Tower, his voice purring. "It will always maintain its pristine condition."

Infidel pulled her hand away. "So, uh, the Jagged Heart's a harpoon? Those are pretty big. You obviously aren't carrying it. I guess that book stores more than just your armor?"

"Yes," said Tower. "It's filled with many types of equipment. And, on the final page, anything I write is instantly duplicated in a matching book in the monastery. They may also add items to their book for my use."

"And that's how you'd trigger the X sanction?" she asked.

He nodded.

"Don't you think it's creepy that we're working with someone who's kinda, sorta dead? I mean, I never got along with my father, but I didn't think he'd get involved with necromancy. I especially didn't think the church would go along with something like this."

"The needs of a king and the needs of the church don't always overlap," said Tower. He looked toward the faint glow of the caldera. It had been especially calm ever since the eruption. "Of course, sometimes they do. The church hates all primal dragons. The king wants this island for its natural wealth." He waved his gauntleted hand toward the forest. "Think of the navy that can be built with such an endless supply of large trees. We've long ago exhausted all useful timber on the Silver Isles, and now the forests on the Isle of Apes are producing fewer and fewer large trees. Anywhere the king searches for new resources, he finds primal dragons standing in the way. But, plans have now been set in motion to rid the world not just of Greatshadow, but of all the dragons. In the not so distant future, King Brightmoon will face no barriers at all in his quest to expand our great civilization."

"Hmm," said Infidel, running her hands along the seams of his chest plate, tracing the joints lightly with her fingernails. "I suppose ruling the world does excuse a little necromancy."

Tower stared deeply into Infidel's eyes. "And you, my lovely princess, *you* are the last surviving link to the bloodline of your father. Our children will have the sole claim to inherit the crown. Think of it, my darling: the product of my seed and your womb will hold dominion over the earth!"

Infidel met his gaze, and said, "This is quite a vision."

"A grand vision," said Tower. "And a true one. I believe with all my heart that our story is the central narrative of the One True Book. Our life and love are the very core of history. It is destiny. Our destiny."

Infidel turned her back to him. "You'll pardon me if I need some time to think about this. This is quite a lot to swallow."

"Would it help if you had something sweet and cream-filled to swallow first?" Tower asked.

At first I assumed this was the worst sexual innuendo I'd ever heard, but Tower surprised me by turning to a new page in the book and tapping it. Instantly the night air was cut through by the scent of vanilla. Infidel's nose twitched as she peeked back over her shoulder. Her face lit up with a huge grin as she spun around.

Tower was holding a silver plate on which set the tallest slice of cake I'd ever seen. The dessert was composed of seven inch-thick layers of golden cake separated by velvety frosting as white as fresh snow. The whole plate was dusted with confectioner's sugar and delicate daisy petals composed of frosting. As Infidel stared at the pastry, I felt a surge of delight to see her smiling so after such a long period of sadness, then a surge of jealousy that I wasn't responsible for her joy.

"I wrote the monks and asked them to hire the finest bakers. They placed the result into my book only hours ago. Enjoy!"

Tower produced a fork as he spoke, but it was too late. Infidel had already snatched up the confection with her fingers and was shoving it into her mouth. She might have been raised in a palace, but she'd had fifteen years in Commonground to shed any table manners. I hoped that Tower might be turned off by the sight of such messy hunger.

Instead, his own eyes as he stared at her frosting covered lips told of a deeper hunger still.

CHAPTER SEVENTEEN
THRONE

THE WAR DRUMS ended at dawn. Silver mist covered the black stones of the courtyard as the sunbeams seeped through the trees. The dragon-hunters woke to a breakfast of dried sausages and bananas.

Father Ver unrolled the golden map on a section of lichen-covered column. Everyone gathered around, chewing their sausages as they looked at the gleaming scroll.

Aurora was the first to break the silence. "So this is really going to happen. We're going face to face with Greatshadow."

Lord Tower nodded. "We've paid a steep price to come this far. Yet, when I look around this courtyard, I'm certain we shall succeed. Never before has the dragon faced a band of adventurers with our combined power."

"It isn't power that will guarantee our victory," said Father Ver. "It's the rightness of our cause. We're the champions of truth, pitting ourselves against the living embodiment of falsehood. We must not fail."

Zetetic opened his mouth, inhaling to speak.

Ver cut him off with a raised hand. "We know your thoughts on the matter."

"Not all of them," said the Deceiver. "You've dragged me back from the grave for this mission. That's an admission that you can't do this without me. I'd like to name my terms."

"You'll do what we tell you," said Father Ver, "or you will die."

"You admit I do have a choice," said Zetetic.

"You won't disobey," said Tower. "You've proven your instincts for self-preservation."

"Which is why I'm not thrilled about being drafted for this suicide mission. But, let's pretend for a moment that there's one chance in a million we'll beat Greatshadow. Our goal, while unlikely, isn't impossible. Assuming we come out of this alive, I have certain demands."

"You're in no position to issue demands," grumbled Father Ver.

Tower said, "I'd like to hear them."

Father Ver raised his eyebrows. Even the Deceiver looked surprised.

Tower said, "Believe it or not, Zetetic, I'd prefer you were a willing member of this party. If there is something you want that we can provide, tell us."

Zetetic looked off balance, as if he hadn't expected Tower to actually listen. He cleared his throat. "Very well. Of all the reasons I've heard for doing this, Relic's motive is the only one that makes sense to me. Look around you. We're standing in the middle of a fallen civilization once more advanced than our own. Within Greatshadow's lair, we'll find artifacts of these people. Our understanding of the world could be forever changed by what we learn of their science, their religion, and their art."

"The fact that their civilization failed is evidence that they had nothing of value to offer us," said Father Ver.

"Nonetheless, if we do survive this, I don't want to see the artifacts simply looted. I'll promise my willing cooperation on one condition: I get to review each item we recover for cultural, historical, and magical significance. I don't want to unearth these treasures merely so that the king can use the jewels to decorate his toilet."

"We cannot grant this," said Father Ver, wasting no time to consider the offer. "We shall bring in monks to catalog the treasure. The mercenaries will be compensated according to their contracts, and what remains will be divided between the church and the king."

"The church and the king are wealthy enough," said Zetetic. "The king will get the island and its natural wealth. The church will grow as it boasts of an evil vanquished. The only treasure I seek is knowledge. I've traveled the world, driven by my hunger to learn more. I've explored palaces beneath the waves, and studied in cities built upon clouds. Greatshadow's hoard is a doorway to a new land: the distant past."

Father Ver shook his head. "We know all we need to of the Vanished Kingdom. The thing we are most certain of is that these poor men followed mistaken religions. Time has erased their failed gods from memory; should any idols of these false faiths be found, we must destroy them so that no weak-minded men can be led astray."

"Your church claims to honor truth above all," said Zetetic. "Yet you seek to erase the truth of earlier times. We should document and study—"

"Enough!" Lord Tower slapped the Gloryhammer into his gauntleted palm. "Father Ver, the Church will remain the final arbiter in distributing the treasure. However, I find no problem with granting the Deceiver what he's asked for. Not control of the treasure, but the opportunity to study it. We must catalog the treasure anyway; Zetetic may oversee this work."

"This had better not slow down our pay," said Menagerie.

"It won't," said Tower.

"I'm surprised you're capitulating on this, Tower," said Zetetic.

"Surprised or not, I'm giving you my word," said the knight. "I want you to fight with your full heart. I want you" — he glanced around the gathering — "all of you, to understand the importance of our mission. As Reeker's death reminds us, Greatshadow's malignant intelligence spies upon mankind through every candle, waiting for any moment of carelessness to strike. After we slay the dragon, mankind need never fear fire again." He looked around the tangled jungle, and shook his head. "A once great kingdom, buried beneath a hostile wilderness. Such a waste, and Greatshadow is to blame. Here, life is brutal and short; the civilized concepts of mercy, compassion, and justice have failed to take hold against these twisted roots. These noble ideas are what we are truly fighting for. When Greatshadow falls, we shall tame this land. The world will no longer have any place where the wicked may hide from the righteous."

"I appreciate the attempt at inspiring us," said Aurora. "What I'm not hearing is how we're going to actually kill the dragon. Your hammer couldn't even touch the fire-drake."

"The drake was nothing but flame. Greatshadow has a body."

"True. But he's not just a body. Assuming we can kill the big lizard part of him, how do we touch his spirit?"

I knew she was digging for information about the Jagged Heart, but Tower didn't give her any satisfaction. "An excellent question," he said. "We will launch our assault on the beast from the ancient temple that lies below." He tapped a star-shaped chamber on the map.

"Why is that going to make any difference?" asked Menagerie.

Zetetic said, "Despite Ver's insistence that his religion has all the answers, all temples are imbued by the collective energies of their worshippers with special properties. The veil between the material and immaterial is especially thin in these places. Thanks to my metaphysical flexibility, I can manipulate the temple energies to open a door to the spirit world. Father Ver is in possession of a Writ of Judgment. I will send him into the spirit world to confront Greatshadow's soul."

"He's that powerful?" Aurora asked.

Father Ver shook his head. "Even if I weren't reading the scroll, the sentence of death written upon it comes from the highest earthly power of the church, the Voice of the Book. The beast's soul will fade when confronted by his truthful verdict as frost retreats before sunlight."

Aurora looked dubious; frost sparkled on her cheeks as the morning brightened.

Lord Tower said, "With Greatshadow's soul destroyed, slaying the beast's body will be my duty."

"Buhuh pluh?" asked No-Face.

Menagerie nodded. "Your plan does seems a little... spare. What happens if the priest fails? What happens if the dragon fries you?"

Tower nodded. "If needed, I may also travel to the spirit realm, since I have a weapon that my harm the dragon's spirit. As for Greatshadow's body, you killed two dragons in Commonground. You're the back-up plan."

"I appreciate your confidence," said Menagerie.

Tower looked back at the map. "Of course, there are challenges before we reach the dragon. Most of this palace used to be above ground. Lava flows have covered much of it; earthquakes have wiped out entire sections of a complex that once covered two square miles. Previous explorers have wiggled through a maze of narrow tunnels to try to survey what they could. However, if the monks have interpreted the map correctly, the depression in the center of the courtyard was once a ceremonial well before it was filled with debris. We can dig straight down one hundred feet through the courtyard to reach deep passageways that may still be intact, then follow these to the temple."

Tower pointed at the spot in the courtyard where they'd have to dig. Menagerie looked at the jumbled boulders then said, "I hope the Gloryhammer can turn into a Gloryshovel. Even though I have a mole tattoo, digging through a hundred feet of rock might take a while."

"We can be down below in ten minutes, if Father Ver doesn't screw with me," said Zetetic.

"Behave and he won't have to," said Tower. "Show us what you can do."

"Very well." Zetetic glanced at No-Face, their gazes locking for the briefest of seconds. "I possess the ability to move rocks through pure mental force."

He held his hands toward the rock pile, his brow furrowed. Everyone looked at the rocks, anticipating a show. Seconds passed, stretching into minutes. Father Ver turned his back to the Deceiver, scowling deeply. Still, nothing happened. Aurora shook her head. You could tell she didn't think Zetetic could do it.

No-Face kept staring. I floated over the boulder-filled pit. I held my ghost breath, catching hint of a faint rumble below. Without warning, fist-sized stones beneath me began to dance, bouncing into the air a few inches at first, then a few feet. A stone the size of a watermelon stood on end, then slowly rose, wobbling, until suddenly it shot out in a long arc over the jungle, vanishing from sight. The ground trembled as stone after stone rose; chunks of rock as big as rowboats were lurching heavenward. Waves of dust rolled over the courtyard as uncounted tons of stone sailed out of sight.

"Damn," I said, looking back at Relic. "I wish I'd known this guy back when I was looting these ruins. I mean, exploring. Exploring these ruins."

You could be exploring the ruins now, thought Relic. *You could confirm that this does, in fact, lead to an open passage.*

I slapped myself on my intangible forehead. What was I waiting for? I dove into the solid ground like it was a swimming pool. Instantly, I regretted it. It was one of the few moments since I'd died that I truly felt dead, cut off from light and air, surrounded by lifeless earth. It took all my willpower to continue sinking into the suffocating darkness. I couldn't help but think about my body, enshrouded by silent blackness, six feet of sandy soil forever pressing down. I hadn't thought much about my old shell, but burial now struck me as a cruel thing to do to a body. Still, what was the alternative? Reeker hadn't made cremation look attractive. If I'd had a say in deciding my final resting place, I'd have asked that my corpse be placed inside a giant glass jar full of pure grain alcohol. Set me in the corner of the *Black Swan* and let life go on around me. Of course, if everyone did this, bars would be pretty overcrowded with pickled mummies. Worse, it'd waste an awful lot of booze.

I have no way of judging how far I sank before my head emerged into the hallway. It glowed with the same pale spirit light I'd found in the pygmy tunnels. Tile murals decorated both walls. Beneath thick layers of grime, once vivid colors depicted a procession of what I assumed to be royalty. The people portrayed were tall and slender, with bone-white skin, the color of pygmy flesh without dye. Both women and men were bare-breasted; both sexes wore bright green skirts rather than pants. The men's legs showed from the mid-thigh down, while the women were covered all the way to the ankle. Everyone portrayed wore copious amounts of jewelry; I peered closer, trying to figure out if the yellow gleam beneath the dust was actual gold, or merely paint. I instinctively scraped at the grime, but, of course, my nails passed right through.

The men were depicted with large jade rings in their noses and ears; the women had no piercings, but their hair was piled high on their heads and bound up in coils of gold. In the background of the mural were a dozen buildings ablaze with color; bright red and yellow flags decorated bamboo mansions, long since rotted away. Beyond the cityscape, the jungle looked much the same, the towering trees flecked with red. Blood-tangle vine must have been a nuisance even then.

The procession was accompanied by animals on leashes — tall dogs with wasp-thin waists, yellow and black tigers, and some big-ass praying mantises. I'd seen plenty of giant bugs in the jungle, but you could have put a saddle on these things.

I leaned closer, studying the legs of the insects. The joints were ringed with small dots, like rivets. They looked familiar. Then it hit me — the bugs were machines, like the mechanical tiger that had given Infidel a hard time. I examined a tiger in the mural: it, too, was plainly mechanical beneath its yellow and black paint. Could Infidel have fought this very same cat?

Before I could explore further, dust began to rain down from the walls as the surrounding earth groaned. Up ahead, shafts of light began to jab into the darkness as the fallen rubble was jerked skyward by the Deceiver's telekinesis. I squinted as I made my way through the dust toward the ever-brightening light. The last of the rocks lifted, revealing a ragged hole in the roof. I peeked to see how high it was, but jumped back as a boa constrictor slithered through the hole, scanning the hallway with copper-colored eyes. Its tongue flicked in and out, tasting the air as its seemingly endless body flowed into the hall.

The serpent erupted into a sudden fit of coughing. After catching its breath, it twisted its head back up into the hole and shouted, "It'sss dusssty, but looksss sssafe!"

The shaft of sunlight suddenly grew a dozen times brighter. I retreated back, shielding my eyes, as Lord Tower landed with a clatter in the center of the hall, the Gloryhammer casting shadows out behind him. He raised the hammer over his head as he turned in a slow circle to study his surroundings. The gold glittering in the mosaic caught his eye, and he wiped away the dust with gauntleted fingers. My hate for him deepened exponentially. It wasn't enough that got to kiss Infidel? He got to explore ruins more effectively as well?

"Paint?" asked the boa.

Tower flicked his right hand, and the gauntlet of the faith armor sprouted razorblade fingernails. He delicately grabbed a single golden tile the size of an olive pit and twisted, popping it free. He rolled it in his palm, letting it catch the light.

"Sssolid gold," said the boa, its tongue flickering near the metal. He looked up and down the hall. "If the gemsssstonesss are alssso real, this hall alone is pricelesss. Once we melt down the metalsss and—"

"You'd do that?" Tower asked. As he spoke, ropes were dropping into the hole from above.

"Do what?" asked the boa. "Melt down the metalsss?"

"As much as I hate to side with Zetetic, it seems wasteful to destroy such a work of art," said Tower.

The boa's nostrils twitched. "I don't sssee how we'll ssspend the money otherwissse. It would be difficult to carry an entire hallway back to Commonground."

Tower placed the gold tile back in place, carefully balancing it so that it wouldn't fall. He didn't say anything; perhaps he was shocked by Menagerie's attitude. I really couldn't claim any moral high ground. If I'd found this wall a year ago, I'd have chipped out the more valuable bits myself.

No-Face and the Deceiver were the next ones down. The Deceiver whistled as he looked at the murals.

No-Face chuckled, then said, "Wuh ruh!"

"Yeah," said the boa, "we're rich."

Zetetic moved toward the dusty wall. "I can clear this dust so we can get a better look." He sucked in a lungful of air, then exhaled, his breath swiftly turning into a gale force wind that blew the dirt from a ten-foot section of the mural, sending everyone else into a sneezing fit. The Deceiver's eyes lit up like a child being offered candy. He leapt to the exposed artwork, tracing his fingers along a yellow circle near the top of the mosaic, a single piece of glazed ceramic nearly a yard across.

"A sun disk!" he said, excited. "It's rare to find these intact,,. Judicious Merchant said that he found so many shattered, he was certain that they'd been destroyed deliberately. He speculated that a new god arose in opposition to the sun god these disks represent."

"All it representsss to me isss money," said the boa. "Large artifacts bring good prices."

"How can you be so crass?" asked Zetetic. He looked at Tower. "This is precisely why we need to protect these treasures."

"Protect them for what?" asked the snake. "The world hasss carried on without them for thousssandsss of yearsss. Who is harmed if thessse thingsss are sold to the highessst bidder?"

"Tower, if the king wants to civilize this island, think of how much easier it will be to draw settlers if there are artistic wonders in place to delight them," said Zetetic.

"You'll draw more people once word sssspreadsss of lossst gold to be found," said the boa.

Aurora and Father Ver were down now; Infidel followed a second later, with Relic clinging to her back.

Father Ver looked at the sun disk. He looked toward Tower, his eyes fixed on the Gloryhammer as he said, "May I?"

Tower handed over the magic weapon as casually as if the priest had asked him to pass him the salt at dinner.

With a grunt, the Truthspeaker swung the hammer, smashing it into the center of the ancient artifact. The disk rained to the floor in a hundred shards.

Father Ver tossed the hammer back to Tower. "The false idols of doomed men aren't treasure; they're physical blasphemy, fit only for destruction."

Zetetic stared at the shattered disk, slack-jawed. His face hardened as he turned his eyes toward the Truthspeaker. He lunged, hands reaching for the holy man's throat as he shouted, "You son of a—"

No-Face caught the Deceiver by the neck and threw him to the ground. He dropped his iron ball, letting the chain catch half an inch from Zetetic's face. The Deceiver flinched.

"I'll behave now," he said.

"Maybe he will," said Menagerie, his snake-eyes gleaming. "But I mussst protessst. That disssk was more valuable intact than broken. We're due a percentage of the treasssure. I mussst insissst that we do not decreassse the value of the artifactsss we find."

"You're the one wanting to melt down the gold," said Tower, sounding exasperated.

"Whuh buh hukha?" asked No-Face.

"He'ssss right," said Menagerie. "We mussst alssso refill the hole ssso that Hookhand cannot loot thisss hall while we explore further."

Tower raised his hand and said, "This debate is over." He glared at Father Ver. "Leave the idols and artwork we pass unmolested." He turned to Menagerie. "You aren't owed a single coin until Greatshadow's dead. Once we've accomplished that mission, we'll secure the area. Until then, ignore any treasure we happen upon."

The boa turned his pointy face away and grumbled, "You're the bossss."

"Gruh," said No-Face, with a shrug. He looked down, then offered Zetetic an outstretched hand to help him back to his feet.

"Lord Tower, if I may offer guidance, this way leads to the King's Court." Relic pointed westward with his spindly arm. I noticed that his cloak was stirring in a slight breeze. Air was flowing around him, the dust in the sunlit circle rising up in a swirl.

Aurora held her hand toward the breeze. "It's hot as a furnace," she said.

"It will only get hotter as we descend," said Relic.

The air cooled as Aurora whispered a prayer. "No sense in being uncomfortable."

"Menagerie, you take point," said Tower. "Heat shouldn't bother you as a snake. Aurora, you're next. Keep cooling the air as it passes you. Deceiver, you and No-Face stay close behind her. Father Ver and myself will follow." He looked to Relic. "You and the War Doll will watch our backs." He glanced down the corridor, holding his hammer high, his eyes searching the shadows. "Everyone stay alert. We have no idea what we might face down here."

"There's a damn dragon, for one thing," muttered Zetetic.

Tower nodded to Menagerie, still in his boa constrictor form. "Move out."

The giant serpent slithered off down the hall much faster than anything without legs should move. Aurora trotted after him, and everyone fell into place behind her. I floated next to Relic and said, "So, have you really been here before?"

Does it matter? thought Relic.

"You said you hate Greatshadow. I thought if you really did come from the Vanished Kingdom, and Greatshadow destroyed civilization back then, it might explain your grudge."

A reasonable theory.

"But is it right?"

Relic shook his head. *Without the primal dragons, there would never have been a Vanished Kingdom. Humans lived as little more than animals before three thousand years ago. But, as the primal dragons merged with their various elemental forces, previously untameable aspects of nature suddenly possessed intelligence. Men had always prayed to gods; they adapted to pray and make offerings to dragons. Luckily for man, dragons respond well to flattery.*

"Then what did destroy this place?"

Men themselves. You saw Father Ver destroy the sun-disk. His is not the first religion ever to loathe other religions. In the final days of the Vanished Kingdom, a god called Nowowon rose in power. He was a god of destruction. You find his image throughout the kingdom carved in obsidian.

"I've found a lot of obsidian statues, but they're always of different creatures."

Nowowon had no fixed form. He took the shape of each follower's greatest fear. His followers hoped to avoid their own destruction by destroying the worshippers of other gods to appease him. In the end they wound up destroying themselves as the entire civilization collapsed; self-destruction gave Nowowon his greatest pleasure.

"And Greatshadow just moved into the ruins?"

Greatshadow was always present. No civilization can exist without the use of fire. In his earliest days as a primal dragon, Greatshadow enjoyed the respect given to him by humanity. But as the Vanished Kingdom aged and grew corrupt, Greatshadow grew increasingly disgusted with mankind. Once the Vanished Kingdom fell, Greatshadow decided he preferred

the wilderness that surrounded him to the company of men.
He's stopped every attempt to restore advanced civilizations on
this island. The pygmies escape his notice by living in harmony
with their surroundings.

I was intrigued by this news, and had a dozen questions, but
before I could ask them the passage we traveled opened into
a huge, circular chamber a hundred yards across, ringed with
columns. We all craned our necks as we entered, looking up at
the high cone-shaped roof. A checkerboard pattern spiraled up
the steep walls, producing a feeling of vertigo.

In the center of the chamber was a raised platform. Upon
this sat a mirrored glass pyramid roughly ten feet along the
base. Sitting upon this, perfectly balanced, was a cube of what
looked to be black, seamless iron the same height. Perched atop
this was an equally large sphere of polished jade, seemingly
carved from a single block of stone. My ghost heart skipped a
beat as I looked at it. I couldn't even begin to guess its value.

Finally, on top of these three, perfect solids, sat a throne of
gold.

"Muh fuh uh," said No-Face, softly.

"It's magnificent," whispered Zetetic, sounding awed as he
looked at the tower of geometric shapes. "I wonder what these
objects must have meant?"

The boa constrictor rose up next to him, its eyes glazed. "I
can tell you what the throne meant," he said. "The man who
ssssat upon that throne ruled the damn world."

Father Ver spat on the dusty floor. "The man who sat on that
throne is dead. No one remembers his name."

As dazzled as I was by the wealth before me, Father Ver's words
struck me. What did wealth mean if you could afford to build
something like this, then vanish so completely from memory?
The man who sat upon that throne had probably thought he was
pretty important, but time had swept him away completely. Since
everything a man might do with his life would be erased by time,
perhaps my grandfather was right. Maybe the only sensible path

was to live naked in a tree, eat fruit and bask in the sun. Not that this had been Father Ver's point at all.

Menagerie, however, had different feelings on the matter. He slithered across the room, his serpentine belly somehow finding purchase on the smooth surfaces of the pyramid.

"Don't climb it!" cried Zetetic. "It's precariously balanced!"

"Precariousss my assss," said Menagerie as he zipped up the cube and slid over the sphere to the throne. "There'sss an iron rod or sssomething ssstuck through the middle to hold everything in place."

He slid his chin on the throne itself. The boa pulled loop after loop of his body onto the seat. In a flicker, Menagerie's human form appeared on the throne. "I know you said the debate about treasure was over, but look at this! We have to take measures to protect our finds. We can't leave this here for Hookhand to just walk in and grab!"

"No one is going to grab it," said Tower. "The sheer weight will protect it from being stolen."

"Are you really willing to take that chance? If you come back tomorrow and it's gone, you'll hate yourself." Menagerie rubbed his hands along the golden arms of the throne.

"I assure you, I'll be able to sleep in peace," said Tower. "Come down at once and let's move on."

Menagerie ground his teeth, glaring at the knight. Then he said, tersely, "As you wish."

He clamped his hands around the armrests as he stood up, his feet on the jade sphere. As he rose, there was a loud click. From beneath the floor, there was a ticking sound, like the world's largest clock counting off seconds.

"That can't be good," said Zetetic.

Menagerie picked up his hands from the armrests. "Nobody panic. It's probably just—"

Before he could finish the sentence, the ticking stopped. The jade globe snapped open, a wedge widening into a giant mouth full of saw-edged green teeth. The mouth proved larger than the footprint of the throne. The golden chair dropped straight down into the maw, carrying Menagerie with it.

The jaws clamped shut with a loud clang that bit right through the throne. The metal posts and backrest spun off through the air, flying twenty feet before clattering loudly on the floor. Menagerie's torso from the belly-button up tumbled through the air. His legs were completely gone. The sphere spun around to face the rest of the party with an eyeless face, as its mouth once more opened in a toothy smile.

CHAPTER EIGHTEEN
DEVOURED BY THE MONSTER

MENAGERIE'S TORSO BOUNCED once on the floor. His left hand flopped limply against a small squiggle tattooed behind his ear and he suddenly vanished. I blinked, wondering where he'd gone, but had no time to dwell on the matter.

The sphere, the cube, and the pyramid had all separated, hovering in the air, spinning to face new targets. The jade sphere shot toward No-Face as a deafening, high-pitched scream erupted from within. With only inches to spare, the faceless mercenary leaped from the path of the green ball, leaving the toothy maw aimed at Father Ver. Yet as No-Face dodged, he let his iron ball and chain trail behind him. The giant mouth snapped down as the weapon passed through its mineral lips. Shards of jade sprayed out as the teeth snapped on the iron links. With a grunt, No-Face planted his feet and jerked the chain taut. The jade orb spun dizzily as it cut an arc, narrowly missing Father Ver. Infidel dropped her pack and leapt into the curving path of the spinning sphere, drawing back her fist.

A thunderclap echoed through the chamber as she landed her punch. The gleaming green stone shattered, sending sharp, fist-sized chunks in all directions. Chewed-up bits of golden throne bounced on the marble floor. What must have been hundreds of concentric platinum hoops, in diameters from ten feet to smaller than a wedding ring, spilled out, rolling everywhere.

There was no sign of Menagerie's legs amid the rubble, though I didn't exactly spend a lot of time looking. My attention was drawn to the cube and the pyramid, which were hanging in the air, unseen motors within whining like a billion mosquitoes. Unlike the sphere, no mouths opened on these solids as they selected targets and launched forward.

The iron cube raced toward Infidel. She reared back to punch it, but the flying cube smashed her in mid-swing, flattening her against its face. The whining, buzzing noise within rose in pitch as it built speed, pushing her with it. With a shock wave that knocked Relic, Father Ver, and the Deceiver from their feet, the cube hammered into the chamber wall.

I thought of the flattened skeletons I'd found embedded in stone and felt sick. Any normal person would be nothing more than a smear of blood after such a blow. Yet, when the cube pulled back, Infidel looked intact; the marble panel behind her was shattered into gravel, and she was driven into the dense volcanic soil behind. She looked dazed, but was plainly alive.

The cube whirled and targeted Lord Tower, zipping in a straight line toward the knight. Tower was hovering an inch or two in the air. Steel spikes snapped out of the soles of his metal boots and he kicked down onto the marble floor, driving the spikes into the stone. The cube hit him with an ear-splitting *WHANG*, driving him backward. Marble fragments flew as Tower's boot carved a long, ragged gouge in the floor. The pitch of the unseen engines grew ever louder, but the cube's speed was visibly diminishing. I wondered if Tower could actually stop it before they reached the wall.

My eyes were drawn elsewhere before I saw the outcome of Tower's braking action. Amidst the larger chunks of chewed-up throne, I spotted what looked like a bit of brownish red intestine wriggling on a scrap of purple silk. I looked closer, in morbid fascination, wondering if Menagerie had been chewed up so completely by the inner workings of the sphere that this was all that was left. I stared closer, and suddenly understood what I was seeing: half an earthworm, pinched off at one end, writhing in pain.

Was there a second half to this worm amid the rubble? Could Menagerie be restored if we could join the two halves? I turned to find Relic to share my theory, but was distracted as the glass pyramid flashed past me.

Unlike the straight paths the sphere and cube had followed, the pyramid moved chaotically through the air, darting a few yards in one direction, then shooting off at a crisp angle without losing speed in defiance of all logic and physics. Its glass faces were cycling through colors, pale blues, bloody reds, banana-yellows. It rang with a sound like off-key chimes as it jerked through the air. No-Face chased after it, trying to shatter it with his ball and chain, but the pyramid would tumble aside before his blows connected, shooting off in some new random direction.

Aurora, meanwhile, was grabbing the fog that surrounded her, shaping and pressing the mist into her palm until she'd packed a ball of ice the size of a grapefruit. She hung back, studying the pyramid's lurching flight path, her eyes narrowed. Perhaps she figured out a pattern, or perhaps it was only luck, but when she reared back and flung the ice-ball, aiming to the left of the pyramid, her target obliged by darting left. The ice-ball hit the triangle face dead center, passing through the glass as if it wasn't even there. Instantly, the neighboring face flashed green as the ice-ball shot out. No-Face, still chasing the dancing pyramid, wound up getting punched right in the gut by the projectile. He stumbled, off balance, clutching his belly.

"Sorry!" shouted Aurora. She turned her eyes away from the pyramid for only a second, but in that second all the faces turned black as it charged her. She looked up, raising an ice-covered fist as the pyramid overtook her. Instead of the crash of glass hitting ice, the collision unfolded with eerie silence as Aurora simply sank into the ebony surface. The pyramid tumbled as it passed over her, kissing the floor where she stood before shooting straight up, once more flashing through a spectrum of bright shades.

Aurora was gone.

Meanwhile, Lord Tower had finally won his contest of momentum against the cube. He now held it motionless in mid-air, with a single hand holding the Gloryhammer across the cube face while his free hand popped open the compartment on his belt that held his magic notebook. The visor of his helmet lifted on its own as he awkwardly flipped through the book with one hand. Finding the page he wanted, he brought the book to his face and bit down on the edge, trapping a page open as he let go with his hand and brought his fingers to the long, skinny item sketched on the page. He drew his hand back, tugging a loop of leather from the paper, followed by a long shaft of narwhale tusk that he kept working out a few feet at a time, continually adjusting his grip. The bone-white shaft proved to be eighteen feet long, tipped with a gleaming heart-shaped blade of pinkish ice.

If this wasn't the Jagged Heart, it's hard to imagine what was.

Tower let the book tumble from his mouth. With a grunt, he pushed the iron cube away from him, tapping it with the Gloryhammer so that it flew back a half dozen yards. The iron block whined as it shot toward the knight once more. Tower brought the tip of the harpoon down, dropping the Gloryhammer to grasp the shaft with both hands.

The iron cube ground to a halt as the ice tip burrowed into its solid face, sinking nearly a foot. Cracks spread across the iron as the whining noise within changed to a growling grind. Tower twisted the shaft and the entire cube shattered. Fragments of springs and gears bounced all around him.

The knight didn't waste any time savoring his victory. Instead, he charged back across the room, his spiked iron boots shooting out sparks as he ran, the harpoon held like a lance. The glass pyramid flashed white on all faces as Tower neared, a bright, burning light nearly impossible to look at.

I turned away just as the light suddenly dimmed and a cacophony of breaking glass reached my ears. I looked back and saw that the pyramid was gone; all that remained was glassy dust scattered across the floor like snowflakes.

"Uhrurruh!" No-Face shouted, dropping to his hands and knees. He ran his fingers through the glass dust. "Uhrurruh!" he cried again.

Tower surveyed the scene. "Is everyone okay?" he asked.

"Aurora was inside the pyramid when you broke it," said Zetetic, now back on his feet. He nudged his boot around in the glassy remains, until he found a splinter the size of a man's thumb. He picked it up and looked at it closely. "She's gone forever, I fear."

"Nuh!" cried No-Face.

Tower, his faceplate still open, turned pale. "I didn't know," he said.

"What could you have done differently if you had known?" said Father Ver, still sitting on the floor. "You couldn't let the thing keep tumbling until it had swallowed us all."

No-Face stood up, his whole body trembling. He stared at Lord Tower with his single, misshapen eye, his fists clenched. He screamed at the knight, "Yuh guhdum muhfugguh! Yuh kuh uhrurruh!"

"It was an accident," said Tower, lowering his faceplate.

Relic was back on his feet, wandering through the rubble that covered the floor. He pushed aside bits of shattered jade and chewed up gold with the tip of his staff. At last he leaned over and picked up a small, moist, wriggling bit of meat, then moved to the other half of the worm I'd spotted on the silk.

"Is this going to work?" I asked. "Can you read Menagerie's thoughts?"

Relic didn't answer me as he placed the two halves together, letting the bisected worms touch at their shared wound.

There was a rapid blur of motion, as the thin, squiggling worms gained mass and muscle. In the span of a heartbeat, the worm was gone and Menagerie sat before us, restored once more. The speed of the recovery left me seeing double.

Only, I wasn't seeing double.

There were two Menageries, sitting facing each other, both the size of pygmies.

"What the hell?" they both asked in unison. Their voices were high-pitched squeaks as they asked, "How did... It wasn't supposed to work like..." They each reached out to touch the other, their fingertips tapping together in mirror symmetry.

Both reached for tattoos on their shins and suddenly two small bears were staring at one another. "Terrific," both bears said, in a resigned tone.

Father Ver walked toward the twin bears and looked down, his eyes narrowed. "You're to blame for this! You were ordered to ignore the treasure. You've cost us the ogress and the War Doll by your disobedience."

Relic shook his head. "The War Doll is still functioning."

Infidel punctuated his sentence by tearing free of her stony outline, staggering onto the floor, still looking dazed.

The Truthspeaker continued to glare down at the small bears. "Disobey again and your contract will be terminated."

The Menageries shifted back into their twin, pint-sized human forms. They both placed their hands across their knees and sighed. They said in their stereo voices, "You don't need to threaten me. No one feels worse about this than I do. The sight of all that gold made me stupid."

"Muh fuh," said No-Face, looming over his fellow Goon. "Nuh whoowa smuh guh?"

"Yeah, you're the smart Goon now," the Menageries said, shaking their heads.

The faceless giant held out his hands. Menagerie took them, and let himselves be pulled back to their feet.

While this was happening, I'm certain that I'm the only one who noticed that the Deceiver had pulled out a piece of cloth and wrapped the largest shard of glass within it, stuffing it into his bag.

"Let's take an hour to rest," said Tower, sliding the harpoon back into the book. "There are prayers of penance I need to perform for having allowed a book to touch the ground. No-Face, you're bleeding; let Father Ver stitch you up." The big man's hands and knees were red with blood from where he dug through the glass fragments searching for Aurora. Finally,

Tower turned to Relic and said, "Make certain your War Doll is still functioning. If you need more time for repairs, let me know."

"Of course," said Relic. He left the others and headed toward the shadows of the hall where we had first entered. Infidel sat there, crouched down out of sight of the others. She'd removed her shining steel bra, which was squashed flat. She was hammering the flattened plates back into cup shapes with her fists, using her knee caps as a guide.

"I'm sick of this," she grumbled softly as Relic approached.

"Patience. You may shed your disguise soon enough."

"I don't mean I'm sick of my disguise. I'm sick of this mission. Stagger and I goofed around in these ruins for a decade before he got killed. This team is dropping like flies. Maybe Aurora and I weren't always friends, but she deserved a better death than that."

Relic squatted down beside her. With his limbs hidden within the confines of his cloak, he looked more like a heap of rotting rags than a man. "We can't be certain that Aurora is dead. Her thoughts simply vanished when the pyramid swallowed her. Perhaps she was transported elsewhere."

I also had my doubts she was dead. Unlike Ivory Blade or Reeker, Aurora hadn't lingered behind as a ghost. Or would a human ghost and an ogre ghost go to the same afterlife? The Great Sea Above she'd described certainly was nothing like the church's version of heaven. Since the ghosts usually only lingered a moment, had I simply missed her in all the excitement?

Infidel tried the repaired cup on for size. It was still dented, but it did vaguely resemble the curve of her breast again. "The Black Swan said that only two people survived this quest, and made it pretty clear I was one of them. Tower's probably the other survivor, given his bag of tricks. It doesn't bother you that your death has been foretold? Why don't you get out while you still can?"

"Whatever the Black Swan saw, she's already altered our fates. It's possible we will all survive, and the dragon will die."

Infidel didn't look at him as she worked on the second bra cup. Her lips were pursed tightly together for several seconds before she said, softly, "Or maybe all of us will die. Even me."

I put my ghostly hand on her shoulder, wanting to comfort her. I'd never heard such despair in her voice.

"I thought I was done with this," she said, hammering the metal on her knee.

I didn't think she was talking about the bra.

Relic nodded. "And now you are afraid again."

She picked up the cup-shaped steel and began to smooth it between her fingers. "I haven't felt like this since I left the palace. I used to be so timid and terrified. I never wanted to feel that way again."

I was surprised to find out she'd been afraid of anything as a child. It seemed counter-intuitive. As a princess, I would have guessed she'd been protected from everything.

"I was treated like a china doll," she said. "I wasn't allowed to play outside because I might fall and get scratched. I couldn't sit too near a window, because the sun might burn my skin. I slept with armed guards stationed at my bed because my father was afraid of kidnappers. My whole family had tasters who sampled our food to make certain it wasn't poison. Being constantly reminded I was so fragile left me in a constant state of terror."

Relic nodded knowingly, but I had trouble imagining a fragile, frightened Infidel.

She sighed. "I wanted to do this treasure hunt as a quick smash and grab, making stuff up as we went along, the way Stagger and I always played it. Events never got out of control when we were together, because we never tried to control them. We just moved on whim and instinct, living fast and fearless. Now, Tower is talking about destiny and history, the Black Swan is playing with people's lives like they're pawns in some game, and it sounds like my father is already studying maps of this island figuring out where to build his new palace. I can't help feeling that all this planning has put things out of control. We're all going to die."

Relic rose up, stretching his back, sinews popping. His hunch disappeared as he rose to the height of an ordinary man. His body was still hidden by the tattered cloak. His eyes glowed like red embers in the shadow of his hood.

"Perhaps you're saying these things hoping I will reassure you," he said, in a stern tone. "I need offer no comfort. All the strength you need to prevail pulses within your veins. You ceased to be a frightened little girl the second you devoured the blood of a primal dragon. A dragon soul shares your body now, a soul more powerful than the sniveling child you once were. Surrender yourself to the dragon inside and our victory is assured."

Infidel shook her head slowly as she tested the second cup. Satisfied, she worked silently with the link of chain that held the cups together, crimping the ends between her fingernails, then slipping the whole thing on from the back like a vest before pinching the final connecting link between the cups shut at the front.

She stood up. Relic, still standing straight, looked down upon her, a good head taller. She peered up into his glowing eyes. "Who the hell are you?" she asked.

"I'm the second survivor of this mission," he said.

"How can you know this? Are you a seer as well as a mind-reader?"

"No," said Relic, as his head lowered once more, returning his outline to his hunchbacked profile. "But you cannot imagine the trials I've endured to reach this moment. There is nothing left for me to fear. Not even Greatshadow."

"So tell me about the trials. Tell me who you are. Why should I keep listening to you?"

Relic shook his head. "I must remain an enigma until we

achieve our goals. Greatshadow can pluck thoughts from the minds of others. If you knew my true identity, he might learn it as well. I'm the one enemy he should fear above all others... because he doesn't even know I exist."

"Why are you his enemy? Why do you hate the dragon so?"

Relic clenched his gnarled fist. "This too, must remain my secret. But know that my hatred for the beast is deep and righteous. Turning back is unthinkable. I cannot live any longer in a world that contains Greatshadow."

I rolled my eyes and said, "I'm really getting tired of your mystery man act. Just answer her questions."

Relic ignored me.

Infidel shrugged. "Fine. I've lived with your mystery man act this long, I can put up with it for another day."

"And your fears? Can you put them behind you?"

She pulled back her shoulders and clenched her fists. "Dragons are cold-blooded. That's the only blood I've got now. So cold my heart's just a block of ice, incapable of fear, or doubt, or remorse. Timid little Innocent has long since been devoured by the monster." She cracked her knuckles, as all emotion drained from her face. She looked like a machine once more. "Let's go kick Greatshadow's scaly ass."

CHAPTER NINETEEN
ROUGH TREATMENT

AFTER EVERYONE HAD rested, we pressed deeper into the palace complex. The rooms we passed through were mostly barren. After all this time, I suppose items made of wood or cloth would have turned to dust, but it was curious that there were no ordinary objects made of stone or ceramic, which would have endured. The emptiness hinted that the people who had dwelled here had time to pack before they abandoned the place. On the other hand, it was tough to ignore the gems and gold embedded in the countless mosaics. Certainly, if people had time to pack up their dinner plates and chamber pots, they would have taken their valuables as well.

With Aurora gone, everyone was sweating profusely. The narrow passageway we followed descended at a rather sharp angle, and stretched for what must have been at least a mile. It made me wonder what the ancients had been digging for.

"It doesn't make sense," the Menageries grumbled. They were once more in their human forms, walking in mirror symmetry; as one miniature Goon swung his left foot forward, the other moved his right.

"What doesn't make sense?" asked Tower.

"We're heading toward a temple, right? This doesn't seem like a good location to attract followers. Why put it so deep inside a mountain?"

"Muhskuh wuh thuh," said No-Face.

The Menageries chuckled, a sound like chattering chipmunks.

"What did he say?" I asked.

The mosquitoes were worse then, answered Relic.

"Obviously, they were a mining culture," said Zetetic. "You

don't produce the gold and gemstones we've seen simply panning in streams. These people spent a lot of time underground."

Relic nodded. "There was spiritual significance to the depths as well. The trees sink their roots deep into the soil. The ancients deduced that the earth was the origin of all life; the ground was regarded as sacred. Digging into the earth produced precious metals and priceless gems, further evidence that the divine dwelled beneath the surface. The deeper they dug, the greater the treasures produced. Temples were built as deep as possible so that the gods could better hear the prayers of the priests."

Father Ver shook his head. "How sad to live oblivious to the truth."

"A truth contained in a book your own church didn't discover until a mere thousand years ago," said Zetetic. "You have plain evidence men existed long before then. Does it strike you as unfair that your Divine Author condemned so many generations of men to ignorance by hiding the book?"

Father Ver started to answer, but Tower raised his gauntlet. "This is the wrong time and place to debate this. According to the map, we've reached the entrance to the temple." He glanced at Relic. "I assume you can verify this?"

Relic nodded. We were in a long narrow room filled with arches covered with pale blue tiles. At the end of the hall there was a circle of stone, nearly fifteen feet across. Relic pointed to the stone and said, "That stone rolls aside. Beyond is a spiral stairway built of human bones leading down seven hundred seventy-seven steps. At the bottom is a natural cavern filled with gleaming crystals hundreds of feet tall; this was the most sacred spot in the kingdom."

I perked up. "If Zetetic is right, and the veil between the spirit world and the realm of the living is thin in temples, could I escape? Could I come back to life?"

Relic didn't look at me as he led the others toward the stone door. He replied mentally, saying, *You've already escaped the pull of the spirit world, Blood-Ghost. Abandon hope; you will never be alive again.*

"You know, you could sugar coat that a little. There's no need to be rude. You still need me as your spy, remember?"

For all the information you've so far gathered, I believe my circumstances would be materially unchanged without you.

I punched him in the back of the head with a phantom fist. It passed right through, but I felt a teeny bit better.

We reached the end of the hall. I'd seen this type of door before, a giant disk of stone sitting inside a matching groove. The ancients were marvelous engineers. Though the stone weighed several tons, no doubt it was so well balanced even a child could move it.

The disk was ringed with cup-sized indentations. Tower placed his hands into the holes, then flexed to roll the stone aside.

The door didn't budge. Maybe it wasn't that well balanced after all.

"It's locked," said Relic.

"I see," said Tower. "How do we unlock it?"

Relic ran his gnarled hand along the blue tiles that decorated the arch surrounding the stone. He found the one he was looking for and pressed it. It slid aside, revealing a shaft about six inches wide. He thrust his skinny arm into it. "There's a lever that releases the..." A muffled *SNAP* caused his sentence to go unfinished. He pulled out his hand, opening his fingers to reveal the rusty remains of an iron rod. He sighed. "Not all ancient artifacts are as well maintained as the War Doll."

He looked back over his shoulder and motioned that Infidel should step forward. She placed her hands into the same holes Tower had tried. The muscles of her back bulged in sculpted relief as she strained to move the door. Whatever mechanism held the stone resisted even her magnificent muscles.

"This looks like a job for a ghost," I said, poking my head into the wall to examine the lock mechanism. Unfortunately, I couldn't make heads or tails of the jumbled of rusted gears and levers embedded in the wall. I drifted through the door completely, into the stairwell on the other side. I discovered that it no longer contained a staircase; the seven hundred and seventy-seven steps of bone must have crumbled to dust, though I could see the spiral holes in the wall where they'd once been anchored. Far below, in what must have been the temple, there was an eerie orange light that looked like boiling lava. The heat was unbearable.

I poked my head back through the door to tell Relic that it looked like the temple had been claimed by the volcano. I flinched when I found the Gloryhammer flying toward my face. Fortunately, it passed straight through my nose and sank into the two-foot-thick slab of stone I was ghosting through. Shards of rock flew everywhere as cracks spread across the surface. I drifted aside as Tower brought the hammer around once more, delivering a second blow. The door crumbled. He kicked aside shattered rock and looked down the shaft on the other side.

"There are no stairs," he said. "I do see a green glow far below."

Green? I looked back down, and found that the previously orange light was, in fact, green. As I watched, the green broke apart into blue and yellow swirls, which were washed away by waves of purple. If this was lava, it was like no lava I'd ever seen.

"Missing stairs are no problem," said twin squeaky voices. A pair of squirrel-sized spider monkeys jumped to Tower's shoulders. "I'll check it out," they said, before leaping into the shaft, bouncing back and forth across the gaps in the stone where the bone stairs once stood.

Since stairs were optional for me as well, I decided I'd beat Menagerie to the bottom of the shaft. I dropped down, passing them, the heat growing in intensity as I descended. The disk of light at the bottom continued to change colors and patterns in a chaotic, unpredictable fashion.

My ghost skin tingled as my body emerged from the shaft. What I saw defied my understanding. Relic had said the temple was in a crystal cavern, but this didn't look like any cavern I'd ever been inside, and there wasn't a crystal in sight. Imagine, if you can, a large, turbulent cloud, ever-changing as it drifts across the sky. Now imagine what it would look like if you were inside the cloud. The stone around me was an undulating, amorphous shape. The walls looked solid, despite their refusal to stand still or maintain a single color. The room was full of bones, no doubt the remnants of the stairwell. Fragments of skulls, femurs, and chalk-white teeth were scattered in all directions, resting on the ceiling and walls as well as the floor, though if I wasn't looking at the round opening of the stairwell, I couldn't be certain what was a floor and what was a wall. I closed my eyes, since the shifting walls left me feeling seasick. It didn't help. I lost all sensation of what was up or down. My ghost form had only a tenuous connection with gravity at best, but here there was nothing at all to orient me. Fortunately, when I envisioned the bone-handled knife, I felt its familiar tug.

I turned my face in its direction, glancing back up the shaft. The spider monkeys had reached the opening to the room, staring at the chaos with wide eyes. Further up the shaft I saw a shadowy figure clambering down the walls like some human spider. As it drew nearer, I saw it was Zetetic.

The monkeys glanced up. Perhaps feeling a sense of obligation to be first into the room, they jumped, dropping lightly to the writhing stone. The monkeys stumbled as the stone shifted beneath them. Though they didn't sink, it looked as if they were riding waves. One of the monkeys managed to rise on all fours, his tail wrapped around a shimmering polka-dotted stalagmite, but was toppled a second later when the pillar sank back into the surface. The confused monkeys tapped the stone beneath them with their knuckles, then rubbed their tiny fists. The stone was hard, despite its fluid nature.

The Deceiver's head popped out of the shaft and looked around. He dropped onto the shifting floor and landed on his knees, giggling. "By the unanswerable questions! False matter!" He looked around, delight in his eyes. "I saw a nugget of it once, preserved inside an enchanted pearl in the palace of the mer-king. I had no idea that such a large volume of the stuff still existed!"

The monkeys had been carried by the shifting floor until one now stood perpendicular to Zetetic, while another was surfing a wave of stone fifty feet away. The monkey near Zetetic looked slightly green as it said, "What the hell is wrong with this place?" He rode the chaotic stone higher, until he was looking straight down on the Deceiver. "Shouldn't one of us be falling?"

The Deceiver shook his head. "Ignore your eyes. Think of down as whatever direction you point the soles of your feet." Zetetic rose on trembling legs, holding his hands out to steady himself. His eyes were closed. A few seconds later, he cautiously opened his eyes. He grinned as the monkey was carried back and forth on currents of stone. "Imagine you are perfectly stationary. You are the center of your world, and let the room orbit around you. Everything is relative here."

The monkey responded by vomiting. The clear, frothy broth pooled around his feet. He closed his eyes and moaned, "Make it stop."

Zetetic shrugged. "I don't know what else to say to help you. Your body is made of true matter. It still obeys the same physical rules it always has. You can control your physical response with simple willpower."

Menagerie was still two very sick little monkeys by the time No-Face, Relic, and Father Ver made it down the shaft on a rope ladder. No-Face and Relic were quickly toppled by the changing landscape. Father Ver managed to remain upright as he dropped from the shaft, frowning as he took in the bodies in motion around him. He responded by holding out his arms and turning around slowly. The stone in a ten-foot disk beneath him flattened out and stopped moving.

He crossed his arms and said, in a firm tone, "I'm standing on the floor."

No-Face, who was directly overhead, suddenly plummeted onto the circle of motionless stone, landing at the Truthspeaker's feet. The monkey who'd been speaking with Zetetic leapt from his perch on the wall and landed on No-Face's chest. I had no idea where the second half of Menagerie had gotten to. It was impossible to estimate the size of the chamber. It seemed to stretch out for miles, but the rules of perspective were completely useless. Relic was just a little speck, seemingly a hundred yards away, then he reached out and tapped the edge of his staff onto the circle that Ver had calmed and suddenly he was close enough to touch, crawling onto the island and collapsing next to No-Face.

Zetetic didn't seem bothered by the sudden emergence of a floor. He continued to ride the shifting stone, as surefooted as a forest-pygmy on a swaying vine. "Fighting it is only going to make you more disoriented."

"Fighting falsehood is my sworn duty," said Father Ver. "The truth of what has happened here is plain. The pagans corrupted the true matter of the cavern, infecting it with falseness, which has flourished in isolation. In the beginning, before the Divine Author dipped the sacred quill in the holy ink, matter was devoid of such truths as width and length and breadth. By worshipping false gods, the ancient priests weakened the walls surrounding them. The stone has gone feral."

"This is going to shock you," said Zetetic, "but I concur. We're surrounded by the original stuff of creation, matter unshaped by mind. With practice, we could mold it to anything we can imagine. This is the greatest treasure we've yet discovered, far more valuable than gold, and you're wasting it by turning it into mere rock."

"Stone must learn to respect the truth that it is stone," said Father Ver, striding forward, calming more of the undulating rock into smooth gray solidity. Soon, he had an oblong island fifty feet long and a few yards wide frozen into rather mundane looking granite.

Relic pulled himself back to his feet and said, "At least there is no question that we have found the perfect location to attack the dragon's spirit. In a place like this, we should have little difficulty ripping the veil between the physical and the spiritual worlds."

Looking around, I realized that everyone was present and accounted for except Tower and Infidel. I flew back up the shaft, homing in on the bone-handled knife. I cut a path through stone and emerged in the hall where I found Tower with his helmet removed, on his knees before Infidel, holding her hand. He was kissing her knuckles.

"My love, before I go below to face the dragon, there is something I must give you."

"Great!" she said. "I hope it's chocolate this time."

Tower brought a gauntlet to his breastplate, directly above his heart, and pressed a small panel there. A tiny door slid open and something glowing fell into his palm.

My eyes bulged as he slipped a dazzling ring studded with diamonds and glorystones onto Infidel's finger. Infidel's mouth fell open slightly, but she made no sound.

"I've carried this over my heart since the day you vanished. I always knew the moment would come when I would have another chance to give it to you."

"Um," said Infidel. "Why now?"

"I've won every battle I've ever fought, my love. Still, I can't underestimate the danger that waits below. It may be that I shall perish. But I would die a happy man if I knew this ring was on your finger, testament to all the world of our eternal love, my princess."

"Ah," she said. "Hmm. Uh, it doesn't really go with my disguise, you know? Father Ver might figure everything out if I go below flashing this around." She slid the ring from her finger.

"You won't be going below," said Tower. "The danger is too great. I want you to go back to the surface. I'll find you after the battle. I couldn't bear to see a single hair on your head singed by the dragon."

"It's a little late for that," she said, running her fingers through her spiky locks."

"That fact that you can jest is testimony to your courageous spirit," said Tower. "Still, I beg you…"

Infidel sighed. "Don't beg."

"But my love for you is—"

"You aren't in love, you idiot," she said, grabbing his gauntlet and dropping the ring into it. "At least, not with me. You don't even have a clue who I am."

"You're Princess Innocent, daughter of—"

"Stop," she said. "You know my family tree. You don't know me."

"But your lineage is part of who you are," said Tower. "Your royal breeding proves that you're a woman of beauty, grace, and wit, matchless in—"

"Please stop talking," she said. "You think I haven't heard this crap growing up? Being a princess means you stop being a real person. You're just an actress following a script written by history. In case you didn't notice, I tore up that script. I'm not sweet little Innocent anymore."

"Oh, I know this," he said, rising, looking down at her with a leer. "You've grown into a very, very naughty girl. You may even require a spank—"

"Try it and I will rip your arms off," she said, smiling sweetly.

He cocked his head, looking confused. "I'm sorry. Since you're wearing leather pants, I assumed you might enjoy such rough treatment."

Infidel sighed, powerfully enough to stir the dust in the room. She closed her eyes, rubbing them as she contemplated her next words. Finally, she said, "It's time to come clean. I'm not going to marry you. I don't like you. At least, not romantically. It's possible we could, I dunno, be friends. You seem like a decent guy who would probably make the right woman happy."

"Yes!" he said, squeezing her hand. "And you are that woman!"

"You're sure of that?"

"With all my heart."

"You know me that well?"

"I've known you since before I met you!"

"What's my favorite color?"

His face went blank. Then, he smiled softly and said, "I remember the green ribbons you wore in your hair. Green is your favorite color."

In fact, she hated green. She didn't enlighten him, however, hitting him quickly with a second question: "What's my favorite food?"

His face brightened. "Cake!"

"A good guess, but the correct answer is fried monkey."

He furrowed his brow, trying to figure out if she was joking. He waved his hand dismissively. "We shall have years to learn this trivia."

She shook her head. "I know I've been giving you mixed signals. You ran into me at a very confusing time. I'm still mourning the death of someone I truly loved, wondering how to move forward without him. Plus, I've been given some unexpected news about my future, and you seemed like you might, maybe, be a candidate for helping fulfil a little prophecy. Any daughter I had with you would at least have pretty eyes."

"Any son you had with me would some day be king!" Tower said. "Think of your destiny!"

"I don't really do destiny. I escaped from my father's plans for my future. The Black Swan told me something about my future that messed with my mind a little, but I really don't have any reason to take her seriously. I thought maybe you played some role in my future, but you care far more about potential kings that might fall out of my womb than you care about me as a person. I'm sorry, but I'm just no longer interested."

"But... but... but..." said Tower, his voice trailing away.

"I should have told you this earlier, but Aurora thought you might have the Jagged Heart and I played along to find out if it was true. Now that she's gone, there's really no need to humor you."

Tower set his jaw as his eyes hardened into an angry stare. "Yes," he said, his voice low and trembling. "Yes, my princess, there is a need for you to humor me. You're still a fugitive, accused of crimes beyond imagining. I'm your sole path to forgiveness."

"Forgiveness is a vastly overrated commodity," she said. "Also, are you really trying to win me over with blackmail?"

Tower said nothing as he put his helmet back on.

"So, what, we fight now?" asked Infidel.

"Yes," said Tower. There was something strange about his voice. I poked part of my face into his helmet for a look. He was crying. "Yes, we fight now. But not each other. Not yet. My first mission is to slay the dragon. Then... then I will return to my sacred duty of smiting infidels." His shoulders sagged. "Flee if you wish. I won't pursue you."

"Flee?" Infidel cracked her knuckles. "There's more proof you don't have a clue who I am."

Flashing a grin, she jumped down the shaft.

DOWN BELOW, THE Truthspeaker had carved out a hundred-foot circle of calm stone amid the chaotic false matter. The cavity seemed even larger than it had before, as if the false matter of the walls was retreating from the holy man. The heat was as horrible as ever; Father Ver's armpits were stained with dark circles of sweat. The second Menagerie spider monkey had rejoined the group; the two tiny primates were fanning one another with triangular wedges of shoulder bones to keep cool.

Infidel dropped from the shaft, landing on the stone island. She looked around, her eyes wide. I floated toward her, wondering if the veil between the spirit world and the material world was as thin as Zetetic claimed. I placed my lips by her ear and whispered, "Your favorite color is black, even though that isn't really a color. I could have answered the monkey question in my sleep. Tower might know your family tree back a dozen generations; I know ten thousand things that make you smile. And when you smile, I smile."

She didn't smile. She didn't respond at all, other than to look toward the shaft just as Lord Tower flew through the opening. He shot off sideways at blinding speed, slamming face first into a wall, sending out a rainbow spray of undulating false-matter gravel. He rose on hands and knees, perpendicular to the others, and said, "By the sacred quill! What madness is this?" A huge stalagmite grew beside him; he placed his hand upon it to try to rise. The stone fell away just as quickly revealing Zetetic, his hands behind his back, looking amused.

"You'll find it difficult to fly. If you're not in contact with a surface, up and down don't really exist. The Gloryhammer has no objective gravity to resist."

The steel spikes in Tower's boots sprung out and dug into the rock. He rose to his full height, using the Gloryhammer as an impromptu cane. He sounded nervous as he asked, "This cursed landscape is where we fight the dragon?"

"Not exactly," said Zetetic. "This is where I send the Truthspeaker into the spirit world, and open a tunnel for you to launch a sneak attack."

"When?" asked Tower.

"I can cast the spells at any time, but I assume you wish to pray or meditate or drink some holy water. Whatever it is the righteous do to prepare themselves for battle."

Tower looked toward Infidel. With his faceplate down, there was no way to tell what he was thinking. After a gaze that lingered long enough to make everyone uncomfortable, the knight said, "I'm as righteous at this moment as I will ever be. Let's do this."

"Now?"

"Now."

Zetetic crossed his arms. "Is there some reason to rush? Maybe you feel ready to fight, but the rest of us are hot, tired, and hungry. Let's set up camp, rest a little, get some food in our bellies."

"Let's not talk about food right now," said Menagerie.

"Agreed," said Tower. "This is no fit place to make camp. The less time we linger, the better. Open the portal."

Zetetic grumbled something beneath his breath, then reached out to grab Tower's gauntlet. He turned toward the calm stone island where the Father Ver stood and towed the knight over the shifting stone to join the others.

"Maybe I'm not hungry," said Menagerie, "but I wouldn't mind a little rest before we face the dragon. What's the hurry?"

"Zetetic is no doubt gambling that more of you will die if we delay our mission," said Father Ver.

Zetetic pursed his lips tightly together.

Father Ver continued, "His powers draw on the beliefs of others. Tower and I offer him no fuel for his corrupt arts. If only the three of us had made it this far, he'd be powerless, since the Deceiver doesn't truly believe his own lies. And, if he were powerless, we'd be unable to open the doorways to the dragon. He imagines this would save his life."

"That's a pretty elaborate theory," said Zetetic.

"We both know it's the truth," said Father Ver.

"Whatever," said Zetetic, with a dismissive wave. He faced the monkeys and No-Face. "I want the two of you to give me your full attention."

The mercenaries turned their heads toward him with weary stares.

"I have... I have the power to open gateways that lead from this chamber to anywhere I wish, even other dimensions."

The monkeys nodded simultaneously. No-Face, in his expressionless stare, also seemed convinced.

The only one who looked doubtful was Zetetic. He studied the ground at his feet, taking a deep breath, before stepping up to Tower. His face was mirrored in the knight's gleaming faceplate as he said, "I'm going to send you to Greatshadow's lair. So far, my mental shields haven't detected any of his telepathic probes. He won't know you're coming, but you only get one shot. Make it count. If you merely wound the dragon, you might condemn the entire world to burn."

Tower nodded. "I've prepared for this moment my whole life. Though some among us may doubt the purity of my intentions, I will not shirk from my duty... or my destiny!"

Tower opened the compartment on his hip and pulled out his magic book, swapping the Gloryhammer for the Jagged Heart. The searing heat of the chamber instantly cooled from hellish to merely unbearable.

"Ready?" Zetetic asked again.

"Do it," said Tower.

Zetetic grabbed the knight by his biceps and suddenly jerked him from his feet, holding him overhead. He looked like he was getting ready to throw the knight, and, as it turned out, that was exactly the plan. With a grunt he hurled Lord Tower at the nearest wall. The stone swirled as Tower approached, forming a vortex, like the cone of air that forms when water drains from a tub. Tower shot down this ever-lengthening vortex, until he became little more than a speck, flying toward a pinpoint of bright white light.

"Your turn," said Zetetic, grabbing Father Ver by the arms. Their gazes met. The Deceiver's voice was little more than a whisper as he said, "You heard the speech. For the sake of mankind, *do not fuck this up!*"

He snatched the holy man from his feet, holding him overhead for a few seconds as his eyes studied the swirling stone, searching for the exact spot where the barrier between dimensions was at its weakest. Suddenly, his eyes brightened. He could see it. I could as well. At the edge of the platform, at a ninety-degree angle from the direction he'd tossed Lord Tower, a vortex of brilliant white light began to spin. I raised my hand to shield my eyes from the radiance, but no one else on the platform save for the Deceiver seemed aware of the light show. The vortex quickly grew, becoming a hole in the air several yards across. From the other side of the hole, I could hear the wail of a terrible wind, a sound that sent shudders through my soul, though, again, the others remained oblivious.

With all his muscles straining, Zetetic tossed the holy man toward the spirit door.

The Truthspeaker never reached the portal. Instead, in mid-flight, he was struck by a flying body that shot out from the vortex Tower had flown down. Father Ver landed on the stone platform face first, then flopped to his back unconscious, revealing a huge gash along his left eyebrow. His twitching legs kicked Zetetic in the ankle and the Deceiver went down as well, cursing as he landed on his butt.

At the far end of the platform, Lord Tower, or something that looked a lot like him, slid to a halt near Infidel's feet. She jumped back, landing on the shifting false matter, spreading her arms to keep her balance. The figure before Infidel wasn't Tower, but instead a statue of the knight carved from dull gray stone. The Jagged Heart was nowhere to be seen. Infidel stared at the statue with a confusion that rivaled my own as the fluid stone beneath her carried her away. She jumped to return to the island, but wound up even further away, thwarted by the room's meandering geometry.

Meanwhile, I heard the rattle of No-Face's chain, the familiar sound that always rang out when he readied himself for a fight. The twin monkeys were suddenly replaced by a pair of snarling wolverines. I looked to the stone vortex, squinting to make out the shadowy figure approaching.

The thing that stalked toward us was human in form, mostly. It was transparent, but not invisible, more like murky water than air, so that anything beyond appeared distorted. The fluid it was composed of had a slight brownish hue, like sewer water. It was carrying the Jagged Heart, but showed no signs of freezing.

As it walked toward us, it shouted, "O stone! Be not so!" It then shrieked with laughter, a high-pitched, slurred barking that reminded me of the forced, empty cackle of a drunken whore who hadn't truly understood her client's joke.

The unpleasant sounds of the liquid man before us were matched by a shrieking behind us. It was the Deceiver, looking at the approaching figure, crying out with terror until his lungs were emptied of the last drop of air.

Just as the Deceiver's voice faded out, the liquid man stepped from the vortex and placed his feet on the stable stone island. Now that he was closer, I recognized he was formed not of water, but of booze — whiskey judging from the smell. He was an impressive figure, as tall and muscular as Aurora had been.

"If you've got a straw handy, I can tackle this," I said to Relic.

He didn't find it funny.

This is the old god I spoke of! he thought back. *Nowowon, the god of destruction!*

"He sounds fun," I said.

Nowowon turned his liquid eyes toward me and said, in a solemn seriousness, "I lived, evil I."

This will not be fun for anyone. Nowowon had no match for cruelty among the old gods. He delighted in tormenting the dead as well as the living.

"Party pooper," I said.

"Party boobytrap!" said Nowowon, licking his liquid lips. "Are we not drawn onward to new era?"

Behind us, Zetetic finished filling his lungs with air, and screamed again.

CHAPTER TWENTY
RAW WAR

FOR A SUPPOSED god, Nowowon didn't impress me. Except for Zetetic freaking out, no one else showed any obvious panic. That may have been because not everyone was paying attention. Father Ver was unconscious from his face-plant and Infidel had her back to the action as her repeated leaps over the false matter kept carrying her random directions and distances. Relic was just staring at Nowowon with the same detached calmness he showed toward most events.

Menagerie in his wolverine bodies and No-Face with his swinging chain didn't look worried as they slowly circled the old god. I wondered what they were seeing? It made sense, in a completely senseless, magical way, that a god of destruction would appear to me as walking whiskey. Self-destruction no doubt had a special place in his heart. He was appearing to me as my greatest weakness. Maybe Menagerie was currently looking at a ten-foot-tall guy made entirely of money. Whatever he was made of, he'd taken the Jagged Heart from Tower, so he wasn't going to be a pushover.

No-Face was first to strike, leaping forward with a noise half war cry, half grunt: "HRUNN!" The iron ball sliced through the air and came down dead center of Nowowon's face, bouncing off without so much as leaving a scratch, at least from my point of view.

Nowowon met the blow with a thrust of the Jagged Heart, moving at blinding speed. No-Face didn't stand a chance; the harpoon impaled his rib cage, driving down into the stone beneath him until the icy blade was completely embedded, leaving only the shaft exposed. Blood bubbled around the wound, then froze, as the ball and chain slipped from his fingers. No-Face sank to his knees, pinned by the shaft, unable to fall completely. No ghost appeared; as horrific as the wound was, he wasn't dead yet.

The wolverines let loose angry howls as they launched themselves at the god, sinking their teeth into his throat. Nowowon grabbed them, then tossed them away, shouting, "Ooze zoo!"

As the beasts spun through the air, they began to break apart into dozens, if not hundreds of animals. Instead of two wolverines hitting the ground, the floor was suddenly covered with countless pint-sized creatures, no larger than they'd been depicted on the original tattoos. There were kitten-sized lions, wolves smaller than mice, and sharks no bigger than goldfish flopping on the floor.

As bad a development as this was, it was followed by something far worse as the miniature animals launched into a feeding frenzy. The lions leapt upon the sharks, the bug-sized boars were stomped by ankle-high elephants, and worm-like anacondas wrapped themselves around tiny eagles. Blood, fur, and feathers flew in a bloody whirlwind.

"Bad animals I slam in a dab," Nowowon laughed as he stomped over the surviving beastlets, smearing them to paste beneath his heel.

No-Face groaned as he writhed on the harpoon, sinking lower, until his trembling, outstretched fingers reached his fallen ball and chain. With a muffled groan, he flung the weapon, bouncing it off the old god's ear.

Nowowon stopped laughing as he paced back over to No-Face. He stared down at the impaled mercenary and growled, "Lived as a dog, reviled? Deliver god as a devil!"

He placed his thick fingers beneath No-Face's chin flap and gave a sudden yank. With a sickening slurp the tumorous mask tore away, revealing... nothing. A completely blank, unblemished mass of skin, unmarred by scars, devoid of mouth, nostrils, or even eyes, despite the fact he'd always had one showing.

"I know how the god's power works!" I shouted at Relic, hoping that my insight might be of some help. "No-Face was afraid there was nothing under his skin flap! Menagerie was afraid that there was nothing human left in him, that he was nothing but a mass of animals!"

Relic nodded. "And Tower feared that his only legacy to the world would be a statue. Nowowon destroys men with their greatest fears."

"I really hope your greatest fear is of something harmless, like squirrels," I said, as Nowowon stalked toward Relic.

Relic looked around the island; the Goons certainly looked dead, even if I hadn't seen their spirits. Zetetic was curled into a fetal ball, sucking on his fist, his face awash with tears and snot. Father Ver was unconscious, Tower was stoned, and Infidel was still leaping around like a drunken jackrabbit. Finally, Relic looked back at me. *Stall him while I mentally guide Infidel back across the shifting terrain.*

I felt his mental hands grab me and hold me in place as he beat a retreat for the edge of the island. I struggled to break free of his invisible grasp, and did so just as Nowowon reached me. The old god grabbed me by the throat and lifted me from my feet. He brought my face to his. I could see right through him; the whiskey fumes of his breath left me dizzy as his lips brushed my ears and whispered, "Murder for a jar of red rum?"

Though he asked it as a question, I was apparently not intended to answer. From nowhere he'd produced a glass pitcher full of what smelled like rum, but looked like blood. He pushed me to the ground, pinning my arms. He pinched my cheeks to force my lips open, and poured the alcoholic blood between my teeth.

The taste... the taste was heavenly. The booze played upon my tongue like a symphony, sweet and bitter, cool and burning, and with each precious drop I swallowed my heart beat stronger.

I grew increasingly aware of the stone beneath me. I moved my legs, feeling my naked foot scrape along the cold stone, chilled as it was by the Jagged Heart embedded not twenty feet away. Goosebumps covered my skin as he freed my arms. I used both hands to grab the glass and sat up, still guzzling the precious fluid, fire burning in my veins. This bloody broth had brought me back to life!

Murder for a jar of red rum? The Black Swan had been right. I'd kill my own mother for more of this. I emptied the glass and ran my tongue around the inner rim, searching for the final molecules of goodness.

I rose, woozy, and held the glass out toward the old god.

"Thank you, sir, may I have another?"

Giggling, Nowowon pointed toward the Jagged Heart and said, "Red rum, sir, is murder."

I nodded, and stumbled toward No-Face's still body and the long harpoon that jutted from his chest. The sound of my feet slapping the stone was a wondrous thing. I nearly wept as my solid fingers closed around the cold shaft of the harpoon. Needles of ice ran up my bare arm, but even this sensation took my breath away. My breath! My breath! I heaved out great clouds of smoke as I strained to free the Jagged Heart from its sheath in No-Face's massive rib cage, and the solid stone beneath.

The ground creaked as I withdrew the frozen weapon. No-Face's body slid down the narwhale tusk slowly. I placed my foot on his neck to pull the harpoon free. There was no question he was dead now. Maybe I had missed his departing spirit in all the excitement.

Or perhaps he'd lingered on until I'd removed the harpoon and, alive once more, I could no longer see ghosts. It wasn't a power I would miss. Of course, who knew how long Nowowon's brew would restore me? I needed to guarantee a second glass. Who to kill? Who to kill to prolong this feeling? Zetetic, who was getting on my nerves with his rabbit-like shrieking? Father Ver, who I didn't like much, and who was an easy target in his slumber?

Relic?

Oh, definitely Relic.

I turned to face the man who'd been jerking me around like a puppet and discovered that he'd fallen into Nowowon's clutches. Nowowon was tearing away the hunchback's robes to reveal... a dragon?

I blinked. The blood rum was blurring my vision ever so slightly, but there was no mistaking what I was looking at. It was a baby dragon only a little larger than the dead one I'd seen in the hands of the lava-pygmy shamans. Unlike the earlier specimen, which had looked healthy save for, you know, being dead, this dragon was badly lamed. Its wings were tiny, twisted knots perched upon its back. Its legs were spindly and bent at odd angles, as if they'd been broken then mended without being set properly. The little dragon hung limp in Nowowon's grasp; the old god had the disfigured dragon's long spindly fingers splayed out in his palm, and was bending them backwards until they snapped, one by one. Had Relic possessed a fear of dragons and been transformed into one by Nowowon? Or had he been a dragon all along, with a fear of being crippled?

"Maim? I? Him I am!" said Nowowon, giggling.

Then, from the corner of my eye, I saw Infidel fly back onto the platform with one final lucky leap, landing near the fallen statue of Tower. She picked up the stone knight by the ankles and charged at the old god. She didn't even glance in my direction. Was I still invisible? Or, was she just locked into combat tunnel vision?

With a savage growl she leapt, swinging the statue like a hammer. She struck Nowowon squarely on the top of his head, driving his skull down into his shoulders, forcing him to drop Relic, assuming that's who the dragon was. The blow also had the effect of sending a spiderweb of cracks across the surface of the statue. Bits of gravel flaked away, revealing gleaming armor beneath.

She raised her knight-club again and hammered the old god once more. Now shards of stone the size of saucers were flaking away from the statue; suddenly, Tower shrugged, and broke completely free of his stony prison. The old god had been driven into the ground up to his knees, and his head was completely flat against his shoulders. Apparently, this wasn't fatal to a god; his arms were still flailing about, trying to grab his assailant. Infidel, still in her battle rage, danced around his groping hands, and either didn't notice or didn't care that her weapon was alive once more. She again swung Tower overhead, and chopped him down to smash the old god even flatter.

"Stop!" Tower cried out, as she raised him once more overhead.

Infidel looked up, confused.

Nowowon's hands found Infidel's ankles and jerked her from her feet. She hit the ground hard, as Tower fell on top of her with a loud crash.

I didn't know what horrors Nowowon might be ready to inflict upon Infidel, and I didn't want to find out. I charged with the Jagged Heart, driving it into his body, which still appeared to be liquid despite the mangling Infidel had inflicted. I sank the weapon in until my fingers reached his fluid skin, and twisted.

In response, two fresh arms emerged from Nowowon's armpits and pulled aside his liquid breastbone, revealing his bashed-in face beneath. He still had his original arms clamped on Infidel's ankles. She was kicking, to no avail. Her fingers left small trenches in the stone as she tried to drag herself away. I'd never seen such fear and confusion in her eyes as she looked back over her shoulder and saw me.

"Stagger?" she asked, her voice trembling.

Having seen the fate of No-Face, Menagerie, and Relic, I didn't dare give Nowowon time to get creative with Infidel's weaknesses, whatever those might be. I yelled out, "Tower! Use the Gloryhammer on this thing!"

Tower scrambled to his feet, reaching for his magic book. The

Armor of Faith had resisted Nowowon's powers, protecting him from full statuefication. Maybe the Gloryhammer would prove equally effective.

"I hope this hurts," I said, wriggling the harpoon around as the Gloryhammer burst into full radiance behind me.

A grin passed over Nowowon's liquid lips. "Won't lovers revolt now?"

"I don't need your help to save her!" Tower cried. The hair stood up on the back of my neck. I spun with all the speed I could muster, tearing the Jagged Heart free, as Tower swung the Gloryhammer not at the old god, but at me. With a speed that shocked both of us, I was able to raise the blade of the harpoon into the path of the enchanted hammer. There was a blinding flash, like the high noon sun dazzling on pure white snow. The force of the impact knocked the Jagged Heart from my fingers. Yet, as the light of the hammer spun off behind me, I realized my blocking action had not only spared my skull, it had knocked the Gloryhammer from the knight's grasp.

Infidel screamed, kicking uselessly as Nowowon's body restored itself, rising above us. He now had six arms; I had a very bad feeling in the pit of my stomach as I saw that one of these arms now grasped the Gloryhammer, and another the Jagged Heart.

Nowowon pinned Infidel's ankles to the ground as he flipped her over on her back. He placed the tip of the Jagged Heart against her sternum as he grew ever larger. The sweat that beaded on her torso instantly froze into little diamonds. He raised the Gloryhammer, ready to drive the world's biggest nail straight through her.

"I'll save you!" Tower cried, reaching for her left arm.

"I've got you," I yelled, grabbing her right hand.

We both pulled with all our might as Nowowon struck.

I lost my grip and had my breath knocked from me as I hit the ground, rolling. Nearby, I heard a loud crash as Tower's armored ass slammed into the rock. I rose on my hands and knees, looking at him. He was flat on his back, staring up at a young girl in a lacy white gown who stood before him. She had a silver tiara atop her brow, studded with emeralds. Green ribbons threaded through her platinum braids. There had still been some of Princess Innocent inside Infidel after all, it seemed.

Where Infidel had been pinned only a second before, there was now only her empty clothes.

It was then I noticed the tree trunk next to me. I gave it a closer look. It wasn't a tree trunk. It was a dark green shin, covered with thick, overlapping scales, like the hide of a rattlesnake.

I looked up. I was sitting between the legs of a woman at least twenty feet tall. Her feet and hands ended in three-clawed talons, sporting dagger-length claws black with dried gore. A long, thick crocodilian tail thrust out from just above her buttocks. A fringe of dark green scales ran up her spine, to join with a mane of what looked like spiky vines.

I made a hasty retreat as the half-giantess, half-dragon reared back and roared, her voice causing the false matter of the cavern to ripple. Her jaws opened much further than an ordinary woman's should have, revealing a mouth full of glistening fangs.

Not that I'm complaining, but in a fair world, the knight in the enchanted armor would have gotten the enraged she-dragon to deal with, while the unarmed naked man got to face off with the little girl in the frilly dress.

Alas, as it turned out, neither of us had a chance to take any action at all. Perhaps a little worried about what he'd unleashed, Nowowon frowned at the giantess. "God damn mad dog," he growled, bringing the Gloryhammer around in a vicious back swing. He caught the dragon-woman in the side of her head, knocking her from her feet, sending her bouncing toward the swirling light of the spirit doorway. There was a loud sucking sound as her tail pointed straight as an arrow toward the gate. Her knife-like nails trailed sparks as the vortex to the spirit world sucked her toward its depths. Her face was a mask of rage, her eyes a bright, glowing green, as jade spittle foamed on her snarling lips. Then, as if understanding there was no escape, she smiled, casting her gaze toward young Princess Innocent. A long, slimy, serpentine tongue flicked from between her lips, flying across the gap toward the girl. The tongue wrapped around Innocent's forearm, then yanked her from her feet swiftly enough to pull her out of her white silk slippers. Innocent screamed at an octave that would have made bats wince as she was sucked into the spirit vortex in the wake of the dragon-lady.

With sickening suddenness, the screaming stopped. The doorway to the spirit world was gone.

Tower leapt at Nowowon, punching him hard in the knee. "Bring her back!"

"No sir! Prefer prison," chortled the old god, before smashing the knight in the head with the Gloryhammer. The metallic chime that rang out from the impact practically made my ears bleed. I could only imagine what it must have sounded like on the inside. Tower fell to his knees, holding his head, and Nowowon pushed him over with an oversized toe. He pinned the knight beneath his foot, then tossed the Jagged Heart so that it imbedded in the ground near my feet.

I didn't flinch. He wasn't trying to strike me.

I still owed him a murder.

"I need another drink to do this," I said, holding out my trembling hands. "All the excitement has left me shaky."

He nodded as he gave me a look of sympathy, an expression out of place on the features of a sadistic god of self-destruction. One of his free hands produced a second jar. "Regal lager," he said, offering it to me.

"Regal lager," I agreed, taking the crimson brew from him. I lifted it to my lips, inhaling one long, intoxicating sniff of the heady aroma. Never had I wanted a drink so badly.

But instead of drinking, I spun around, covered a dozen feet in three long strides, and dumped the ice-cold liquor on Father Ver's face.

The priest's eyes snapped open, his bloodied brow furrowed in confusion as he focused on me. "You're the boy who ran away after stealing the poor box," he said.

Considering that had been damn near forty years ago, I was more impressed than offended by the greeting. The bastard really was good at seeing truth.

"False god!" I said, pointing in Nowowon's direction. "Get him!"

"Was it a rat I saw?" asked Nowowon. He snapped his fingers and, instantly, my heart stopped. I moaned as my body faded back to its spectral form.

If Father Ver was bothered by my vanishing act, he showed no sign of it. Instead he rose, wiped the blood from his eyes, then straightened his shoulders to look at the old god.

"No! It is opposition!" cried Nowowon, as he shrank back down to the height of an ordinary man. He brandished the Gloryhammer in both hands and growled, "Raw war!"

"War is not necessary," said Father Ver. "You'll drop the hammer. It isn't yours."

The Gloryhammer slipped from the old god's shaking fingers.

Father Ver walked toward Nowowon, stepping over the gibbering form of the Deceiver. He looked down on the man with contempt, but took pity as he said, "Your vision isn't real. You've been caught in a mental trap. Arise."

Zetetic's eyes opened. He pulled his drool-covered fist from his mouth and gave it a puzzled look.

Father Ver thrust an accusing finger at Nowowon.

"You do not belong here! You are a false being, and have no place in this world!"

Nowowon walked backward toward the vortex of stone, looking at it nervously, as if he was considering making a break for it. But he sounded defiant as he looked back at the Truthspeaker and shouted, "Evil dogma! I am God, live!"

"We both know that isn't true," said Father Ver, as Tower crawled to retrieve the Gloryhammer. "I sense a summoning spell at work. Someone has trapped you here against your will. You faded from the memory of men long ago. There are no believers to sustain you."

"O no! O no! O no!" the old god screamed as he shrank before the force of the Truthspeaker's words.

"You are a fraud," said Father Ver, as the old god shrank to waist height.

"You are a perversion," he said, reducing Nowowon to the size of a house cat.

Father Ver looked down on the diminutive old god and crossed his arms. "You aren't even worth crushing beneath my sandal. You're a lie, and no one believes you any more."

Nowowon squealed as he shrank to the size of a mouse, then a cockroach, then a fly. Lord Tower's spiked metal boot suddenly slammed down, driving into the solid stone.

"I'm not wearing sandals," he said, casting the Truthspeaker a sideways glance.

Zetetic ran up, snatching the Jagged Heart from the ground. "Why is there a crippled baby dragon over there? Why is the spirit gate closed? What the hell happened? I thought the world had come to an end!"

"Why would you think that?" asked Tower.

"I threw you both through your gates. Greatshadow was ready for us. He killed you both and came into the chamber and killed the rest of us. I survived because I had told No-Face that fire couldn't burn me. But when I left this place, I found nothing but ash as far as the eye could see. I traveled the world, entirely alone, for decades without finding another survivor. Even the mermen and ice-ogres were gone. The primal dragons had joined together to strip the earth of all sentient life."

"You were trapped in a deception by the old god," said the small dragon, rising up on his misshapen legs with the help of his gnarled cane. This was definitely Relic's voice, and now there was no mistaking this dragon's eyes were the same eyes I'd spied through the burlap hood. "Nowowon knew that you were vulnerable to assault with a highly detailed hallucination. You were trapped by what was essentially a lie."

"It lasted forty years!" said Zetetic, waving the Jagged Heart in Relic's face for emphasis. "And who the hell are you? Why is no-one telling me why there's a dragon here?"

He was answered with a deep voice that made the ground tremble.

"There's a dragon here because you woke me from my slumber."

Everyone turned to the vortex of stone.

A scaly head the size of a ship had squeezed through the hole. It was a deep, glowing red, the color of embers shimmering beneath a blanket of dark ash. Sulfurous smoke rose from the creature's nostrils. The dragon glared at us with eyes that burned like foundry furnaces, with a heat that caused Father Ver's robes to send up tendrils of white smoke from fifty feet away.

All we could do was stare back, the moment frozen, as Greatshadow opened his enormous maw, revealing teeth like ivory stalactites and a tongue like a carpet of lava. Wind howled through me as Greatshadow sucked in air like a bellows.

CHAPTER TWENTY-ONE

OILY BLACK SMOKE

AND THEN THERE was fire, a great red wave of flickering tendrils engulfing us in a flood of heat and light. Imagine a coal-fired oven, stoked to a cherry red, with a pot of oil boiling furiously upon it. Imagine plunging your head into this pot, the burning oil working its way into your nostrils and ear canals, into your tear ducts, searing every pore. My spectral teeth burned, my tongue scalded, and there was nothing to do but keep screaming, though I couldn't even hear my own voice. Once, I'd ridden out a hurricane in my small boat and the roar of the wind had been so loud it loosened my bowels. This devouring flame howled far louder, a crescendo appropriate for announcing the end of the world.

And the smell. As a veteran explorer of volcanoes, I knew all too well the brimstone stench and the peculiar acid tang of molten rock. Add to this the stink of vaporized hair and flesh crackling on the bone and you still cannot imagine the foulness of the atmosphere.

As suddenly as it had begun, the flame passed. The pain jangling my phantom nerves collapsed from incapacitating to merely agonizing. Blinking away the ghost tears in my scalded eyes, it appeared that little had changed. The four figures who'd been present before were still there: Relic, revealed as a dragon, was unharmed, save that his staff was but a heap of white ashes at his feet. He was standing where Infidel's clothes had been; they were completely gone. There was no sign of the bone-handled knife, though I still felt its tug... from Relic's mouth?

The Deceiver had survived as well, crouched down, hugging the Jagged Heart to his chest, its aura of supernatural cold sparing him from the flame. Tower, too, was untouched; his Armor of Faith gleamed even brighter, as if the flames had cleansed it of the dust and grime it had gathered on our journey. Somehow, Father Ver, standing just behind the knight, wasn't even singed even though his robes had burned away.

In fact, the only party member missing was No-Face's corpse. There wasn't even a pile of ash, just a small rivulet of serpentine liquid metal flowing where his ball and chain had once been.

Father Ver turned toward me. As I studied his face, I realized I could see Tower through him. I wasn't looking at a man. I was looking at a ghost.

The phantom glared at me, and said, "You cannot be my guide."

"Nice to see you too," I said. "Look, you might be here for only a few seconds, so let's get to the point: it looks like you're still heading for the spirit world. When you get there, I need you to rescue Infidel. I mean, the War Doll."

"You mean Princess Innocent."

"You knew?"

He frowned deeply. "This was just one of many obvious truths I turned a blind eye toward with the goal of ridding the world of Greatshadow."

"But how could you know? Relic was reading your mind and said you were fooled."

"I sensed his mental probes instantly," Father Ver said. "It was a simple matter to command him to see in my mind whatever he wished to see."

I crossed my arms and shook my head, imitating the same pose of disapproval I had encountered so frequently in my youth. "So you not only kept quiet about things you knew weren't true, you actively took part in a deception. For shame."

"Your judgment matters to me not in the slightest," said Father Ver. "Tower was my friend. I would not deny him his chance to find his lost love. In the end, the Divine Author will deliver the final verdict on my choices. Let us hope... let us hope it was His intention to write a romance."

I opened my mouth to respond, but he looked heavenward, not caring whether I spoke to him or not. He spread his arms wide as his face was bathed in light from above. I looked to see its source, but there was nothing there.

"Ah," he said, in a tone half joy, half sorrow. "So that's the truth of it."

He pressed his lips together in a wistful smile as the outline of his face wavered. Then he was gone, and all that was left were a few blackened teeth where he had stood.

My attention returned to the danger at hand. I didn't want to be around if Greatshadow unleashed another inferno. Fortunately, while I had been chatting, Tower had sprung into action, leaping into the air and flying straight toward the dragon. In scale, it was like a bee diving toward a bear's nose. With both hands, he slammed the Gloryhammer into the center of Greatshadow's snout. Like a bear stung on the nose, Greatshadow winced and drew his head back. The false-matter tunnel warped and wobbled, allowing the impossibly large beast free movement as he retreated. Tower grabbed the rim of a scaly nostril with his razor-tipped left gauntlet, refusing to give the dragon a second of relief as he rained blow after blow on the creature's nose.

As Greatshadow departed, Relic spat the bone-handled knife from his mouth into his hand. It had been completely untouched by the flames. The misshaped little dragon shouted to the Deceiver, "We must give chase! Tower needs the Jagged Heart!"

"You're out of your mind!" shouted Zetetic. "I'd be dead if I wasn't carrying this. And why should I listen to you? You're a dragon!"

"A dragon maimed by Greatshadow," snarled Relic as he wiggled his stunted wings and limped toward the Deceiver. "A dragon whose sole purpose is to see his father suffer and die for the cruelties he's inflicted."

"Father? You're Greatshadow's son?"

"Possibly."

"How can you not be sure?"

"I'm definitely his offspring. But I'm uncertain if I'm his son or daughter. Since my genitals are internal and I've not yet matured, this remains—"

"Stop." Zetetic scrunched up his face and rubbed his closed eyes. "Just stop."

"You're uncomfortable discussing sexual biology?" asked Relic.

Zetetic sighed. "It's one of my favorite topics. But, maybe, right now isn't the best time to get into this?"

"Agreed. We must help Tower."

Tower was a fair distance away at this point, still maintaining his assault. There was little Greatshadow could do to remove his annoying assailant while he was in the tunnel, but the second he pulled his head free into the larger chamber beyond, a talon with claws longer than the Jagged Heart swatted Tower away.

The far end of the tunnel became a solid sheet of flame as Greatshadow tried a second time to melt the knight.

"Make yourself immune to flame," said Relic, grabbing Zetetic by the arm and tugging him.

"I can't!" cried the Deceiver, planting his feet wide to resist. "There's no one left to believe my lies! Your reptilian mind is useless to me!"

"Lie to Menagerie. He's still alive," said Relic.

"What?" I said.

"What?" said Zetetic.

"No shape-shifting blood magician would neglect to include a tick among his forms," said Relic. "I sense him now, dug in behind your knee. Nowowon's magic has robbed him of his humanity, but the Goon is an accomplished survivor."

Zetetic lifted the hem of his robe and bent over, using the Jagged Heart to balance himself as he twisted to see the back of his leg. Sure enough, there was a little black speck there. "Do ticks have ears? Can he hear me?"

Relic was silent as he stared at the bug.

He shook his head. "Unfortunately, his mental state has been greatly damaged. Perhaps he may recover once he has consumed sufficient blood, but, for now, your skepticism is justified. He'll be of no use to you."

"Do you have a second plan?" asked Zetetic.

"As a matter of fact," said Relic, running the sharp edge of the bone-handled knife along his palm. He sucked in air as a line of bright blood bubbled up.

I was floating near him, watching with interest, a bit off vertical amid the room's distorted landscape. I fell about a yard as I materialized, landing on the cracked black stone. I instantly leapt up with a yelp; the stone was hot as a furnace. I jumped closer to Zetetic and the Jagged Heart, and while my feet were spared a scalding, I became keenly aware of my nakedness and the possibility of losing toes and other more valued parts to frostbite. I hopped a few feet away, into a zone where the ground was more bearable.

"Stagger is a ghost haunting this knife. His soul manifests physically when the knife drinks the enchanted blood of dragons."

Zetetic furrowed his brow. Then he shrugged, and said, "I've seen crazier stuff. But if I must work with a dead man, I'd rather not be confronted with his private bits. Luckily, I have the power to summon clothing from thin air."

Instantly, I was dressed in finery; a cream silk shirt tucked into black satin britches with calf-high boots of soft leather. The whole thing was topped with a rather flamboyant red velvet cape.

"That's handy," I said. "Have you ever thought of earning a living as a tailor?"

"It wouldn't work. One limitation of my art is that I can never convince people of the same lie twice."

"There's no time for discussion!" said Relic. "We must get the harpoon to Tower. With every passing second, Greatshadow grows closer to victory."

Zetetic chewed his lower lip. He looked to be in genuine agony as he said, "Every fiber of my being is screaming I should run. But... Nowowon's little hallucination trap may not have worked the way Greatshadow would have wanted. We can't end this merely by wounding the beast, or even annoying him. Humanity may pay the ultimate price for our failure. I'm in."

"Wait," I said, grabbing Zetetic by the arm. "If you can't convince people of the same thing twice, how do we get to the spirit world? How do we kill Greatshadow's soul without Ver's scroll, and, more important to me, how do we rescue Infidel?"

"Who's Infidel?"

"The War Doll, formerly Princess Innocent Brightmoon," said Relic, holding the blade in his intact claw as he allowed drops of blood to drip one by one onto the bone-handled knife. His blood boiled and bubbled, etching the steel as it vaporized, but he timed his bleeding so that another drop had fallen before the first evaporated. "By now the dragon half of her nature has no doubt consumed the last remnants of her human self. She cannot be rescued. Killing Greatshadow's soul can be accomplished with the Jagged Heart; as Aurora revealed, it's been crafted to slay spirits. As for getting the harpoon to the spirit world, there is a magical item in Greatshadow's lair we can use."

"How do you know this?" I asked.

"Even in my egg, I could read minds. I was hatched with many of Greatshadow's memories. From the moment I first breathed air, I already had a full command of language and a deep understanding of his mystic arts."

"Precocious little scamp," said Zetetic. "Let's hope you know what you're talking about. Hurry!"

The two of them set off at a fast jog down the tunnel. I hung behind for a second, staring at the spot in the air where I'd last seen Infidel, and decided my only chance of seeing her again was to cast my lot with these two.

About a hundred yards down the tunnel, we were all knocked from our feet. A wave of lava swept into the far end of the passage, rushing toward us in a glowing river. Fortunately, since I was behind the Jagged Heart, I was spared from the heat, which rolled toward us as a shimmering wave, but stopped the second it reached the air around the enchanted weapon. The lava stopped flowing as well, freezing into a low wall about three feet tall. Behind it, the molten rock began to drain away, back into the chamber beyond.

I strained to see, missing my power to just float around and look at whatever interested me. As we climbed onto the wall and rushed forward, with the ground cooling and crackling as we advanced, what I could catch a glimpse of interested me greatly. I saw Greatshadow stumbling, bleeding profusely from the side of his head, his blood coming out in great surges of liquid fire.

We arrived at a large ledge on the inner lip of a volcanic caldera open to the sky. Before us was a bubbling lake of magma stretching off as far as I could see, which wasn't all that far due to the haze of sulfurous smoke. Greatshadow had dropped to all fours, shaking his head to clear it. His eyes had a glassy look. His sheer size was almost impossible to comprehend; not even whales were this large. He was more like a landmass than a living being, though the muscles rippling beneath his crimson hide revealed the truth of his animal nature.

Above us, beyond the sulfur clouds, the sun blazed brightly. Only I quickly realized that it wasn't the sun; the light was moving far too swiftly across the sky. Suddenly the glowing object burst through the clouds. It was Lord Tower, blazing down with the speed of a shooting star. He slammed, hammer-first, into the dragon's head. The addition of speed turned Tower into something more dangerous than a bee — he was now like a bullet shot from the sling of an expert marksman, and his momentum was enough to drive his invulnerable armor deep into the dragon's skull.

The blow flattened Greatshadow, driving him down into the burning mire. He unleashed a low, mournful howl as he struggled to rise. Magma-like blood bubbled from a series of holes near the fringe of spikes along the ridge of his skull. His eyes seemed unfocused as his limbs jerked spastically.

"Plainly, we're not needed here at all," said Zetetic, turning back toward the tunnel.

"Die!" Relic shouted. It took me a second to realize he wasn't shouting at the Deceiver. Instead, he was shaking his bony fist at Greatshadow. "Your suffering is like wine to me! I drink in your agony as you die! Die! Die!"

Tower clawed back out of the hole he'd dug into Greatshadow, covered in flaming gore. He rose into the air, twirling, throwing off a halo of muck. When he stopped spinning he was clean again, his silver armor a dazzling light show reflecting the Gloryhammer, the lava, and Greatshadow's pulsing blood.

"Your final page has been written, Greatshadow!" Tower shouted, his voice echoing from the walls of rock surrounding the battlefield. "Your name shall vanish from the One True Book!" Tower shot into the air, vanishing into the haze as he rose toward heaven to summon speed.

"Do it!" screamed Relic. "Kill him! Kill him!"

The resentment I felt toward my own negligent father suddenly seemed rather mild.

Zetetic's retreat had halted only a few feet into the tunnel. He was looking back at Greatshadow. Apparently, the opportunity to witness the death of a primal dragon was overriding his desire to flee.

Greatshadow's glazed eyes suddenly focused on the ledge we stood on. With a voice like a rumbling earthquake he growled as he spotted Relic, "This was your doing!"

"Yes!" screamed Relic, spittle flying. "I've plotted your

demise since the day you tossed my twisted body onto the volcano's slopes! Once you die, I shall become the new primal dragon of fire! No one will deny me my destiny!"

"Indeed?" said Greatshadow, his voice firm despite the fact he still flopped helplessly in the lava, unable to rise. "You've shielded your mind from me, but your dead companion has no mental defenses. I've just learned that the knight's armor is made of prayer."

He cast his gaze skyward as Tower reached his apex, the brightest object in all the heavens.

Relic's waving fist froze in mid-air. A sudden look of horror filled his reptilian eyes.

"The monks would be too disciplined to light a candle," he mumbled, sounding almost as if he was speaking to himself.

"I'm pretty sure none of them smoke," I said.

"They don't even cook there," said Zetetic. "All their food is prepared in a nearby village and brought to them daily."

"In that village, there is a bakery, with an oven that never grows cold," Greatshadow said, sinking deeper into the lava as the light shot back down toward him. Tower punched through the clouds, his speed so great that a thunderclap sounded in his wake. Yet, as impressive as his speed was, he suddenly had no target. Greatshadow vanished completely beneath the bubbling rock with little more than a ripple. Tower punched into the glowing surface, throwing up a white-hot splash of magma.

For ten seconds, everything was quiet.

Then, the Gloryhammer shot up into the air, pulling Lord Tower from his blazing bath. Tower spun to clear his armor then surveyed the lava beneath him, searching for his foe.

His foe found him first, as a flame-wreathed talon punched from the surface and snapped around the knight like a man snatching an annoying fly. Greatshadow rose from the syrupy rock with a growl and slammed his talon down on the stone ledge we stood on, knocking us all from our feet. Tower was pinned beneath the impossible bulk of the massive lizard as Greatshadow brought his head to the platform and said, in very satisfied tones: "Embers rise constantly from the furnace of this bakery. They dance above the chimney like turbulent stars. A few may travel far, holding their heat until they land. Sometimes, such embers set roofs aflame."

"Rrraahhhhg!" screamed Relic, as the bone-handled knife dropped from his talon. He fell to all fours and charged the larger dragon. He opened his jaws wide, to almost a perfect ninety-degree angle, before he sunk them into Greatshadow's knuckle.

He shook his head from side to side, tearing at flesh, though in scale, he was doing about as much damage to Greatshadow as Menagerie was doing to Zetetic. "Da! Da! Da!" he raged. I think he meant, "Die! Die! Die!" Though, considering the relationship, perhaps not.

"You annoy me," said Greatshadow, flicking Relic with his talon and sending him flying far across the lava.

Around this time, the last of Relic's blood bubbled away from the bone-handled knife and I faded from existence. I watched with despair as my hands once more turned to mist, though I was slightly intrigued that, for some reason, this time I wasn't naked. Zetetic's clothing had made the transition with me back to the ghost zone I dwelled in.

Tower had grabbed one of Greatshadow's nails and was bending it back. He said, in booming, heroic tones, "You're bleeding, dragon. Your strength wanes with each heartbeat. Death is near!"

Tower was right. For the primal dragon of fire, Greatshadow didn't look so hot. He had big, gory holes in the side of his face, and his blood gushed out by the bucketful. His vitals fluids no longer glowed like flame, but were now a thick brown-red stream that spilled down onto the knight's face, splattering across the platform. I looked to where the knife had fallen, to see if there was a chance any of the drops might hit it.

The knife was gone.

I spun around.

Zetetic was nowhere to be seen.

"Your allies... have abandoned you," said Greatshadow, his voice strained.

"A pure heart may face evil alone," said Tower, defiant, as the strength of the Armor of Faith snapped the nail he wrestled with. He reached out and sank spiky fingers into the stone and began to drag himself free of Greatshadow's weakening grasp.

"You aren't... alone," said Greatshadow. "Three hundred monks pray... for your victory."

"Which is why I cannot fail!"

"The monastery has a library with ten centuries full of ancient books, dry as kindling," said Greatshadow, as his eyelids drooped. "There is an open window. And now... there is fire."

"Die!" screamed Relic as he rose from the lava near Greatshadow's hips, climbing the dragon like a mountain, pausing every few feet to take a nip from his hide.

The prayer-driven gears within Tower's armor purred at a louder pitch as he finally kicked himself free of the dragon's failing grasp. He lifted the Gloryhammer above his head and shouted, "This ends now!"

At that moment, the metallic ring that covered the thumb on his left gauntlet vanished.

"One of the faithful... has abandoned his post," said Greatshadow. Suddenly, a bolt popped out of the plate covering Tower's left kneecap. "He is not alone in loving books more than duty."

Tower answered by swinging the Gloryhammer with all his might toward Greatshadow's mocking tongue. Greatshadow's front teeth splintered with a wet sound that made me cringe. The dragon drew in a shallow breath as his mouth closed around the Gloryhammer and Tower's hands.

The dragon's scaly cheeks puffed out as he exhaled. A jet of white flame shot thirty feet out from Tower's left kneecap, quickly fading into a stream of oily black smoke.

Greatshadow spit out the Gloryhammer and stared at the

smoking husk of armor standing before him. With a creak, the armor tilted to the left, then toppled, landing with a clatter as it broke into scattered pieces. The interior was covered with soot half an inch thick.

Relic was now almost to Greatshadow's neck. The larger dragon grabbed the annoying assailant gingerly between two claws and placed him on the ledge amidst the scattered armor parts.

"Die! You must die!" screamed Relic.

"I sense I may have — in some fashion — offended you," said Greatshadow.

"You discovered me fresh from the egg and snapped my bones between your talons! You tossed my half-dead body from the caldera onto the slopes for the pygmies to scavenge! I was nothing but the unwelcome waste of your perversions, tossed away like trash! You will suffer! You will pay!"

Greatshadow rolled the tiny dragon between his talons, turning him to his back, taking a misshapen wing and snapping it once more. Relic screamed in agony as Greatshadow twisted the flesh back and forth, until a sharp bone punched through the surface.

"Little Brokenwing," said Greatshadow, tossing him onto the platform so that he bounced near the mouth of the tunnel. "Let the pain you feel at this moment linger. You have cost me dearly today. Nowowon required four centuries of incantations to properly enslave as my watchdog. You took him from me. I've worn my original body for thirty centuries, but the damage done by the knight may yet rob me of it. I saw your cowardly ally in possession of the Jagged Heart. You would dare bring *her* weapon to my lair, knowing what you know of our history?"

"I dare any price!" Relic hissed through clenched teeth. "Beginning with the pygmies who came to butcher my corpse, I have left a trail of death and destruction in my wake. My hate for you is a fire that can never be quenched!"

Greatshadow's mention of cowardly allies made me wonder

where Zetetic had gone. Assuming he had the bone-handled knife, I felt for the familiar tug, and instantly found it. I flashed down the tunnel only a few yards. Zetetic was pressed to the wall, his face drained of all color; the red D tattooed on his forehead looked pink. He was shivering, and not just because he had both arms wrapped around the Jagged Heart, hugging it like he was a frightened toddler. He had the bone-handled knife clutched in his right hand and what looked like a shard of glass in his left. He stared toward the opening of the ledge where Greatshadow busied himself with tormenting his overly ambitious offspring.

Greatshadow's blood seeped and bubbled across the stone like a dark river.

Setting his jaw, Zetetic leapt from the shadows, diving toward the stream of boiling ichor. He slapped the flat of the knife blade into the fluid. Instantly I was on my ass before him, meeting his frightened gaze. From the corner of my eye, I saw Greatshadow turning toward us, drawing a breath. The Jagged Heart had saved Zetetic before, but the dragon was so close that Zetetic's long, frazzled ponytail fluttered as the beast inhaled. This blast was coming at point blank range.

With a voice squeaking with terror he gazed deeply into my eyes and announced, "I understand the interspatial geometry of the ancients!"

He snapped the gleaming glass in his left hand, which I now saw to be a mirror.

At that second, Greatshadow breathed, a great blinding gush of fire licking around me in all directions. Yet, I wasn't burned. The flames danced behind me, swirled above me, spun before me, but I remained safe in a bubble of cool air.

The conflagration died away. It seemed to me that Greatshadow, in his weakened state, had lost much of the power of his flame. He looked odd as I stared at him, distorted and wavy. Then I realized I was seeing him through a wall of pure ice at least a yard thick.

The wall of ice had materialized from the tip of the Jagged Heart. The Jagged Heart was being held by a humanoid figure nine feet tall, broad across the shoulders, wearing a long black walrus-hide coat. I looked up and saw the mostly bald, blue-white scalp and the curve of ivory tusks. Never had I been so happy to see a woman whose last words to me had been a not so subtle threat of butchery.

Aurora looked down at me. As usual, her expression was one of utter coolness; she seemed unflustered that she'd just emerged from some unfathomable extra-dimensional prison to find herself face to face with a primal dragon. "I'll ask later what you're doing here," she said, shifting the shaft of the harpoon from her right hand to the left. "Right now, it's time for Greatshadow to meet someone who knows how to use this thing."

CHAPTER TWENTY-TWO
WORST NIGHTMARE

AURORA LUNGED, THE Jagged Heart held above her head, aiming for the gap between Greatshadow's eyes. The dragon pulled away, pressing down on the stone ledge with his massive claw. The volcanic rock cracked beneath his weight, creating a deep pit a yard wide just where Aurora's oversized boot should have landed. She fell as the ground between her and Greatshadow gave way.

Greatshadow plunged into the magma lake once more. I ran to the hole where Aurora had vanished. She'd dropped about twenty feet; her heels were balanced on a six inch lip of stone. Fresh lava bubbled below her, fiery red.

I pulled off my cloak and dropped to my chest, my arms dangling over the edge to allow the hem to reach her.

"Climb up!" I shouted.

"Infidel thinks you're dead, you bastard!" Aurora said as she grabbed the thick velvet cloth. "Why the hell are you still alive? What on earth are you doing here? For that matter, what the hell am I doing here?"

Zetetic looked over the edge as Aurora began to climb up the cloak. My arms felt like they'd be pulled from their sockets. Zetetic said, "The pyramid trapped you in an interstitial realm where time doesn't exist as a dimension. I freed you."

"And while you're pondering that, you should know I'm a ghost, but turn solid when dragon blood gets on my knife," I explained, my voice strained as I struggled not to drop her. "I may dematerialize at any second, so hurry."

Aurora furrowed her brow as she climbed. "I can't decide which of you is making less sense. Let me talk to someone sane. Where's Infidel?"

"The spirit realm," said Zetetic.

"She's dead?"

The Deceiver stroked his chin as he contemplated the question, then said, "I don't believe a word has been invented that describes her condition. She's been split into physically manifested dual aspects of her psyche then thrust bodily into a non-material realm of souls."

"You are not allowed to answer any more of my questions," Aurora grumbled as she grabbed the rocky ledge next to my shoulder with her sausage-sized fingers. My teeth chattered as she clambered over me back onto the relative safety of the ledge. "Where'd the damn dragon get off to?"

Relic crawled from the tunnel toward the bone-handled knife. He answered Aurora through teeth clenched with pain: "Greatshadow is bathing in magma to cauterize his wounds."

Aurora tensed as she saw the small dragon. She raised the Jagged Heart, looking ready to put him out of his misery.

"Wait!" said Zetetic, grabbing her arm. "He's a friend."

"I wouldn't go that far," I said.

"He's an enemy of our enemy," said Zetetic.

Relic reached the knife and moved it from the vaporizing dark-brown pool it lay in, touching it to the sticky red blood coating his shoulder from his broken wing. The fresh fluid filled me with a surge of energy.

"So, can Greatshadow just wait us out?" I asked. "Could he stay under the magma forever?"

"Actually, no," said Relic. "Despite the fact my father dwells in a volcano, the elemental force he's merged with isn't magma, it's fire. His physical body and his internal flames both require air. He must surface soon."

Zetetic looked around. "Soon may not be soon enough," he said. "Tower's armor is disappearing piece by piece."

He was right. Tower's chest plate was still there, along with various nuts, bolts, and gears, but the bulk of the armor had vanished. As I watched, the hip compartment that held the magic book flickered, then turned to smoke, leaving the leather-bound volume within sitting on the barren ground. Zetetic tore off a piece of his robes and fashioned them into impromptu mittens, lifting the book.

"Technically, I'm not touching it," he said as he flipped through the book. He shook his head slowly as he studied the pages. "Not that having this will do me any good. Greatshadow is no doubt burning the monastery to the ground, killing everyone inside. When the last monk praying to keep my heart beating is slain I'll be dead, permanently this time."

"Greatshadow may have plucked that information from Stagger's mind," said Relic. "Perhaps he thinks if he waits long enough, he can face one less foe. Aurora is our best hope now. She can use the magic of the Jagged Heart to slay Greatshadow."

"This still doesn't make sense to me," I said. "Fire melts ice. Why is an icy fragment of Hush more powerful than a whole dragon?"

"Hush isn't the dragon of ice," said Aurora. "She's the dragon of cold."

"So?"

"To understand the true nature of reality, you need only look into the night sky. Darkness is the permanent state of things; light is merely a fleeting local phenomenon. The same is true of heat and fire. Flames can rage brightly for but a moment. Just as darkness will always win out over light, cold is the eternal backdrop that existed before fire, and will endure after. Flame can never win any permanent victory against cold."

"The true power of the weapon lies in more than simply its elemental chill," said Relic. "Greatshadow is the dragon who broke Hush's heart. Its frosty bitterness embodies the seething hatred Hush feels toward Greatshadow. It can, and will, slay him."

"I know a lot of dragon history, but I've never heard that," said Zetetic.

Before Relic could provide us with a history lesson, Greatshadow burst from the surface of the bubbling magma, his neck rising up fifty feet, a hundred, as he drew a deep breath into his mighty lungs. He was wreathed in fresh flames, his skin aglow with his newly stoked energies. The ground beneath us trembled as the lava pool began to rise.

Relic shook his head, looking as if he might be about to cry. "He's opened fresh lava vents beneath the surface! If the volcano erupts, we'll all perish!"

Aurora craned her neck up, drawing the harpoon back. Greatshadow spread his enormous wings, beating them in a powerful downstroke. Globs of molten rock rained around us as a foundry wind nearly swept us from our feet.

"His head's too far away!" Aurora shouted over the gale. "I can throw a harpoon a hundred yards on a good day, but not straight up!"

"You could if you were bigger!" Zetetic leapt in front of her. "Fortunately, I have the power to make you a giantess with an enchanted kiss!" He stood on his tip toes, grabbed her cheeks, and mashed his puckered lips between her tusks.

A wall of flame shot down toward us as Greatshadow exhaled once more. As before, the flame was thwarted by a shield of ice as Aurora grew rapidly, doubling to sixteen feet, then thirty, as Zetetic grabbed Relic by the tail and dragged him back toward the tunnel.

I lingered behind for half a second to watch as Aurora topped out close to ninety feet tall. The Jagged Heart had grown with her, taller than any tree. Her long black coat flapped as she leaned back to throw, the hem catching me like a sail, knocking me from my feet. Flat on my back, I watched as she let the harpoon fly, aiming toward Greatshadow's open maw as the jet of flames died away.

The Jagged Heart flashed up like reverse lightning, trailing snow, entering the dragon's cavernous jaws and punching into the roof of his mouth. His head tilted sideways as he shrieked in pain. The bright, crystalline tip of the harpoon jutted from the top of his skull. His eyes rolled up, as if trying to focus on it.

Finally, Greatshadow shuddered, his body wracked with a death spasm. Zetetic ran from the tunnel and grabbed my hand, dragging me back toward relative safety as the dragon began to fall. Magma splashed up in a raging tidal wave as his body collapsed. Aurora, no longer in possession of the Jagged Heart, dropped to her hands and knees and tried to squeeze her massive bulk into the tunnel.

She was too late. The molten wave fell upon her and she screamed as her giant shoulders slammed into the tunnel entrance, plugging it, saving Zetetic, Relic, and myself from the magma bath.

I ran to her as the magic that had transformed her drained away. She returned to her normal size, inside a large cave that was a perfect negative outline of her body. The lava had hardened into solid stone on touching her, but not before it had burned away much of her skin. Her face had been spared, at least, and she was still alive as I dropped to my knees in front of her. "Hang on!" I screamed. "Zetetic can fix you!"

Her words were nothing but a whisper as she answered, "Th-the Heart... i-it must b-be returned..." The last of her breath passed between her ivory tusks as her eyes closed.

I pursed my lips together, fighting to keep from crying. She'd never intended to fight Greatshadow when this all began. She'd never done a thing to deserve this fate.

Relic hobbled next to me, the bone-handled knife in his bleeding claw. "There is no time for mourning," said the small dragon. "Greatshadow's body is dead. We must act swiftly to kill his elemental spirit, before he can grow a new shell."

Zetetic wandered around the cave left by Aurora, staring up at specks of light that dotted the ceiling. He climbed a wall and thrust his fingers into one of the lights, which proved to be a hole in a paper-thin sheet of rock. He flaked it away in big handfuls, and soon had a large enough gap to climb through.

"Follow me," he said, as he wriggled out.

Relic leapt onto the wall and clambered after him. Despite

his injuries and the obvious pain of every movement, the little dragon still seemed much stronger and faster than I was. I guess even a lamed dragon was a better physical specimen than an ordinary man. Or, at least in better shape than me. I was panting, my arms trembling, by the time I managed to drag myself through the hole. My legs were quivering as I walked out onto a freshly formed plain of soot-black rock still spiderwebbed with tendrils of bright red lava. The volcano seemed to have lost a great deal of its energy with Greatshadow gone. Still, I danced around, grateful I had boots. As long as I kept moving, the heat was merely blistering instead of crippling.

In the center of the rapidly cooling lava, amid rock that cracked and popped as it gave up its heat, was Greatshadow's enormous head and shoulders, frozen into the solidifying stone. One wing jutted into the air behind him like a giant black sail. The deep brick-red of his scalp was now pink beneath a layer of thick frost. The Jagged Heart had returned to its normal size and lay upon his snout as if it had been dropped there by some hopelessly lost whaler.

Zetetic ran across the smoking plain, jumping over glowing cracks, scrambling up Greatshadow's scaly hide. Though it was entirely the wrong thing to be thinking about, I couldn't help but gawk at the sheer size of the dragon's skull as my internal booze calculator tried to figure out how many rounds I could buy at the *Black Swan* if I could somehow cash it in. A lot. A whole damn lot. Numbers weren't my strong suit.

Zetetic stood between the dragon's eyes as he snatched up the Jagged Heart. "Got it!" he shouted. "Now, we just need to get a warrior to the spirit world to finish off the dragon!"

Relic nodded, standing before the Greatshadow's toothy jaws, staring up at Zetetic. "Stagger will have to do."

"Have to do what?" I asked.

"Go to the spirit world to kill Greatshadow," said Zetetic, tossing the harpoon at me. I jumped back as the tip buried into the stone where I'd just stood.

"You almost killed me!" I shouted.

"I don't think that's possible," the Deceiver said. "You aren't alive, remember? No court would convict me."

I grabbed the harpoon and yanked it free. I held it toward Relic. "You're the one with the daddy-grudge. You do it."

"Nowowon has broken my claws. It's agonizing to hold this knife; I could never wield the harpoon effectively," said Relic. "And Zetetic is too cowardly to be trusted with the mission."

"I have no argument with that statement whatsoever," said the Deceiver.

"I'm not exactly a prime physical specimen myself," I said, wiping sweat from my brow. "And I'll fight any man who says I'm not a yellow-bellied coward!"

"You may not need to fight the dragon yourself," said Zetetic. "The War Doll — I mean, Infidel — is already in the spirit realm. The gate she passed through leads to the specific abstract reality where Greatshadow's soul resides. She did show a certain talent for violence. If she's somehow recovered from her psychic split, you could have her complete the mission."

My immediate thought was, screw the mission. Except for the whole end-of-the-world-by-fire thing, what did I care if Greatshadow's soul was killed? But the thought that I could be reunited with Infidel in the spirit world made my heart beat faster. I didn't want her to die, but, if she was already a spirit, I'd rather be on the other side with her than trapped here as a ghost.

"Okay," I said, holding the harpoon in a two-handed grasp. "You've made your case. How do I get to Infidel? Zetetic can't open another spirit gate. If there was a magic item here that could open the portal, isn't it buried under about a thousand feet of rock now?"

"Oh," said Relic. "That was a lie."

"Nice," said Zetetic.

"Then there's not some object here with the power to send me to the land of the dead?" I asked, confused.

"I wouldn't say that's true either," said Relic, walking toward me, wincing as he shifted the bone-handled knife around in his claw to grasp it by the hilt instead of the blade.

Before I understood his intention he stabbed me, the blade punching though my left nipple. In a second of time that dribbled by like molasses I felt the knife tear through my pectoral muscles, skim between my ribs, slice the edge of my left lung, and puncture my heart, halting it mid-beat.

The world went black.

I LIFTED MY throbbing head from my folded arms and looked around the bar at the *Black Swan*. I blinked my bleary eyes, attempting to focus in the dim light. The lanterns barely flickered behind soot-grimed crystal globes. A score of empty tankards were set out around me in a semi-circle of pewter and glass. My whole body was stiff and cold as I stretched, working out the kinks in my back.

I rubbed my sleep-fogged eyes, then studied the bottles behind the bar, choosing what I'd drink next. I frowned when I realized all the bottles looked empty. Everything was covered with dust. Busty, one of the regular serving wenches, was at the far end of the bar, her back to me.

"I just had the worst nightmare," I said. My tongue felt thick in my mouth, covered with a dry, pasty scum. "Bring me a beer, would you, luv?"

She wouldn't. At least, she didn't. She just stood there, still as a statue. I got up from the stool and staggered toward her, keeping one hand on the bar for balance. I reached the end of the bar and suddenly sobered up.

Busty was nothing but a dusty skeleton, still standing upright, staring blankly ahead with empty sockets. Her frilly blouse hung like a sack, the generous bustline now dangling to reveal a desiccated breastbone. I spun around, surveying the silent room. There were a hundred people packed into every corner, all dead, their skeletons frozen in rough approximation of daily motion. Players gathered around a table, faded cards forever clasped in their bony fingers. A whore leaned on the shoulder of a client in a corner booth, her mummified cheeks stained with rouge, her dusty wig askew atop her skull.

"Hello?" I said, to the silent room.

No one answered.

However, as I strained to listen, in the distance I heard a long, low howl, like the baying of a wolf. I crept across the dusty floorboards to the door, looking out onto the familiar skyline of the Isle of Fire.

Only, it wasn't quite as I remembered. The boats surrounding me were all derelict husks, floating in water the color of red wine. A rotting, tilted pier ran toward the banks of the bay. The damage done by Greatshadow's attack on Commonground was nowhere to be seen. Instead, the slopes of the island were still covered with a thick jade canopy of trees, rising to a volcano from which plumes of stark white steam boiled heavenward. The sky was a light gray slate, devoid of a sun, or even clearly defined clouds. The island that lay before me seemed out of scale, smaller somehow.

I crouched down, startled, as the animalistic howl once more rolled over the bay. Wolves weren't native to the Isle of Fire, though they haunted the mountains near the monastery where I'd spent my childhood. I'd gone to sleep many a night pondering the meanings of their different songs; sometimes, they sang toward the moon to tell tales of loneliness and lost loves. Sometimes, their songs were almost joyous, a simple declaration of, "I'm alive! I'm here! And I'm a wolf!" That song was easy to distinguish from a harsher, more sinister war cry, when they howled to frighten prey, to startle them into running. This was that last type of howl.

I glanced back to the bar. The Jagged Heart was lying on the floor beside my stool. I looked down, surprised to find I was still wearing the finery Zetetic had conjured. To my greater surprise, I found the bone-handled knife jutting from my chest. I didn't feel a thing as I grasped the hilt and popped it free. No blood flowed from the wound.

"Relic?" I said, wondering if he could still hear me.

The only answer was the gentle lapping of the wine-dark sea.

Going back inside, I grabbed the Jagged Heart. I wondered how it had made the transition. I'd been holding it when I was stabbed, but when I first died, I'd passed over naked. Maybe the difference was that Relic hadn't stabbed a living man to dispatch me to the ghost realms. He'd stabbed a materialized spirit. If I ever met the Divine Author, it seemed like a good thing to ask Him about over a pint of beer. Assuming the Divine Author drinks.

What am I saying? He's a writer. Of course He drinks.

Alas, He wasn't here at the moment, and my quick pillaging pass behind the bar showed that beer wasn't present either. If this were paradise, the sea outside would have been made of actual wine, but I suspected I would be in for an unpleasant surprise if I tested that. I was going to be doing this dragon hunt sober, damn it.

Back outside, I headed up the boardwalk toward the forest. Like the bar, it was eerily silent: no bugs buzzing, no bullfrogs bleating, no birds providing a serenade. I pushed through underbrush studded with fearsome thorns. The Jagged Heart proved better than a machete; vines and limbs studded with wooden needles froze solid as I touched them, snapping with only the slightest touch. Once I was through the brush, I was surrounded by towering trees, their smooth, perfectly formed trunks stretching high overhead into a curtain of unbroken green. It was dark as a moonless night, but my eyes soon adjusted to the dimness.

From high up the slope, the howl of the unseen beast once more rolled through the air. As the sound faded, I thought I could hear a *crunch, crunch, crunch* in the distance, the footsteps of something large creeping amongst the trees. I had a pretty good idea what might be making the noise.

Somewhere out in the darkness was the monster who'd lived inside the woman I'd loved.

I skulked up the slopes, holding the harpoon like a halberd, a weapon I had absolutely no experience with. Not that I had much experience with any weapons. Infidel had been my principal mode of defense, which was for the best. Given how often I'd been drunk when our fights broke out, if I'd tried handling anything sharp I'd probably eventually have stabbed myself.

I heard a *shuff, shuff, shuff* of something moving through the leaves and pressed up closely against an ancient tree trunk thick enough to hide an elephant. I peeked around, listening closely to see if the noise was drawing closer.

Shuff, shuff, shuff. It was right on the other side of the tree.

When I met the she-dragon, would I kill her? Could I? What if I tried to talk to her? Would she recognize me or just try to eat me?

Trusting that I would know what to do when the moment came, I grasped the harpoon and raced around the tree at top speed, which, thanks to my cape snagging on the trunk, wasn't all that fast. Still, it was fast enough to terrify the little girl in the lacy dress I found pressed up against the tree on the far side. Her eyes popped wide and her mouth gaped into an almost perfect 'O' as she filled her lungs, ready to scream. I dropped the Jagged Heart and jumped toward her, hands outstretched, knocking her to the ground as I clamped my hand over her mouth. Air gushed around my fingers as her muffled scream tickled my palm.

"Shhh!" I hissed, as quietly as I could manage. "Shhh! Do you want your other half to hear?"

Tears welled in her eyes as she shook her head 'no.'

I couldn't believe how tiny she was, pinned beneath me. Infidel had actually been somewhat petite, I guess, but it was easy to forget this when she was juggling around bruisers and brutes. Princess Innocent was a whole lot shorter and her arms were thin as broomsticks. My hand practically covered her whole face.

"I'm going to let go," I whispered. "Don't scream."

She trembled as I pulled my hand free. I helped her stand, while I rose to my knees so we'd be on eye level.

"Are you all right?" I asked. Her dress was torn in a dozen places, and her cheeks were covered with scratches. Her long silver hair was a mess.

"Who are you?" she whispered.

"You don't remember?"

She shook her head.

I weighed my words carefully. I had dreamed, should I ever reunite with Infidel, I'd confess my love and kiss her hard enough to make us both dizzy. That seemed highly inappropriate now, given her reversion to such a young age. "I was... I was a friend. My name is Stagger."

"You smell bad," she said, scrunching up her nose.

No doubt I did. Growing up in a palace, Innocent had probably never met anyone who sweated.

"Have you seen your other half?" I asked. "Is she near?"

She furrowed her brow, looking confused.

"The she-dragon," I said. "She brought you here."

"She wants to eat me," said Innocent. "But I'm good at hiding."

Which was true enough. The princess had hidden inside Infidel all these years without me suspecting a thing.

As I thought this, an idea occurred to me. Innocent had been hiding inside Infidel. Could she do so again? What if... what if the way to join her two halves back together was simply to let the dragon once more devour the princess?

"The way you're looking at me scares me," said Innocent.

I pursed my lips as I pondered my options.

Whatever was showing on my face couldn't have been good, because Innocent suddenly burst into tears. She went limp, almost fainting, as she fell against my chest, sobbing. I wrapped my arms around her, stroking her hair.

"It's okay," I whispered. "It's okay. I'll protect you. I won't let the monster hurt you."

And that was that. The vile thought of feeding this little girl to the she-dragon was banished back to whatever dark pit in my brain it had crawled from. Some fatherly instinct welled within me and I knew with absolute certainty I'd willingly die to protect this girl.

"I'm s-so tired," she sobbed. "I've b-been running and running and running."

Again, this was true for Infidel as well. The whole time I'd known her, I'd thought of her as a fighter, but, in truth, she'd lived every moment on the run from her own past. How had I been so blind?

"You won't have to run any more," I whispered, setting my jaw firmly. "I'll fight the monster for you."

I hugged her for a long time, her face pressed against my chest, until her sobs died down to whimpers, then sniffles. I finally pulled away from her, still on my knees, my hands on her shoulders as I said, "Everything is going to be fine. I'm your friend, and I'll take care of you."

She didn't say anything. She didn't move. Her mouth hung half open as her eyes were fixed at a point in space somewhere over my shoulder.

I didn't have to turn around to know what was standing behind me.

CHAPTER TWENTY-THREE
THE WORLD CAN WAIT

I DOVE ASIDE as a three-clawed foot stomped down where I'd stood, causing the earth to shudder. My flight was brought to a choking halt by the red velvet cape, caught beneath the she-dragon's heel. I should have dumped the cloak the second the damn thing had been inflicted on me. I fiddled with the collar for half a second before slicing the clasp open with the bone-handled knife. I dropped the blade as I scrambled toward the Jagged Heart. The ground was slippery with frost. I slid across ice-etched leaves, my hand outstretched. A giant claw punched into the soil in front of me, forming a scaly fence. I slammed into it, the harpoon only inches beyond my grasp.

The she-dragon leaned down, her jaws dripping sap-like spittle, the tangles of her hair dangling like vines. Bright yellow eyes stared into mine as she paused in reptilian concentration. Did she recognize me?

"Infidel!" I shouted. "It's me, Stagger!"

Her oversized fingers wrapped around my throat as she snatched me off the ground. Her nose was merely two holes flat against her face, like the nose of a snake. The emerald green scales that glittered around her eyes were weirdly beautiful, in a terrifying, inhuman way.

"I love you!" I shouted. "You loved me!"

The creature licked her lips, her eyes twinkling with the same delighted hunger I'd seen in Infidel's face when Tower had produced the cake. Her head tilted back as her jaws opened to an impossible angle. I flailed helplessly as she brought me toward her jagged teeth.

"Leave him alone!" a tiny voice shouted below my feet.

The she-dragon closed her mouth and looked down. From the corner of my eye, I glimpsed Princess Innocent with her hands on her hips.

"He's my friend and I won't let you hurt him," the princess shouted, a stern look in her eyes.

A low growl rumbled from the she-dragon's chest as she eyed the annoying creature.

The princess stomped her feet, obviously furious at the delay. "My daddy's the king and you have to do what I say! Put him down!"

"You really should listen to her," I squeaked.

The she-dragon responded by flinging me aside. I went flying above the canopy of trees, feeling profound déjà vu as I reached the apex of my flight and began to plummet toward the blood-tangle vines far below. My re-entry was thoroughly unpleasant. If I'd truly been alive, it's possible it would even have been fatal, as I slammed into a tree trunk hard enough to knock off bark. But, just as the wound had been clean when I pulled the bone-handled knife from my ribs, the cuts and scrapes that crosshatched my arms beneath the shredded remains of my sleeves didn't ooze a single drop of blood.

I rose on rubbery legs as a high-pitched shriek of pain reached my ears. I struggled back up the slope, limping, my ankle twisted, though the pain I felt was muted by the same general gauziness that wreathed all my senses in death. Then, for no apparent reason, my ankle suddenly hurt like the devil. In fact, my entire body felt like I'd gone two rounds in a pit fight with No-Face. Blood bubbled up from my various cuts, though almost a minute had passed since the wounds had been inflicted.

A hundred yards ahead there was another ear-piercing scream, far louder than before.

"Infidel!" I shouted, hopping back up the slope with all the speed I could muster. "Infidel!"

At last I spotted the elephantine tree I'd hidden behind only a few minutes before. I moved to one side and saw the Jagged Heart still on the ground, near freshly fallen trees.

I hopped a little further, my heart growing cold as I realized how utterly silent the forest had become. The shrieking I'd heard earlier had stopped, and now the quietness was broken only by a wet, crunching sound, repeating every few seconds, a sound that I imagined might come from the jaws of a she-dragon devouring meat and gristle.

Braced for the worst, I stepped into the clearing.

Sitting atop one of the fallen trees, her face covered in bright green goo, was Princess Innocent. She lifted the bone-handled knife overhead and gave a solid punch down with both hands, planting it to the hilt in the tree trunk, creating the sound I'd heard. I wondered if, for some reason, my blood was pumping in my body because the knife blade was wet again, though with what looked like green slime instead of blood.

I then realized the tree trunk the princess was hacking into was covered in dark green scales and shaped like a woman. It wasn't sap coating the knife.

I sagged, resting my hands on my knees, catching my breath, as Princess Innocent placed her mouth against the fresh wound she'd gouged in the she-dragon and sucked up the oozing blood. With every mouthful, she grew a little larger. The gown she wore tightened, then split along the seams.

After a moment the princess sat back and wiped the bright green blood from her face. She had a woman's body now, over a foot taller than when she'd started her feast, with magnificent breasts I instantly recognized. Before me was the woman I'd known all these years, her silver hair long and gleaming, her skin pale beneath blood and shredded gown, completely free of pygmy dyes. Innocent looked like Infidel once more.

I smiled at the perfect logic of the magic unfolding before me. Infidel hadn't been created when a dragon devoured a princess.

Infidel had been born when a princess devoured a dragon.

Infidel looked slightly drunk, oblivious to her surroundings as the dragon blood settled into her belly. Yet, as she surveyed the forest with her glazed eyes, her face broke into a giant grin as her gaze reached me. She cried, "Stagger!"

"Infidel!" I answered, throwing my arms open as I hobbled toward her.

She jumped from the corpse and bounded toward me like a sprightly gazelle. I flinched as she reached me, her arms wrapping around me, braced for significant damage to my ribs. However, her hug, while robust, seemed to have only ordinary strength behind it. I bent my face down to gaze at her in wonder, but instantly closed my eyes as she pressed her lips to mine. The green blood still on her cheeks smelled like papaya. Her sticky tongue slid between my teeth. I hugged her back with all my might and kissed her till we were both dizzy.

Not metaphorically dizzy, mind you, but actual stumble-and-collapse-from-lack-of-air dizzy. We fell, landing atop the red cape that lay over the leafy earth like a bedspread. Only the impact of the ground made our lips pull apart. I was on top of her, staring down into her sea-gray eyes and all the words and wisdom and wonder that they contained. Her body beneath mine was hot as a furnace. Where our skin met through our tattered clothing, it was slippery from dragon blood and my own blood and a copious amount of sweat. Our breaths intermingled as we studied each other's faces and for the span of several heartbeats it felt as if all was right with the universe.

Except, alas, it wasn't.

"As much as I hate to ruin this moment, the world might come to a fiery end if we don't go kill Greatshadow's spirit," I whispered.

"The world can wait," she replied, as she placed her hand in my tangled hair and drew my mouth to hers once more.

Fortunately, she'd left the bone-handled knife in the dragon's blood. For the events which followed, it was useful to be in full, unmuted possession of all my senses, and to have a heart free to pump blood to wherever it was needed.

As we kissed, her gentle fingers slowly pulled away the damaged rags that had once been my shirt. My own fingers slipped into the strained seams of her gown and completed the tearing, freeing her from her silken confinement.

And then...

And then...

And then...

Shall I tell you how she looked, bare beneath me, the body of an angel wearing the grin of a devil, hungry for pleasure? Shall I tell you of the noises that came from deep within her, the guttural growls, the sibilant songs, the barely-voiced moans as my mouth fell against her skin? Shall I tell you how she tasted, all sweetness and salt, of the wine that was her sweat and spit and tears? Or how she smelled, like earth, like ocean, like sunlight, a symphony of aromas where every scent note built to a perfect crescendo?

And shall I tell you how she felt? Do I even possess the vocabulary to describe the smooth, slick landscape of her body, the warm terrain so full of curves and creases, the silken softness overlaying muscle and bone of breathtaking artfulness? Can I possibly find the vocabulary to describe the magic of feeling her heart beating as I pressed my lips against her throat, the steady *thump, thump, thump* a drum beating out a single message of *life, life, life,* so elegant and simple it moved me to tears?

No. No, I don't believe I can tell you of these things, and I don't believe that I should.

But they happened all the same.

SINCE I CANNOT tell you about the unspeaking wonder of the moments that followed my reunion with Infidel, allow me to fill you in on what was occurring back in the real world with Relic and Zetetic. While I wasn't personally witness to these events, I have since learned enough to reconstruct the moment: Zetetic and Relic had freed the Gloryhammer from where it was partially trapped beneath freshly cooling lava. I had wondered if the Gloryhammer would vanish like Tower's armor, but apparently it was a far older creation, an enchanted weapon with a history dating back centuries, and Zetetic recounted this history to Relic with his usual enthusiasm for obscure magical lore.

As they spoke, Zetetic and Relic retreated to a perch atop Greatshadow's skull, which rose like a little island from the lava plane. They amused themselves for a time by pulling possessions out of Tower's sketchbook, including the Immaculate Attire, which Zetetic used as a seat on the still-hot skull. Several more slices of cake in various flavors were also retrieved, which they devoured with gusto.

As daylight faded they passed the time speculating as to what was happening elsewhere. For instance, Zetetic put forth the theory the fire Greatshadow had started in the monastery must have been brought under control, even though the last bolts from Tower's armor had finally faded away. Some monks had survived, Zetetic argued, since his heart was still beating.

Relic chuckled lowly in response and said, "You never died."

"I was hanged," said Zetetic.

"Yes. But your neck didn't break. You suffocated, and merely passed out."

"My neck was pure agony for a week after," said Zetetic. "It certainly felt broken."

"No doubt you'd injured some ligaments," said Relic. "But Father Ver knew the truth. When they hung you, the noose was designed to suffocate you without severing your spine. You passed out from asphyxiation, feeling as if you were dying. When you woke up, you were told of your death, though it had never occurred. No monks have ever had to pray to keep you alive. I snatched the truth from Ivory Blade's mind."

"Oh," said Zetetic, then burst out into raucous laughter.

"You're relieved you need not fear imminent death?"

Zetetic wiped a tear from his eye. "There's that. But I also appreciate the irony. How appropriate that I should be ensnared with a simple lie."

They both sat quietly for a while, listening to the crackle of the stone cooling around them, until Zetetic asked, "How are we going to know if Stagger succeeds?"

"We shall know when the world doesn't end," said Relic.

"It's not ending right now."

"That we know of," said Relic.

Zetetic nodded, pondering this. Then he said, "Do you think Stagger ever found the she-dragon or the princess?"

"Let us hope not," said Relic.

"Why?"

"Because the princess would distract him. He would probably try to protect her from danger, which means he might not do what is needed to slay Greatshadow."

"But maybe he'll find the she-dragon," said Zetetic.

Relic sighed. "In that case, the creature is probably chewing his flesh right now."

And, in a way, he was right, since as my reunion with Infidel unfolded, I became increasingly decorated with bite marks.

But I'm not telling you of such things, am I?

ONCE WE WERE too exhausted to continue the more athletic portion of our reunion, we wrapped our tenderized bodies in the red cloak, our limbs entangled as we slipped into a dreamy haze in which time lost all grip upon us. Infidel's face was pressed up against my chest, listening to my heartbeat. She was so still and quiet I thought she'd gone to sleep, until she whispered, "You smell nice."

I chuckled. "Innocent didn't think so."

"Innocent didn't know what was good for her. You, Stagger, are good for me. I was so lucky to know you."

"Why are you speaking in the past tense?" I asked.

"You're still dead, right? That wasn't just some bad dream?"

My mouth went dry. "It wasn't a dream," I whispered. "I am dead. But I never left you; I've been with you every moment, haunting the bone-handled knife. And now we can be together forever."

"Can we?" she asked, sounding skeptical.

"Can't we?" I asked. "I guess, honestly, I don't know. I don't understand how things work here in the spirit world. Maybe there will never be any ending here."

"But I don't belong here," she said. "I'm still alive. At least, I think I am. There's this... tug... inside me. I feel like my time here is limited. Eventually, I'll be drawn back to the real world."

"I understand," I said. "I wish I could come with you."

"I don't see why you can't, if I can take the knife back. Haunting the blade that killed you. That's kind of weird."

"This coming from a woman with a belly full of dragon's blood."

Infidel sat up, frowning as she noticed the tangled green ribbons in her long hair. As she worked to unknot them, she said, "The first time I swallowed Verdant's blood, it was dried up and concentrated. I could feel the power surging through my body. This time, it turned me back to my correct age, but I don't feel super-strong." She ran her fingers along a line of hickeys on her neck. "And I'm definitely not invulnerable."

"Maybe things work differently here. Hopefully you'll be back to your arm-ripping self when you get home."

She looked up the slope toward the caldera. "I wish I knew how to get home. The only path I can think of leads straight through Greatshadow. The dragon must know how to travel between the spirit world and the material world, or Zetetic wouldn't be worried."

"We still have the Jagged Heart," I said. "Even with just normal strength, we can take him."

She sighed as she pulled the last ribbon free from her hair and tossed it away. "That's so sad about Aurora," she said, referring to a conversation we'd had during an earlier pause.

I sat up and rubbed her back. "She was a good friend."

"She was my only friend," said Infidel. "Except you."

"I'll always be with you," I said.

She nodded gazing off into the distance. "Especially if the Black Swan is right."

"About what? The dragon apocalypse?"

Infidel rolled her eyes. "About us having a daughter."

Somehow, despite everything that we'd done together since our reunion, that possibility hadn't crossed my mind. Could I really impregnate Infidel? Did this half-alive, materialized phantom body of mine have that power?

"You're quiet," she said, as I grew lost in thought. "Don't you want her to be yours?"

I smiled as I lay back, pulling her down with me. "I want it so much, I think we should take at least one more run at increasing the odds."

And then there was another hour that I can't talk about.

"Stagger must have gotten the job done by now," said Zetetic. By now it had gotten really dark in the caldera. Outside the small circle of light cast by the Gloryhammer, ghostly flames flickered and danced above cracks in the ground, as gases beneath the earth seeped free and ignited.

"I'm not so certain," said Relic. "I don't feel... a release."

"A release?"

"Like all dragons, I'm attuned to elemental forces. Greatshadow is still present in the flames surrounding us. He simply hasn't gathered the strength yet to control them."

"If he died, you could take over the element of flame? Just like that?"

Relic shrugged. "It would require time. How much is difficult to say."

"How long did it take Greatshadow to master the element?"

"Though I have many of his memories, I can't judge the time, since time as we know it wasn't invented when my father was young."

Zetetic looked perplexed.

"Before Glorious merged his spirit with the sun, the sun's path was more chaotic. Years and days had no fixed length. Glorious inadvertently gave birth to human civilization when he guided the sun into a fixed path, making seasons predictable, and agriculture possible."

"Amazing," said Zetetic.

"Still, to answer your question as best I can, I expect it will take a decade or more to merge my soul with fire."

"A decade doesn't seem very long to achieve such power."

"To you, perhaps. I've only been alive a few months. A decade seems unbearably long."

Zetetic stroked his chin as he contemplated the small dragon. "You're an interesting infant, Relic."

"I don't want to be called Relic any more."

"Why not?"

"I used that name because I never was given another. But my father finally fulfilled this simple obligation, at least. He called me Brokenwing."

"So he did. Little Brokenwing."

"I won't be using the 'little,'" said the dragon, somewhat indignant.

"So, if Stagger fails, what are we going to do?" asked Zetetic.

Relic shook his head. "There's no point in asking. Stagger is our only hope."

Zetetic looked up into the darkness. "I wonder what's taking so long to get the job done?"

If I'd been there to answer, I'd have reminded him that at fifty, my body isn't quite as robust as it once was. It takes a little longer to get the job done.

AND EVEN LONGER to get the job done a third time. This dayless, nightless land provided few clues as to how much time had passed as we rested, utterly exhausted.

Infidel was using my hairy belly as a pillow, looking up at me with a dreamy gaze. Suddenly, her eyes widened.

"It's so obvious!" she said, jumping to her feet.

"What's obvious?"

"Dragon's blood! You come back to life when the knife touches dragon's blood. And, you came back to life when Nowowon gave you a drink of blood. So, to come back to life permanently, you need to drink dragon's blood!"

I sat up, scratching my head. "You think it's that easy?"

"Who's the brain in this operation?" she said, placing her hands on her hips.

"Um," I said, deciding to pretend I didn't understand the question. Anyway, what could it hurt? She scrambled toward the fallen body of her dragon-self.

"Ow, ow, ow!" she said as she crossed over the ground. "Lots of sharp rocks under these leaves. I'm not used to being tender-footed."

"You want to wear my boots?" I asked, wrestling to put on what remained of my pants.

"I'd slip right out of those things," she said, scrambling onto the dragon corpse. "I'll wrap my feet in some cloth from the cape. Right now, you need to suck some dragon-blood."

She grabbed the bone-handled knife, struggling to free it. She gouged a new hole on the side of the hip. Gore the consistency and color of pea soup oozed out.

My lips were tender from Infidel's nibbles, but I heroically pressed them to the scaly hide of the corpse and sucked. The blood was sticky, as difficult to swallow as molasses, and the fruity flavor I had tasted on Infidel's tongue had a sourness when drank directly that grew more unbearable the longer it sat in my mouth. It took a few moments to force down a cup of the stuff.

"Ugg," I said, wiping my lips. "I'm used to putting bad things in my mouth, but this is fairly rotten."

"How do you feel?" she asked.

"Fantastic!" I said. "But I've felt that way ever since we've been back together. Just being able to talk to you again is more magical than dragon's blood."

"Maybe you won't notice any changes to your body until we get back to the real world," she said, studying my bruised frame with a critical eye.

"That's probably how it works," I said, hoping it was true.

She sat down on the she-dragon's log-like foot and began to cut the lower edges of my cape into strips with the knife. She wrapped her feet in the thick velvet, forming what could have passed as ballerina slippers. They looked surprisingly functional; Infidel had a lot of experience improvising with clothing. She took what remained of my shirt, tore off the shredded sleeves, and wore it like a tunic, cinching it at the waist with a belt made from the braided sleeve rags.

I dressed while she worked, slipping my boots back on. Since I was shirtless, I decided I'd wear what was left of the cape. I brushed off the twigs and leaves, and noticed a snarl of long, tangled hair. I looked at it closer, unable to tell if it had come out of my scalp or hers, and finally decided it was a little of both. Inspired by the intertwined fibers, I began to wrap the long strands around my little finger, tucking and twisting them until I formed a small braided ring. It barely fit on my little finger. I braided another, slightly larger. I finished my efforts just as she jumped down from the log.

I dropped to one knee before her and took her hand.

"I don't know if this counts, since there's no church, no priest, and, alas, no wedding cake. But, my parents never got married, and I want our daughter to grow up respectable. So, Infidel, with this ring, I thee wed, if you'll have me."

I paused before I slipped the smaller hair ring onto her finger, looking into her face. Her eyes were wet as she nodded and said, "I do."

The ring fit perfectly; the silver in her hair and the gray in mine even gave it a bit of sparkle. "It's not exactly gold and glorystone," I said.

"It's far more precious," she whispered, pulling me close. I handed her the larger ring. She slipped it onto my finger.

At this point, I should probably switch to another interlude in the material world, but, alas, there really wasn't anything interesting going on there. So I'll just skip ahead to the part where we got dressed again.

She finished binding up her slippers as I finished fixing the clasp on my cape. She tossed me the bone-handled knife, which I stuck in my belt, then went to grab the Jagged Heart.

"Wow," she said, lifting it, a bit off balance. "It's kind of heavy."

"Yeah," I said. "I should probably carry it. You carry the knife."

"Nah. Even if I don't have supernatural strength, I still have more experience jabbing holes in things than you do."

"Conceded."

She looked toward the caldera. "You're certain the world will be destroyed if we don't do this?"

"I'm not certain of anything. But Zetetic thinks it's a real possibility."

"Yeah, but he's, you know, a Deceiver. He's got the tattoo on his forehead and everything. What if he's tricking us into doing something awful?"

"I don't have an answer for that. But what's our alternative?"

She shrugged, but still didn't look eager to tramp up the slope.

"We have the best reason of all for doing this," I said. "Assuming you're pregnant, I don't want my daughter being born in the land of the dead. For her sake, we have to get you home safely, and we have to make sure that there's still a world left for us to raise her in."

Infidel nodded as she pressed her lips together in a look of grim determination.

"Let's go find this oversized iguana and get out of here," she said, marching up the slope, the harpoon resting on her shoulder like a soldier's pike.

*   *   *

THE PECULIAR GEOGRAPHY of this corner of the afterlife meant we didn't have far to go. Barely a hundred yards passed before we pushed through a wall of thorny brush onto a steep rocky ridge that led to the caldera. We advanced arm in arm, in part because it's the way lovers like to walk, and in part because we were each having trouble walking individually. My ankle still hurt like hell and Infidel was leaving bloody footprints from where thorns had punched through her satin shoes. Not to mention, we were both tender and chaffed and raw. In places.

As we limped our way past the lip of the caldera, we looked down over a field of black rock, dotted with vents of steam. In the center of this barren landscape there was what looked to be the remains of the world's largest bonfire, a half-mile-long hill of soot-covered coals and glowing embers wreathed in a skin of pale blue flames.

The bonfire crackled with sparks as we approached. There was a peculiar rumble, low and rhythmic, that I had difficulty identifying. Then, Infidel grabbed my shoulder and pulled my ear down to lip level. She whispered, softly, "Is that fire snoring?"

I nodded. Of course it was snoring. This was Greatshadow's spirit and it was asleep. Infidel always crashed into a corpse-like slumber after a tough battle. Greatshadow probably did the same.

Our eyes locked. Would it really be this easy? Did we just have to sneak up on an exhausted dragon and punch the Jagged Heart between his eyes?

Infidel placed her hand on the back of my neck. She tilted her face to meet mine and gave me a long, lingering kiss. In the aftermath I stared at her, moon-eyed. There was frost in her long platinum locks. Her breath came out as mist. And her eyes, her eyes glistened like deep and mysterious pools in a cavern as she said, softly, "Trust me."

I nodded. There was never any doubt. My fate, her fate, the

fate of our daughter, the fate of all mankind: I surrendered them willingly into her hands.

She motioned for me to wait where we stood, a good fifty yards from the smoldering flames, as she lowered the harpoon to attack position and crept forward. I held my breath as she inched closer, my eyes flickering from her to the slumbering dragon. Now that I understood the true nature of the flaming hill before us, it was easy to make out the dragon's long neck and ship-sized head. Infidel was marching straight toward his mouth.

Thirty feet away, she knelt, placing the harpoon on the ground before her.

"Greatshadow," she said, in a very loud voice. "Wake up."

She didn't reach for the Jagged Heart as enormous eyes flickered open, great orbs glowing like furnaces, to focus on her with a hate-filled stare.

CHAPTER TWENTY-FOUR
WE FELL

"YOU'VE BEEN SENT to kill me," said Greatshadow, smoke rising from his jaws. His teeth looked like ash-covered logs glowing with internal fires.

"Yes," said Infidel, still kneeling, her head bowed low. "But I'm not going to. I don't wish to hurt you."

"Yet you've brought the accursed Heart to my elemental realm. Merely looking upon it causes my soul to weaken. You must know the agony it brings me."

Infidel shook her head. "I'm sorry. I didn't personally bring the harpoon here, though I was told it could hurt you. I confess, however, I don't really understand why."

The ashen heap that was once the most feared dragon in the world turned his enormous head away, so that the Jagged Heart was no longer within his line of sight.

"It's a part of her," he sighed, his voice crackling like a campfire stirred by a breeze. "Long ago, before we dragons entangled our souls with the elements, we were mortal creatures. Like all beasts, the most important goal of our lives was to mate. Unlike other beasts, we dragons prided ourselves on the spiritual nature of our relationships. We weren't mere animals, puppets of our instincts and lusts. We based our coupling on refined courtships that ensured that we were perfectly paired: mentally, spiritually, magically, and physically."

"I was told that you and Hush were lovers?"

Greatshadow shook his ragged head as cinders fell from his eyes like dark tears. "More than lovers. Alone, we were incomplete beings; together, we were one perfect soul. Her cold balanced my heat. My wrathful nature was calmed by her grace, while my brash and sudden passions could stir her cool and logical heart. When we lay entangled together in our coupling, staring into one another's eyes, there was no loneliness. We were a universe in total, beyond all cares. Or so I thought." Greatshadow swallowed hard as the ground trembled beneath my feet.

Infidel cast a glance back at me. I studied her face for some clue as to why she hadn't attacked. I longed for Relic's telepathy. I didn't know why she was taking this risk. And yet... and yet she gave me a slight nod, with her eyes locked on mine, and the message was plain. *Trust me.*

I nodded back, and waited.

Greatshadow's voice was almost a whisper as he said. "Our universe was not so complete as I thought. There was... another. As I stared into the eyes of Hush, she dreamed she was looking into the eyes of Glorious, the dragon who was to become the elemental partner of the sun. My flames, it seems, were not enough for Hush. Her cold, logical heart judged that Glorious would be her perfect mate. So, she abandoned me, and flew to him, to profess her love."

"I'm sorry," said Infidel.

"What is there to be sorry for?" Greatshadow growled. "It proved a great stroke of good fortune, at least for those of us who were to become the primal dragons. Glorious rejected Hush; he was on the verge of merging his spirit with the sun, and had no time for such trivia as love.

"In her anger, Hush struck Glorious, killing his body, which freed his soul to fully merge with the sun. Such was the violence of Hush's blow that fragments of solar material fell to earth."

"The glorystones," said Infidel.

Greatshadow nodded. "While I was not yet the dragon of fire, I studied all flame, and saw the blaze of the glorystones as they fell. I flew to investigate and found Hush standing over the mortal shell of Glorious. Hush tried to convince me that Glorious had attacked her, but my telepathy was superior, and I saw the truth. My rage was so great that I felt my soul burst into flame; I became the elemental embodiment of wrath. My first act upon wielding this power was to lash out at Hush for her betrayal. Even then, her mastery of cold helped protect her from my physical assault, but the emotional pain of that moment forever altered her. Understanding the source of my primal rage, her heart literally froze when she realized she had driven away the one dragon who had truly loved her. As her ice-bound heart shattered into a thousand sharp shards, the unfathomable chill that filled the vacant spot within her soul triggered Hush's transformation into the primal dragon of cold."

"I'm sorry you've felt such pain," said Infidel.

Greatshadow let loose a low rumble that might have been a rueful chuckle. "We've become much greater beings as a result of her betrayal. Though I wonder, at times, if we aren't also something less."

He cast a baleful glare at the harpoon. "Just as everything I cherish eventually turns to ash, everything exposed to her cold heart will eventually wither and perish. Even I."

"If I knew how, I would remove it from this place to stop it from hurting you," said Infidel.

"I know," said Greatshadow. "I see your thoughts so plainly. You have not come here with hatred in your heart."

"No," she said. "I set out on this quest to find comfort for my own broken heart, not because I held any animosity toward you."

"You came to steal my treasure," he said.

"Yes."

"But you've decided you no longer want it."

Infidel touched the band of hair on her finger.

"Gold and glorystones are wealth, not treasure. I can see that I was surrounded by genuine treasures all along. I just had to learn how to recognize them."

"How sorrowful to find these truths only once you are in the realm of the dead," Greatshadow said.

"But I'm not dead." Infidel looked up to meet his gaze. "I arrived here by accident and I need to go back. You must possess the power to send me home. You have the ability to travel between the spiritual and physical worlds, or else Zetetic wouldn't be so worried."

"Traveling between the worlds comes at a cost," said Greatshadow.

"Name the price," she said. "Send us back and I promise that we'll never bother you again. I promise to take the Jagged Heart as far away from you as possible, and I promise to fight anyone who even whispers of making an attempt to kill you."

"You would kill my offspring? The one you call Relic?"

"Consider it done," she said, snapping her fingers.

Greatshadow pondered for a long moment. "No. Tell the pathetic broken-wing that I shall have my revenge at the time and place of my choosing. The thought of the sleepless nights the young one shall endure pleases me. A swift death shall not slake my smoldering rage."

"Consider the message delivered," she said. "Just send us back."

Greatshadow eyed the Jagged Heart. "You must take this weapon from this place. I cannot recover while its bitterness poisons the energies of this land."

She gingerly lifted the harpoon, making sure not to point the tip toward him.

"Some people are worried you'll destroy the world because of what we've done to you," she said, softly. "I could have killed you as you slept. I chose mercy instead."

"Mercy is not a quality often attributed to flame," growled Greatshadow.

"Is it not?" asked Infidel. "Many a wound has been cauterized by fire. Meat half gone to rot becomes a safe meal once it's cooked. Men could not survive harsh winters without your help. There is more to flame than wrath and destruction."

"Too many men think this way," said Greatshadow, sounding

indignant at what I thought had been a compliment. His eyes began to blaze as he said, "Men believe they have tamed me, trapping me in hearths to bake their bread and in foundries to forge their steel. They forget that I am a wild thing that will not remain in a cage. I have killed many men to remind others of this truth."

"Perhaps you need reminding, too," she said.

The dragon tilted his head in a quizzical look.

Infidel said, "The wind, the sea, the frozen wastes... these elements are used by men, but none are worthy of the partnership that man has formed with flame. Thanks to mankind, fire is everywhere. In the middle of the trackless ocean, fire can be found in lanterns aboard a ship. On the most frigid, snow-capped mountain, you'll find fires glowing on hearths. Right now, even at this moment when you are at your weakest, men are lighting candles, torches, and bonfires, all of which help to restore you. There is far more fire in the world due to the actions of men than there would be without us. You may be a wild thing that doesn't wish to be tamed, but certainly, even the wildest beast enjoys being fed. We nourish you with coal from far beneath the earth, we cut down forests to fill our fireplaces, and sometimes we even offer you our dead."

Greatshadow nodded grudgingly. "You are wise, Princess Innocent, though you tell me a truth I already know. Even in my darkest moments of smoldering anger, I dare not destroy mankind. In a world without men, I would be very hungry indeed."

"I don't know that I'm wise," said Infidel. "I just think we're alike in some ways. We both hate anyone who tries to tame us, but understand we sometimes must do things we don't want to do in order to keep a full belly."

Greatshadow lifted his head high, sparks flying from his jaws as he roared, a sound like a blast furnace in great, puffing gusts. The noise nearly deafened me, but I felt no fear. It was obvious from the expression in his eyes that he was laughing.

"That a mere mortal thinks she is in any way like me is an amusing notion, Princess," said the dragon. "It has been many centuries since I laughed so freely. You have earned your journey home."

With these words, he extended his talon and used a long glowing claw to trace a large circle upon the ground before him. The stone inside that circle fell away, revealing a black pit, full of stars.

"The material world lies through this portal," said Greatshadow.

Infidel turned her head toward me and motioned with her eyes that I should join her. I ran up and clasped her hand, giving her a swift kiss. She dragged me closer to the ring of fire. Fortunately, the Jagged Heart shielded us from the heat. Hand in hand, we stared into the abyss.

"Is it safe to jump?" I asked.

"When have we ever worried about that?" she said with a grin, falling forward, her fingers wrapped in mine. She dangled on the edge for the barest instant as my weight held her. Then, in total confidence, I leaned forward and we tumbled into the darkness.

INFIDEL RELEASED THE Jagged Heart and it fell beside us in a lazy spin. We hugged each other tightly as we flew past stars, past moons and suns and comets. We tumbled though airless voids, hugging one another in terror, awe, and wonder. We were neither in the spirit realm nor the ordinary world of matter; we were two isolated souls, entangled, entwined, a whole and complete universe where seconds and hours had no meaning. Yet, despite our inability to measure time, our eternity of togetherness drew to a close as a great blue jewel of a world emerged from the void beneath us. We clung to each other as the world grew large enough for us to make out the shapes of landmasses beneath the wispy white oceans of clouds. We fell toward a small green speck amidst a vast blue sea, the wind tangling our hair as we slowly emerged from the abstract realms. Far below, we spotted a smoking caldera atop a high mountain that seemed to be the bulls-eye where we'd land.

We looked into each other's eyes. There was no hope of speaking amid the howl of the wind whipping past us. We both knew that Greatshadow had cared nothing for our safety by sending us back along this path. Dropping to earth was no problem for him; he had wings. It was going to take more than a net of vines to save us this time.

Despite this knowledge, all I felt looking into Infidel's face was joy that we would once more be together in the land of the living, however brief that experience might be.

She kissed me.

I kissed her back.

Her lips grew softer and softer until, suddenly they were gone. My arms closed around empty air. I opened my eyes and she was still inches away, her eyes wide, searching. I raised my hand to her cheek and it passed right through, as if she was a ghost.

Or as if I was. Infidel had fully emerged into the physical realm, and I was left behind, still a phantom.

"Infidel!" I screamed, as she dropped away, feeling the full tug of gravity. The Jagged Heart flashed past me, following its parallel path. I hovered in mid-air, no longer touched by gravity. I felt for the spirit tether of the bone-handled knife to pull me closer to Infidel but didn't move at all. I looked down, and saw the knife tucked in my belt. My link to the material world was trapped with me on the other side.

I gave chase with all the speed I could muster, drawing close enough that I could see genuine fear in Infidel's eyes as she tumbled toward the black caldera below. Even if Infidel had still been invulnerable, I don't know if she could have survived a landing on volcanic stone without a net of vines to cushion her.

Then, rising from the caldera in a pale blue mist, a humanoid shape flew to intercept Infidel a half-mile above the ground. The foggy wraith reached out with ethereal fingers, stroking the shaft of the Jagged Heart. Light flashed from the tip of the harpoon, striking the stone below, and suddenly there was a hill of snow heaped a hundred feet tall, its base sizzling on the black rock. A second later, Infidel punched into the snow mound, leaving the perfect outline of her splayed limbs in the surface. The Jagged Heart dropped into the snow several yards distant, far enough away I didn't worry she'd been impaled.

The ghost of Aurora continued to drift upward, raising a hand in greeting as she saw me. "You can see why my people built a temple around the harpoon."

"Will she be alright?" I asked, staring down into the hole Infidel had left in the snow mountain. I couldn't see anything in the shadows. The whole pile was melting at a frightening pace, an ever-growing puddle boiling off at the edges.

"It was like she fell onto a mountain of feathers," said Aurora.

"I can't tell you how happy I am to see you. You've stuck around longer than the others did after they died," I said. "Does that mean I'll have some company from now on?"

She shook her head. "I couldn't leave until I saw the Jagged Heart had returned from the land of the dead. I assume your efforts were successful?"

I shrugged. "We'll need to wait a few weeks to find out if she's pregnant."

Aurora gave me a blank stare.

"Oh! You mean did we kill Greatshadow?"

She nodded.

"She let him live. He let us go."

She raised a blue eyebrow. "Why?"

I shrugged. "She had her reasons." I didn't want to admit that I didn't fully understand Infidel's choices. I hoped Aurora wouldn't ask any follow-up questions.

Aurora looked north. "It doesn't matter. The call of my

ancestors is strong. I hear the songs they sing as they chase the ghost whales in the Great Sea Above. I want to join their hunt."

"Go," I said. "The Jagged Heart is in good hands. We'll see that it gets home."

Aurora gave me a smile that said, *I know,* then faded from my sight.

A half-mile below, Infidel climbed from a pile of slushy snow now only a few yards high. Her lips and fingertips were completely blue. She stumbled forward, dragging the Jagged Heart behind her, limping toward the circle of light atop the dragon skull where Zetetic and Relic waited. I flew toward Relic and said, "You're in big trouble."

He didn't respond.

"Hey!" I shouted, waving my fingers in front of him.

Nothing. Yet, I was still relatively solid, as a phantom goes. I could see my own fingers, and was pleased to see I was still wearing my braided wedding ring. I seemed to have my full phantom body; I even had the clothing Zetetic had dressed me in. Why couldn't Relic hear me? Or, maybe he could, and was just being spiteful?

Infidel climbed up onto the skull, her teeth chattering. She tossed the harpoon to Zetetic and said, "You. Carry this. Carry it over there, in fact. I'm freezing."

He nodded and backed up about ten feet, so that she was no longer in the range of the harpoon's aura of cold. He said, "You've changed since last we met. I like you with long hair. You could use a comb, though."

"I could use a jacket even more. Brrr." She leaned down and picked up the Immaculate Attire. "I wondered where this went." She slipped the pants and vest on and the magical leather adjusted to fit her. With her arms outstretched as she dressed, her eyes lingered for a moment on the braid of hair still on her finger. I wondered why it had made the transition while mine didn't?

Infidel didn't dwell on the ring for long, however. Instead, while she pulled on the boots that went with the armor, she eyed Relic (we didn't yet know he'd changed his name). "Your daddy is going to kill you one day. But he wants to build suspense first."

"Greatshadow's alive? How can he still be alive?"

"You're the mind reader. You already know why I did what I did."

His reptilian eyes narrowed into slits as he stared at her. "I... I can't read your thoughts."

She looked surprised.

"Oh no," said Relic, rising up. "I could feel it earlier. During his sadistic assault, his spirit moved within me, ripping my mind as he snapped my body. But, with no other minds near that I could look within, I didn't realize what he'd done. He's torn the part of my mind that senses the thoughts of others! I'm blind!"

"It won't matter once you're dead," said Infidel.

"Isn't it enough he crippled me physically?" Relic growled, as his eyes burned like cinders. "He had to cripple my mind as well?"

Zetetic cleared his throat. "You may not be as crippled as you think. One of my teachers was the world's foremost scholar on dragons. I could introduce you to him, if you'd like. He's studied dragon skeletons at every stage of development. Reptiles possess amazing powers of regeneration. He might know how to break your bones and reset them properly."

"That sounds painful," said Relic.

Zetetic shrugged. "Just a suggestion."

Relic nodded. "I will... consider the offer."

He looked back toward Infidel. "I don't suppose my father... that he... did he, by chance..."

"What?" she asked.

"Did he happen to mention my gender? Did he refer to me as 'my son' or 'my daughter?'"

"Um, no. He called you 'offspring.'"

Relic looked crushed by this news.

Infidel leaned over and picked up the Gloryhammer. She slung it over her shoulder. "This is mine now."

"Really?" asked Relic. "What gives you a claim to it?"

"The fact that I will flatten anyone who tries to take it from me."

"I find your reasoning quite persuasive," said Zetetic.

Infidel's feet lifted from the ground a few wobbling inches. The light of the Gloryhammer gleamed on the silver trim of her new boots. "This hammer will come in handy. Flying will make getting to Aurora's homeland a lot faster."

"Why are you going there?" asked Zetetic.

"To return the Jagged Heart," she said. "Stagger told me that Aurora's dying words were a plea to see that the harpoon was returned to its rightful home. I intend to make that happen. I need to do this mission fast. I can't afford to spend a few months aboard a ship."

"Why not?" asked Zetetic.

"She thinks she's pregnant," said Relic.

"I thought you couldn't read minds," she said.

"I knew of the Black Swan's prophecy. I take it you reunited with Stagger?"

"I have the Jagged Heart, don't I?"

"But he remains in the realm of the dead?"

She frowned, looking down at the braided band on her finger. "He sort of... faded out on the way back. But... but I..." She swallowed hard. "He'll always be with me in my heart."

"I'm here," I whispered near her cheek. "I'll always be here."

"The bone-handled knife is gone?" asked Relic.

She looked a little pale as she nodded slowly.

"Then he's lost forever," said Relic.

Infidel rose a few feet higher in the air, looking straight overhead, toward the last place she saw me. "He trusted me," she said, her voice faint. Then, she looked down, her face firm with resolve. "And I will spend every day of my life proving I deserve that trust. My leap-before-I-look days are behind me. I'm going to be a great mother."

"Says the woman who just made a spur of the moment decision to fly to the North Pole via enchanted mallet," said Zetetic.

"Just for that, I'm not giving you a ride out of this volcano."

"That's fine. I have the power to fly and am finally over my fear of heights," he said, as their gazes locked. He jumped into the air, and stayed there. "You warmed up?"

"Warm enough," she said.

He tossed her the Jagged Heart, which she caught in one hand. Her flight grew wobbly as she rose another couple of yards in the air. "Thinking-ahead Infidel sure wishes she had Tower's little magic book to carry the harpoon," she said.

Zetetic shrugged as he rose to her level. "Too bad it got burned up when Tower's armor disintegrated."

"No!" I shouted. "He has it!"

But, I hadn't mentioned this to Infidel, so she merely said, "I guess I can rig up some kind of sling."

Zetetic sank back down and offered a hand to Relic. "Can I offer you a ride?"

Relic sighed as he raised the claw that Nowowon had mangled least. "Any place in the world is safer than here."

I floated next to Infidel as the three of them rose like balloons toward the edge of the caldera. The shadows of the vast pit fell away as we reached the sky and found the sun rising on the eastern ocean. Pale golden rays danced over a shimmering sea, bathing the treetops below with a radiance that made the dewy canopy look as if someone had spilled a bucket of glistening jewels.

And I finally got it. I understood what Infidel had meant when she said she'd already discovered Greatshadow's treasure. It was the island itself, the last wilderness, and I knew, with the same certainty that I knew that stone is hard and fire is hot and water is wet, that there would be no better place on the planet for our daughter to grow up.

"I'm dying to hear the details of what happened in the spirit realm," Zetetic said.

"What happened between Stagger and me is private, you creep," said Infidel, sounding genuinely offended.

Zetetic shook his head. "I mean, the details of your confrontation with Greatshadow. The Jagged Heart should have killed him. You got close enough for conversation; presumably you were close enough to strike. Why didn't you finish him? You've gambled the safety of the world by sparing him. What possible reason could have stayed your hand?"

"If I'd killed Greatshadow, all this would be gone," she said, her eyes scanning the jungle as they slowly flew down the slope at about the pace of a good jog, heading toward Commonground. "My father's men would come and set up lumber mills and mines. Before you know it, there would be farms everywhere. The priests would follow and build churches, and in a couple of years, this place would start to look civilized."

"Indeed," said Zetetic. "That was precisely the plan."

"But it wasn't my plan. I've spent the best years of my life here, and I like the island as it is: untamed and untamable. I grew up in a world of castle walls and armed guards and endless rules that shackled the soul as well as the body. I've had a taste of freedom now and will never give it up. I want to raise my daughter in a world that still has a place where the wicked may hide from the righteous."

Zetetic slowed a bit. "Damn," he said, with a nod. "That's not a bad reason at all."

Infidel shrugged, with an expression that told me she didn't particularly care if he approved of her reasons or not. She flew on a little ways, until, suddenly, she looked back over her shoulder, her eyes wistful as she stared at the sky above the caldera, toward the spot where I'd vanished.

Then her distant gaze shifted, looking much closer, not quite to where I hovered, but not so far off either.

"You aren't in this alone," I said, with a reassuring smile.

I'm sure it was only a coincidence that, at that exact second, she smiled back.

THE END

ACKNOWLEDGEMENTS

FIRST, THE INSPIRATION: I started writing Greatshadow in the summer of 2009. At the heart of the story was a tale about a man and a woman who were secretly in love, but who never confessed that love out of fear of ruining their longstanding friendship. One reason that this story flowed so naturally from me was that I was caught up in exactly this situation. I spent nearly all my free time with a woman named Cheryl Morgan, a woman who I'd met only a few months after my previous girlfriend, Laura Herrmann, had passed away. When we met, I simply wasn't in the right state of mind to pursue a new romantic relationship. Once I said we could just be friends, to my surprise, Cheryl wound up becoming my friend. Most of my life experience had taught me that the day a man and a woman agree to be friends, it's pretty much the end of them speaking to one another. But, Cheryl and I wound up as best buddies. She was all that I could ask for in a friend. Which meant that, when I was interested in a romantic relationship again, I was afraid to bring up the subject. We had a really good thing going. A genuine friendship isn't something to be trifled with.

And yet, there I was, writing a book about two star-crossed lovers kept apart by their reluctance to confess what they truly felt. It was impossible to write the fiction without constantly thinking about my reality. So, I'm happy to report that writing this novel forced me to finally talk to Cheryl about my true feelings, and discover that she felt the same way. We were married on November 11, 2011. So, let me give heartfelt thanks to Cheryl for being wonderful and patient with me, and providing me with the emotions that stand at the core of this tale.

Of course, inspiration is only half the job of writing a book. The other half is the actual slog of putting down words on paper then revising them again and again and again. In these labors, I was ably assisted by my wonderful team of dedicated wise-readers: Laurel Amberdine, Ada Brown, Cindy Hannikman, Will Ferris, Cathy Bollinger, Jesse Bernier, Dona Nova, Jenney O'Callaghan, Joey Puente, and, of course, Cheryl Morgan. Once I had the book in its nearly final stage, I sent it off my friend Jeremy Cavin, who gave me suggestions that I think really helped elevate the novel. My editor, Jonathan Oliver at Solaris, deserves credit for helping me put the final finishing touches on the manuscript. I must also thank my agent, John Berlyne, for fighting to see Greatshadow published as the first part of a larger series. And, thanks goes to Gerard Miley, for helping bring the book to life with his fantastic cover. (And wait until you see the cover for Hush!)

If you've enjoyed Greatshadow, I hope you'll stick around for future books in the series. Greatshadow isn't the only primal dragon to be targeted by the Church of the Book. In the next book, Infidel will confront Hush, the primal dragon of cold, Rott, the primal dragon of decay, and Glorious, the primal dragon of the sun. One of these dragons will meet their final fate due to the machinations of the church, an event that won't go unnoticed by the other dragons. Is the dragon apocalypse finally at hand?

ABOUT THE AUTHOR

James Maxey lives in Hillsborough, NC with his lovely bride Cheryl and a clowder of unruly cats. He is the author of the Bitterwood fantasy trilogy, *Bitterwood*, *Dragonforge*, and *Dragonseed*, as well as the superhero novels *Nobody Gets the Girl* and *Burn Baby Burn*. His short fiction has appeared in dozens of anthologies and magazines such as *Asimov's* and *Orson Scott Card's Intergalactic Medicine Show*. The best of these stories appears in the collection *There is No Wheel*. For more information about James, and to follow the progress of further books chronicling the *Dragon Apocalypse*, visit dragonprophet.blogspot.com.

Now read the first chapter from
the next novel in this exciting series…

HUSH

BOOK TWO *of the* DRAGON APOCALYPSE

JAMES MAXEY

SOLARIS

CHAPTER ONE
A DANGEROUS SPLINTER

A PRINCESS, A shape-shifter, and a ghost walked into a bar.

The room fell silent as all eyes turned toward the princess. The bar was the Black Swan, the most prestigious saloon in the boat city of Commonground. While the house wasn't as packed as it would be come midnight, there were still scores of hard core gamblers crowded around the poker tables. Ordinarily, you could have marched a two-headed tiger through the joint and not gotten these players to glance up from their cards. But the princess, known in these parts as Infidel, was known to be much more dangerous than a two-headed tiger.

Infidel was an imposing figure as she stood in the doorway with the sun low in the red sky behind her. The first thing anyone would notice about her was that she was a woman who wore her three decades well, with sculpted curves, generous platinum curls, and enigmatic gray eyes. The money hungry men in the room wouldn't linger long on her face, however. She was dressed in the priceless Immaculate Attire crafted for Queen Alabaster Brightmoon nearly three centuries before. Formed from the hide of the last unicorn, the legendary armor was milky white and trimmed with silver. The enchanted leather clung to Infidel's body like a second skin. Slung over her shoulder was another famed artifact of the Silver Isles, the Gloryhammer, glowing with a pale white light.

Despite her impressive armaments, it was Infidel's reputation that brought the room to a standstill. On her first night in this bar ten years ago she'd ripped off the arm of a bruiser twice her size. The whole town soon learned that this young woman possessed magical strength and skin so tough that swords couldn't scratch her. Even as her fame grew, her beauty had tempted many a fool to a place an unwelcome hand upon her. Commonground had an unusual quantity of one-armed sailors.

I say this as the biggest fool of all. My name is Abstemious Merchant, though everyone in Commonground called me Stagger. For ten years, I was Infidel's constant companion, staring at her moon-eyed when she wasn't looking. I was far too cowardly to confess my love. Yet, fate can be kind to fools and cowards. Beneath Infidel's white leather gauntlet, on her left hand, she wears a ring of woven gray hair. This is my hair. I wear a matching small braid of a platinum-hued locks. These serve as our wedding bands, since at the time of our betrothal there were no jewelers handy.

Fate's kindness, you see, is balanced by a wicked sense of humor. In this unfolding joke, I'm the ghost. In death, as in life, I follow her everywhere.

As a phantom, I'm unseen and unheard. If I could have spoken to Infidel, I would have advised to wear a cloak and cowl into this place, despite the tropical heat outside. Wearing the Immaculate Attire in this city of thieves was the equivalent of walking through a lion's den wearing a suit sewn from steaks. Worse, someone in this town might be smart enough to ask why she was bothering to wear armor at all. She'd recently lost her magical strength and invulnerability, and if word spread her former enemies would turn out in droves. Plus, as her husband, I wasn't thrilled with the way the skin-tight armor accented her breathtaking assets. For supposedly Immaculate Attire, the outfit certainly lent itself to dirty thoughts.

Infidel's silver trimmed boots clicked on the polished oak floor as she walked through the room. Ordinarily stone-faced poker players openly gawked and drooled, though I tried to assure myself they were hungering for the Gloryhammer in all its refulgent splendor. Glorystones are fragments of the sun. They're rarer than diamonds and twice as hard. The Gloryhammer is literally priceless. All the gold in the world couldn't buy it. The Tower clan, a family of famous knights, had passed down the weapon for generations. Alas, the last surviving male of the line had recently been reduced to soot. Infidel now owned the hammer under the legal precedent of finders, keepers.

Infidel didn't look back at the gawking crowd as she arrived at the bar. Battle Ox was bartending. Battle was a half-seed, meaning his mother had visited a blood house to imbue her yet-to-be conceived child with animalistic traits. If the magic was done properly, a half-seed ox child would be big, strong, and tenacious. Do the magic wrong, and you get Battle Ox — a full blown minotaur with horns wider than his considerably broad shoulders.

In more civilized parts of the world, an infant born with a bovine face would have been put to death as a horrid abomination against nature. In Commonground, Battle's visage seldom merited a second glance. Despite the name inflicted by the pun-happy denizens of Commonground, Battle was a rather gentle vegetarian. While he would willingly eject a rowdy patron if the need arose, his true calling in life was drawing beers with perfect heads of foam. My mouth watered at the smell of the amber fluid.

Battle nodded at my wife. "A lot of people here won't be happy to see you back" he said, with his gruff, bass voice. "Odds were running ten to one that Greatshadow would fry you."

Infidel leaned on the bar. "How did anyone know we were going to slay the dragon? The mission was a secret."

Battle shrugged as he picked up a glass and a towel. "The Black Swan started taking bets on the outcome of your dragon hunt the second you left town. The volcano's been belching lava for the last week, so we figure Greatshadow was still alive."

"Well, maybe he is and maybe he isn't," she said. "The Black Swan will get the full details. Tell her I need to see her. Now."

Battle put down the glass he was cleaning. "You ever learn the word 'please?'"

"Don't mess with me. I've got one hour to get back to the Freewind and don't have time to waste. I've got something the Black Swan needs to see immediately."

Battle shook his furry head. "No can do. She's already in a meeting. Going to be a lot longer than an hour."

Infidel unclasped the top three buttons of her leather armor and peeled it back, showing the top of her cleavage. Battle's eyes bulged.

"You see this?" Infidel pointed to a black speck the size of an apple seed that nestled in the ampleness of her décolletage.

"Uh...," said Battle, his mouth hanging open.

"This is Menagerie. What's left of him."

Remember the shape-shifter who came into the bar with us? Menagerie used to be the most feared mercenary in Commonground. A blood-magician of unparalleled skill, Menagerie could turn into any of the scores of animals that used to decorate his tattooed flesh. Menagerie had barely survived our dragon hunt. Since shape-shifting into this tick form, he'd yet to change back into a man. A telepath of our acquaintance informed us that Menagerie had been so traumatized by his brush with death that his mind was shattered.

Battle couldn't know any of this, of course, but Infidel didn't have to produce any further explanations. Men are willing to believe almost anything while they're looking at a woman's breasts.

"I'm the only one that can hear him since he's latched onto me," she said while his eyes were still fixed on her. "The Black Swan has a potion that will change him back to human, and he has to drink it within the next five minutes or he'll die. Do you want to tell the Black Swan she's lost her most valuable employee because you were too timid to interrupt a meeting?"

Battle frowned. No, no he did not want this, was the message I was seeing in his eyes. But he also looked as if he had his doubts. Infidel wasn't particularly gifted at lying. If Battle asked any follow up questions, Infidel would probably be in trouble.

Fortunately, Battle was too cleavage-addled to notice any holes in her story. He grunted, "Wait here," then went through the curtain that covered the doorway behind the beer kegs, leaving Infidel alone. At least as alone as a woman can be with a brain-damaged shape-shifter sipping her blood and her invisible dead husband hovering close behind.

Infidel turned around, leaning back against the bar.

Every eye in the house was staring at her.

Even though the Black Swan was the classiest joint in Commonground, it was still a den where desperate men gathered to try to make an easy fortune. Their already questionable judgment was numbed further by generous tankards of booze. Ordinarily, order was maintained by the Black Swan's infamous hired muscle, the Three Goons. Even when the Goons weren't present, their reputation kept most people in line.

Of course, except for Menagerie, the Goons were now dead. If the patrons knew about the dragon hunt, did they also know that the bar's most feared enforcers weren't coming back?

Infidel reached over her shoulder and grabbed the Gloryhammer. Instantly, its enchantment kicked in. Her skin glowed faintly as she lifted off the floor ever so subtly. In addition to granting her flight, the hammer also enhanced her strength. The boost was nothing like her former arm-ripping power, but anyone looking at her had to be sizing up their odds of getting their skulls smashed.

The odds were too high even for this room full of hardened gamblers. One by one, all eyes looked back at the cards in their hands. The roulette wheel was spun again, dice were jiggled in cups, and in under a minute the saloon had resumed its normal routine. Infidel slowly drifted back down to the floor.

Then Hookhand and his Machete Quartet walked in from the street. If I'd still had a heartbeat, it would have skipped. I had history with Hookhand. When I was alive, my primary revenue came from locating ruins in the jungle and salvaging lost treasures. Hookhand used to make his living by having an uncanny knack for showing up just as I was climbing out of some god-forsaken tomb with a sack full of artifacts, which I would trade in exchange for not being nailed to a tree and flayed. This arrangement lasted for years until Infidel started adventuring with me. In the intervening decade, there've been about seventeen different members of the Machete Quartet. Infidel normally doesn't let them suffer for too long. Hookhand hasn't been as lucky. When he first came to Commonground, he was known as Fairchild the Nimble. Now, he's got one eye, his nose is squashed against his cheek, and he walks with a prominent limp. He's got maybe six teeth left, and, of course, where he once had a right hand he now has a hook, a big nasty one of the sort you might use to gaff a large fish.

Despite a decade of serving as Infidel's punching bag, Hookhand was still a feared figure in the city. His gang was made of street urchins he recruited just after they hit puberty, when they're strong and agile enough to swing a machete like it's a dagger, but still too young to have any fear of life and limb. Once they join the quartet they become Kid White, Kid Blue, Kid Green, and Kid Black, based on the color bandana they wear. Hookhand doesn't like to waste a lot of time memorizing names.

In theory, the black bandana is worn by the gang member with the most seniority, but I didn't recognize this kid at all. If I'd seen him before, I would have remembered; the boy was obviously a half-seed, part hound-dog by the look of him. He had an ugly pair of canine teeth, but any air of menace was diluted by his floppy ears.

"Well, well," said Hookhand as he spied Infidel. "If it ain't ol' Ripper herself. I see you killed the knight. Quite a prize, that hammer. Quite a prize indeed."

Infidel nodded to acknowledge the words. She leaned forward, resting her hand on the shaft of the Gloryhammer like it was a cane. She said, "Surprised to see you back in town. I thought you were up on the mountain, robbing pygmies."

"The volcano's been spitting lava ever since we saw you and your friends fly out. Looks like you made the dragon mad. I made the executive decision to place some distance between us and the caldera." Hookhand looked around the room. "Where are your friends?"

"Who are you talking about?" Infidel asked. "I don't have time for coyness."

"Zetetic the Deceiver. He was right by your side, carrying a baby dragon."

"Your eye's playing tricks on you." Infidel shook her head. "Never met the guy."

"Zetetic has a large red 'D' tattooed in the middle of his forehead. He's easy to recognize, even 200 feet in the air."

"Your depth perception isn't what it used to be," said Infidel.

"True enough." Hookhand slowly limped toward her. His gang spread out to the far ends of the bar. There was no way that Infidel could keep all four of them in her field of vision. There was a time that wouldn't have mattered; a machete would have just bounced off her invulnerable hide. While the Immaculate Attire protected her body, at some point in the convoluted chain of ownership from Queen Alabaster Brightmoon to Infidel, the helmet had disappeared. Infidel's head and neck were completely vulnerable. But Hookhand couldn't know this, could he?

Hookhand stopped about eight feet away. Infidel didn't look perturbed. Was this just for appearances, or was she overly confident?

"I want Zetetic," said Hookhand.

"You want to turn him in for the price on his head? Old news. He's working for the Church of the Book now. They don't want him dead any more."

"I thought you didn't know him," said Hookhand.

"I don't," said Infidel. "But you know I bounty hunt. I stay informed."

Zetetic had split company with Infidel shortly after getting back to Commonground. He'd promised Brokenwing, the only other survivor of our ill-fated dragon hunt, a visit with a former teacher who was the world's foremost authority on dragon anatomy. Since Brokenwing was a rather badly mangled young dragon, they'd departed on their quest with understandable alacrity.

"If you like to stay informed, here are a few facts for you," said Hookhand. "We saw eight people go into the Shattered Palace. You were part of a dragon hunt organized by Lord Tower and Father Ver."

Infidel laughed. "Father Ver's a truthspeaker and Lord Tower's the most respected knight of the church. I, as my nickname implies, am a notorious infidel. A knight and a priest wouldn't be caught dead in my company."

"I think getting caught dead is precisely what happened," said Hookhand. "You were disguised as some kind of mechanical woman to fool them. It doesn't take a genius to figure out what happened. You and Zetetic betrayed the others. You're carrying Tower's hammer and dressed in armor that used to be worn by Ivory Blade. I didn't see Blade go into the Shattered Palace, but I'm guessing I'd find his corpse if I went poking around."

Blade had died a good week before we reached the dragon's lair. But, despite the fact that his conclusions were off, Hookhand had some surprisingly good intelligence. How did he know so much?

I studied his thugs closer. In addition to Kid Black being part blood-hound, Kid Green had distinctly hawkish features, including freakishly alert eyes and feathery sideburns. Kid Blue's overly long arms clued me in he had some monkey blood. Kid White had some jaguar in him, judging from his cat-eyes and the mottled patches in his close-cropped hair. A hound, a hawk, a monkey, and a jaguar would make damn good spies out in the jungle. By now, Kid Black, the dog-boy, and Kid White, the half-jaguar, were at opposite ends of the bar, machetes drawn. There was no way Infidel could watch both of them at once.

Infidel retained her cool as she pressed a gauntleted fist into her palm and cracked her knuckles. The sound echoed around the room. Half the gamblers abandoned their chips and headed for the door. Infidel's brawls were sometimes hard on bystanders.

Infidel took the hammer in both hands and once more her skin went luminous. She said, "Lord Tower could fly. He had impenetrable armor made of solid prayer. If you take your accusations seriously, you might tell these children to get where I can see them. If I could kill someone like Tower, what makes you think these kids have a chance?"

"Tower wouldn't fight dirty," said Hookhand, snapping his fingers. The Machete Quartet lunged, but Infidel had anticipated the signal. The hammer flared to solar brightness as she shot up ten feet, snapping to a halt just beneath a broad ceiling beam. Most of the machete blows that connected hit her boots, leaving little more than scuff marks that were swiftly erased by the armor's magic. Kid Blue, the monkey boy, reacted to Infidel's flight by dropping his machete and hooking his long, skinny fingers into the heel of her right boot. He used his momentum to swing his legs overhead, grabbing her belt with his toes, then flipping up to grab the shaft of the hammer with both hands. Kicking into her chest, he grunted as he tried to pull the weapon from her grasp. The speed and power of the assault caught Infidel off guard and she lost her grip with her left hand, though her right hand held on.

The monkey child placed a foot on Infidel's face as he struggled to twist the hammer away. Infidel responded by opening her mouth and sinking her pearly whites deep into Kid Blue's heel. A shudder ran along my intangible spine. Biting the bare foot of someone who'd been walking around the docks of Commonground was the most reckless thing I'd ever seen Infidel do, and I'd watched her dive headfirst into the jaws of a dragon. But, the tactic worked. Kid Blue shrieked as he let go of the hammer, dropping back down to the floor, where he landed on his outstretched hands and somersaulted back to his feet. Nimble little devil.

But, the jaguar kid was no slouch either. With Kid Blue clear, Kid White sprang flat footed from the floor to the bar to the shelf of liquors behind, then shot toward Infidel like an arrow, with a savage swing of his machete. The chiming of the booze bottles as he kicked off caused Infidel to look over her shoulder and she spun in time to block the machete blow with the Gloryhammer. She jerked her knee up to connect a solid blow to the kid's chin. The half-seed was stunned and fell hard, landing spine-first on the back of a wooden chair, his body folding backward at an acute angle that made me wince.

Infidel pointed the hammer toward Hookhand. Her eyes were narrow slits of murder as she shot toward him. But in her rage she either didn't notice or didn't care that a slender tube of bamboo had appeared in his hand. He sucked in air as he raised it to his lips. He blew so hard I thought his eye was going to pop out of his skull. A cloud of red powder caught Infidel right in the face as Hookhand dove to the side. Infidel gasped as she hit the cloud, then grunted as she slammed into the floor. Her armored shoulder took the brunt of the blow, but the impact was enough to topple chairs around the room. She bounced across the oak planks, losing her grip on the hammer. Her eyes were scrunched tightly together as she slid to a halt on her back.

As a ghost, my senses are muted, but even my nostrils burned from the cayenne cloud that hung in the air. Infidel's face was blood-red with the pepper. She tried to breathe but her throat closed after the barest gasp. Even when she'd had impenetrable skin, she couldn't have shrugged off an attack like this.

Kid Blue, the monkey child, sprang across the room and

landed on Infidel's right hand, pinning it. Kids Black and White followed suit, pinning her left arm and both legs, respectively. If she'd still been super-strong, she could have flicked them off like fleas. Now, her limbs trembled, but her weak spasms couldn't shake them.

The Gloryhammer hung in mid-air, where it had come to rest after bouncing off the floor. Hookhand snatched it with his good hand. His eye went wide as the hammer's power filled him. He tilted back his head and laughed. "At last! At last!"

His feet left the floor as he moved toward her. "I've watched a lot of machetes bounce off that pretty head of yours," he said. "I've dreamed a long time about seeing your brains splattered across these planks. Considerate of you to deliver the perfect tool to get the job done."

Hookhand continued to drift toward her, approaching at a speed fairly described as lackadaisical. Was he trying to prolong the moment? Was flight with the hammer harder than Infidel made it look? Or was Hookhand still a little afraid of her?

"Hold her tight, boys," he said, pausing a few arm lengths away.

"She's weak as a kitten, boss," said Kid Black, the dog-boy who trapped her left arm beneath his knee as he ran his hairy knuckles through her hair. She twisted her head away from his fingers, still unable to open her eyes. She'd started breathing again, rapid shallow spasms that had to be filling her lungs with fire. Sweat poured off her brow and bright red snot ran from both nostrils; I couldn't tell if this was blood or cayenne. Any normal person would have been moved to either pity or revulsion by the sight, but Kid Black was staring at her with barely disguised lust. "Such pretty hair. So soft. So pretty, pretty soft."

"She won't be soft when she catches her breath," said Hookhand

"She's weak now," said Kid Black, stroking her chin, then tracing his fingers down the ivory arc of her throat. The top buttons of her armor were still undone. "Weak and helpless."

"Just like a dog," snickered Kid Blue. "Always looking for something to hump."

"I thought he was always looking for something to eat," said Kid White.

"She could be both," said Kid Black, folding the top of the leather breast plate down to reveal her pale cleavage. He lowered his long narrow face to her throat and licked at her sweat.

I screamed in my rage, my impotence to alter things in the living world stabbing at me like a knife.

Hookhand held back, his eye a little glassy as he watched Kid Black run his hairy hand along the top of Infidel's cleavage. Infidel's face was already scrunched up as much as humanly possible, and pinned as she was I couldn't tell if she was even aware of this assault. Was she even awake, or had crashing into the floor knocked her senseless?

"Wake up!" I screamed, my ghost voice hauntingly silent in the room. "Wake up! Wake up! Wake up!"

"Ow," said Kid Black, yanking his hand away.

"What?" asked Kid Green.

"Something bit me."

"Wake... up..." my voice trailed off as I saw that the tick on Infidel's breast had vanished.

Kid Black put the edge of his hand into his mouth to gnaw at the tiny parasite digging into him.

Then his head came apart.

Menagerie could change shape faster than the eye could follow. His powers flowed from blood magic; his human form had been covered scalp to toe in tattoos inked with the blood of the animals they represented. He'd been able to switch between these forms instantly, and even vast differences in sizes hadn't been a barrier to his magic. He'd been able to change from mouse to elephant just as swiftly as he could between lion and tiger. I'd never before pondered what would happen if he'd entered a person's mouth the size of a tick, then turned into a full-sized blood-hound. As it happened, Menagerie's expanding body proved powerful enough to rip Kid Black's skull open from the inside out.

Kid Black flopped backward, his lower jaw missing, his upper jaw cracked open in such a way that I could see his brains. As his body hit the floor, his ghost seemed to be knocked loose. His spirit rose above his corporeal form, looking bewildered. Since dying, I've had the ability to see ghosts as they depart the mortal world, and occasionally to converse with them. I felt like saying something particularly nasty to this spirit. I know this dog-boy was just street trash, a freak, never standing a chance at a normal life, but any pity I might have been able to summon had vanished the instant he started pawing my wife. Unable to summon sufficiently nasty curses from my normally abundant lexicon, I lifted my middle finger to his spirit as it flickered and faded.

The hound dog that had sprung fully formed from Kid Black's mouth growled as he faced Hookhand. Hookhand shook off his confusion about what he'd just witnessed with remarkable speed and swung the hammer overhead, aiming for the dog's skull. The hound lunged forward, sinking his teeth into Hookhand's groin as the hammer splintered the floorboards.

Infidel's eyes jerked open, bloodshot and brimming with tears. Her blurry gaze fixed on Kid Blue, who was still pinning down her right forearm with both his hands. The monkey child had his eyes on Hookhand, probably wondering where he was going to swing the hammer next, and failed to notice Infidel's left hand was now free. Infidel reached for the scabbard on her hip. Two seconds later, a dagger was hilt deep in the center of the monkey-child's chest. He looked at her with sad eyes as he toppled over. His spirit stuck around no longer than the dog-boy's.

Infidel sat up, fixing her gaze on Kid White. Sweat from her brow washed a fresh flood of cayenne into her eyes and once more her lids scrunched shut as she gasped in pain. Kid White leapt up, bringing his machete overhead two handed, preparing to cleave her skull in half.

Hookhand was still swinging the Gloryhammer wildly. A sledgehammer is a remarkably inappropriate instrument for removing a dog from one's crotch. It is, however, a surprisingly effective tool for bashing in the head of your own henchman if you're not careful. The hammer connected with Kid White's skull with a sound a watermelon might make after it was thrown off a roof. The machete held by Kid White flew into the air as he fell lifeless.

I watched with a sick feeling in the pit of my stomach as the tumbling machete fell toward Infidel's blinded face. Then a huge, three-fingered hand flashed through the air and snatched the machete in mid-flight. It was Battle Ox. He turned with a snort toward Hookhand, who was floating now, using the flight power of the hammer as poorly as it could possibly be used, smashing furniture right and left with his all-powerful weapon as the hound dog between his legs twisted out of the path of every blow.

With a swift, precise chop of the machete, Battle lopped off Hookhand's remaining hand at the wrist. The hammer spun up to the chandelier, smashing the crystal, but Battle Ox's thick hide protected him from the rain of shards.

Hookhand wasn't so lucky. A finger length dart of glass sank into his remaining eye. He fell to the ground, crying in pain, until Battle brought his whimpering to an end. Hookhand's ghost bubbled up from his corpse. Usually, spirits resembled the bodies that housed them, but Hookhand's spirit was small and gnarled, a scarred broken thing that stank of rot and despair. His pathetic yellow eyes fixed on me as his toothless mouth voiced my name. I lunged toward him and he shot downward, percolating through cracks in the floor board, dragged down to whatever hell awaited. The hound dog sensed that his opponent was no longer a threat and released his locked jaws. He loped back over toward Infidel.

Battle ran back to the bar and snatched a bottle of whiskey. He pulled off the stopper as he approached Infidel. The hound leapt into his path, hackles raised, snarling.

"This is the only thing that's going to wash off that pepper," said Battle. "Water will just make it burn worse."

"He's right," I said to Menagerie.

The hound went silent as I spoke, then stepped aside.

"Hold still," said Battle as he knelt, taking Infidel's chin in his massive hand. "This is going to feel worse for a minute, but it might save your eyes."

Infidel seemed to understand, growing still as Battle tilted the bottle over her face, letting it come in a deluge that washed away most of the cayenne. He motioned for one of the bar maids to bring him a second bottle. The light in the room was dizzying as the Gloryhammer bounced around in the rafters, casting stark shadows. Battle's eyes narrowed as he studied Infidel's face. Infidel had a splinter of wood jammed into her cheek from her impact with the floor. A half dozen other small cuts speckled her face from where fragments of chandelier had hit her.

He washed away the remaining pepper with most of the second bottle. A barmaid handed him a dishtowel and he used it to wipe Infidel's face. She sat up and grabbed the towel, taking control of cleaning the last of the cayenne from the creases around her eyes. She let out a long sigh as she forced her eyes open and looked down into the towel, flecked with blood.

A few seconds of silence passed as she pulled the splinter from her cheek. It was, by any objective standard, a trivial wound. But, I could tell from Infidel's eyes that she understood that this splinter might be the most dangerous injury she'd ever received. Her secret was revealed. Given the speed rumors spread through the city, it was only a matter of hours before everyone learned she'd lost her powers.

"I thought you couldn't be cut," Battle said.

"You've seen me bleed before," Infidel whispered, her voice still weak from pain. "That assassin with the shadow blade. The right magic can break my skin."

"The floor ain't magic," he said. Battle put the whiskey bottle into her hands and he helped her to her feet. A bare inch of fluid still sloshed in the bottle. "Drink the rest of it."

"Can't," she said. "I might be pregnant. Maybe it's an old wives tale that whiskey will hurt the baby, but I'm not taking chances."

"Damn!" said Battle, shaking his horns. "She did it to me again!"

"What?"

"The Black Swan. She bet me you'd have a baby this year. I mean, Stagger's dead. If he'd still been around, maybe, but I just can't believe it otherwise. Who—?"

"Stagger's the father," said Infidel as she managed to stand on her own. Her eyes were still bloodshot, but worked well enough that she spotted the Gloryhammer bouncing around in the rafters.

"Help me grab that," she said to Battle. "The Black Swan's probably going to bill me for the damned chandelier. Better stop that thing before it floats behind the bar and takes out the inventory."

"Right," said Battle, grabbing her by the hips and lifting her overhead. She stretched her fingers as far as she could, barely touching the shaft of the hammer. Yet, the barest touch was all she needed to regain control. It slid fully into her grasp and she floated to the floor under her own power.

The hound dog came up to her and sat before her, its tongue hanging out.

"Whose dog?" she asked.

"Um, ain't that Menagerie?" Battle asked. "I saw him leap out of what was left of Kid Black's skull."

Infidel looked down at her chest, running her fingers along the red bump where the tick had once rested.

"Menagerie?" she asked the dog.

The dog said nothing. Menagerie had always been able to talk before, no matter what animal shape he'd worn.

"Menagerie?" I said. The dog tilted its head in my general

direction, but still said nothing. There was intelligence in his eyes, but dog level intelligence, none of the tactical genius that normally burned in the shape-shifter's visage.

"We'd better get him to the Black Swan fast," said Battle Ox. "She's working on the potion now."

"Riiiight," said Infidel, sounding confused. "Right, the potion."

She placed the whiskey on the bar as she followed Battle. I wasn't surprised she'd refused the drink. She hadn't drank much before. It's not so tough to give up something that you never enjoyed in the first place. But, I wondered, when Hookhand first showed up... were Infidel's taunts meant to scare him off? Or was she trying to provoke him? This was her first fight since losing her powers. Had she chosen an opponent she'd routinely beaten in the past to test her new combat style with the hammer and armor? Imagining Infidel going the next nine months without a brawl was a lot tougher than imagining her going nine months without a drink. Once word got out that she was vulnerable, was there any place in the world she'd be safe?

HUSH

BOOK TWO *of the* DRAGON APOCALYPSE

JAMES MAXEY

Coming July 2012
UK ISBN: 978-1-78108-016-0 • £7.99
US ISBN: 978-1-78108-017-7 • $8.99